THE DEVIL'S DEN

The inside of the *looca*-den even surpassed its entrance in squalor. Bunks coated with ancient straw lined the walls, stacked so closely upon one another that the people lying in them could not hope to sit up. The air was tinted blue from *looca*-smoke, and the lack of windows left the room dark and stifling.

As the blue smoke swirled around her, Athaya reached out tentatively, and her mind instantly recoiled. The air was alive with hideousness, crackling with the currents of twisted and tortured minds, irrational thoughts and delusions—a cacophony of gibberish that sent ice streaming through her veins.

Ranulf gave her elbow a comforting squeeze. "There's all kinds of madness in the world besides a wizard's *mekahn*," he said quietly. "We'll have to sort out the kind we're after."

Then it came, like a scream out of the darkness.

Athaya cast out to the disturbed young man's mind. "His paths are almost formed," she whispered, "but I think we've caught him in time."

"God, they're coming again," the man gibbered. Then he closed his eyes and lashed out, striking Ranulf on the jaw before crying out: "*Ignis confestim sit!*" And from the tips of his fingers, a single bolt of green fire struck the ground, igniting the dry straw . . .

By Julie Dean Smith
Published by Ballantine Books:

A Caithan Crusade
   CALL OF MADNESS
   MISSION OF MAGIC

MISSION
OF
MAGIC

Julie Dean Smith

A Del Rey Book
BALLANTINE BOOKS • NEW YORK

A Del Rey Book
Published by Ballantine Books

Library of Congress Catalog Card Number: 91-91809

ISBN 0-345-36627-1

Manufactured in the United States of America

First Edition: June 1991

Cover Art by Michael Herring

To the Old Dazzler

Acknowledgment

The author is grateful to Charles Witke, Professor of Greek and Latin at the University of Michigan in Ann Arbor, for his on-going assistance with the incantations used by the Lorngeld. *Gratias tibi ago!*

"What will it lead to? This I cannot know. But great magics—indeed, great endeavors of any kind—threaten vast ruin, but lure with the promise of vast reward."
—CREDONY OF TENOSCE
  Reflections upon the Discovery of Translocation

CHAPTER 1

✳✳

"**B**LASPHEMY," THE ARCHBISHOP MUTTERED INDIGnantly, twisting his face up into a meaty scowl. He set aside the chicken leg he had been chewing on and turned the page of an ancient book, leaving a greasy, coin-sized thumbprint on the yellowed parchment. "Proud, self-glorifying heresy, that's what it is."

"So you keep saying," the man across from him grumbled, his concentration once again shattered by the prelate's incessant babble. Durek Trelane, king of Caithe and lord of the Isle of Sare, shifted his weight in the hard-backed chair and let out a grunt of pain as he tried to work the stiffness from the muscles in his neck. He had never been fond of bookish pursuits and despised nothing more than being confined in a small, airless chamber thick with the smell of old leather and ink. Even the roaring fire nearby could not entirely chase away the icy bitterness of a late January evening.

But today his studies had a purpose far beyond mere edification, so he was willing to tolerate some discomfort for their sake—even though his archbishop's company was proving far more tiresome than either the uncomfortable chair or the chill. Pulling the heavy black mantle closer around his shoulders, he took a gulp of mulled wine from his silver goblet, closing his eyes briefly while the cinnamon warmth flowed through him, and then turned his face away to discourage the clergyman from any further attempts at unwanted conversation.

Archbishop Ventan, however, was not quite so easily daunted. Not a minute later, he made an impatient huffing sound and clicked his tongue noisily. "Just listen to this: 'The Lord sheds blessings of magic on a chosen few, and they are called upon in turn to bless others and use their gift to the betterment of the world.' Can you believe that? What rubbish! How does one better the world, might I inquire, by unleashing all matter of madness and destruction upon it? Ludicrous."

"I didn't ask you to criticize it. Just read it, will you?" A vague hint of warning had crept into his voice, but the archbishop didn't seem to notice.

"With respect, my Lord, I must protest," Ventan declared, closing the volume hard so that a thick cloud of dust rose from its pages. "Those books of magic contain nothing but wickedness. They—"

"They may be of help to us in the future, Daniel, and that's the last complaint I intend to hear from you on the subject." The king threw the archbishop a damning glare and thrust his own book aside, knowing he would never finish the essay he was reading unless he was left alone. He rubbed his eyes wearily, forcing stinging tears to soothe away the dryness.

"But *wizardry* . . ." Ventan murmured, unable to suppress a shudder. He nervously scanned the chamber as if afraid some random magic might yet linger there. Yet if anything lingered in that chamber, it was nothing more than three months of dust— left untouched because few dared enter that private set of rooms for fear that the one who once lived there might still haunt them. The king, however, did not believe in ghosts or other foolish fancies—those who dared might claim he believed in nothing requiring half so much imagination—and spent many of his winter hours here, diligently searching through the musty records for any scrap of knowledge that might help him learn more about magic and those who practiced its hellish arts.

Evidence of his work was clear; the sparsely furnished room displayed a wild disorder that would have appalled its former occupant had the wizard Rhodri been alive to see it. Open books lay scattered across the shelves, and loose sheets of parchment filled with crabbed scribbles littered the floor around the center table where Durek and the archbishop sat. The windows were slick with smoky grime, and cobwebs hung limply from the ceiling beams like tattered lace. But the king quietly tolerated these signs of neglect and knew that when his studies here were done, he would have the room closed off permanently, its history and existence locked away like a corpse in a sealed tomb.

Seeing Ventan drawing breath to fuel another speech, Durek cut him off with a sharp gesture. "I don't condone magic any more than you do, Daniel. You know that. But a man doesn't wait to study the arts of war until *after* he's fallen under attack. The more we can learn about these wizards, the better prepared we'll be to deal with them if we have to."

Durek got up from his chair and stretched, tendons snapping like footsteps on dry twigs. "I never thought of Rhodri as much of a scholar, but there are enough books here to fill a library. I've already found some notes on corbal crystals—like that one you used to have—and several pages about something called a 'vision sphere.' But some of his other notes . . ." Durek frowned and shook his head. "It's almost as if he were tracking some sort of experiment. I gather that my father was involved somehow, but Rhodri's writing is so full of cryptic remarks—not to mention being illegible to begin with—that I can't make any sense of it."

"All wizards are mad, my lord," the archbishop stated resolutely. "And Rhodri was probably worse than most." Ventan reclaimed his chicken leg from the silver tray in the center of the table and took another bite, chewing angrily as he spoke. "Kelwyn would have done better to rid himself of that wizard straight away rather than let him work mischief for twenty years. Why, toward the end your father was actually *serious* about wanting to abolish the sacrament of absolution! That never would have happened if he'd not been given magic. The power seduced him, just as it seduces all who encounter it." The archbishop swallowed noisily. "And look what came of it."

Durek lapsed into moody silence, thinking back with bitter regret on the many arguments he'd had with Kelwyn, futilely trying to make him see reason. Durek had always deeply respected his father—even if he could not quite bring himself to love him—and could not comprehend how a man so universally acknowledged to be one of Caithe's most extraordinary kings could have made such a grievous error in judgment. Throughout his life, Kelwyn had consistently proved his skills as a shrewd tactician and an excellent warrior, earning even the grudging respect of those rebellious nobles he had been forced to subdue in order to bring the long-needed peace that Caithe now enjoyed. In retrospect, it was easy to think that he could have brought his kingdom under a single rule with his inborn gifts alone, without risking his soul by dabbling in magic.

Durek felt his muscles tense up at the mere thought of magic. Yes, that's what it all came down to. If only his father hadn't been so stubborn about those wizards. *Those damned, mind-plagued wizards!* Kelwyn had been determined to revoke the sacred rite of absolution—a preposterous idea!—and worse, he wanted to legalize the teaching of magic to the Lorngeld. All this in spite of constant appeals by his eldest son and the Curia that such a course of action was useless—that all wizards were children of the Devil and could not be saved except by renouncing their gift and offering up their lives to God. And Kelwyn's refusal to believe that one simple fact had been his downfall, for he had been brutally murdered by one of the very wizards he sought to protect.

And worst of all, that wizard had been his only daughter, Athaya.

Durek's reverie was broken by a muffled groan as Ventan got up from his chair and padded across the carpet toward the fire. The hem of his black cassock hovered several inches above the floor due to an overly abundant stomach, revealing two mutton-like ankles and a pair of costly velvet slippers embroidered with gold. He turned to warm his back against the flames, and when the light was right, Durek could see small spots of grease rimming the archbishop's sleeves where he had furtively wiped his mouth.

"It's late, Majesty," he said with a sigh. "Shouldn't you get some rest?"

"I appreciate your concern," Durek replied graciously, knowing full well that Ventan was merely grasping for an excuse to leave, "but I want to finish that essay I was reading before I retire. And you can start sifting through that stack of papers over there." The king motioned to a disconcertingly large bundle of creamy pages loosely banded together with a purple cord. "The ink on them hasn't started to fade yet—they must be fairly recent."

Swallowing another sigh, the prelate gathered up the papers

from the shelf and grudgingly began to sort through them. He handled them carefully, touching only their outermost edges as if afraid the paper itself might carry some sort of contagion other than mere knowledge.

Having finally obtained an atmosphere of quiet, Durek promptly found it impossible to concentrate. As the minutes passed, the fire began to crackle much too loudly, and he heard the clatter of each tiny hailstone that the winds flung against the chamber's leaded-glass windows. Even the crisp sound that came each time he turned a page of his book began to distract him. Briefly, he considered giving up and going to bed, yet despised the notion of doing exactly what Ventan was hoping he would do.

Then he realized the source of his problem. A room containing Archbishop Ventan should never be so quiet.

Durek looked up curiously. He half expected to find the archbishop dozing, although that should have produced at least a muffled snore or two. But Ventan was very much awake. Bushy gray brows were furrowed deeply inward, his face frozen with the startled look of a man who has just read a public notice of his own death. Whatever the archbishop was reading, it had him utterly absorbed.

"What have you got there? Anything I should see?"

Durek's unexpected inquiry made the prelate start. Quickly regaining his composure, Ventan set the paper aside and made a placating rumble in the back of his throat. "Oh, I don't think it merits your attention."

"I'll be the judge of—oh, what is it now?" he snapped in response to the tentative rapping on the chamber door.

A nervous-looking sentry took one step inside the wizard's chamber, visibly reluctant to venture from the safety of the doorway. "I regret the intrusion—"

"I thought I gave orders not to be disturbed."

"You did, Majesty," the young man replied, dropping an apologetic bow, "but I checked with Lord Gessinger, and he thought—"

"Mosel Gessinger had a thought?" Ventan put in under his breath. "God has wrought yet another miracle."

"—thought you'd want to hear about this right away," the sentry finished, clearly trying not to smile at the archbishop's barb. "Captain Parr and his squadron have just returned from the border."

The king's eyes flashed with sudden animation. He sat bolt upright and winced as a sharp twinge of pain from a protesting muscle shot through him. "For once, Gessinger was right. I'll see the captain immediately. Send him in."

The sentry quickly ushered in a brisk young man dressed in the bloodred livery of the King's Guard. The only decoration on his uniform was his brass-linked collar of office declaring him the captain of Durek's corps of personal guards—a post he had held just over three months. Razor-fine hair was combed neatly back from sharp-boned cheeks, and he looked at his king with intense, unblinking brown eyes, like those of an owl who is most alert in the deepest part of the night.

Durek rose to his feet. "You have a report to make, Captain?"

"We traced them to Beysdon, sire," he began in a cold, unemotional voice, getting straight to the point instead of bothering with a florid preamble as Ventan would have done. "It's a small fishing village about a day's ride from the border wall. They purchased horses in Feckham and took the seacoast road north. One of the dockhands said that a man and woman answering to their description boarded a Sarian trading ship sometime during the last week of November." The captain paused to give his next pronouncement the proper effect. "The ship was scheduled to dock in Torvik a few days later."

"Torvik," Durek muttered darkly. "The closest Reykan port to Ath Luaine."

Archbishop Ventan laced his pudgy, sausagelike fingers together and set them atop his belly. "Your sister is most certainly seeking refuge in Osfonin's court."

"No doubt, although he's an utter fool for taking her in. But I think he'll listen to reason," Durek added with an icy glitter in his eye.

"Most certainly," Ventan agreed. "I doubt Osfonin will consider Athaya's safety worth the price of a Caithan invasion."

Captain Parr cleared his throat, subtly reminding the others that he was still present. "If I may, Majesty," he continued. "There was someone else with them. From the information I was able to pick up, I'm certain it was Kale Eavon—one of the two men who disappeared the same night as the princess' escape.''

''And one of Graylen's favorites,'' Durek observed, scowling as he thought back to Parr's predecessor. Tyler Graylen—Athaya's erstwhile lover—whose treasonous head had been displayed on an iron pike atop the gatehouse, and then taken down a month later to rejoin the rest of his body in an unmarked grave. Graylen had been known to inspire a great deal of loyalty in his men. That much could be said for him, at any rate. No doubt one of them had been misguided enough to place his loyalties with Athaya even after his captain was executed, thinking to do him one final service.

Durek gave the owl-eyed guardsman a brief nod of dismissal. ''Thank you, Captain. You've done well. I'll send for you in the morning to give you further orders.''

As the captain bowed crisply and departed, Durek rummaged among Rhodri's things until he located a clean sheet of honey-colored parchment and a fresh pot of ink. He dipped a slender white quill into the ink pot and eagerly scribbled down a few words in his blocky, childlike hand. He had waited far too long to compose this particular letter, and even though he knew that a strongly worded missive to the Reykan king would take more time than he was willing to spend on it tonight, he felt compelled to at least put down the first few lines.

It had been over three months since his sister's flight from Caithe. Three months since she had murdered their father with magic and propelled her oldest brother to the throne. And tracing her had taken longer than Durek ever thought possible. His best guardsmen had been searching under every rock and clod of dirt for Athaya and her Reykan cohort, Jaren McLaud, ever since October, asking in every village for news of them, and praying for God's protection from their evil spells and magics— magics that had left the last wizard at Delfar Castle nothing more than a smattering of flesh on a dungeon wall, although Durek, allowing himself a malicious smile, regarded Rhodri's demise as no great loss to his court.

''She will have to be tried, of course,'' Ventan remarked, craning his fleshy neck in an attempt to read what the king was scribbling. ''Even if it is only a formality.''

''Never fear, my friend,'' Durek said with dangerous calm. His lifted his hand, and beads of ink slid from the end of the quill like drops of black blood. "She'll answer to me for what she's done. And if I ever get my hands on that damned Reykan wizard who taught her these things, I swear I'll—" He broke off, his face suddenly crimson with rage. Biting back a curse, he flung the quill aside, sending it skittering across the polished cherrywood table.

"They are both already doomed, your Majesty," the archbishop pointed out, shaking his head in an unconvincing display of remorse. "They must be punished, of course, but the fact remains that whatever you do to them in this life will amount to nothing compared to what awaits them in the next. God shall condemn them to the lowest reaches of hell for dabbling in the Devil's magic. And despite your sister's royal blood, I fear not even the Church can save her now."

"Somehow I don't think Athaya will mind in the least when she finds out you've excommunicated her," Durek said without bothering to look up. Then he emitted a short, mirthless laugh. "In fact, if I know my sister, she'll probably take it as a compliment."

Ventan thrust out his lower lip, his dignity ruffled by the very idea. "Yes, the queen dowager said as much herself." The archbishop paused for a moment and then added, "Dagara will want to know what the captain has learned."

"That goes without saying," Durek murmured. But while his stepmother's reaction to the news would be predictably venomous, Durek knew that his brother's reaction would prove harder to judge. Nicolas had kept to himself these past few months, attending few court functions and taking many of his meals in his chambers so that he could sulk in solitude. But his sullenness was a refreshing change compared to what he had been like those first few weeks after Tyler's death. Durek had not expected that such bitter fury could be found in one whose greatest delight was stealing kisses from young ladies in dimly lit castle corridors. Still, his anger seemed to be fading over time, and although it was a great deal to hope for, Durek thought that his brother was slowly beginning to see reason. Nicolas never mentioned Athaya's name to anyone and sank into a deep, brooding silence whenever the subject of the Lorngeld arose.

Brushing aside the ink-blotted paper, Durek got up from his desk and went to the window, gazing at the city of Delfarham sprawling out beneath him. The cobbled streets were layered with a thin sheet of ice from the evening's storm and were slowly being covered by a heavy snowfall that blanketed the slate-tiled roofs and gleamed purplish blue in the moonlight. The fortress around him was quiet—unusually quiet, even for this hour of the night—and Durek would have felt completely at peace were it not for the nagging problem of Athaya preying on his mind.

With luck, however, that problem would soon be resolved. Behind him, Archbishop Ventan picked up the abandoned sheet of parchment and began reading it absently. "The queen will object, of course."

"Yes, she'll object. *If* she knows about it." Durek turned slowly and gave the archbishop a telling glare. "But I don't know anyone who's planning to ride all the way to Halsey to tell her, do you?"

"No, Majesty," Ventan replied, wide-eyed. "And in her condition, I don't believe it would be wise to upset her with such news. Her first pregnancy was not an easy one, and the second shows signs of being little better."

Durek frowned, a line of worry forming between his brows. Cecile concerned him—not enough to move his court to Halsey to be with her, of course, but enough so that he occasionally thought of her and of the child she would bear him come the summer. The queen had become irritable and sullen as autumn progressed, and not all of that could be ascribed to the child she carried. Like Nicolas, she was slow to face the unpleasant truth that her dear Athaya was little better than a common outlaw and damned for her magic besides. He had fought with her more than once on the subject, the result of their last encounter being his insistence that the warmer southern climate might improve her temper and that she should take immediate advantage of it.

Suddenly impatient, Durek snatched the sheet of parchment from Ventan's grasp and stalked toward the door. "Come along, Daniel. I want to start drafting this letter tonight. Besides, this room grows more frigid every hour."

Realizing that he was not going to get to bed anytime soon, the archbishop extinguished the reading candle with a resigned puff of breath, irritably fanning away the fragrant tendrils of smoke that curled upward from the wick. He took one last bite from the abandoned chicken leg, then rapidly restacked the pile of papers on the table.

"Daniel?" The king's voice echoed harshly off the stone walls in the outside corridor.

"Coming, my Lord," the archbishop replied, looping the purple cord around the pages he'd been sorting. But before he reached the door, he abruptly turned back to retrieve from that bundle the paper that had so intrigued him before Captain Parr's timely interruption.

After a quick glance to insure that Durek had gone, Archbishop Ventan hastily crumpled the page and moved to toss it into the fire. But he checked himself at the last moment, his eyes darting warily around the chamber, suddenly fearful that destroying a wizard's possessions might cause some sort of hideous spell to be unleashed. With a nervous dispatch, Ventan flattened out the page, folded it twice, and tucked it inside a dusty, leatherbound book. Then, with a self-satisfied nod, he slid the volume into the far reaches of the cluttered bookshelves and hurried from the chamber.

CHAPTER 2

❋

"**Y**OU'RE OVERDOING IT ON THE RAIN, ATHAYA," the old wizard instructed, shaking his head as he watched the torrents of icy drops beating down on the dreary winter landscape. "I didn't ask for a flood, you know. And your thunder sounds much too hollow. Round out the tone—make it richer, like a pipe organ. Let the sound reverberate." He clicked his tongue softly. "That last one sounded like a fishwife beating two tin pots together."

Trying not to scowl visibly, Athaya closed her eyes and worked the spell again, changing the inflection of her voice and subtly altering the circular gesture she made with her hands. In answer to her command, dark clouds swirled in the sky above, changing to an even deeper shade of gray. A silent flash of yellow light illuminated the sky like the glint of a mirror turned toward a lamp and was followed a few moments later by a clap of thunder, this time smooth and deep, rolling like ocean waves. And as Master Hedric had requested, the sound echoed over the crags surrounding Ath Luaine, tumbling over itself until it gradually died away in the distance.

Athaya tucked her thumbs inside the gem-studded girdle around her hips and smiled. "There," she said proudly, turning back to her teacher. "What did you think of—"

Her words were brutally drowned out by a crack of thunder

11

that sent shock waves through her bones. In the same instant, a renegade streak of lightning lashed out of the darkened clouds and struck an oak tree fifty yards from the tower in which she stood.

"Pay attention to what you're doing!" Hedric snapped, the harshness in his voice more a result of being genuinely startled than from any real anger. He poked his white-thatched head out of the arched window and furrowed his brows at the blackened oak, now cleaved neatly in two and filling the air with the smoky scent of scorched wood.

Sighing, he pointed a crooked finger at her. "You can't be careless with this sort of thing."

"I didn't mean to—"

"Don't try to show off until you know what you're doing."

"But I wasn't—"

"That's enough, Athaya," he said, waving the Caithan princess silent. He studied her pensively for a moment. "Perhaps you need a short rest. Come, banish your spell, and I'll make us some tea."

Athaya swallowed any further protests and dispersed the storm clouds, scattering them to the north and restoring the leaden, overcast sky that had lingered over the valley for days. After four months of the Master's tutelage, Athaya knew better than to contradict him. Ordering her to learn and recite from memory the names and reigns of each Overlord since the founding of the Circle—Hedric's attempt to instill in her a healthy sense of respect after one particularly heated burst of temper six weeks ago—had convinced her of that. But even though she had learned to curb her tongue for the most part, there were still times when she chafed under the weight of his constant demands—times when she wanted to snap back at him and tell him that he asked too much; that she simply couldn't learn everything he wanted her to know; that she was too tired to practice her illusion spells or read yet another lesson from her books. She wanted to cry out that she was the princess of Caithe and that no one had a right to treat her like a bonded apprentice. But if Hedric was even remotely impressed with her title he never showed it. He knew, as did she, that while her veins pulsed with royal blood, Hedric was one of the elite Circle of Masters and outranked her to no small extent in the arena of wizardry.

Although he had proved to be patient and even tempered,

Hedric was in no way an easy taskmaster. He had not pushed her too hard at first, of course, knowing what she had been through in Caithe. The death of her father and of Tyler—coming so soon after she had barely accepted the fact she was a wizard at all—had very nearly undone all the progress she'd made with her gift, and threatened to plunge her back into the dark madness of the *mekahn* where she would no longer have to deal with her pain.

It had taken several weeks of quiet rest before she could face the challenges of her training again, and even then Hedric was exceedingly delicate in working with her. But now that her grief had lessened, and the pain, though not gone, had begun to subside, Hedric pressed her to explore the full extent of her talents and did not hesitate to show his disappointment if she failed to do her best at all times, explaining, when he thought she deserved to hear it, that the deeper his faith ran in the abilities of his students, the harder he was determined to be with them.

Athaya smiled inwardly. *Based on that,* she mused, *he must positively worship me.*

The hem of the Master's deep green robe swished softly among the dust and rushes on the ancient floor as he puttered about the fireplace, setting withered sticks to blazing with a whispered word and hanging a pot of water over the fire to boil. Unlacing the thongs of a burlap sack set near the hearth, he drew out two packets of Selvallenese tea and placed them in the shallow cups. When the water began to bubble, he poured it over the packets to release a sweet orange scent.

Wrapping cold hands around her cup, Athaya sank into a weather-beaten chair across from Hedric, grateful for the brief respite from her lessons. They had been at the ruined tower for hours, laboriously testing her skills at weather-spells. The tower itself was a deserted lookout post from a time long before the spires of Glendol Palace had been erected in Ath Luaine and lay in a barren valley a few miles northeast of the city—a spot ideal for practicing such spells, since there was no arable farmland to flood and only one village close enough to be inconvenienced by the torrential rains intermittently called by Hedric's pupils. And Master Hedric, conscientious about keeping an even score, habitually insured several days of temperate air and sunshine in the valley after one of his student's weather lessons, just so those few countrymen living nearby wouldn't feel put-upon by the often ineptly crafted storms.

Mollified by the warm tea, Hedric folded his hands in his lap and smiled at her. "Actually, Athaya, that was one of the strongest storm-spells I've ever seen. Better than I could do at your age."

Athaya didn't reply right away, since Hedric's rare expressions of praise were usually followed by a sobering dose of criticism. This time was no exception. His smile soon faded, and he fell silent for a while, studying the glazed clay teacup with unnecessary intensity.

"I know you're nervous about tonight, Athaya, but you have to learn to control such feelings. They interfere with your spellwork. If, heaven help you, you're ever forced to resort to battle-magic, your enemy certainly isn't going to wait for you to calm down and prepare yourself before he attacks you. Dealing with distractions is part of what you have to learn."

"Being brought before the Circle of Masters is more than just a distraction," she protested, staring bleakly into her teacup. "I can't believe you waited until this morning to tell me."

"What? And have your concentration shattered any longer than was necessary? In light of what you've done to that poor oak, I probably shouldn't have given you any advance warning at all."

Athaya's shoulders sagged heavily. Even the rigors of her lessons were infinitely more appealing than the prospect of an evening under the Circle's ominous scrutiny. That assembly of powerful wizards had always seemed like a myth to her—something people talked about but never actually saw, like God or heaven. The only member of the Circle she had ever met was Hedric, and other than that, she knew of them by reputation alone. But their reputation was obviously well earned. She knew of at least one wizard who would have done anything to join their number, including dabbling in forbidden spells and very nearly sending her and Jaren to their deaths in the process. But although Rhodri was nearly six months dead, Athaya could not forget how desperately he had wanted to count himself among the magical elite and secure the Circle's favor. Their opinions obviously carried weight, and the wizard who fell foul of them would likely be the sorrier for it.

"What are they going to ask me about?"

Hedric drained off the rest of his tea and set the cup aside. "Well, I already told them that you plan to go back to Caithe one day and start making some changes regarding how the Lorngeld are treated there. I expect they'll want more details on just how you plan to go about that. And I won't lie to you, Athaya," he added, his voice growing more troubled, "at least one member of the Circle is extremely suspicious about your past. He's not altogether convinced that Kelwyn's death—or Rhodri's, for that matter—was an accident."

Athaya felt a hot rush of outrage sear through her. If her teacup had been made of glass, her furious grip would have shattered it. "But that's absurd! How could anyone possibly think I'd do something like that on purpose?"

"I know it's ridiculous," Hedric replied calmly, with just a trace of derision. "I only mentioned it so you wouldn't be caught off guard if the subject came up. I've witnessed your occasional outbursts of temper, my dear, and I don't think having one during a Circle meeting would be at all productive. But the majority of the Circle doesn't think ill of you, so try not to let the opinion of one uninformed wizard upset you."

Burying her face in her hands, Athaya suddenly felt more disconsolate than ever. "I don't think I'm ready for this. Can't we put it off for a while?"

"No, Athaya. I've already put it off longer than they've liked. The Circle first asked to see you last fall, right after the news of Kelwyn's death reached Reyka, but I knew such a confrontation would have been too hard on you then. But it's been four months now, and they're getting impatient."

Athaya opened her mouth but abruptly closed it again, realizing that her protests would be just as fruitless as all of her stubborn, petulant refusals to learn the craft of magic had once been. Never mind that she was, in retrospect, infinitely grateful that those protests hadn't accomplished a thing.

Hedric slowly leaned forward, and the loud creak of his splintered oak chair sounded like snapping bones. Athaya felt a tingle of discomfort skirt down the back of her neck. Although he hadn't said a word, she knew that Hedric was preparing to broach the one subject that both of them had been avoiding all afternoon.

"And what of the other spell I asked you to prepare for me today?"

The air in the small chamber suddenly grew colder, and Athaya felt gooseflesh forming on her arms. She had sworn never to work that spell again—not since the first and only time she had cast it. The fiery green coils of lightning that she once unwittingly commanded to fly from her fingertips had been deadly—she recalled with horrid clarity how they viciously wrapped themselves around her father's body, crackling and writhing as they burned and sucked away his life's breath. Without knowing how she had done it, she tapped into a power too great for her then-meager control, and was forced to stand by helplessly while he pleaded for her mercy. But all his cries came to nothing. Granted, the spell had been broken by her brother's timely entrance, but only after the damage to Kelwyn had been done. Not two hours later he was dead, and Athaya was left with a weight on her conscience that she would carry the rest of her life.

And Durek, of course, had not believed a word of it when she explained that it was Kelwyn who began the battle—Kelwyn who lashed out first. He struck his daughter in uncontrolled anger, using a spell of killing force to avenge a host of imagined evils, caught as he was in a tangled web of madness spun by his borrowed and decaying magic. Athaya's only option was self-defense, but untrained as she was, she had gone too far, and pumped far too much power through the fiery coils without any knowledge of how to banish them.

Athaya's throat constricted, and her words came out barely above a whisper. "Master Hedric, I already told you that I never want to work that spell again. Please understand . . . it brings back memories I'd rather forget. I'm afraid—"

"Which is precisely why you must prove to yourself that you can do it without harming anyone." His expression was sympathetic but unswervingly firm. "I have confidence in you, Athaya. So does Jaren. You must learn to have that same confidence in yourself."

"But—"

"I purposely waited a few months before asking you to do this for the same reasons you mentioned. But I think you're ready now, and Jaren tells me you've read everything that's been written about the spell. Perhaps you'd feel more relaxed trying it with him?" he suggested, sensing he had found another reason for her reluctance. "I could send to the palace for him—"

"No," she cut in, with a bit more force than she'd intended. Noting Hedric's questioning gaze, she tried to force a smile. "No, don't . . . bother him."

More relaxed? she thought, averting her eyes. *Believe me, Master Hedric, that would only make things worse.*

Hedric looked as if he were about to ask her something and then quickly thought better of it. "I hope that means you agree to try, because we're not going back to the palace until you do." He picked up an empty saddle pack from the floor and held it up. "And since we've already eaten the lunch we brought with us, we're bound to get quite hungry if you persist in arguing for the rest of the day."

Athaya shuddered as if icy fingers had brushed the back of her neck. Still, she nodded glumly. It would do no good to argue with him. She had tried before, and always failed. Grudgingly, she conceded that Master Hedric was as stubborn as she was— a fact that might have truly impressed her under any other circumstances.

"Just don't let me hurt you . . ." she said, turning pleading eyes toward him. *God knows I've hurt too many people already.*

"You won't. I'm a fairly decent wizard myself, you know," he added offhandedly. "I can deflect your spell if I have to." He offered her a comforting pat on the arm. "Your father never had that chance."

Hedric got up and moved behind her, forcing some of the tension away by kneading her knotted shoulder muscles with his hands. "Just start small, Athaya. Try to weave the coils around your teacup."

Athaya felt beads of sweat forming on her forehead as she stepped inside her paths and focused her concentration on the spell she sought. Most days, the mere knowledge that a vast, hidden world of magic was inside of her just waiting to be explored gave her a thrill of excitement—a childlike excitement unmatched since the long-ago days when she and Nicolas would venture down to the shore beneath Delfar Castle, exploring secret coves in perpetual hope of finding treasures abandoned by Sarian pirates. But at times like this, when her studies touched upon the darker spells that could maim and kill, she realized that there were as many horrible and dangerous things inside of her as there were treasures, and that she could no more be rid of them than she could be rid of her own heart, or bones, or blood.

She fixed her eyes on the dimly lit path-walls around her, imbued with familiar yet unknown symbols that spoke to some part of her in a language that her conscious mind would never know. The closer she came to that place in her paths where the deadly spell was kept, the more nervous she became. Then she faced the wall of runes—a wall she saw only in the eye of her mind—and took a deep breath and let the markings speak.

She bit down hard on her lip as she saw the trails of fire begin to spark and form, flowing from her fingertips like the tendrils of mist from a vision sphere. Although she knew what to expect, the sight gave her a start and the coils sputtered for an instant. But with Hedric's quiet encouragement, Athaya fought back the urge to panic and guided the ropelike fire into a circle around the base of her cup, listening to it crackle and spit as it quickly set her tea to boiling.

"Pull back a bit, Athaya," Hedric whispered, frowning at the angry brown bubbles. He waved away a cloud of steam. "Don't try so hard."

Somehow unable to speak, Athaya managed to nod. Forcing herself to relax, she tried to make the flames expand without pushing any more power through them. But as she'd seen before, she wasn't a good judge of her own strength, and the fiery coils snapped out in a series of arcs, curling down the table legs and slithering across the floor like dozens of venomous snakes. The fire wasn't hot—at least not anymore—but she had seen what it had done to her tea and had no desire to lose control and broil herself and Hedric by accident. Yet the more she worried about the dangers, the warmer the coils seemed to grow.

"It's getting too strong—" Her voice had a faint edge of hysteria to it, and if she wasn't careful, she knew she would start laughing.

"It's just like a rope, Athaya. It doesn't have to be harmful. Don't pump too much power through it—that's what makes it so dangerous."

Athaya tried to pull back, but she was growing entranced by her creation, unable to look away or think coherently. The temperature of the room seemed to rise as she envisioned the fiery ropes binding her father's writhing body, draining him of strength and life, torturing his mind into one last instant of sanity as he begged for mercy. With detached curiosity, she watched as the flames snaked across the floor toward her. And somehow, it didn't seem to matter when she saw them wrapping around her own feet, imprisoning her in a trap of her own design . . .

"Athaya, take control." Hedric's voice was gentle, but there was a shade of anxiousness in it. "You have the power, not the spell itself."

In the corner of her eye, she saw Hedric stand, readying himself to counter her spell by force of will if he had to. But she knew that despite his assertions, he was old, and his powers, as Jaren once told her, were not what they had been in his youth. Without any training at all, she had once used these coils to kill a man in the prime of life—a man who had always been strong and robust. A man who had cried for mercy at the last moment, and been granted none.

She tried to simply stop, as she had that first time—to break the spell by breaking her concentration—but despite Hedric's earlier remark, her attentions were not so easily shattered after months of discipline and practice in crafting and sustaining spells, and she was unable to shake the vivid visions. The memories crowded in too quickly, and with too much force, and this time, she feared it would take as much conscious effort to end the spell as it had to cast it.

In a flurry of desperate confusion, Athaya rushed through the labyrinthine passageways of her mind in search of a counterspell. In search of *escape*. She would never be able to forgive herself if Hedric came to harm trying to control her power to protect her from herself.

Fleeing deeper into her paths, she turned into a dark corridor and halted in front of a solid wall—a dead end. She must have made a wrong turn somewhere in her rush to return to the source of the fire-spell. But how to get back? Much as she tried, she could not remember how to retrace her steps. She was flustered now—not knowing how to escape from herself and unwilling to accept that she never could.

Panic rose like bile in her throat—she had never been so deep in her paths before—and she retreated into an unfamiliar alcove to gather her wits. But before she drew in her next breath, she knew there was something here. The sensation came over her like a cool wind on a summer afternoon. She had found a route of escape—she could sense the feelings of release all around her, a way to flee from the horror she was creating. The runes on the alcove wall spoke of flight; of escape; of freedom from this place; of sanctuary and peace. She could see only blackness, but instead of causing fear it inspired hope, like a glimpse of sun on a blustery day.

"Let it go, Athaya," Hedric's voice came again. Her head suddenly felt stuffed with wool as he began to smother her spell by force of will.

No, don't! she pleaded wildly. Like memories of a childhood nightmare, the faces of Tyler and her father loomed up from beyond the veil. *Stay away! I'll only hurt you. I hurt everyone I touch!*

If Hedric spoke to her again after that, Athaya never heard him. All she could think of was the powerful urge to escape and the heart-soaring thrill of knowing she had found a way. She choked down a mouthful of air to steady herself, then let herself go with a whisper.

"Hinc libera me . . ."

Athaya barely felt the violent lurch when it came, like a drunken man so numbed by wine that tumbling down a staircase causes no pain. The chair beneath her seemed to drop away, and she felt sucked into another realm, gripped by a force more powerful, more pervasive, than anything she had ever imagined. Blinding, white light was all around her, and swirling within it was a disorienting kaleidoscope of images, all in vivid colors, but each racing past her too quickly for recognition. Battered by a cacophony of noise, Athaya felt her body tingle as it melted away, leaving only her consciousness behind.

Then came another jolt, and the world dissolved in a wave of vertigo, forcing her back into her body and confining her within her senses. Gasping for breath, she felt like a babe suddenly expelled from the womb, too bewildered and tired to cry.

It was over in a heartbeat's time. Now the scent of beeswax and leather hung in the air, and motes of dust tickled at her nostrils. Something solid was beneath her again, and she heard the quiet hissing of a nearby fire.

And from somewhere very far away, she thought she heard a gasp of astonishment, and the clatter of an earthenware teacup exploding into fragments.

CHAPTER 3

✵

A THAYA'S MIND WAS BLANK, THE ONLY THOUGHT IN IT
being her awareness that she wasn't quite awake, but
hadn't exactly fallen asleep. Her eyes felt full of sand, and
her temples throbbed as if protesting a nagging hangover.
There was a queasy, unsettled feeling lingering in her stomach.

It took only seconds for memory to flare up like a torch in
dry straw. She gasped and squeezed her eyes closed tighter than
they already were, terrified that she might witness the damage
her wild spell had wrought. Her hands curled into tight fists,
and only then did she realize that they were empty and cold and
that no streams of deadly fire flowed from them.

"Master Hedric," she ventured tentatively, her voice unsteady, "is everything all right?"

The silence that followed made her sick with dread, her first
thought being that there was no one left to answer—that her spell
had done what she feared it would, and sent yet another innocent
man to his death.

Then she heard the quiet rustle of cloth and the sound of
someone swallowing very hard.

"Hedric isn't here," came a voice no steadier than hers had
been. "It's me . . . Jaren."

Athaya didn't bother to react, convinced she must be hearing
things. It couldn't possibly be Jaren. Just this morning, he told

21

her he would be doing some research in Hedric's library all afternoon. And on a day as chill and gloomy as this, no one—not even Jaren, who claimed to love the cold—would have ridden out from the palace unless his business was pressing.

She opened her eyes a crack, but as she took in the scene before her, they gradually widened in stunned disbelief. *This has to be some sort of hallucination*, she thought, still groggy. How else could she explain sitting across from Jaren at a reading table in Hedric's library—a room several miles from the tower she'd been in a few moments ago. Jaren, or whatever illusion of him that was here with her, was seated sideways in his chair, legs flung casually over the armrest. Light from the reading lamp formed a gold halo on his sandy blond hair, and a thick, gilt-edged book rested forgotten in his lap, the ancient pages speckling his deep blue tunic with dust. His face was frozen in utter astonishment, and until he snapped his gaping jaw closed, Athaya wasn't sure he was capable of moving at all.

Tentatively, she reached out and touched the edge of the walnut reading table, surprised to find that it felt as solid as it looked. *If I'm hallucinating*, she considered, *then I'm doing it amazingly well.*

"What are you doing here?" she blurted out. Then, realizing that it wasn't his location that was in question, she added, "Oh, what am I saying . . . what am *I* doing here?"

Jaren drew in a deep breath and let it out slowly. "I don't know. You were just . . . here. I was studying these path-maps when I heard a . . . I don't know how to describe it . . . a faint, ringing sound. At first I thought I'd imagined it, but then I saw the air shimmer—right there where you're sitting—and the next minute you appeared." Jaren shifted around in his chair and leaned toward her apprehensively. "Just what kind of spells were you and Hedric working on?"

Athaya pushed herself out of the cushioned chair and began walking in agitated circles around the small library, nervous hands busily smoothing out skirts already free of wrinkles. "He wanted me to practice the fire-coils. I didn't want to, but you know how stubborn he can be." She saw Jaren's mouth curl up in a grin, but if he was considering making a comment about her own disposition, he decided against it.

"I don't know what happened, exactly," she went on. "I started losing control of the coils, so I tried to find a way of stopping them. But I don't know how that made me end up here. And now I have a headache," she added grumpily, pressing her fingers against her temples. The rest of her didn't feel much better—her chest felt heavy and her limbs were starting to cramp, almost as if she had crossed the whole three miles between the tower and the palace at a full run.

Tired of pacing, Athaya sat down on the edge of the window seat across from the reading tables and anxiously fingered the tassels on one of the small, embroidered pillows.

"I remember wanting to get away—I was afraid Hedric might get hurt by the spell—but I certainly don't recall asking to go anywhere in particular."

"Then I wonder why you ended up here?" Jaren mused, not really anticipating an answer.

Athaya started to voice the expected "I don't know," but her mouth never formed the words. She had learned from experience—and not always pleasant ones—that her magic was inextricably linked to facets of her mind of which she wasn't always conscious, nor always proud. Any answers she sought about why her spells worked the way they did, whether for good or ill, were within her grasp if only she chose to look for them.

Athaya glanced over the library, with its peaceful collection of books and blankets of stubborn dust. It made sense. A room of quiet repose . . . who wouldn't feel sheltered here?

But as she gazed about the cozy room, her eyes eventually rested on Jaren, and on the golden halo of lamplight playing about his hair. In a flash of insight, and with that peculiar, out-of-time awareness of encountering a profound truth, she realized that it was not this *place* she had sought at all.

She only wanted to be where Jaren was.

Why did I come here? she repeated inwardly. *Because I always do, Jaren. I always come to you. So you can tell me that everything's going to be all right. When my father died, and Tyler . . . you were there for me. I feel safe with you.*

Athaya suddenly felt herself stiffen, conscious of the danger and uncertainty gnawing at the edges of her brain.

Or at least I used to.

"I wanted to go somewhere safe," she said at last, when all her thoughts had run their course. "I suppose the library seemed as safe a place as any." It wasn't quite a lie—just a careful pruning of the truth.

Then a more practical concern asserted itself. "What must Master Hedric be thinking right now?" she asked. "I never exactly told him I was leaving."

"You'd better let him know you're all right. He won't admit it, but he's probably worried sick about you."

Nodding, Athaya settled back among the pillows in the window seat and held her palms apart, quietly whispering the command that would call her vision sphere. The strands of fog were surprisingly slow in coming, and for one breathless moment, she feared they might not come at all. Long after the sphere should have formed, milky trails of whiteness hung limply from her fingertips, as if she had tried to brush aside a sticky mass of cobwebs.

"I must be rattled," she mumbled to herself. "I've cast this spell a hundred times." Concentrating harder, she pushed more energy through the spell. But even after several minutes the essence still refused to mold itself into a globe, floating listlessly about her hands like wisps of smoke in a drafty corridor.

Baffled, she frowned at her hands as if unused to seeing them at the ends of her arms. Inside, her heartbeat quickened with concern. "Something's wrong," she whispered, banishing what paltry evidence of a sphere there was. "My magic has never been this weak before."

Jaren slid out of his chair and came to sit next to her on the window seat. He clasped her hands between his, and didn't seem to notice when she flinched slightly at his touch. "Don't panic, Athaya. Whatever spell you used to get here had to be awfully potent. You probably just drained your strength. Mind if I take a look?"

There was an awkward interval of silence as Athaya groped for some excuse to refuse, but her need to understand what was happening to her outweighed all other concerns. She gave her permission, albeit reluctantly, and Jaren gently touched his fingertips to her forehead.

She was used to his presence by now—that familiar, brushing sensation of another mind in hers, like the dream of an embrace. Lately, though, there was something else, and unlike their earliest workings together, she now had to make a conscious effort not to sever the link.

Relax, Athaya, he sent soothingly. *You're awfully tense . . . just relax.*

As the winter months progressed, Athaya had grown unavoidably aware of the emotions that bubbled over from Jaren's mind into hers whenever they joined together like this. Either she was growing more perceptive as her skills increased, or, perhaps more likely, Jaren was simply unwilling—or unable—to hide his thoughts from her anymore. He had been careful to shield them at first, not wanting to disrupt the pace of her studies with Hedric, but his efforts were fast becoming as futile as trying to grow an oak inside a flowerpot. And the fact that he never spoke openly of them only served to make them more intense when she sensed them secondhand.

But why, she wondered for the hundredth time, was she suddenly so unsettled by Jaren's feelings for her? Why now, months after she had first learned of them? She had known that Jaren cared for her even before Tyler died—in fact, Tyler had been the one to tell her so. But instead of the inner serenity that she expected to feel at knowing she was loved, Athaya was only conscious of a nameless, growing fear—a fear she would recognize if she would simply turn to face it.

And that, she knew, was certainly no way to react to one who had done so much for her. Jaren had literally kept her alive during the grueling flight from Caithe to Reyka—a journey more horrible than even the worst of her childhood nightmares. Even now, her dreams were littered with images from that time: images of traveling by night and sleeping by day and of the utter exhaustion she endured day after day, drained by the constant need to keep moving, of the nights the king's soldiers had combed the seacoast road, asking questions in every village about a black-haired woman and her Reykan companion, and forcing them to shun the alerted populace in favor of barns and ruined cottages that could be shielded with wards; of Jaren's quiet presence at her side, always patient with her outbursts and angry tears whenever the memories of Tyler and her father became too much to bear. And—an oddly pleasant memory amid the rest—a vision of waking every morning with Jaren at her side, huddled under the same blankets for warmth against the crisp October nights, and feeling comforted and safe, if only for a few fleeting moments.

Everything looks normal, he remarked, jolting her out of her reverie as he withdrew. "Just give it some time." The sanguine look on his face told her that he had gleaned nothing of the direction her thoughts had taken during their contact.

After a moment's pause, Jaren motioned her to wait and slipped out of the library. His footsteps echoed down the spiral stair to the base of Hedric's tower residence, and Athaya heard the faint sound of low voices as he spoke to one of the sentries customarily posted there. He returned a few minutes later, smiling.

"I sent a rider out to tell Hedric you're safe with me. Even if he's already used his sphere to find you, the message should keep him from worrying."

Athaya had to credit Jaren's thoughtfulness in not using his own sphere to contact Hedric while hers was so unusually frail. It was a small thing, but it revealed more about him than anything else could have at that moment.

"Let's just wait until Master Hedric gets back," Jaren went on. "Maybe he can explain what happened. Or," he added, his eyes alight with enthusiasm, "maybe we can find out ourselves." He hurried back to the reading table and scooped up the book he had abandoned there. "I didn't think there *was* a spell for traveling from one place to another, but," he added with a grin, "I guess there has to be, doesn't there?"

Settling down beside her on the window seat—very close beside her, Athaya noted—Jaren opened the thick book and flipped distractedly through its pages. "I was studying these path-maps before you . . . 'dropped in.' Maybe there's a spell like yours in Master Credony's sketches."

Athaya peered over Jaren's shoulder as he turned to a page littered with a maze of intersecting lines, each labeled in barely legible script. She had often seen Hedric use such maps as a reference in the course of her studies. He explained that by using drawings of how one wizard's set of paths is structured, he could guide her through territory that neither of them was familiar with, and reduce the number of unpleasant surprises that might come when experimenting with new spells.

"These maps that Master Credony made of his own paths may be centuries old, but they come closest to your general pattern. And he was one of the most powerful adepts in our history," Jaren added respectfully, reminding Athaya once again of the potential she carried within herself. "If anyone knew about a spell for traveling, it would have been Master Credony."

Grateful to have something to occupy her mind, Athaya got up and collected several volumes of Credony's ancient works from the shelves and stacked them on the reading table. She did not rejoin Jaren in the window seat, however, but elected to read at the table, and when Jaren glanced up in mild disappointment, she quickly turned her back to him and began to read.

Within the hour, the rusty creak of the door latch announced Master Hedric's return to the library, his cloak powdery with new-fallen snow. Athaya had been sketching maps of her own paths in an attempt to locate the spell that had accidentally transported her to the palace, but when she saw Hedric in the doorway, she quickly brushed the papers aside and jumped to her feet, silently wondering what sort of lecture was in store for her this time.

"I've had students try to avoid their lessons with me before," Hedric scolded lightly, "but never with quite so much . . . flair."

Athaya felt her cheeks grow hot. "I'm terribly sorry, Master Hedric. I never meant to—"

"Oh, don't apologize," he said, genially waving off her excuses. Instead of being angry, Hedric was grinning ear to ear. "In fact, you should be quite proud of yourself."

"Proud?" she echoed. "Proud of what? I lost control of my spell and panicked."

"I know, Athaya. And we shall talk about that later," he added sternly. "But what you did after that was quite extraordinary."

I should hope so, Athaya thought to herself. *I'd certainly hate to think these sorts of unplanned excursions happen as a matter of course.*

"You can explain all of this?"

"Easily," he said. He gestured toward the stack of books on the table. "In fact, Master Credony has already done so. You, my dear, possess the spell for translocation."

Before Athaya could make any sort of response, Jaren jumped from the window seat and took a seat at the table. He gazed at her with newfound respect, as if he'd only just learned that she was born of royal blood. "I've been reading through Credony's essays for hours and haven't found so much as a casual reference to such a thing."

"I'm not surprised," Hedric replied dryly. "General opinion holds that the spell is a myth. Those Masters who established the standard texts and curriculum at Wizard's College found Credony's notes on the subject far too esoteric and poorly researched for general study, so there are precious few copies of them. I have a copy here somewhere, but it might take me awhile to locate it."

Athaya stared at both of them blankly. Now that she had grown accustomed to the idea of using magic to do otherwise inexplicable things, the thought of being able to move instantly from one place to another didn't seem as incredible as it might have a year ago.

"So . . . the spell isn't common?" she ventured.

"By all means, no," Hedric replied. "Oh, maybe wizards do it all the time in children's stories, but the talent for translocating is actually extremely rare. Credony purportedly could do it, and there are unsubstantiated rumors about one or two other wizards since his time, but no one presently on the Circle can translocate or has ever heard of anyone who could. Most of them uphold the consensus that the spell is a myth and that Credony was losing his wits when he wrote of it. Ah, but you'll prove otherwise," he added, eyes sparkling.

Somehow Athaya expected she was going to have enough difficulty getting along with the Circle without revealing this new talent and cultivating a reputation as an upstart, but she decided not to worry about that until she had to. Besides, she wasn't even sure she could work the spell again, since she didn't have a clue as to how she'd done it in the first place.

"But I don't remember asking to be trans . . . whatever it was. 'Translocated.' "

"You *did* want to escape, however." The muscles of his face were taut, as if he were making a physical effort to remember every detail of her experience. "That's the last sensation I read from you before you vanished."

Athaya nodded. "I was afraid. And I just wanted to get away from everything. The fire-spell, the Circle meeting . . . it was all getting to be too much."

"Perhaps I shouldn't have pressed you, then," Hedric conceded after a while. "You may have been more nervous about tonight's meeting than I realized. I'm sorry."

Jaren patted her shoulder reassuringly. "Don't worry about

making a good impression on the Circle," he said, with all the confidence that comes of giving advice on a problem not one's own. "They're not too intimidating once you get to know them."

Hedric lifted one of his bushy white brows. "I'm glad you feel that way, Jaren," he said approvingly. "They've asked you to be there tonight as well."

Jaren looked up sharply, a pained look creasing his features. "What? Oh, Master Hedric, I'd really rather not. I have a lot of work to do . . . you know, these maps and all . . ." His voice trailed off as he realized from Hedric's bemused but unflinching stare that any further protest would be pointless. "Why didn't you tell me before?"

"Because you've been my assistant for over five years, Jaren, and not once have you ever been happy about coming to a Circle meeting when I've asked you to. I didn't want to give you enough time to invent a decent excuse."

Jaren slouched down in his chair despondently. "It's not the Circle itself, so much," he murmured after a while. "It's the Overlord. I don't think he likes me very much."

"Oh, don't let that worry you. I don't think Basil likes anybody. Especially me. You just have to learn to get used to him."

Before Jaren could utter another complaint, Hedric turned back to Athaya. "We're still going to work on those fire-coils," he warned, "but we'll go slowly. Actually, you *did* manage to counter the spell before you disappeared, so you might not need as much practice as you think. Right now I'm more concerned with the translocation spell. That could prove far more useful to you in the future."

Athaya's mind began to reel with the potential of such a talent. If nothing else, she could travel between Caithe and Reyka in a matter of moments, instead of enduring an entire fortnight on horseback. "So I can go anywhere I want to just by casting a spell?" she asked, astounded that it could be that simple.

Hedric coked his head to one side. "Theoretically. But Credony had only begun researching the spell when he died, so there's very little written about it. He speculates, for instance, that wizards can only go to places they've seen or been to before. I can't guarantee he's right, but it's a logical guess."

"Then once I figure out exactly how the spell works, I'd better write it down," Athaya said, secretly giddy with the knowledge that she might shed light on an element of magic that generations of wizards had not. Perhaps her own essay on the subject might one day be added to the already prodigious amount of magical lore in Hedric's library.

"You'd best be careful, though," Hedric warned her, pointing a crooked finger in her face. "It was only your good fortune to discover the spell when you wanted to somewhere safe, like this library. What if your thoughts had drifted instead to a desert in Cruachi, or worse, to your brother's audience chamber in Delfarham? You could have just as easily ended up there, with no inkling of how to get back."

Athaya shivered as if someone had just sprinkled snow down her back. That possibility had never occurred to her. The last thing she needed was to transport herself right into Durek's lap by mistake. And with her powers so weak, she would have been utterly at his mercy, unable to return even had she known how.

"If you want to experiment with this spell further, make sure you don't go far and that either Jaren or I knows what you're planning." He lowered his chin and held her gaze firmly. "As I said before, don't try to show off until you know what you're doing."

Athaya nodded obediently, unwilling to refute him this time. "There's something I know about the spell already," she said soberly. "It made my power terribly weak. I tried to call my sphere shortly after I got here and all I got were a few strands."

Jaren leaned forward and rested his elbows on his thighs. "Probably a temporary loss of strength, don't you think?"

"I hope that's all it is," Hedric replied, creasing his brows into a frown. "Granted, he was near death at the time, but perhaps there's some other reason why Master Credony failed to research this spell thoroughly. Try your sphere now, Athaya," he instructed hastily, before any of them could grow needlessly alarmed. "It's been over an hour since you translocated."

Athaya lifted her hands, conscious of the moisture on her palms as she prepared to try the simple spell again. While the strands of mist did not come as rapidly as they should have, they appeared much more quickly than before. The resulting globe was fragile and not quite round, but at least it displayed progress in the right direction.

"It's stronger now," Athaya whispered. "And I don't feel quite so tired."

"You probably put more strength into the spell than you realized," Hedric said. "Especially if you channeled the energy from the fire-spell directly into the translocation. I suppose a temporary loss of strength is only to be expected."

Athaya dispersed the sphere so that her power could restore itself more quickly. "That's a relief. At first, it took a long time for the strands to appear at all, and all sorts of crazy things went through my mind. I thought I might have done something to take my power away, or locked it up somehow so I couldn't get to it."

Athaya laughed at those absurd notions, but to her surprise, Hedric did not share her amusement. He gazed at her peculiarly, with perhaps a faint touch of vexation, and for one uncomfortable moment, Athaya felt like a diplomat whose poor mastery of a foreign tongue has led him to say something unintentionally horrible to his host.

"Master Hedric?"

The old wizard grunted noncommitally. "Oh, bother," he murmured to himself. "I forgot to tell you about that."

"What?"

For a moment, it looked as if he might explain, but then he got to his feet and shuffled toward the bookshelves, diligently running a finger across the leather spines.

"I'm afraid it will have to wait," he said over his shoulder. "It's too complicated to go into now, but it's really quite important." He gestured toward the door in a not-so-subtle invitation for his two young guests to leave. "If you'll excuse me, I need to find something." He stepped up onto a low stool to search the higher shelves.

"I'll get it," Jaren offered, rising to his feet.

The Master's refusal was firm. "No, Jaren. This isn't something you can handle for me."

Jaren backed away looking puzzled, and Athaya doubted that there had ever been a time when his assistance was so flatly denied.

"Now go on," Hedric said, waving them away, "or you'll barely have time to change and get a bite to eat before the Circle meeting. Eight o'clock in my study, both of you."

After a hasty supper and an anxious hour rummaging through her wardrobe for an appropriate gown, Athaya left her chambers to meet Jaren. The deep purple gown and exquisite rope of pearls, both gifts from Osfonin's daughter Katya, made her feel slightly more confident than she had earlier in the day, and her spirits were almost light as she strode regally into the Great Hall.

To her dismay, the feeling was pitifully short lived.

Jaren was not alone in the Hall. Prince Felgin, heir to the crown of Reyka, was beside him, draped casually over a chair on the dais. A reddish witchlight hovered a few inches above his head, and he absently batted it to and fro like a toy, an incongruously serious expression marring his bearded face. Nearby, Jaren leaned against the edge of the trestle table, already dressed for the Circle meeting in a black velvet doublet and a crisp white shirt.

But it wasn't the sight of either of them that distressed her. It was the presence of Ian McLaud, the duke of Ulard, who was speaking in low tones to his son, palms held up as if futilely trying to press a point. The duke was a broad-shouldered man in his early sixties, an old soldier by the look of him, who carried himself with the assurance of one who knows exactly how the world's affairs ought to be managed and has little tolerance for those who disagree. Jaren, however, was not at all receptive to whatever the duke was saying, and stared at the floor with his arms crossed defiantly across his chest as he patiently waited for his father to finish.

"Aye, I understand what you're saying, son," he was saying, his voice clear and crisp as if long accustomed to giving orders. "I was young once, myself. But you know what they say. A shot or two of Sarian whiskey's a fine thing every now and again, but if you drink it morning, noon, and night, it's bound to be the death of you."

Jaren flushed red, scandalized. "*Father!* How dare you compare her to—"

"With respect, Lord Ian," Felgin broke in smoothly, "don't you think you're being overly harsh? None of it was her fault."

"I don't care whose fault it was, my prince. The fact is, she's trouble. And I don't want trouble coming to the only one of my four sons that has been blessed with the Lord's gift."

Immediately, Athaya sensed that this was a conversation she would rather not hear, and slowly backed away, hoping to slip out of the hall unnoticed.

"I asked to go with her, Father," Jaren said, his voice edged with a muted hostility that Athaya had never heard before. "She needed to be trained, and Hedric was too old to go. And if you think I'm going to stay here while she risks her life for what she believes in, you're wrong. Before she leaves, I have every intention of—''

Just then, Jaren caught sight of her in the doorway and the rest of his words evaporated like a puddle on a hot afternoon. Felgin and Lord Ian both turned in unison, and Athaya whispered a curse under her breath, knowing it was too late to make a decorous exit.

"Athaya . . .'' Jaren tried to sound casual, but Athaya could see that his hands were tightly curled into fists. "Have you been waiting there long?''

She shook her head, and Jaren's features visibly relaxed.

"It must be time to go,'' he said, descending the dais steps to join her.

"Yes, it's nearly eight o'clock. Good evening, Felgin.''

"A better one for me than for you, I expect,'' he teased, banishing the witchlight. "But don't let old Basil scare you. He acts more pompous than he really is.''

Athaya couldn't help grinning. "Rather like you, then,'' she observed.

The prince sighed negligently. "Ah, but not half so handsome.''

Laughing, Athaya conceded the point. Then, as a matter of courtesy, she inclined her head to Jaren's father. "Lord Ian.''

The duke offered her a frosty, if polite, nod. "Princess.''

Athaya made no further attempt to engage him in conversation. Ever since he had arrived at the palace in January for Osfonin's winter council, Jaren's father had shown himself not at all fond of her, and although he was never discourteous, he never went out of his way to be gracious, either. He regarded her with cool indifference, as he would an impoverished relative who'd lost his fortune out of stupidity rather than bad luck, and his manner held an undercurrent of profound disapproval that she could recognize instantly, having lived the better part of her life under the weight of such silent condemnation.

Jaren was quick to sense the tension between them and eagerly took Athaya's arm. "We have to go, Father. You know how the Overlord is when people are late.''

Lord Ian nodded brusquely, making it clear that he would permit only a man of the Overlord's stature to interrupt his personal affairs. "We'll finish this discussion later, Jaren," he declared, his tone leaving no room for contradiction.

Jaren stole a sidelong glance at Athaya, and for a moment looked as if he might object. But he soon swallowed whatever he had been about to say, unwilling to provoke further argument in front of her.

"All right," he said with obvious reluctance. "I'll stop by your apartments after the meeting."

Athaya offered a word of farewell to Felgin, who merely extended his hand in benediction like a priest blessing the troops before the battle.

Jaren took a fast pace out of the hall, and Athaya had to hurry to keep up with him. They passed through the smoky, torchlit corridors without saying a word, but the silence soon grew uncomfortable. Athaya gestured to his garb and smiled.

"I should have worn black tonight, too. I feel as if I'm going to my own funeral."

That elicited a reluctant smile in return. "It won't be too bad," he said as they approached the timeworn steps leading up to Hedric's study in the south tower. "I shouldn't have made an issue of it before."

"But what you said bothers me. If this Basil fellow finds *you* objectionable, Jaren, then I have a feeling he'll positively hate *me*."

Jaren laughed softly. "Don't worry. Basil and I just don't get along too well, that's all. Frankly, I think he resents the fact that I was trained by a Master and he wasn't, especially since I didn't show any particular promise. But my father was a friend of Hedric's and the king's, and . . . well, that's politics for you. Basil never refers to it directly, but he has this way of making me feel as if I ought to apologize for my position here. Like he's judging me all the time. It's unnerving."

"I know what you mean," she said, trying not to sound overly critical. "That's exactly how I feel around your father."

Jaren's mood abruptly soured, and his tone turned peevish. "Now, Athaya, I've told you before—"

"He hates me, Jaren, and the only one who won't admit that is you." She strode ahead of him and began climbing the narrow steps to Hedric's study, her hand pressed against the newel for support. "I almost got you killed last fall and he knows it."

"He doesn't hate you," Jaren muttered.

Athaya stopped on the stair and threw him a pointed glare over her shoulder. "He just compared me to a cup of bad whiskey."

There was an awkward pause, and Jaren's guilty expression left no doubt as to whom he and Lord Ian had been discussing in the Great Hall. "You heard."

"Lord knows it isn't the worst thing anybody's ever said about me," Athaya added, resuming her stride, "but it definitely leaves me with the impression that he'd rather you stay as far away from me as possible."

"He'll come around eventually," Jaren said sullenly. "Just give him time."

If I gave him from now until judgment day, it wouldn't be enough, Athaya mumbled to herself, but didn't pursue the subject. With the Circle of Masters lying in wait for her, she would have to find another time to consider how to win the duke's good opinion—if, indeed, it could be won at all.

CHAPTER 4

❊❊

WHEN ATHAYA AND JAREN ARRIVED, MASTER HEDRIC was already in his study, sweeping a ball of dust into the corner with a broom of bundled straw. He had scattered several candles and small lamps around the room, and their glow, combined with that of the fire, made the room a welcome retreat on such a dark winter evening. Hedric offered them a brief nod of greeting, then gestured for Jaren to help him push the worktable against the far wall, leaving the center of the low-ceilinged chamber bare.

"When will they be here?" Athaya asked, idly scanning the myriad jars and stacks of papers still littered about the chamber. Despite the lofty status of his fellow Circle members, Hedric obviously hadn't deemed it necessary to tidy up overmuch on their behalf.

"Oh, they're not coming here. We're going to them—in a manner of speaking." He gave a brief nod of satisfaction at the room's disheveled appearance and set the broom aside. "We'll be gathering at the Circle Chamber. It's located in Tenosce—a smallish city about a week's ride northeast of here. It's been our traditional meeting place ever since Wizard's College became part of the university there four centuries ago."

"A week's ride? But I thought the meeting was tonight."

"It is. And that means you have one more lesson to learn—and quickly."

He reached into his robe and handed her a flat, polished stone, different hues of gold and brown swirling together in a delicate pattern. On one side, it looked like a simple piece of agate, but on the other, she noticed that tiny runes had been carved into the rock.

"What is it?" she asked, turning the stone over in her hands.

He smiled crookedly. "Your invitation."

Leaving Jaren behind—who presumably knew how to use such stones—Hedric guided her to the center of the room and produced another stone from his pocket. He slowly ran his fingers over the runes, then extended his hands out to the sides as if trying to embrace the wind.

In a matter of seconds, tendrils of mist, just like those of a vision sphere, flowed from his palms. But instead of forming the traditional globe, the white essence gradually shaped itself into an oblong—a rectangular doorway running the full length of Hedric's body and matching the width of his outstretched arms. When complete, the oblong seemed to solidify, looking more like a pane of glass than insubstantial mist. It reminded Athaya of a winter window etched with frost, through which one could see nothing but swirling fog and snow.

Then Hedric turned away from his creation and held up his piece of stone. "It's a ward key," Hedric explained. "It's used to open a gateway through the protective wards surrounding the Circle Chamber. This gateway—we call it a panel—is somewhat like a vision sphere. There are a few technical differences," he went on with a shrug, "but the principle is roughly the same." He tapped his fingers against the oblong and it rang like fine crystal.

"But if everyone uses these panels, then why have the Chamber at all?"

"Those members of the Circle who can attend in person are encouraged to—panels can be somewhat tiring to maintain, and if the meetings run long, tempers tend to get short. But this being the middle of winter, I'd expect that only Basil and Tonia will actually get there. Basil lives in Tenosce and Tonia is from Ulard, a few miles north. Friend of Jaren's family, by the way," he added, casting a smile at his assistant. "But enough of that.

We've only got a few minutes, and I want to make sure I've set the key properly so you can activate it.''

At his cue, Athaya did exactly as he had done, touching the key to activate the spell within, and then holding her arms out to define the boundaries of the panel. Rest and a hot meal had helped restore her power after the afternoon's experiment with translocation, and it took only a minimal amount of effort to release the stone's preset spell. In minutes, she stood before an oblong of glasslike mist, identical to Hedric's but scaled down to her own height.

Nodding his satisfaction, Hedric turned away from the pair of misty oblongs and reclined into his favorite chair—the one that always reminded Athaya of a living tree that was only serving as a chair out of its own benevolence. ''You can leave the panel alone for now. When the Overlord calls for us, then we'll forge the visual link to the Chamber.''

Athaya cast a questioning look at Jaren, who hadn't said a word since they'd entered the library. She assumed he was still brooding about his talk with Lord Ian, as he had made no move to create his own panel.

''I only have one ward key besides my own,'' Hedric said, picking out her thought, ''and I can only set it to one person at a time. The two of you will have to share that panel.''

Just then, the library grew dim as the panels lost their silvery glow and turned a deep, smoky gray. Athaya flashed a worried look at Hedric, but he merely nodded and struggled back to his feet, his bones cracking faintly. ''Nothing's wrong, my dear. They're ready for us, that's all.''

Athaya positioned herself in front of the second panel, and Jaren stepped up behind her, close enough so that the pale light enveloped them both.

Then the murky depths of both panels suddenly flashed white, like unexpected lightning in the middle of the night. Athaya jumped back in surprise, and Jaren steadied her with his arms, holding on to her just a moment longer than he needed to once she regained her balance.

''Yes, yes, we're coming,'' Hedric grumbled as he settled himself in front of his panel. ''They've opened the gateway on their end, Athaya. Just touch the key to your panel to open your end.''

Following Hedric's lead, Athaya pressed the rune-carved side of the stone against the misty glass. With a soft click, the white haze instantly dissolved, revealing a multisided chamber like the chapter house of a small monastery. For a moment, Athaya forgot the serious nature of the meeting, so entranced was she by the room's simple beauty. Smooth, sandstone pillars ringed the room, soaring upward to support a graceful domed roof. Brass-plated candelabras were set near each of the pillars, each holding dozens of slender white tapers that gave off a soothing glow. The only aspect of the room that was at all ornate was the polished marble floor, its multicolored enamel inlay showing a cross flared at each of its four points, with each containing three interlocking circles—the same symbol that decorated the door of Hedric's study.

The serenity that the Chamber's beauty inspired in her did not last long. Spaced between the pillars, like a ring of playing cards come to life, were the panels of the other wizards of the Circle. They formed a striking array, and Athaya's gaze shifted in turn from the black-skinned giant in a yellow turban, to the sleek-looking woman with olive skin and seductive eyes, to the shrewd-looking gentleman sipping something from a flask, and finally to a white-haired icicle of a woman clad in a variety of exotic furs. They assessed her silently, their faces revealing nothing.

In the center of the circular chamber were two more figures, heads bowed close as they spoke in low tones to one another. The first was a rumpled-looking woman of middle years whose weathered face gave the distinct impression of having been crudely formed out of clay and left to harden in the sun. A simple russet gown hung loosely on her shapeless frame, the material wrinkled in places as if she'd been napping in it and hadn't found time to change before coming to the Chamber. In striking contrast, the man beside her was clad in an elegantly flowing blue robe accented with marten's fur and adorned by a collar of silver links. His hands and features were smooth and firm, like sculpted marble, and though little of it remained, not a hair on his head was out of place. Without breaking the oppressive silence that had fallen over the Chamber, he turned his piercing blue eyes to Athaya, pressing his thin lips together in stiff formality.

And this, Athaya thought with dismay, *can only be Overlord Basil.* Sleek blue robes billowed out behind him as he strode toward her, and even though she knew that the Overlord was actually in a city many miles away, she instinctively drew back. Worst of all, his steady, intimidating stare left little doubt as to which member of the Circle held such grave misgivings about her past.

No wonder Hedric hadn't told her.

"You are Athaya Trelane, princess of Caithe," Basil said, profoundly unimpressed.

Athaya tried to square her shoulders but only managed to create the impression that she had a cramp in her back. "I am."

"I have heard of you."

Athaya blinked. *And what you've heard isn't good, I take it.*

"You remember my assistant, Jaren McLaud, of course," Hedric said hastily, and Athaya was grateful for the brief respite from the Overlord's stony gaze. Basil's eyes flickered momentarily to Jaren.

"I do." His tone was neither approving nor disapproving; a kind of expressionless monotone that one could interpret a hundred different ways. Jaren murmured a few polite words of greeting, and Basil accepted them with a faint air of noblesse oblige before focusing his attentions back on Athaya.

"Do you know why we have summoned you?"

"With respect, Lord Basil," Hedric cut in again, "don't you think we could at least introduce her to everyone first?"

The Overlord looked at him blandly. If he was annoyed at having his breach of courtesy pointed out, the only visible sign was that his slender fingers curled more tightly around the collar of silver links at his throat. "As you wish, Master Hedric."

As Basil made each cursory introduction, Hedric sent a mental comment of his own to Athaya, much to the consternation of the Overlord, who could tell by her expressions what Hedric was doing and suspected that his comments were not entirely favorable. The rumpled woman beside him, however, looked highly amused, and Athaya even caught her tossing a conspiratorial wink to Hedric when the Overlord wasn't looking.

"This is Master Selga," Basil began, gesturing to the wintry-looking woman with the white hair and ice-blue eyes.

Not a bad sort, Hedric added, *but she's new to the Circle and tends to be a little snobbish about her talent.*

"And Master Arzan—" The ebony man in yellow silks, seated on a tasseled pillow.

A horse-breeder from Cruachi. A fine magician, but not much imagination.

Basil crossed the room and motioned to the next pair of panels. "And this is Master Genesco—"

A tea merchant, which explains why I always have a decent supply of it in spite of all the raiding on the trade routes. Drives a hard bargain, though. Even with his friends.

"Master Kiva—" The sultry one with well-oiled skin.

Ah, yes. Master Kiva. Nobody knows exactly what she does. Something illegal, I expect. Or at least she likes us to think so.

The Overlord's tone suddenly sounded more resigned. "And Master Tonia—"

Hedric's voice warmed noticeably as Lord Basil gestured to the shabbily clad woman at his side. *Probably the most level-headed, sensible one of us all. She can be brusque at times, but don't let it put you off—mostly I think she acts that way just to annoy Basil. In case you haven't noticed, he can be somewhat overbearing.*

Athaya began to laugh, then quickly covered it with a cough when she caught Basil's completely mirthless stare. She couldn't help thinking that if Basil were to ever meet her brother Durek, they would be able to spend many happy hours discussing their mutually unfavorable opinions of her.

Before Basil took charge of the gathering, however, Master Tonia sauntered up to Athaya's panel, nodding a greeting to her before peering over her shoulder to Jaren.

"It's been a few years, Jaren," Tonia said, molding her clay-like features into a sincere smile. "I don't think I've seen you in . . . oh, what's it been? Two years?"

"About that, Master Tonia. Is the farm doing well?"

"Oh my, yes," she replied with a chuckle. "Bought myself three more pigs last year, and—"

"I think we've had quite enough of the preliminaries," Basil announced, flicking an impatient glance at Tonia. "We have business to discuss . . . *if* that's all right with you?"

"Have it your way," she said with a mild shrug. Then, under her breath, she murmured, "You always do."

"My friends," Hedric began formally, addressing the entire Circle, "you have asked me to bring Athaya here so she could tell you in her own words what happened in Caithe last fall. I, in turn, would ask you to reserve judgment upon her until you have heard everything she has to say. I think there may be some unfair misperceptions about her that need to be cleared up." He didn't look at Basil as he spoke, but he didn't have to.

At Hedric's prompting, and with the eyes of the Circle upon her, Athaya swallowed hard, took a deep breath, and told her story as best she could. The longer she spoke, the more the tumultuous days of last autumn came back to her, and she remembered details of her experiences that she had thought long forgotten. She spoke of the time Hedric first told her what she was, and how, after denying it for so long, she had gradually allowed Jaren to teach her about her gift, and instill in her a profound respect for it. Then, trying to keep her voice from breaking, she told them of the disastrous accident with her spells that had caused Kelwyn's death, and of Rhodri's unexpected appearance at the funeral that led to her subsequent arrest. And finally, straining under the memory, she spoke of the offer Rhodri made to her—to give away her power or see Tyler die that day, with her and Jaren soon to follow—and how she had succumbed to his demands, unable to let the man she loved die for the sake of magic, and how it had left her powerless—

"And you say this ritual killed him?" the wizard Genesco asked, gazing at her without censure. "After he tried to take your magic?"

"Yes." She tried to block the gruesome vision of shattered flesh and bone from her mind. "I'd rather not describe exactly how."

From the panel on the opposite side of the room, Selga haughtily tossed back her long tresses of white hair. "Rhodri should have expected such an outcome. Did he think the Lord God would neglect to insure that wizards cannot hoard a treasury of magic like men hoard storerooms of gold?"

"You don't have to be so confounded pompous about it, Selga," Master Tonia grumbled.

"If you please," Basil scolded, holding up his hand for silence and allowing Athaya to finish.

"There's not much more to tell. After Jaren helped me recover my power, we escaped from the castle and made our way here. And I've been studying with Master Hedric ever since."

Basil nodded faintly. "Jaren, would you tell us exactly how this 'recovery' was effected?"

Athaya felt Jaren's hand tighten on her arm as he spoke, but his voice was steady and calm as he addressed the Circle, detailing how she had traced her paths to their source to trigger the magic's return. "The power was restored the moment Rhodri was dead," he explained, "but Athaya couldn't use it until after she'd touched it directly."

"Curious," the Overlord remarked, and then paused to consider their testimonies for several minutes. The chamber fell silent, and Athaya's gaze flickered to Hedric for a moment, who gave her a reassuring nod.

After what seemed like hours, Basil drew in a deep breath, pacing in a slow circle around the Chamber. "You do not deny that your magic was responsible for King Kelwyn's death?" His voice carried a note of surprise, as if he had not expected her to admit such a thing.

"I don't deny it, Lord Basil. But that king was also my father. If I could have prevented his death, I would have. I just didn't know how. He used magic against me and I simply tried to defend myself. I never meant to—"

"You tell us it was an accident, yet we have no proof of that."

Exactly what Durek had thought! Even though Hedric had warned her this might come up, the old accusation sent burning resentment coursing through her. She was on the verge of blurting out something unforgivably rude when Jaren whispered a steadying word in her ear, urging her to keep calm.

She dug her nails into her palms as she spoke, hoping the pain would lessen her rage. "If it's proof you want, why not read my thoughts? Look at my memories and see for yourself."

"Believe me, Athaya, I would do just that if we were in physical contact. And I may yet, at some future time. But for now we will have to forgo such a reading. Hedric could do it, certainly, but . . ." He didn't bother to finish, but his meaning was clear enough. Basil wasn't about to trust Hedric with such a delicate task if he couldn't be trusted to keep his students from dabbling in forbidden rituals.

"Actually, Basil, she might be able to drop in for a reading if you'd like her to." The look on Hedric's face was decidedly mischievous. "It seems as if she possesses the spell for translocation. You know—the one everyone keeps insisting is a myth."

The Overlord's nostrils flared in astonishment, and he made an indelicate sputtering sound with his lips. But he displayed

exceptional control and expertly brushed off the unforeseen pronouncement, unwilling to be upstaged by someone of Athaya's
dubious stature.

"Absurd," Genesco declared, peering absently into his flask
and then taking a small sip. "That's nothing but a child's tale."

"Then that child's tale caused Athaya to vanish during one of
her lessons today and reappear three miles away," Hedric replied. "She doesn't know exactly how she did it, but Jaren and
I are both witnesses."

Master Tonia scowled at the Overlord in frustration. "Basil,
aren't you listening? If this is true, then Athaya has stumbled
across one of the rarest spells in existence! Are you going to
ignore it just because you have reservations about the one who
did it?"

"I'm not ignoring anything, Tonia," he replied shortly, "but
we're here to discuss her past and her future, not what she learned
this afternoon."

"But the thought-reading . . ." she protested. "Or don't you
want to know the truth? Maybe you're happy enough thinking
the worst of her?"

"If I may, Master Tonia," the wizard Arzan interjected, deftly
defusing the argument, "a reading isn't even necessary at this
point. Everything the princess has related to us happened months
ago. By this time, she could have convinced herself that it was
the truth, even if it was not." The whites of his eyes were stark
against his deep black skin and seemed to glow in contrast. "A
reading would prove nothing."

Basil's eyes warmed slightly, visibly grateful.

"I'll grant that this discovery is of singular importance, Master Tonia," Basil conceded, glancing at Athaya as if she were a
curious artifact, and not flesh and blood, "but it is not the subject of tonight's gathering. Perhaps at some other time, we can
pursue it more fully . . . after she has learned more about the
spell and its properties. For now, let us return to the topic at
hand."

Hedric was somewhat perturbed to see the news of his pupil's
rare talent brushed aside so quickly, but even he had to admit
that there was precious little Athaya could say about the spell at
this point except that it existed.

"I see a disturbing pattern emerging here," came a bemused
voice from across the Chamber. Master Kiva raised two thin

brows, each perfectly shaped with kohl. "Why is it always your students that get themselves into such trouble, Hedric? First Rhodri, now this one—"

Although she was clearly teasing him, Hedric's face flushed with color. "I'd like to point out that Rhodri was ultimately responsible for this entire fiasco. If he hadn't been so hell-bent on proving that power could be safely transferred to someone born without it, then Athaya and Jaren never would have come so close to getting themselves killed."

Basil's expression was grave. "Take care not to let your personal feelings about Rhodri color your judgment, Hedric. After all, you were the only one who found fault with his nomination to the Circle at the time. We have no definitive proof that he was responsible for King Kelwyn's magic, or—"

"No proof?" Athaya cried out suddenly, unable to believe what she was hearing. "But he told me so himself! Everyone in Caithe knew of it!"

"And he wrote to me and admitted everything," Hedric added, remembering the letter that Athaya had brought with her on her first visit to Reyka. "It was all an experiment—a bid for a seat on this Circle. It was always his obsession—"

"And can you produce this letter?" Basil said, eyeing him warily.

Hedric paused for a moment before whispering a curse. "No. I was furious at his insolence, so I burned it."

"Ah. So once again we have only Athaya's word that Rhodri's death, like Kelwyn's, happened the way she said it did."

"But *I* was there," Jaren protested.

"And did you actually witness either of these deaths?"

"Well . . . no," he admitted. "But I was with her shortly afterward each time and I saw the condition she was in. She couldn't have faked that, Lord Basil. Or had time to invent anything other than the truth."

"As you say. But that is your opinion. Not proof."

"How can you stand there and flatly accuse her of murder?" Hedric retorted, now visibly angry. "You know how uncontrollable the *mekahn* can be in its late stages. Or maybe you don't at that," he added in frustration, "since hardly anyone in Reyka sees the symptoms at their worst anymore. We're all too damned sheltered. But you must know the Caithan clergy's stand on wizardry. What happened to Kelwyn was a tragic accident.

And as for Rhodri, why on earth would she have attacked him if not in self-defense?''

Basil's eyes narrowed dangerously. "Why, indeed. Must I remind you, Hedric, that there are those who don't share our particular views on the nature of our gift?''

Hedric was startled into silence for a moment. He hadn't expected Basil's suspicions to have extended quite that far. "No, you needn't—"

"The cultists in Sare, for instance. They think magic is divine, yes, but they also think it gives the Lorngeld a God-given right to rule over everybody else. Thank God there aren't many of them," Basil added with a snort of disgust. "But as we know, the Caithan kings also carry the traditional title 'Lord of the Isle of Sare,' howevermuch they may govern the island in name only. For all we know, Athaya could be in league with them—setting herself up as ruler in her homeland. Caithe hasn't got a single wizard in it, as far as we know. It would be easy for her to—"

"That's *enough*!" Athaya declared, fueling her voice with every shred of royal upbringing at her command. She could—and had—endured insults of all kinds, but this was too much to ignore. "I have no designs on the Caithan crown, my Lord, and for you to assume such a thing is blind insolence of the worst kind. I may as well accuse *you* of all manner of plotting and conspiracy to attain the lordship of this Circle . . . or can you *prove* to me that there was none?''

"Athaya!" Hedric shouted, stunned at both Basil's accusation and her violent outburst. "Athaya, be silent!"

The furious edge of his tone killed her next words even as she formed them. Breathing hard to steady herself, she dropped her eyes to the floor, infinitely grateful that his next remarks were not directed at her, but Basil.

"I think we've strayed from the subject again," Hedric said with forced calm.

The Overlord's face was oddly still, but the crease in his brow revealed an awareness that he had perhaps voiced too many of his suspicions. He let out a puff of a sigh, as if he'd just been told that his dinner would be slightly late.

"Very well, let us return to the central issue.''

Basil stepped in front of Athaya's panel and folded his sculpted hands together. To her surprise, he seemed to regard her with more respect than he had before, as if through her outburst she had somehow passed some sort of test.

"Suffice it to say, Athaya, that your past is somewhat controversial. I doubt that any good can come from debating something that none of us can change. But we can discuss the future. Hedric has told us that you have agreed to take the Caithan situation into your own hands. In light of that, this Circle has an interest in knowing what your plans are for Caithe. What will you do when you return?"

It was the first time Basil had addressed her without that edge of contempt—not to mention the first time he'd elected to use her given name—and she found herself slightly more at ease in his presence.

"I'll teach whoever I can. It will start slowly, but the more people I can train, the more I can send out to train others. We'll have to work secretly at first, until we gather enough support. And I want to locate my father's former allies and ask for their help. There weren't many of them, but one or two were quite influential. Perhaps I can convince them to donate money to found a Wizard's College in Caithe."

"An ambitious project for one determined young lady," Basil's remark was dry, but Athaya sensed a measure of admiration in it.

"I don't plan to send her off alone," Hedric pointed out. "As you know, I've contacted a few people that may be suited for the task and I've had one or two inquiries from those who have heard rumors about Athaya's intentions and are interested in joining her."

"And I'm certainly going to go," Jaren added resolutely, placing a hand on her shoulder.

Athaya felt as if a cold lump of coal had suddenly been dropped into her stomach. All at once she felt trapped—caught between Jaren and the panel with no route of escape. She edged forward slightly, awkwardly conscious of his touch, but before her thoughts could coalesce any further, the Overlord spoke again.

"I'm aware of Jaren's experience as a tutor, Athaya, but are you in any way qualified to teach inexperienced wizards?"

Athaya didn't answer right away, but after a moment's pause, she decided that it was a moot point. "I don't know, Lord Basil," she answered honestly. She met his gaze steadily. "But it's better than letting them die."

She saw the Overlord's brow go up, but he did not seem at all displeased with her response. In fact, he looked mildly impressed—as impressed as he would ever be with anything, she reasoned—and even nodded approvingly.

"Master Hedric can, of course, guide you in this. He's taught more wizards than even I can count, and most of them have done quite well." Athaya could sense that despite the friction between them, the Overlord truly respected Hedric's skill. "But I can't stress enough the importance of ethics," he cautioned. "Wielding such a power as we all possess involves far more than technical expertise."

"I know that all too well," she replied. That had been Rhodri's greatest fault—using powers without regard to their moral implications. As the victim of such negligence, she had vowed long ago that instilling a respect for ethics in all of her future pupils would be of highest priority.

Turning away from her, Basil asked the Circle if they had any further questions before their guests were dismissed, but the silent exchange of glances that ensued convinced Athaya that the Masters were inclined to suspend their discussions until she was gone.

"Lord Basil," Hedric said, "if you please, there's one more matter I'd like to bring to the Circle's attention before Athaya leaves."

"Very well, what is it?"

Hedric looked away from his panel to where Athaya and Jaren were standing. "Jaren, I'd like to ask you to go now. This is a private matter."

Jaren balked for only an instant before he obediently accepted his dismissal. His hands grasped her protectively for a moment, then released her to whatever Hedric was planning. He stepped out of the light of her panel, and Athaya heard the study door close softly behind her.

Basil looked vaguely puzzled by such secrecy. "What's this all about?"

"A matter involving Circle spells, my lord."

The Overlord flashed him a glare of warning. "You know better than that, Hedric. You were right to send your assistant away, but you will have to send Athaya out as well if you're planning to discuss the secrets of this council."

"This matter directly involves her, Basil. There's one of the Circle spells I think she should be taught, and—"

"What?" came Master Genesco's startled voice.

"Impossible," Selga declared, again tossing back her pale tresses.

Basil glowered. "Absolutely not. And you know better than to even bring up the subject."

"I have my reasons," Hedric insisted. "Can't I at least offer them?"

"Go ahead," Tonia piped up. "You've roused my curiosity, even if he hasn't got any." She jerked a thumb in the Overlord's direction.

"Yes, do go on," Kiva urged, as if eager to disrupt the meeting further.

Basil closed his eyes in resignation and made a curt gesture for Hedric to continue.

"It is true that Athaya has many weapons at her disposal should she need to defend herself in Caithe. But if she were openly threatened, one of her best defenses could be the sealing spell. A time may come when she'll be forced to hide what she is for her own safety."

"His words have merit," Arzan said candidly. "I would wish that spell at my disposal if I found myself in a land as inhospitable to wizards as Caithe."

Selga threw up her hands impatiently. "And where would that get you? Who would unlock the seal?"

"*What* seal?" Athaya blurted out, painfully conscious that she was very much left out of the conversation.

"A power seal, Athaya," Hedric said. "You reminded me of it this afternoon when you told me how weak your magic was after the translocation and how you thought you might have done something to impair it. A sealing spell is a way of locking away your powers so they can't be used."

Athaya frowned at him. "What kind of an advantage is that?"

"A great one if you happened to encounter any corbal crystals. With your power sealed away, the gem has no effect. You'd react to it just as you did before the *mekahn*, as if it were no different than any other gem. And unless there just happened to be another wizard nearby who could see that you have paths, no one would be able to identify you as one of the Lorngeld. That simple fact might just save your life if you get into trouble."

"Something you're bound to do," Master Kiva observed, but Athaya could tell from the friendly glint in her eye that she was only teasing, and more, that she felt a close affinity for those who make a habit of stirring up trouble.

"But why is it such a secret?" Athaya asked.

Basil regarded her with an air of foreboding. "A handful of spells—like the seal—are confined to the Circle because the potential for abuse is so great. They do have some benefits, however, and unlike the rite of assumption, have not been forbidden outright. You see, Athaya," he went on, growing even more grave, "you can not only place a seal on yourself, but you can place one on another wizard as well. Granted, they'd have to be fairly weak or defenseless not to be able to resist such an attack, but it can still be done. And if you refused to release them—"

Basil shook his head, but did not elaborate.

"The existence of the spell itself isn't a secret," Hedric explained, seeing Athaya's face still clouded with confusion. "We would have run across it eventually in the course of your studies. What I could *not* do was teach you how to cast the sealing spell, nor give you access to what has been written about its properties. Not without the Circle's permission." Hedric turned back to Basil and inclined his head. "Which I would like to request formally."

After a moment's consideration, the Overlord stepped up to each panel, privately conversing with each member to gain his or her opinion. Athaya strained to hear what they were saying, but caught nothing but a low buzz of voices. Nearly a quarter hour passed before he had obtained everyone's opinion and returned to Hedric's panel.

"Very well, Hedric. In light of the unusual circumstances, you have this council's permission, reluctantly given, I assure you, and under the express condition that you make sure to stress how extremely dangerous this spell can be."

"Thank you, Lord Basil. I'll go over all the details with her tomorrow."

"Wait—*how* dangerous?" Athaya asked, suddenly aware that there was more going on here than she'd realized.

Hedric waved her silent. "Later, Athaya. Later."

"It's growing late, and we still have some private matters to discuss," Basil said. He fixed his eye on Athaya, directing his next remarks to her. "I doubt there will be cause for us to meet again until after you have returned to Caithe, but believe me, this Circle shall anxiously await reports of your progress." The words were polite, but the curve of his lip insinuated that there had better *be* some progress, or she would come to regret it. "We will be watching you."

At first, Athaya was annoyed by his demeanor, but after considering it further, she realized that he was vaguely afraid of her—not of her power, but of the uncontrollable element she represented; something inside his domain, but entirely out of his reach.

"You made that sound like some sort of threat," she said lightly, intending it as a jest.

Basil stared directly at her with a cat's unblinking gaze. All of his earlier sternness and severity flowed back in full measure, and he pulled himself up to his full height.

"I meant to."

The Overlord stepped back, and in the next instant, Athaya's panel abruptly went to black. She had been summarily dismissed.

Then, from Hedric's panel, she heard Basil's voice again. "Now what's all this nonsense about translocation?"

With her part in the meeting over, Athaya left the study and ascended the steps to the library to wait for Hedric.

Late that same night, Athaya lingered in the library to read what she could about the sealing spell before her lesson with Hedric the next day. She had been wide awake right after the meeting—being told that she was about to learn an extremely dangerous spell had not been conducive to sleep—and wanted to read as much as she could while apart from Jaren, so she would not have to hide the books from him later and avoid answering whatever innocent questions he might ask about what she was studying. Not that he could have peered over her shoulder to find out. Those books containing details about Circle spells had been spelled so that the words would look like gibberish to those not approved to read them. After the meeting, Hedric had keyed the books to her and retired for the night, delaying their discussion about the sealing spell until morning.

When she could keep her eyes open no longer, Athaya finally decided to quit the library and seek out her own bed. She had no idea how late it was, but not long ago she had heard the thunder of hoofbeats in the courtyard, so there was obviously someone still up and about. She blew out all the candles and doused the fire, then proceeded down the dark, spiral staircase.

As she reached the base of the tower steps, she caught a furtive movement in the shadows ahead. An instant later, an arm reached out of the darkness toward her, and she jumped back with a strangled cry, poised to flee.

"Who's there?"

"Keep your voice down and come with me," Felgin whispered urgently. His hand clamped down hard around her arm, and he hustled her back up the narrow, timeworn steps so quickly that she could barely keep her footing.

"But where are we—"

"Shh!"

He all but dragged her back inside Hedric's study, his face set with grim determination. "Wait here. And whatever you do, don't leave this room."

Athaya jerked her arm away from him with growing impatience. "Felgin, for heaven's sake, what's going on?"

Her voice carried down the stairwell, and Felgin angrily put a finger to his lips, urging her to keep quiet until he was sure that no one else was lingering on the steps outside.

"Some not-so-friendly Caithan soldiers arrived a few minutes ago," he told her. "And you can be damned sure they're not on any kind of social call at your brother's behest."

Athaya's vision blurred for an instant, and she clutched the back of a chair to steady herself. "What do they want?"

"What else? They know you're here and they want Osfonin to turn you over to them. You're going to stay right here until I come back and tell you it's safe, understand?"

Without waiting for a response, Felgin slipped out of the room and locked the door behind him. Athaya listened to the sound of his footsteps retreating down the stairs, trying to ignore the frantic pounding of her heart. She had always known that it was only a matter of time before Durek realized where she was, but she never dreamed he'd send an official delegation demanding her return. On the contrary, she would have expected him to be grateful for her self-imposed exile. And now the king of Reyka was placed in a precarious situation. Osfonin could turn her over to the soldiers and leave her to whatever fate Durek saw fit, or

lie to the Caithan king to protect her and take the risk of falling
under attack. She might be his friend, but she was not a Reykan
by birth, and Athaya knew full well that Osfonin's first duty was
to his own people.

The next hour passed with agonizing slowness. Athaya jumped
at the slightest sound and was too wary to even light the room
with candles for fear someone would suspect her presence. A
ribbon of pale moonlight streamed though the leaded-glass window and fell across the floor, bathing the room in silver. Huddled in the window seat, she was angry at herself for trembling
and tried to convince herself that even if she was sent back to
Caithe in the company of Durek's men, she still had her magic
at her disposal and could no doubt manage to elude them.

It was then that she picked up the faint murmur of voices on
the other side of the door; voices of those taking care not to be
overheard. Her heart leaped into her throat when she heard the
metal scrape of the lock being turned aside. The door swung
open slowly, the old hinges letting out a low, ominous groan.
At first she saw only a feathered plume atop a shiny helmet, but
then a man appeared, clad in a shirt of chain mail covered with
a deep red surcoat. The visor of his helmet was down, as if he
were preparing for battle.

"So there you are," the man said, his words muffled behind
the visor. He raised a gloved finger and pointed it accusingly at
her. "Fugitive from the king's justice."

"Stay back," she warned. Mustering her courage, she poised
herself to cast a shielding spell in the event of an attack. "I'm
warning you—"

Athaya was caught off guard by the man's unexpected but
strangely familiar laughter. It was only then that she noticed the
Trelanian royal crest emblazoned on his surcoat and the jeweled
coronet encircling his helmet. Then he pulled up the visor and
grinned, revealing a face framed by wayward locks of sandy-
brown hair. With a flourish, he held out his arms like a per-
former awaiting applause.

"You can put me under any spell you like, little sister."

CHAPTER 5

✻✻✻

THAYA WAS SO STUNNED THAT FOR A MOMENT SHE COULD
do nothing but stare stupidly in front of her, frantically
wondering if the figure before her wasn't some kind of
illusion—a trick of the mind caused by an overlong day. But no
illusion could match the boyish grin that she knew so well, or
the mischievous twinkle in his eye that made him so irresistibly
popular with every young lady in Delfarham. Like being rudely
jolted from a dream, Athaya quickly shook off her trancelike
state of disbelief and threw herself into his outstretched arms
with a squeal of delight.

"Nicolas!"

He returned her embrace with vigor, laughing with delight as
he lifted her off her feet and hurled her around.

"Where did you . . . I mean, how did you . . ."

Before she could gather her wits enough to make some sense
out of the garbled words, Felgin's hooded face popped inside
the door.

"I'll come back for you in about an hour," he said to Nicolas.
The Reykan prince couldn't help smiling at the sight of the warm
reunion before him, although he frowned in an attempt to convey the seriousness of their situation. "Just keep it down, all
right?"

Once Felgin had left them, Nicolas deposited his helmet and

54

gloves on Hedric's worktable and kicked off his black leather boots next to the darkened fireplace.

"God's breath, Athaya, it's freezing in here!" he exclaimed, realizing that there wasn't a single source of heat in the room. He gave her a good-natured scowl. "Couldn't you have fled to a more temperate city?"

Taking the hint, Athaya went to the fireplace and placed an armful of kindling atop the cold logs, setting the stack to blaze with a touch and a whisper. Nicolas watched this procedure with delight, taking an unusual amount of pleasure in what to Athaya was a fairly routine chore.

Athaya brushed a patch of powdery soot from her sleeve as she and Nicolas settled down into a pair of cushioned chairs near the hearth. She smiled at him broadly. "Now that I've recovered from the shock of seeing you, will you tell me what on earth you're doing here?"

"Didn't they tell you?" he replied, curling his lips down in distaste to indicate his unfavorable opinion of the mission. He ran his fingers through flattened locks of hair in a futile attempt at making it look acceptable. "I've brought an order of extradition for you. Compliments of our favorite brother."

"Long live the king," she murmured, with a noticeable lack of enthusiasm.

"I promised him I'd try to persuade you to come home."

Athaya looked up sharply. Her first instinct was to wonder what threats Durek had delivered in order to force Nicolas into doing such a thing, but the bemused expression on his face told her that he had no intentions of taking the king's order seriously. Relieved, she let out a short, humorless laugh. "Come home for what? My execution?"

"Not a very tempting offer, is it?" he said with a careless wave of his hand. "But I had to agree to try. It's the only reason he said I could come."

"Frankly, I'm surprised he let you come at all, no matter what you promised him. I didn't think he trusted you that much."

"Trust, little sister?" he responded dryly. "Maybe that explains why he sent his guard captain and two dozen soldiers along to 'protect' me." Nicolas rolled his eyes, offended but hardly surprised by his brother's watchfulness. "Besides, I'm not the official spokesman of the group. That's Lord Gessinger's job, the pitiful old coot. Dagara nagged him to death until he

agreed to volunteer. God knows nobody else was anxious
to . . . let's see, how did Archbishop Ventan put it? To 'risk his
eternal soul by venturing into a land plagued by heretics.' ''

"I just can't believe those two are related," Athaya said,
pointedly withholding comment on the archbishop's misguided
opinions. "Dagara is as shrewish as they come, but her brother
is about as lively as a cup of warm milk. I can't imagine what
good Gessinger is to the king's council when he tries his best to
fade into the background and say as little as possible."

Nicolas smirked his agreement, then stretched out his legs
and wriggled his toes inside the thick woolen hose. "He and
the others are still down in the hall. I think his Majesty would
have made them camp outside the palace but for the fact that
I'm with them—Osfonin was less than thrilled to hear we'd arrived, especially at this hour. Right now, I'd imagine that he's
busy telling them all that he hasn't the remotest idea where you
are, while Gessinger is fumbling for a diplomatic way of letting
him know he's lying. I knew it would grow tiresome rather
quickly, so I drew Felgin aside the moment we got here and
persuaded him to take me to you. He tried to play dumb at first,
but once I reminded him that it was me who helped get you and
Jaren out of Delfarham in the first place, he figured I could be
trusted." For a moment, Nicolas grew solemn. "Strange how
a man I barely know, and a Reykan wizard at that, puts more
trust in me than my own brother."

Athaya nodded, knowing full well how he felt. "Won't the
others wonder where you've gone?"

Nicolas shrugged casually. "Oh, I doubt it. I'll just tell them
I was off chasing girls or some such thing. Since Durek already
thinks I'm frivolous and stupid, his guardsmen are more than
willing to think so, too. Besides," he added, raising a brow, "I
may just chase a girl or two while I'm here. I've seen several
likely candidates already."

With a playful grin, Nicolas swung his bootless feet aimlessly,
creating an exaggerated illusion of utter boredom. Then he let
out a lingering sigh.

"So, are you going to come back with us?"

After adjusting to the rapid change of subject, Athaya shook
her head gravely. She tried to contain a smile so as not to ruin
the masquerade. "No, Nicolas, I'm not."

"Good!" he declared, slapping his hands together as if to rid them of dust. "Now at least Durek can't accuse me of not asking." He quickly scanned the room, surveying the contents of Hedric's numerous shelves. "Got anything to drink around here?"

Laughing, Athaya went to one of the cupboards and fetched a flagon of wine and two polished pewter cups, certain that under the circumstances Master Hedric would not mind their helping themselves to his provisions. She handed one cup to Nicolas, and they touched the rims together in a delicate chime.

Nicolas drained his cup quickly, nodding his pleasure with the unfamiliar vintage. Then his features grew more taut as he put aside his usual carefree demeanor for a more solemn one. Despite what Durek might think, Athaya knew that Nicky was neither frivolous nor stupid, and was quite capable of being serious when the situation merited it. The secret of his charm, however, was that he found such situations rare. He hid it well, but Athaya could detect the desperate concern in his eyes and noted the way his hands anxiously caressed the smooth pewter goblet.

"Tell me what's happened, Athaya. Are you well?"

"Well enough for a fugitive, I suppose. I spend most of my time studying magic with Master Hedric. He doesn't say so very often, but he thinks I'm doing all right. And I'll never be able to repay Osfonin's kindness in allowing me to stay here. He could have easily turned me away."

Nicolas refilled his cup from the flagon. "So where's Jaren? I haven't seen him since I got here."

"I have no idea," Athaya said worriedly. She hadn't thought to ask Felgin if Jaren was in hiding as well. "He didn't exactly make friends with Father's guardsmen last fall. I hope he doesn't run into any of them in a dark corridor someplace. It could get . . . unpleasant."

"For whom? The guardsmen?" Nicolas quipped, openly confident that Jaren's arcane talents would give him the advantage in any such confrontation. "I'm just glad that somebody's been here looking after you in my place. Jaren struck me as a decent sort. And I think he likes you," he added, winking at her.

Oh, Nicolas, if only you knew the half of it, she thought somberly, unable to take much comfort in his innocent remark. She shifted her weight uneasily in her chair. "Tell me what's happening at home," she said, eager to change the subject.

As she had expected, news of her part in Kelwyn's death and of the accidental fire that swept through the cathedral during his funeral had spread throughout the country like a contagion, with the tale growing more and more bizarre the farther it traveled from the capital. The more vocal bishops of the Curia had been more than willing to feed the rumors, too, being fervently convinced that this was only further proof that magic was indeed spawned from the depths of hell and those who used it the servants of the Devil. It was difficult for Athaya to keep a tight rein on her anger as Nicolas spoke, but she managed to hold her tongue, sullenly brooding over the fact that if she'd had a less-than-sterling reputation in Caithe before, it was now infinitely worse.

"And there's one more thing," Nicolas added hesitantly, watching for her reaction. "Ventan's excommunicated you."

Under any other circumstances, Athaya might have felt fear—even stark terror—at being publicly declared a heretic, at knowing she was excluded from all sacraments of the Church that, according to the priests, would insure her salvation. *But if that excludes me from the sacrament of absolution,* she added inwardly, *then I'm all for it.*

To Nicolas' surprise, a strange, almost peaceful smile crept over Athaya's face. "I knew he'd do that. But you know, Nicolas . . ." She struggled with her words, unsure of exactly what she needed to express, but knowing it was important—something she felt in the very marrow of her bones. "Ventan may say I'm damned now, but in all those years of sitting through his sermons and reciting the prayers I was taught to say, I never felt as if I was going to be saved to begin with. I never felt anything. Except boredom, of course," she added wryly. Her eyes took on a faraway look. "But studying my magic has given me more reason to think that maybe there really *is* something called God watching over us. I can't explain it. I'm not even sure I understand it. But I can sense it somehow."

Athaya laughed self-consciously. "I'm sorry. This really isn't the time for me to bore you with talk of my spiritual growth. Go on—tell me the rest."

In what she considered a much more pleasant subject than Archbishop Ventan's negative opinion of the state of her soul,

Athaya was delighted to hear that Cecile was going to have another baby and was strangely glad that her sister-in-law would be away from Durek for a while.

"But it's causing some grumbling in the city," Nicolas added. "Cecile has always been popular with the people, and they don't like the circumstances under which she left." He paused, gazing at his sister pointedly. "Cecile didn't leave Delfarham by choice, you know."

"What do you mean?" Athaya asked, startled. As far as she knew, Cecile hadn't an enemy in the world, and certainly none who would wish to see her removed from court.

"Putting it simply, Durek knows that she's still fond of you in spite of your magic and he doesn't like it one bit. He sent her away so she could reconsider her opinions of you. Frankly, there's not much she can do without turning the whole thing into an ugly, public scandal. If she speaks up on your behalf, she's as much as denouncing the whole Church at the same time. Not to mention denouncing Durek, too."

"I'd never expect her to do that for me, Nicolas," Athaya told him gently. "I wouldn't expect it from you, either."

"I know. But I wish I could do something, even though I'm not sure what. It hurts more than you know just to sit back and listen to everyone slander you. And if I have to listen to one more of Dagara's speeches about the shame you've brought down on the family—" Nicolas didn't bother to finish, completing the sentiment by rolling his eyes in disgust. "She couldn't care less about the family reputation, or, I suspect, the fact that Kelwyn is dead at all. The only thing she's upset about is that the burns she suffered in the fire have forced her to walk with a cane. Her limp isn't that bad, but she acts as if her life is effectively over because of it. The Innocent Victim is becoming one of the better roles in her repertoire."

"I always thought she'd make a fine actress," Athaya murmured. "Especially since Durek has consistently proven to be such a receptive audience. And what of him?" she asked, brushing aside the persistently unpleasant subject of her stepmother. "Has he been making life difficult for you?"

"Oh, not really. He barely speaks to me except to ask why I don't marry an heiress and get out of his sight. But I think he's taken Father's death harder than either of us would have expected." Nicolas looked into the flames as if he were seeing a vision of the past. "He never loved Father, but I'm not sure Durek was as ready to be king as he wanted everyone to believe. He's fairly good at covering his insecurities with a lot of bluster, but deep down I think he's terrified that if people start comparing him to Kelwyn, he won't come off looking so good."

"That might be more a matter of bad timing than any fault of his," she pointed out, trying to be diplomatic. "Almost anyone would look bad coming after Kelwyn. By all accounts, Father was a great king. Even the Reykans think so."

When he returned his gaze to her, Athaya could see the concern in his eyes. "I think that's why Durek is so intent on finding you. If he could, in his words, 'bring down the wizard who brought down Kelwyn,' then nobody could ever accuse him of being ineffectual."

Reluctantly, Athaya nodded her agreement, although she had every intention of balking Durek's plans.

"His guardsmen spent months looking for you," he went on. "They finally traced you here, thanks to that slippery little bastard who's taken Tyler's place—" Nicolas broke off quickly. "I'm sorry, Athaya. I didn't mean to bring that up so bluntly."

"It's all right, Nicky. The pain's not quite so fresh now." She picked up the wine flagon from the floor and refilled her cup, swirling it around for a while before taking a brief sip. "Sometimes I think Hedric pushes me as hard as he does just so I won't have time to brood about what happened . . . and I have to admit it's helped. There's nothing I can do to bring him back. Nobody's magic is that strong."

Athaya sank back into her chair, growing wistful. "Tyler hasn't even been gone six months, but sometimes I feel . . . I don't know, as if all my memories of him are only dreams . . ." She shrugged off the rest of her thought, discomfited by the direction it was taking. It seemed unfeeling, as if starting to heal meant starting to forget as well. "Maybe it's just because I'm here, and not in Caithe. I'm sure the memories will come back stronger once I'm home."

Nicolas sat bolt upright, and the sudden movement almost caused Athaya to drop her wine cup into her lap. "Once you're— Athaya, what are you saying? You can't go back there."

"I have to, Nicky. Oh, not with you and Durek's soldiers," she amended hastily, "but there's something I have to do. Something important." She leaned forward, reaching out to grasp his hand. "I can't tell you much about it—it's safer for you if you don't know."

"It isn't hard to guess, little sister," he replied, giving her hand a gentle squeeze. "You're going back to stir up a pot of trouble, aren't you? To start teaching magic to the Lorngeld?"

Athaya nodded. "Somebody needs to do it."

She pulled herself out of the comfortable chair and walked in a broad circle around the room, lightly brushing her fingertips over the array of items stored there, half hidden by the dim firelight: jars of powders and liquids whose purposes Hedric had never satisfactorily explained to her, scraps of paper upon which were written the Master's half-formed ideas and theories of his craft, and dozens of gilt-edged books whose contents she had become painfully familiar with over the last few months. All were relics of an art she had learned to love and respect, even if many of its mysteries were still unknown to her.

She picked up a time-worn copy of the *Book of Sages*—the most well-known and highly respected collection of essays on the subject of magic. "I can't keep this knowledge all to myself, Nicolas. There are people who desperately need it. I have to pass it on." She ran her fingers across the ancient pages, now smooth as silk. "I owe it to Father. And to Tyler."

"But can't you wait until things calm down at home first?"

Athaya turned to him, her eyes fierce with resolve. "Every day I wait is another day when someone is going to die because no one's there to help them live. No one to teach the Lorngeld how to avoid the madness that their magic brings when it manifests. No one to stop them from lashing out with their untrained spells." Athaya choked on her breath, struggling to go on. "No one to stop them from killing people they love because they don't know what they're doing."

She searched her brother's face for a response and was puzzled at what she saw. He was gazing at her as if he'd never seen her before, as if she were someone he'd met long ago, but couldn't quite place.

"What's the matter?"

Nicolas remained quiet for several moments, studying her with a degree of intensity that Durek never would have dreamed him capable of. Then he slowly got to his feet and went to stand beside her.

"You've changed, Athaya," he told her softly. "I think you've finally grown up. I thought about doing it myself once but it all seemed rather pointless,'' he added lightly, but with a trace of sadness, as if he had lost something in her gain. He flashed her a grin, but his pensiveness soon returned. ''Ever since we were kids you've always been sort of lost, as if you never really knew what to do with yourself. I felt as if I needed to protect you—to keep you from getting in more trouble other than what you managed to find on your own. But you're so much more confident now. It's as if you've found something that you've been looking for all your life.''

''I have,'' she said, casting her eyes over the books and jars and half-filled ink pots scattered throughout Hedric's study. She looked up and smiled at him. ''But that doesn't mean I won't get into trouble the minute your back is turned.''

''I have no doubt of that,'' he said, clearly worried, but managing to laugh it off. He reached out and gave her a hug only slightly less forceful than the one she'd received earlier. ''Father would be so proud of you right now. You're more like him than any of us, little sister. I never realized that until today.''

Athaya felt her breath catch in her throat, and her eyes glazed over with warm tears. Nothing Nicolas had ever said to her had been spoken with such conviction, or had struck her with more force. Durek was a fool indeed if he truly thought his younger brother was a dull-witted encumbrance, for Nicolas was one of the finest, most loving human beings Athaya had ever known.

''It's time for me to keep the promise I made. I can't hide in Reyka forever, and I don't want to take advantage of Osfonin's protection. If Durek got angry enough, or found proof that I was being sheltered here, he might do something rash. Ever since the day of Father's funeral, I've heard rumors that Ventan and the Bishop's Curia have been clamoring for Durek to launch a crusade against the Reykans. I don't want to be responsible for a disaster like that.''

Nicolas sighed heavily. ''They're more than just rumors. The Curia is starting to gain the support of the council. Not enough so that Durek needs to make a decision on it yet, but the followers they've managed to get are quite vocal.''

''And I don't want to be the catalyst that sets them off. I don't want to give them the excuse they need to march in here and start slaughtering wizards.''

Nicolas brushed her forehead with a kiss. "Do what you have to, Athaya. You've got my blessing, if it'll do you any good."

Athaya gave him a sidelong glance. "Not going to try and talk me out of it?"

"Oh, no, little sister," he replied, his eyes twinkling. "I learned many years ago never to try and talk you out of *any-thing.*"

In the Great Hall of Glendol Palace, on the opposite side of the fortress from Master Hedric's study, Lord Mosel Gessinger was awkwardly fumbling with the red ribbons binding the scroll that his king had entrusted to him. It took several minutes for the gaunt, small-boned lord to uncurl the heavy vellum and another moment to adjust the distance between the paper and his aging eyes so that he could make out the words inscribed there. He was a naturally soft-spoken man, and when he finally began to read, those gathered in the hall had to strain to hear him.

"To his most esteemed Royal Majesty, Osfonin of Reyka, from his Majesty Durek Trelane, King of Caithe and Lord of the Isle of Sare, greetings . . ."

"Skip to the meat of it, sir," Osfonin grumbled, drawing a dark blue mantle close around his broad shoulders. He knew that he should be showing his guest better courtesy, but he was hardly in the mood to do so. What should this foreign lord expect, appearing on the palace doorstep just before midnight? By this time, Osfonin had hoped to be deep under a pile of quilts, sleeping soundly, but instead he sat rigid in his throne on the dais, glowering in frustration as he waited for Durek's spokesman to voice the demands that he had always known would come. His only surprise was that it had taken this long for them to arrive. He drummed his fingers impatiently on the throne's ornately carved armrest, and each motion caused Lord Gessinger to grow slightly more flustered, eventually repeating the same sentence twice.

". . . wishes to remind you of the laws regarding magic in Caithe, and of the grievous crimes committed by our sister in this regard. It is in consideration of her soul that we . . ."

While Gessinger droned on, Osfonin's gaze wandered across the Hall, first to Felgin, seated on the dais at his right, and then to Lord Ian McLaud, whose soldier's ear had been among the first to hear the clatter of new arrivals in the courtyard. And although Osfonin had not requested it, twice the normal number of guards had materialized about his person, exhibiting as little trust in the Caithans as the visitors had in their hosts. The king had briefly considered sending for Master Hedric as well, but since none of these Caithans were wizards—a fact they would doubtless be proud of—he felt that Felgin's presence would be sufficient in the event that any less traditional means of defense became necessary.

". . . concluded that it is to your court that the princess was most likely to go, and through the efforts of our most loyal servants, we have obtained evidence . . ."

As Lord Gessinger reached the heart of his speech, the tension in the musty hall became almost palpable. Each nervous cough or rustle of the rushes on the floor sent Caithan hands twitching involuntarily toward weapons which were no longer there, having been left outside the doors of the hall as custom demanded.

"A bit jumpy, aren't they," Felgin whispered in his father's ear. One corner of his mouth tipped up sardonically. "Could it be they dislike our methods of lighting?"

The king tried not to smile as his eyes flickered upward to the ring of reddish witchlights hovering in a circle just below the rustic, timber-beamed ceiling. He knew that Felgin had put them there on purpose, but he had not requested their removal, considering it a harmless measure of revenge for having his much-needed sleep so long delayed. Every few minutes, some wary member of the Caithan delegation peered up at the witchlights suspiciously, half expecting the small orbs of brilliant fire to give imminent birth to demons, imps, or, worse, the Dark Angel himself.

The Hall fell silent for a moment, and Lord Gessinger cleared his throat rather sheepishly, almost reluctant to come to the end of his speech and impart his king's orders.

"We therefore demand the return of our sister to answer charges of high treason for the murder of his late Majesty, Kelwyn Trelane, and—"

Having remained silent long enough, Osfonin snorted impatiently. "And when did it become my duty to track the whereabouts of the Caithan king's relatives?"

Seemingly unaware that his king had just been ridiculed, Lord Gessinger continued reading Durek's demands. "We further warn that if the wizard who assisted in her escape is ever seen in Caithe again, his life is summarily forfeit.''

Just then, the tapestries behind the dais shifted, and a slender figure emerged from the shadows.

"You'd be referring to me, then."

Jaren descended the dais steps slowly, glancing aside at his father only long enough to see the look of furious apprehension on his face.

"Son, stay back," Ian whispered urgently. "These men are no friends of yours."

Silently motioning that he'd be safe enough, Jaren proceeded down the steps until he stood squarely in front of the Caithan ambassador. Feeling a twinge of pity, he offered Gessinger an unexpectedly warm smile—the poor man looked so thin that one strong wind might very well reduce him to dust.

"Good evening, Lord Gessinger. I'm Jaren McLaud." He held out his hand in greeting, and the Caithan stared at it for a moment, as if surprised that a wizard would have a normal five-fingered hand instead of a claw of some kind. Then, not knowing what horrible fate might be in store for him if he refused the proffered hand, Gessinger hastily reached out and accepted it.

Behind him, Captain Parr simmered openly, glaring at the young wizard with thinly veiled contempt. The unusual glint in his eye revealed that Jaren was not feeling well disposed toward the man who had betrayed Tyler Graylen to his king, and here, safe in his own homeland, he could afford to needle the new captain a bit.

"And I certainly remember you, Lieutenant Parr." He flicked a glance at the brass-linked collar of office around Parr's neck. "Ah. It's 'Captain' now, I take it?" Spoken by the son of a duke, the observation came off with a vaguely condescending air, and Parr gritted his teeth with wounded pride.

"I'm certain that King Osfonin can offer you far more comfortable quarters during your stay with us than I'm afraid I received during my recent visit to Delfarham," Jaren went on, the image—and the smell—of that fetid dungeon still unpleasantly vivid in his mind.

"You deserved worse than that," the captain rumbled under his breath, soft enough so that only those closest to Jaren and Lord Gessinger could hear. "Devil's whelp . . ."

Sensing from the murder in Parr's eyes that Jaren had perhaps been given sufficient opportunity to greet the court's guests, Osfonin rose to his feet. "Jaren, would you kindly tell these gentlemen that Princess Athaya is not here. I have explained this once, but they seem to distrust me."

"Certainly, sire," he responded genially, turning back to Gessinger and Parr. "I hate to disappoint you, but I haven't any idea where your princess has gone. We parted ways after our ship docked in Torvik last November, and I haven't seen her since." He shrugged negligently. "She could be on the far side of Selvallen by now."

While Lord Gessinger formulated a polite but skeptical response, the captain glared fire at Jaren. His fingers coiled into tight fists, and had there been a dagger at his belt, it would by now have been well on its way to Jaren's throat.

"Your Majesty," Gessinger began placatingly, "if we could but discuss this further—"

"And discuss it we will, but in the morning when we are all better rested." The king's tone left no doubt that the gathering was adjourned. As he rose, he gestured to the tall, mail-clad soldier posted at the end of the dais. "Lars, see that our guests are given suitable accommodation."

With that, the king strode purposefully out of the Hall, with Felgin, Jaren, and Lord Ian trailing along behind. He looked back only once, and tried not to chuckle as he saw Felgin's ring of witchlights suddenly drop out of the air like a broken chandelier, sending startled Caithans scattering toward the walls in fear of being touched by the Devil's magic.

"Do you think they believed you?" Felgin murmured in Jaren's ear, once they reached the outside corridor.

Jaren's only reply was an intensely cynical glare.

"You'd do well to keep away from Athaya this week," Felgin went on. "That captain will be watching you every chance he gets." Then the prince lowered his voice so that Lord Ian, following a few yards behind them, would not hear. "That is, if you think you can survive seven whole days without seeing her," he teased.

"I'll manage," Jaren replied. "Besides, if all my plans work out, Athaya and I will have plenty of time together once the Caithans are gone." He couldn't suppress an ebullient smile. "Plenty of time."

* * *

The Caithan guardsmen were installed in the castle gatehouse, while Lord Gessinger—and Prince Nicolas, if he ever deigned to appear again—were assigned more comfortable quarters in the guest wing. Two members of that delegation had not yet retired, however, and lingered in a private corner of the moonlit courtyard, speaking as quietly as they could in consideration of the Reykan soldiers standing a polite distance away, ready to escort them to their beds.

"That McLaud bastard is lying through his teeth, I just know it," Parr spat, each word forming a cloud of ice in the crisp night air. If he could have been granted any wish at that moment, it would have been to see Jaren's head on a pike, in the fashion of his former superior.

Lord Gessinger shook his head in mild dismay. "Be careful, Captain. He's a duke's son *and* a wizard. Not a good enemy to cultivate."

"But he *knows* where Princess Athaya is—I'd stake my life on it! And it wouldn't surprise me if she's somewhere inside these very walls," he added, glowering at the massive stone fortress around him. "Why else would Prince Nicolas have vanished so quickly?"

Gessinger furrowed his brows. "Remember yourself, Captain," he cautioned. His warning, however, was effectively diluted by the blandness of his tone. "It is quite unwise to voice negative opinions about one's prince."

"It's a damned sight better than never voicing any opinion at all!" Parr snapped back. Then, quickly realizing that offending one of Durek's councillors would be no benefit to his career, he grudgingly bowed his head. "My apologies, my Lord. I spoke out of turn."

Gessinger waved off the apology with an air of puzzled embarrassment. "I just don't see why you're so adamant about finding the princess. One might think there is more to it than simply desiring to obey the king's order. You have to admit that if it wasn't for Athaya, you'd still be lieutenant to Tyler Graylen, not captain of the squadron."

Parr blinked his disbelief. Was it possible that Gessinger was truly as stupid as the court thought him? "Why so adamant?" he repeated incredulously. "How can you even ask that? She's a wizard! That's a crime enough in itself, even if she hadn't murdered King Kelwyn. And the fact that she refused Archbishop Ventan's offer of absolution only proves how twisted and sick she's become. She has to be caught before she infects anyone else with her fanatical ideas."

Gessinger merely sighed with tired resignation. "Mmm . . . yes. I suppose."

"I can't go back to Caithe without learning something, my Lord. I've worked hard to get where I am, and the king has finally taken notice of me. He's given me a great responsibility, and I won't fail him."

"And you won't refuse whatever reward he extended to you if you succeed, will you?" Gessinger observed.

"There's nothing wrong with ambition," Parr replied curtly. "Especially for those of us who weren't born with a title tacked onto our names."

Again, Gessinger let the veiled insult pass and preferred to yawn instead. "It's late, Captain, and I must retire. We must be on the alert every moment we're here, and for that we need our rest."

Under the watchful eye of their Reykan escorts, Gessinger retreated inside the fortress while Captain Parr broodingly crossed the courtyard toward his own rooms in the gatehouse, boots crunching on new snow like horseshoes on gravel. On his way, he snapped a slender icicle from the eaves of the stables and toyed with it as he walked as if it were a dagger.

In the center of the yard he stopped, turning to look up at the spires of the palace. Methodically, he passed his gaze over each one of the windows, his eyes narrowing as he scanned the ancient fortress. All seemed calm in the frigid starlight, and only the most distant of sounds could be heard . . . the neigh of a restless horse, the latching of a window shutter, a snowy owl hooting its wisdom for anyone who would listen. But in the midst of that seeming calm, he knew, was the object of his quest.

"I know you're here somewhere, Princess," he murmured to himself. "No matter what that hell-spawned wizard Jaren says." He gripped the icicle with both hands and snapped it cleanly in two, tossing the pieces carelessly aside as if they were bones gnawed clean of meat. Then he turned his eyes toward the moon, and spoke as if swearing fealty to it. "The king has put his faith in me," he vowed resolutely, unconcerned by the curious stares of the Reykan guards lingering nearby. "And I won't go back to Caithe empty handed."

CHAPTER 6

✳

W ITH DUREK'S SOLDIERS IN THE PALACE, ATHAYA RE-
mained in seclusion in her rooms even though it left
her little better than a prisoner in honorable confinement. She dared not risk moving through the castle even under
a cloaking spell, fearful that, just as Rhodri had done during her
father's funeral, someone might catch her reflection in an unnoticed mirror or well-polished surface. And while she might
have been able to make excellent use of her translocation spell,
Hedric warned her that she'd had no practice with it, and might
find herself reappearing somewhere other than her intended des-
tination—perhaps in full view of those Caithans who were being
told repeatedly that she wasn't anywhere near Ath Luaine. So
for the meantime, she accepted her voluntary imprisonment,
grudgingly realizing that her situation could be considerably
worse. Still, even after the first day, she had memorized every
inch of the wall tapestry, noted every frayed bit of brocade on
the draperies and bedcovers, and rearranged the chairs by the
hearth a half-dozen times.

On her second day in hiding, two days after the Circle meeting—which, in all the excitement of Nicolas' arrival, she had
almost forgotten—Master Hedric came to her chambers and began instructing her on the sealing spell. One thing she had not
forgotten was Hedric's mention of how dangerous the spell could

be, and she was much more alert than usual during his discourse on the subject.

"Putting it bluntly, the spell can be lethal," Hedric informed her, showing no hint of surprise when her eyes grew round with alarm. "Once your power is sealed, all of your spells are out of reach—including the one that releases the seal. It's like locking yourself in a room and leaving the key on the other side. Another wizard—one who knows the spell—has to unlock the door and let you out."

"But isn't that just more of an inconvenience than anything else?" Athaya asked, shifting to a more comfortable position in her cushioned chair by the fire. "All you'd have to do is wait until you could find someone who knew how to release the seal."

Hedric's weathered features grew grim. "I'm afraid you wouldn't have the luxury of time, Athaya. Oh, a few days wouldn't matter. Probably not even a few weeks. But if you leave the seal unattended for too long, the pressure of your power will keep building—much as it does during the *mekahn*. You'd start experiencing the same sort of mental disruptions, except with your power trapped, there would be no way of releasing the excess energy even in a destructive way. At its worst, once the madness sets in, the pressure can rupture."

Athaya swallowed noisily. "And what happens then?"

"Nothing. That's the last thing that would ever happen to you. You'd be dead shortly after it occurred."

Athaya stopped breathing for an instant, suddenly quite tempted to forgo learning about the sealing spell and take her chances with a corbal crystal. At least that was a known quantity—a threat that could be smashed into fragments or hidden in the dark. Hedric, however, sensed her trepidation and quickly went on with the lesson before she had a chance to object.

"The first thing you need to remember is that the sealing spell requires physical contact to work. To work on someone else, that is," he added. "If you're not touching anyone, the spell affects you instead. But it's not quite as easy as it sounds. Unless the subject is willing, or unless the spellcaster is extremely talented, it's very difficult to hinder another wizard's magic with a seal. It's easier to do if they're asleep or unconscious, but otherwise, wizards' powers are quite good at protecting themselves. When threatened, magic usually speaks up."

He reached out for her hand to forge the necessary contact for the spell, and Athaya offered it reluctantly. She was always discomfited when Hedric spoke of magic as if it were a living entity inside her—something that shared her body and acted according to her will only out of a sense of benevolence. She knew that she held ultimate control over whatever power was inside her, but there were times when she suspected that her magic was still far more potent than she was.

"Just try not to resist," Hedric cautioned, "or the experience will be unpleasant for both of us."

Athaya nodded, but found that relaxing wasn't easy. She should have felt some measure of excitement at learning a spell unknown to anyone outside of the Circle, but that knowledge only served to fill her with dread. When Hedric touched her mind, she flinched in apprehension, but after a few soothing whispers, he managed to calm her enough to do his working. Her apprehension refused to vanish entirely, however, and a moment later she felt gripped, as if someone had wrapped a hand around her mind and held it fast. Even though she tried to submit, knowing Hedric would not harm her, her first reaction was to struggle, all the while knowing that it was too late to get away.

"Obsera hanc potentiam."

At first she felt nothing but a vague sensation that something inside her was tightening somehow. Then it came—a quick but sharp wrenching, like a muscle spasm in the center of her brain. Her apprehension was gone; the urge to struggle had faded. Instead, she felt surrounded by an eerie, placid calm, like hearing the silence of the woodlands for the first time after a lifetime in a crowded and noise-cluttered city.

"Well?" Hedric asked. "How do you feel?"

"Like my head is stuffed with wool," she complained, wrinkling her nose as if about to sneeze. "It's not painful, just distracting. And I feel a little off-balance—as if I drank a glass of wine too fast." She wrinkled her nose again, slowly growing used to the sensation.

"Anything else?" Hedric prompted.

Athaya looked up, slightly apologetic. "Just before you set the seal, I felt afraid. I tried not to resist, but couldn't help it."

"That's just instinct," he assured her. "Your magic sensed the threat and tried to warn you. If nothing else, it's a sign that you're healthy.'' Hedric gave her hand a gentle squeeze and quickly cast the counterspell. *"Aperi potentiam,"* he whispered.

Once released, Athaya felt as if the windows had suddenly been thrown open to a sickroom, letting a cool spring breeze chase away stifling air thick with incense. The sense of imbalance was gone, and there was a pleasant tingling sensation as her power flowed back from its prison, as if her blood was filled with tiny bubbles.

"Better now?'' he asked, and nodded his approval when she got up and walked about the room without a trace of dizziness.

Using Credony's ancient path-maps as a guide, she and Hedric soon located her own sealing spell, buried deep within her paths. For the next hour, she practiced setting and releasing the power seal on Master Hedric, and while he complained that her first attempt was far too forceful and gave him a nasty headache, he professed to be reasonably pleased with her progress.

"Now I want you to set a seal on yourself,'' he said. "After all, that's what you'll have to do in an emergency. But keep in mind that timing is everything. The moment you suspect there is a corbal crystal nearby, you'll need to cast the seal before the gem starts interfering with your power. Once your paths start to cross, you won't be able to act.''

Athaya let go of Hedric's hand and cast the seal on her own powers, both pleased and disturbed when the woolen feeling of stuffiness and imbalance came over her. It was gratifying to know she was capable of wielding the spell, but somewhat frightening to think of its implications.

As if echoing her thoughts, Hedric's features grew grave. "Now remember what I told you before. Never leave a seal active any longer than you absolutely have to. Granted, it won't actually harm you for quite some time, but there's no sense taking chances. You remember how disruptive the *mekahn* can be, and the effects of a seal aren't any better. It's true you wouldn't be able to set off any spells by accident, but it's also true that the condition of your mind would decay more rapidly since your power wouldn't be able to find any means of release.''

Hedric adjusted his position in his chair, but his eyes never left her. "If you do get 'stranded' like this, there is something you can do to stave off the disruptions. Remember all that memorization I require you to do? Reciting all the names of the Circle Lords and how long they governed? Well, it does have a purpose." For a moment, there was a crack in his stern facade. "Other than to make you wish I'd drop off the edge of the earth and stop tormenting you, that is. Memorization is a form of discipline, Athaya. It strengthens the mind just as physical exertions strengthen the body. A disciplined mind allows a wizard to concentrate more effectively on whatever spell he happens to be casting."

Athaya bit her lip warily, hoping Hedric would not ask her to repeat that ghastly recitation again. Already the first few lines echoed unpleasantly in her head. *Credony, lord of the first Circle, twenty-six years; Sidra, lord of the second Circle, eleven years; Malcon, lord of the third . . .* and so on, and so on, until she thought she would go mad. Again.

"Such discipline—controlling your thoughts and not letting your unconscious get the upper hand—is also the best defense against the sealing spell," he went on. "It can hold off the worst of the symptoms, at least for a while. It *is* true that a handful of wizards have managed to escape the effects of a sealing spell with their lives and their sanity," he conceded, "but the odds would definitely be against you. Such a feat takes a kind of mental discipline and strength that few people have—especially those at your level of training, adept or not. In most cases, the pressure of sealed power becomes too great, and eventually ruptures, much like a broken blood vessel."

And that's the last thing that would ever happen to you, Athaya thought, as Hedric's grim warning echoed again in her mind. *You'd be dead shortly after it occurred.*

Hedric released her seal, and Athaya was once again clear-headed, tingling inside with the return of her power. She relaxed into the cushioned chair and let the fire warm her face, content that her lesson had gone well, but Hedric was not so serene, and leaned forward intently, his face grave.

"Now listen well, Athaya. Circle spells are the sole domain of its members, and making an exception in your case is extremely rare. You must not share your knowledge of this spell with anyone. Not Prince Felgin, not even Jaren. Oh, they both know that the sealing spell exists, but your knowledge of how to cast it must remain between you, me, and the members of the Circle. Is that clear?"

Athaya nodded obediently. "Perfectly clear."

"And heed my warnings about the dangers of this spell," he concluded firmly, "even if you ignore everything else I've ever told you." Then, for the first time, he smiled openly. "Which, of course, you would never dream of doing."

He left her shortly thereafter, assigning her a generous amount of reading for tomorrow's lesson, but it was a long time before Athaya could unclutter her thoughts enough to make any progress. It was comforting to know that there was a means of defense against a corbal crystal, even though the sealing spell would have to be cast before the crystal was actually present. If she were to stumble upon one accidentally, there would be no time to protect herself. Still, she mused, it was better than nothing.

But even more than by the potential benefits of such a spell, Athaya was gripped by strong feelings of revulsion, as if Hedric had just given her meticulous instructions on how to perform a particularly gruesome form of suicide. If this was an example of the kinds of spells in the Circle's safekeeping, she told herself resolutely, then she was quite sure she never wanted to know about any of the others.

At the end of the week, just as Athaya was beginning to think that she would be trapped inside her rooms forever, one of Osfonin's blue-liveried pages arrived to escort her to the king's private receiving chamber. Grateful for the respite from her confinement, Athaya eagerly followed the boy through the back passages of the palace, finally entering the king's chamber through a seldom-used side door. It was well past the dinner hour, and the snug, wainscotted room was lit by several candelabras in addition to the large fire burning briskly in the fireplace.

Osfonin was joined by Felgin, Jaren, Nicolas, and Katya, and Athaya held in a wry smile when she saw that her brother and the Reykan princess were seated quite close to one another on a cushioned cherrywood bench. The entire party looked up in unison when she entered, with Jaren and Felgin exchanging a vaguely knowing glance, and Athaya was left with the peculiar impression that she had been the subject of discussion until only a few moments ago.

"Ah, Athaya, do come in." The king motioned her to a comfortable chair by the fire. "I have arranged for your Caithan friends to be occupied tonight so that you could join us in rela-

tive safety. My captain, Lars, will see that Parr and his men are
suitably amused with cards, dice, wine, and . . . whatever else
they require,'' he added tactfully, flicking a discreet glance to
his young daughter. ''Your brother, I fear, felt unwell, and chose
instead to retire early.''

''Oh, they won't come looking for me,'' Nicolas said, noting
Athaya's frown of reservation. ''After a week of peering around
corners and not finding you lurking in them, I think Durek's
men are growing resigned to the fact that they'll be going home
empty handed.''

''And they will be departing in the morning,'' Osfonin added
firmly, openly relieved. ''I offered them a week's hospitality,
and those agonizing seven days are now over. Tomorrow I shall
send them back to Caithe, and they will carry with them my
assurances, Athaya, that I would have been happy to honor King
Durek's request for your extradition if I had the faintest idea
where you were.''

Athaya felt herself grow lighter as the weight of that worry
was lifted from her shoulders. ''That's a greater kindness than
I deserve, your Majesty. Thank you.''

''Durek won't believe a word of it, of course,'' Nicolas
pointed out, ''but he's not a hothead. He doesn't act without
thinking things through and weighing all the risks. In that respect, at least, he's a lot like Kelwyn. I don't think he'd dare
send his army into Reyka without solid proof that Athaya was
here.''

''Even though his bishops keep petitioning him to sponsor a
crusade against us?'' Felgin pointed out mildly. ''Even if they
can't prove Athaya is here, the suspicion alone might be excuse
enough for Durek to give in.''

Athaya remained silent, unable to give Felgin the assurances
he wanted. It saddened her to admit it, but she knew Durek less
than she ever had. And if he was seeking some way of proving
to all of Caithe that he was a worthy successor to his father, as
Nicolas had suggested, then perhaps he would be tempted to
give in to the pressures around him, to make his mark in history
by attempting to destroy what he and his Church believed to be
a cursed race.

Nicolas, however, was more confident. ''I still don't think
he'd take a gamble like that and risk losing. No matter what the
bishops say about . . .'' His voice trailed off into oblivion as an

idea slowly formed in his mind. And as it formed, a grin curled across his face and his eyes began to dance.

Athaya was instantly on her guard. She had seen this expression before. It was often on his face right after he'd thought of a particularly clever practical joke, and she had been the victim of enough of them throughout her childhood to recognize the warning signs.

"I know that look, Nicky. What on earth are you up to?"

Nicolas managed a creditable semblance of wide-eyed innocence. "Come now, Athaya, what makes you think I'm 'up' to anything? For your information, I've just thought of a way to guarantee that Durek keeps his army out of Reyka."

"Have you now?" Osfonin asked, his interest aroused. "Then by all means, don't keep us in suspense."

Whistling to himself, Nicolas got to his feet and strolled to the mantel. His smile grew broader as the idea became more and more appealing to him. "I've enjoyed myself thoroughly since I've been here, your Majesty. You and Felgin have been gracious hosts, and your daughter Katya has also done her best to make me feel quite welcome." He nodded quite pleasantly to the young princess, who absently twirled a lock of auburn hair around one finger. "In fact, I've had such a pleasant time in Reyka that I'm not entirely sure I want to leave."

Katya let out a short gasp of delight, but when she realized it had been audible she hurriedly dropped her eyes and began rearranging her emerald-green skirts.

Nicolas flashed a quick look of triumph to Athaya before he went on, laughing when he saw how completely he had taken her by surprise. "I've suddenly become quite fascinated with this country. And it's been ages since I've traveled outside Caithe . . ." He turned to offer the king his most winning smile. "As long as I'm enjoying a little holiday here, I think Durek will save himself the trouble of an invasion. Even though my brother thinks I'm an absolute fool most of the time, he'd never do anything that would purposely endanger my life."

"He certainly doesn't bear that same sort of affection for Athaya," Osfonin pointed out doubtfully, although the warmth in his eyes revealed that he thought well of Nicolas' idea.

"Well, no," the Caithan prince admitted. "Durek's problems with Athaya go deeper than just her magic. He's always objected to her unconventionality. Her habit of possessing opinions about things instead of simply mouthing what other people tell her to.''

"She's never been guilty of that," Jaren remarked dryly, offering Athaya a crooked smile to show he was only teasing.

Athaya, however, was too absorbed with her brother's pronouncement to pay any mind to Jaren's barbs. "But you can't stay!" she blurted out, finally finding her tongue. "You can't openly disobey him like that."

"Oh, but that's the wonder of it! I won't be disobeying him at all." Nicolas used every bit of self-control he had to keep from laughing aloud. "Durek ordered me to come here and speak to you, Athaya, but he never expressly asked that I return."

"Nicolas—"

"Besides, who are you to spout off about disobeying the king? He's already ordered you to come home for trial and you've refused him. I'd venture to say that's a bit more serious than my altering my travel plans."

Athaya opened her mouth to object, but realized that she couldn't argue against such a blatant truth. Still, she feared that, as usual, Nicolas was being entirely too optimistic about the situation.

"I appreciate your offering to stay—really, I do. But don't make the mistake of overestimating Durek's regard for you. I did once and it very nearly got me killed. What makes you think he would hold back his army just to protect you?"

"Because he needs me—at least for now. If nothing else, I'm an additional barrier between you and the crown. He's only got one son, and while Mailen is a healthy child . . . well, morbid as it sounds, it's never wise for a king to rest all his hopes on a single heir. You can bet that he's praying for Cecile's next child to be a boy. If anything happens to him, he wants to know that there are plenty of people standing in the way of you and the throne—even if one of them is me. The way he sees it, you becoming queen would spell utter disaster for Caithe."

Athaya felt a hot prickle of irritation underneath her skin. Durek's fears sounded painfully similar to the accusations Lord Basil had made when he speculated that she might use her powers to make a bid for the Caithan throne.

"I've never wanted to be queen and you know it," she declared, angrily folding her arms across her chest.

"Oh, I know that. But Durek doesn't. Archbishop Ventan and Dagara have managed to convince him that as a wizard, you'd do anything to take control of the country and send everyone to the Devil by making it legal to teach magic to the Lorngeld. The archbishop thinks that once that happens . . ." Nicolas paused, lowering his head to form a double chin in imitation of Ventan. " 'Then the wrath of God will descend upon us in all its fury, blighting the earth with plague and pestilence as punishment for our sins.' "

Athaya rolled her eyes at the utter hypocrisy of that statement. "Doesn't it occur to him that plenty of disastrous things happen every day for no other reason than the Lorngeld *don't* learn to use their magic?" she cried. "Besides, the Lorngeld in Reyka have used their power for centuries, and I certainly haven't seen any swarms of locusts or been caught in any floods lately."

"You don't have to convince me," he said, holding his hands up in a gesture of surrender. "You have to convince them."

"And that's exactly what I'm going to do." Pushing herself out of her chair, Athaya went to stand before Osfonin with her hands clasped formally in front of her. "I can't thank you enough for what you've done—surely it was more than I ever deserved. But I won't endanger you any more. Once I'm sure that Lord Gessinger and his men are well ahead of me, I'm going back to Caithe."

Katya looked as if she'd been struck. "Oh, Athaya, can't you find some other way? It's just too dangerous! I'll be so worried—"

"Silence, Katya," the king scolded gently. "Athaya knows what she must do. Hedric has told me of her goals and I couldn't respect them more." He rose from his seat and took Athaya's hands between his. "And I'll do what I can to help. I know that Hedric has busied himself for months trying to find a handful of wizards brave enough to accompany you. Perhaps I can assist him in that. I know Jaren plans to return with you, but the two of you can't possibly manage alone."

Athaya balked for a moment, and a distant look passed over her face as if she were backing away from him without moving.

"Actually, Hedric has decided on a few men already," Jaren said. "While Athaya has been closeted away with her studies, Hedric and I have been contacting the candidates. I've been explaining to them how serious the situation in Caithe really is and what the risks are, and frankly, that scares a lot of them off, but we've found two experienced wizards who have committed to the venture. And since they both live near Tenosce, Master Tonia has agreed to bring them to the palace next week so we can all start making plans.''

''I'm damned tempted to invite myself to that meeting,'' Felgin said grumpily, glancing from Athaya to Jaren and back again. ''I'll feel useless lounging around this place while the two of you are off trying to change the world.''

Osfonin regarded his son dryly. ''Perhaps you can spend the time looking for a wife as you ought to have done years ago,'' he suggested. ''I can excuse the omission in your younger brother, but not in my heir.''

''And you can fill a few days teaching me some new dicing games,'' Nicolas said cheerfully. ''I need to master something that Athaya doesn't know—she's gotten too good at chess and cards, and I want to start winning some of the money back that I've lost over the years.''

''A worthy goal,'' Osfonin remarked, trying to stifle his amusement. ''And you are welcome to remain as my guest for as long as it takes to reach it. But I must warn you,'' he added with mock gravity, ''if you wish your visit to serve its true purpose by keeping Durek's army at home, you had best stay until the campaign season is past. But that won't be until November, and this is only March. You would be in for a long stay.''

Seemingly ignorant of the light in Katya's eyes, Nicolas let out an exaggerated sigh. ''Oh, I think I can suffer through it somehow.''

Athaya dared not watch the proceedings herself, but late the next day, Nicolas told her how shocked Lord Gessinger and the other Caithans had been when told that he would be remaining behind as a guest of the Reykan court. No weapons had been drawn—that would have been a near-suicidal gesture—but it was clear that most of the men refused to believe that Nicolas was staying of his own free will. In a discordantly meek tone, Lord Gessinger warned that Durek would exact a terrible revenge for such an insult, but Osfonin cordially suggested that he would do well to get some wizards in his army first, as the Reykan forces were quite adequately supplied with them. This fact, which had not occurred to Gessinger before, caused the duke to abandon whatever further protests he had been preparing to make.

Nicolas had defused the situation as best he could, finally managing to persuade the Caithans that he was most definitely not a hostage, but was only remaining behind in case Athaya happened to come to Ath Luaine. He had, as he said, a duty to fulfill and was not going to disappoint his brother by coming home with news of failure. And to the prince's private delight, Lord Gessinger had believed every word and had departed for Caithe wishing him a pleasant stay and assuring him that Durek would be most happy to hear that he had begun to see reason where Princess Athaya was concerned.

"I was wonderful," Nicolas gloated shamelessly as he and Athaya sat in her chambers finishing a private supper together. "It was a performance even Dagara couldn't have surpassed. I expressed just the right amount of repentance, and the exact degree of shame I should have been expected to show when I explained that I'd finally realized Durek was right in wanting you to be punished for what you'd done. I even managed to blink up a tear or two, just for emphasis. Oh, I almost burst out laughing at the fun of it."

"I get the feeling that Osfonin enjoyed it as much as you did."

"Yes, I think he did at that. But I expect that all good kings are, by nature, good actors. He and I should get along famously these next few months."

"If you manage to spend any time at all away from Katya," Athaya remarked.

Nicolas winked at her. "Come now, Athaya. Didn't I tell you I was going to chase girls while I was here?"

He got up and retrieved his boots from the corner where he'd abandoned them upon his arrival. "I'm afraid I have to leave you now, little sister. I have a very important engagement."

"I'll bet you do," she replied wryly.

"It's nothing clandestine, so stop looking at me like a jealous wife. I'm simply meeting Felgin and Jaren in the Great Hall for a few rounds of dice." He rattled the purse at his belt. "This should be much heavier a few hours from now."

"I've seen you play dice, Nicky. You'd better leave it here if you don't want it empty by morning." She let out a lingering sigh. "I'd love to join you, but I haven't finished the essays that Master Hedric wants me to read for tomorrow."

"I'm glad to hear it," he replied. "If you were with us, we'd never be able to talk about you behind your back." He eyes twinkled just enough to convince her that he and his companions were planning to do exactly that, then slipped out of the room before the wadded napkin she threw at him could strike home.

Late that same night, Athaya curled up near the fire in a white satin dressing gown, occasionally sipping from a cup of mulled wine. A winter storm was brewing outside, and she had draped a thick woolen blanket over her shoulders to ward off the bitter drafts that crept through the cracks in the shutters. She had spent the last two hours studying the documented effects of leaving a sealing spell on too long—an account begun by an overly curious wizard and completed by the pupil who had found what was left of him a few months later. It was not a pleasant essay, and she might have felt more at ease had she been reading tales of ghosts and demons that haunted the halls of old castles. Accordingly, she jumped in fright when she heard the rapping on her door, her heart lurching into her throat.

"It's open," she called out after catching her breath, and quickly set the disturbing volume aside.

Having grown used to the firelight, she hadn't realized how dark the rest of the room was until she looked toward the door. Still, she knew Jaren's silhouette immediately. He pushed the door closed quietly and helped himself to the chair beside her. He was more formally dressed than she might have expected at this hour, as if he'd just come from a court banquet instead of a casual game of dice with Nicolas, and Athaya couldn't remember ever having seen him in that particular blue doublet before. His silver wizard's brooch was pinned to his collar and gleamed as if it had been freshly polished.

"It's late," she offered, since Jaren didn't seem inclined to begin the conversation, "why are you still up?"

"I could ask you the same thing, but Nicolas told me you'd be studying for another few hours." He reached into the small leather bag hanging from his belt and drew out a handful of silver Caithan coins. "Your brother had poor luck with the dice tonight."

He poured the coins back into the purse, then gazed at her expectantly. There was an awkward pause, and Athaya felt as if she was supposed to say something, but hadn't a clue as to what.

She couldn't identify exactly how, but Jaren looked different tonight. There was a sparkle in his eyes that didn't have anything to do with the firelight—as if he'd come to tell her a secret that no one else in the world knew. Mystified, she reached for her cup of mulled wine, but Jaren was quick to scoop it up for her and place it into her hands.

"I haven't seen you much this past week," he said, sinking down into the hearth chair opposite her.

Athaya shrugged. "Nobody has," she replied simply. "Until Gessinger and the others left, I was pretty much stuck here." He didn't make any sort of comment, so she asked, "What have you been doing?"

"Keeping an eye on the Caithans, mostly. Lord Gessinger was the only one who'd speak to me—probably because he was afraid not to—but Parr and his guardsmen just glared at me as if trying to measure my neck for a noose."

"I hope you didn't provoke them."

"Oh, maybe a little. But frankly, they weren't worth it."

There was another awkward pause, and Jaren scuffed his boots back and forth on the carpet, too restless to enjoy the comfort that the overstuffed chair afforded. This time, Athaya decided to wait as long as it took for him to say whatever it was he'd come here to say, all the while thinking how peculiarly he was acting. Jaren was rarely this secretive or hesitant about speaking his mind.

"Your brother and I talked quite a bit earlier tonight," he said at last, and Athaya could tell by the way he folded and unfolded his hands that he was starting to approach the real reason for his visit. "We got to know each other better—there wasn't much time for that in Delfarham last fall . . ." He broke off, looking at her directly. "And we talked about you."

"That couldn't have been too exciting," she remarked.

"Enlightening, perhaps. We have a few thoughts in common."

Athaya frowned, increasingly convinced that she had absolutely no idea what was going on. "Such as?"

"Such as, we both want you to do what you're setting out to do in Caithe. And we had some stories to share of what happened the last time we got on the wrong end of your temper." He laughed at the face she made, but his serious mood quickly returned. Not solemn, but merely earnest and intense, as if he had something of profound importance to say and was determined to choose his words carefully.

"But most of all, we both want you to be happy. Last year wasn't a good one for you, Athaya. We'd like to see this one be better."

"I wouldn't mind that myself," she muttered softly, her eyes shifting absently to the flames that were beginning to die down in the fireplace.

Then Jaren was at her side, his hand extended. "Come here."

To her surprise, he seemed to take delight in the blank look of confusion that spread over her face. He lifted the cup from her hands and set it down on the hearth, then drew her out of the chair and led her to the window seat, its alcove only barely illuminated by the fire. Fierce winds rattled the shutters, and hailstones hurled themselves angrily against the glass, making harsh, scratching sounds like the claws of an animal trying to get in out of the cold. Even from underneath her thick blanket, Athaya could feel the icy drafts, but Jaren seemed oblivious to them. His face was flushed, warmed by some inner fire of his own.

But it wasn't until he laced his fingers inside of hers that she realized what was happening. Suddenly the wine she'd drunk began to sour in her stomach, and despite the drafts from the window, she felt the room grow much too hot.

"I don't think it's been much of a secret how I feel about you, Athaya," he said softly, his eyes lowered. "I haven't come right out and told you, but I know you must have picked it up during our workings and just didn't say anything so you wouldn't embarrass me."

He didn't look up, and Athaya could only be grateful for that. She wasn't sure she could hide the growing dread in her eyes. She wanted to say something to make him stop before he said another word, but it was as if she had suddenly lost the use of her tongue; as if her capacity for speech had been locked away with some other kind of sealing spell.

"I've been thinking about you quite a lot these days," he went on. "About what my life has been like since the first time I met you in that tavern in Delfarham. We've been through a lot together, you and I, and most of it . . . well, it's been rather harrowing. I've tried to be there for you when you needed me, and . . . I guess what I'm trying to say is that I always want to be there for you. I know it's only been a few months, but . . ."

This time he met her eyes, and broke off, his train of thought diffusing into the air like smoke.

"I can't believe this . . . I've been rehearsing this for weeks and now I can't even say it." He shook his head and let out a wisp of nervous laughter. "All I'm trying to ask, Athaya, is . . ." He folded both her hands inside of his. ". . . is if you'll marry me. If you'll do me the honor of becoming my wife."

The words echoed in her mind like the doleful sound of chapel bells on a gray winter dawn—bells that didn't speak of new beginnings, but only of endings. For an instant, she felt suspended in time, trapped inside eternity with no way out.

Now I'm supposed to be happy, she told herself. *I'm supposed to jump to my feet and tell him that I was praying he would ask me that, and that I'll love him forever, and that he's just made me the happiest woman in the world . . .*

But the happiness she should have felt did not come. She looked into the depths of his eyes, where the reflected flames from the fireplace danced, and saw only a growing and threatening terror. . . and she remembered a dream she once had, of a fire in the hall of Delfarham, with desperate people screaming for her help. And then she saw an image even more horrifying than that—of an autumn courtyard blanketed with moonlight, and of a pike on the gatehouse tower, showing her the fate of the last man she had loved. And that had been no dream . . .

"I didn't say it right, did I?" Jaren blurted out abruptly, visibly shaken by her silence. He squeezed his eyes shut and slapped one hand over his forehead, as if hoping for the chance to drop through the floor and never be seen again. "Oh, I knew I should have practiced on Katya first. I've never proposed to anybody before, and I didn't know what to say . . ."

"It's all right, Jaren," she managed to say, trying to assuage his fears. "You said everything just fine." But her own voice sounded alien to her, and she doubted if it would comfort him.

"I wasn't going to ask you yet," he said, words tumbling out like a river overflowing its banks, "but now that we're going back to Caithe . . . well, we can't very well get married there, can we? Even if you weren't excommunicated, I'm sure there would be a slight problem finding a priest who'd agree to marry a pair of wizards."

He held her hands tighter just then, as if afraid she might slip away. "And I know it'll be dangerous. You don't need to warn me—I've seen it firsthand. The minute news of what we're doing gets around, Durek and the Curia will swoop down on us like vultures on carrion. I just want to make sure we truly belong to one another. That we have our share of happiness in case—" He paused to swallow. "—in case something awful happens. In case one of us doesn't make it."

With shaking fingers, he began to unclasp the brooch from his collar. "I want to give you a token . . . something you can keep until I can exchange it with a ring . . ." But before he could undo the clasp, Athaya stayed his hand, unable to let him go on any further.

"Jaren, stop. Please don't."

Athaya had to look away, focusing her eyes instead on the earthenware cup on the hearth, still half-filled with wine. She felt poised on the edge of a cliff, surrounded by fog, knowing that one step in the wrong direction would send her plummeting down to the abyss below.

"I've startled you, haven't I?" he said softly, trying to inject some confidence into his voice. "I know it might have been better to ease into this gradually—maybe drop a few hints here and there—but I thought we'd have more time . . ."

His voice gradually trailed away. Now he knew something was wrong. "Athaya, what's the matter?"

What's the matter? she cried inwardly. *Nothing. Everything. How can you even ask me that? Oh God, I was afraid you might do this, and now I don't know what to say . . .*

Slowly, as if her joints ached, she got up from the window seat and leaned against the cold stone wall with her back to him. He made no move to join her. In the silence that ensued, she did not even hear him breathe.

"Jaren, I'm sorry. I can't marry you."

She didn't have to turn around to know what his face would have shown. Disbelief. Confusion. Wounded pride. And in her mind's eye, she saw all of those expressions cross his features one by one. But she didn't dare look herself.

His next words came very softly. "I don't understand."

Athaya didn't respond, afraid her voice might break. She pressed her body against the cold stone wall, hoping it would help numb the pain.

She heard the soft rustle of cloth, then sensed Jaren's presence behind her. "Is it . . . does this have anything to do with Tyler?" he said tentatively. "I know I could never take his place . . . I don't expect to. But at least let me try to make you happy . . ."

Athaya shook her head, allowing her hair to fall across her face, hiding it like a black veil. "It's not that. There was a time I never thought I could say this, but I think I'm over that now. As much as anyone ever gets over it."

"But then . . . why?"

She heard it in his voice again, the exposed pain—the growing fear that she did not return the feelings he professed. But strangely enough, he never asked her that. Either he had been fairly sure that she did return them, or he didn't want to know otherwise.

Oh, Jaren, how can I possibly explain everything you've been to me? But don't you see? That's just it! That's why it can never be . . .

He put his hands on her shoulders, absently arranging the folds of the blanket resting there. "I asked too soon. I should have waited. Once we're back in Caithe . . . once you've had more time to think, then we can talk about it again. Maybe in the summer—"

"No, Jaren. Listen. Please." She finally turned to face him, steeling herself for what she had to say next. "There's something I've been meaning to tell you for a while now." She backed away a step, as if preparing to flee. "I'm grateful for everything you've done, Jaren: teaching me my magic when I didn't want to learn, being there for me when Kelwyn and Tyler died . . . I can't possibly tell you what that means to me. But I just can't marry you." She paused to take a deep breath, bracing herself against the wall. "And I don't want you to come back to Caithe with me."

If she thought he looked defeated before, that announcement gave new meaning to the word. Every ray of light went out of his eyes, as if someone had just proved to him that there was no God.

He shook his head in disbelief. "You can't mean that."

"I've thought about it for a long time, and I'm sure. I want you to stay here."

"Stay here?" he repeated, his quiet calm starting to crack with despair. "And leave you to go back to Caithe all alone?"

"Jaren, you know perfectly well that I won't be alone. You told Osfonin that yourself only yesterday."

Ignoring her words, Jaren fell back against the wall as if gradually losing the strength to stand. "What am I supposed to do?"

Athaya retreated to her chair by the hearth, feeling decades older than when she had risen from it only minutes before. "Go back to the way you were last year. Before you ever got mixed up with me."

"What?" he said, aghast. "How? I'm in love with you . . . for heaven's sake, Athaya, I just asked you to *marry* me. How am I supposed to simply forget about you after everything that's happened?"

"I'm not asking you to forget," she said, careful to keep the emotion out of her voice. "I'm only saying that you should find someone else to be your wife. You've risked your life for me once, Jaren. I won't ask you to do it again." She turned away, fixing her eyes on the ruby embers in the fireplace. "You have to stay, Jaren. There are people here who need you."

Like a candle snuffed out with a breath, the last flicker of hope died inside of him. "And you don't."

Before she could say anything more, he turned and left her, too hurt and humiliated to face her another moment longer. She listened for his footsteps in the corridor, but the wind had increased in force and she could not hear them.

With an eerie sense of tranquility, Athaya picked up the book she'd been reading earlier and set it back on her lap. She absently flipped through its pages, though with the fire nearly dead, it was far too dark to read. But the peace of the night had been irreparably rent, and in a sudden burst of rage, all of her pent-up emotion exploded like a spark set to tinder. Athaya flung the volume against the far wall with all her strength, watching in furious satisfaction as the binding split apart, sending yellowed pages fluttering in the air like autumn leaves, which gradually floated to rest and settled into dead heaps on the carpet.

Then she ran to the window and unlocked the shutters, twice cutting her finger on the latch, then furiously opened the heavy glass panels as well. The force of the wind sent them crashing back against the walls on either side, sending cracks coursing over the glass like hoarfrost. As tears turned to ice on her cheeks, she let the wind blast her with its fury, ripping the blanket from her shoulders and scattering her hair wildly about her head.

"What more do you want from me?" she cried out, her words all but lost in the howling winds. "What *more*?"

And as heavy flakes of snow whirled into the chamber, stinging her skin and soaking her gown, she called out to the storm to make her heart and mind grow numb along with her body, so that the pain of what she had been forced to do would go away and she would feel nothing.

CHAPTER 7

✹✷✹

"OD'S BREATH, ATHAYA, WHAT ON EARTH ARE YOU doing?"

Nicolas crossed the room in four swift strides and slammed the shutters closed, securely locking the biting wind outside. Then he grabbed Athaya by the arm and dragged her in front of the sparse, ruby-colored embers in the fireplace.

"What are you trying to do, kill yourself? It's freezing out there. And look—the floor is covered with snow and you're not even wearing any slippers . . ."

He spent the next few minutes fussing over her like a nursemaid, but Athaya paid little attention to him, staring straight ahead as if her mind had been frozen, every emotion whipped out of her by the force of the winter storm.

Nicolas fetched the blanket from the corner where the wind had deposited it and wrapped it snugly around her shoulders, then forced her feet into a pair of deerskin slippers. Like an angry father, he ordered her to sit down and then knelt in front of her and began rubbing the feeling back into her fingers, blowing hot breath on them every few moments.

When he was convinced that she was warm enough, he stood up in front of her, thumbs thrust into his belt, looking down in reproach. "I thought wizards only went crazy during this *mekahn* that everybody talks about. Apparently I was wrong."

Athaya didn't bother to reply, but merely gazed absently about the room, noticing for the first time that the wind had strewn the pages of her book over every conceivable portion of it. She would have to put the volume back together, she supposed, or Hedric would be quite angry.

"Why are you here?" she asked tiredly, rubbing her eyes as if Nicolas were an unpleasant illusion that she was trying to dispel.

"Because I usually take it upon myself to tell you when you've done something abysmally stupid, Athaya, and this is definitely one of those times."

"I'm entitled to open a window if I want to," she said, petulantly thrusting her lip out.

Nicolas glared at her severely. "That isn't what I meant."

With an air of exhausted contrition, she burrowed deeper inside the blanket, suddenly aware of the needles beneath her skin as warmth crept back into half-frozen flesh. "You know?"

"Of course I know! What do you think Jaren and I talked about while we were dicing? And I was so sure you'd say yes that I've been waiting out in the corridor all night to congratulate the both of you." Nicolas shook his head in stunned disbelief. "I don't know what you said to him, Athaya, but he was destroyed when I saw him. Thoroughly destroyed."

Athaya closed her eyes tight and sighed miserably. She didn't think it was possible to feel worse than she had when Jaren left her, but she had obviously been wrong.

"I feel as if this is all my fault," Nicolas moaned. "He wasn't going to ask you yet, but Felgin and I talked him into it." He picked up the iron rod near the fireplace and began poking at the embers, trying to stir them back to life. "Why didn't we just keep our mouths shut?"

"It doesn't matter," Athaya said quietly. "Jaren would have asked sooner or later, and I would have given him the same answer. Besides, I couldn't very well have waited until the day I planned to leave for Caithe to tell him that I wasn't taking him with me."

Nicolas spun around on his heel, eyes wide with shock. Jaren clearly hadn't told him the whole story. "What?"

"You heard me. And stop staring at me like I'm some sort of deranged criminal. It wasn't an easy decision."

During the silence that ensued, Nicolas replaced the poker

into its rack and came to stand behind her, resting his hands on the back of the chair. "Are you sure it's the right one?"

"Yes."

"Mmm. That must explain why your book is scattered all over the room."

"Oh, stop harping on me, Nicolas," she snapped. "Just go away and leave me alone."

"Alone? To do what? Die of frostbite? Listen, Athaya, I've been looking out for you ever since we were kids and I'm not about to stop now. Not when you've just made the most bone-headed decision of your life."

Athaya burrowed even deeper inside the folds of the blanket, wishing she had the energy to work a translocation spell and take herself to the other side of the world. She couldn't remember the last time Nicolas had been so upset with her about anything, and her stomach was knotting up with tension.

Sensing that she was slowly withdrawing from him, Nicolas' anger faded, and he touched her shoulder gently. "If you don't think you're ready yet, just tell him so. I think he'll understand. After all, it's only been six months since Tyler died, and—"

"It doesn't have anything to do with that," she said, just a shade too quickly. "Besides, I told you before . . . I'm past that now. Although I feel guilty about it sometimes," she added with a frown, "as if it isn't quite fair."

"Fair to whom? Believe me, Athaya, I'm not trying to diminish what you felt for Tyler. Lord knows I loved him, too. But it certainly wouldn't be a betrayal of his memory for you to care for someone else. He'd tell you the same thing if he could."

Athaya sighed heavily. Usually Nicolas didn't try so hard to press a point, finding his own peace of mind preferable to winning a dispute. But he was obviously in one of his more persistent moods, so it appeared she was going to have to explain everything after all.

"All right, I'll admit this does have something to do with Tyler. But not the way you're assuming." She looked up, trying not to let the anguish show on her face. "It's not that I don't care for Jaren. I do, believe me. I just can't marry him."

Exasperated, Nicolas threw up his hands. "Why *not*?"

"I could love him if I let myself," she said, flinching at the admission as if it caused her physical pain. "But I can't do that to him. I can't encourage him. One man has already gone to his

death simply because he made the mistake of getting too attached to me. Frankly, Nicolas, I'd rather have Jaren stay here
and stay alive than trail after me and end up getting killed.'' She
wrung her hands together, silently pleading for Nicolas to believe her. ''Turning him away was one of the hardest things I've
ever done, but at least I'll know he's safe.''

Nicolas was quiet for a long time, but just as Athaya thought
he was about to start arguing again, he simply patted her arm
and smiled.

''You just don't see it, do you?''

Athaya furrowed her brow. ''See what?''

''Athaya, you wouldn't be so torn up about this if it wasn't
already too late. If you weren't already hopelessly in love with
him.''

Athaya squirmed in her chair, discomfited by that thought.
Jaren had been a confidant, a teacher, and a friend unlike any
other she'd ever had. But she never really thought about being
in love with him, other than to speculate on the heartache it
would lead to if she were, and that specter so frightened her that
she had never dared to look beyond it.

''You can't live in terror of other people loving you,'' Nicolas
went on. ''They'll do it anyway, with or without your leave.
And if you push them away, you're only hurting yourself . . .
and them, too. It's as if you're telling Jaren he's not good enough
for you. That the happiness you'd have with him isn't worth the
risk.''

Athaya jerked back as if she'd been stabbed. ''No, Nicky, it's
not that! It's *me*. Don't you see? He'll only get in trouble with
me. I have to stop this before it's too late. Before it gets any
worse.''

''Good Lord, Athaya, the man's in love with you and you're
making it sound like some sort of disease.''

''It's a fatal one in my case,'' she muttered sullenly.

''Oh, now you're just wallowing in self-pity,'' he replied
sharply. ''Life hurts sometimes, Athaya. And if you never risk
getting hurt, then you're never going to gain anything that makes
you truly happy, either.''

Athaya bolted to her feet and whipped around in a sudden
fury, clutching her blanket in front of her like a shield. ''And
when have you ever risked anything, Nicolas?'' she shot back.
''When? The only risk you've ever taken in your life is wagering

twenty crowns on a game of dice instead of ten! How dare you stand there and tell me simply to pick myself up and go on when you don't know how I feel. You have no idea what I've been through these last six months!''

Nicolas looked struck, trapped in that fleeting instant between being stabbed and waiting for the pain to come. ''I lost my father, too, Athaya. And Tyler.'' He looked away just then, as if it pained him to look at her. ''And I might lose you, for all I know.''

Immediately, Athaya went hot with shame and sank despondently back into her chair, feeling more miserable than ever. ''Oh, God, I'm sorry, Nicolas. I didn't mean that.''

''I know you didn't,'' he assured her. ''But don't you realize that I'm going through the same thing you are right now? Don't you think I'd rather that you stayed here, safe and sound, and forgot all about going back to Caithe? God knows I'll be worried about you every second that you're gone, but I know you have to go. Because what you plan to do is more important than my own selfish reasons for wanting you to stay.''

He rested against the back of her chair and put an arm around her shoulder. ''Listen to me, Athaya. You tried to protect Tyler by not telling him you were one of the Lorngeld. But he cared too much to let you drive him off. Do you really think Jaren will be any different? Athaya, if he's truly in love with you, he'll follow you anyway. And he won't give up until he makes you see how wrong you are.''

Athaya began to chew on the end of a thumbnail. Nicolas' arguments were growing entirely too logical and persuasive. ''Did anyone else know he came here tonight?'' she asked, hoping to change the subject.

''Besides me? Just Felgin. Katya has her suspicions, but she's kept them quiet.''

''Then please don't tell anyone else. Jaren probably feels bad enough as it is without having the whole palace know what's happened. And whatever you do, don't repeat any of this to him,'' she warned. ''If he knows I'm just trying to protect him, then I'll never be able to make him stay here where he belongs.''

''He belongs with you, Athaya. He knows that, even if you don't.''

Athaya sighed deeply. Suddenly she felt drained and empty,

wanting nothing more than to sink into a heavy sleep and forget this entire evening. "Nicky, please go. I'd like to be alone now."

To her surprise, Nicolas leaned over and brushed her cheek with a kiss. When he reached the door, he paused. "I didn't come here to upset you, Athaya. I only want you to be happy. You haven't had much of that, I'm afraid."

"I will be happy," she protested. It was growing harder than ever to stifle her tears, rendering her words a mockery. "I'll be happy knowing that Jaren is safe. That he won't go to his death by following me."

"I understand," he replied. "But let me just say one last thing. You're going back to Caithe to start a revolution, Athaya. Everyone who follows you is going to be risking his or her life, and the lives of people they care about. And a lot of people are going to die for you before your work is done." He shifted his weight against the door, his eyes never leaving her. "What if nobody listened to you because they were too afraid that those they loved might believe what you have to say and endanger themselves by learning their magic or by hiding someone from absolution?" Nicolas gazed at her steadily. "Somehow, Athaya, I think you're expecting other people to risk things that you're not willing to."

The door closed softly, and Athaya made no move as she watched the last embers of the fire turn black. The winter storm still raged outside, bitter winds throwing hailstones against the window, but now the clamor seemed to echo Nicolas' words, trying to force its way through locked shutters and into her mind, scratching and wailing, refusing to be ignored.

One week after Jaren's proposal—a period of time in which they saw one another only in public and exchanged only the briefest of greetings—Athaya paced nervously across the carpet in Hedric's study waiting for the arrival of those wizards he had selected to accompany her back to Caithe. The afternoon sky was an oppressive gray, and the late-winter snow fell heavy and wet, turning the packed earth in the courtyard below to streams of icy mud. Secretly, Athaya hoped the weather would delay the wizards' arrival. She was more anxious about this gathering than she had been about meeting the Circle of Masters, and when her hands were not persistently smoothing her deep purple skirts, they were absently picking at random wisps of ebony hair that poked out from beneath her chaplet.

Halting her pacing for a moment, Athaya exchanged a brief glance with the gray-haired guardsman lingering near the door. Kale Eavon, formerly of the Caithan army, was now the captain of her own troop of royal guards, all of one in number. He said very little—talkativeness was not in his nature—but his mere presence was a comfort. He offered her shy smiles of encouragement from time to time, an incongruously boyish gesture in a man nearly fifty years of age, and one that marked him as that rare kind of soldier who fights from a deep commitment to peace and not from a passion for battle.

"I'm glad you're coming with me, Kale," she told him, suddenly breaking the silence that had hung in the chamber for nearly a quarter hour. "I didn't feel right asking you to—it was a relief when you came to me instead."

The guardsman shrugged his embarrassment, as if not considering his deed worthy of notice. "I'm not sure I believe the same as you do, my Lady," he said with a hint of apology in his voice. "The idea of magic being a good thing . . . it's not what I was taught, you see." His words came out in uneven spurts, unaccustomed as he was to composing such a lengthy speech. "But I do know one thing. Captain Graylen was a good man. I'd have followed him to hell and back as many times as he wished it. If he believed in you, then so can I."

Athaya felt a warm rush of gladness wash through her, wondering what she had ever done to merit such devotion. "Durek will execute you for treason if you're caught," she warned him, wanting to make sure he had considered all of the implications of his return.

He gave her another of his shy smiles, like a young boy flustered at being noticed by a pretty girl. "With respect, your Highness, he could do the same to you."

Athaya laughed lightly. "Ah, well, so he could." She closed the shutters to block out the dismal landscape, then turned to him with a look of mock severity, one finger raised. "But I should thank you not to remind me of that too often."

After another few minutes of waiting, Athaya heard footsteps in the outside corridor, and Hedric promptly emerged from the adjoining library to greet his guests. He had barely opened his mouth to say hello when Master Tonia burst into the study like a blast of wind and unceremoniously dumped her damp cloak over the nearest chair.

"It can stop snowing any time it wants to, so far as I'm concerned," she muttered, shaking out a thinning mass of gray-streaked hair that had been flattened by the weight of the cloak's cowl. "Too bad I don't know any translocation spells," she added, tossing a wink at Athaya. "Old Basil's green with envy over that one, believe you me."

After exchanging polite greetings with Master Tonia, Athaya looked past her, studying the two figures in ice-crusted cloaks that lingered near the door. Puzzled, she drew her brows inward. She'd been expecting a teacher and a former soldier, but neither of the newcomers looked even remotely like a military man, and one was far too young to have claimed any profession at all.

Hedric motioned his guests inside and took their cloaks, casting a kindly but somewhat mystified glance at the younger of the two. "Didn't you bring Ranulf with you?" he asked Tonia, peering out into the corridor.

"Oh, he'll be along. He saw a belt that caught his fancy in a shop window and started haggling over the price. I told him it was too damned cold to wait, so the rest of us went ahead." She raised her brows expectantly at Hedric. "So how long do we have to stand here shivering before you offer us some mulled wine?"

While Hedric and Kale went into the next room to accede to this kindly demand, Athaya offered the three newcomers chairs by the fire, quietly studying the two men—or rather, one man and a boy—in Tonia's company as they took their places. The man was lean and sinewy, roughly of an age with Felgin, and like the prince, his entire aspect was one of refined gentility, from the dark, well-trimmed hair that fell into a precise curl around his chin, to the finely pared nails and impeccable posture. A somber gray mantle, marked on the collar with an unfamiliar insignia, flowed gracefully from his shoulders, and his eyes held a persistent squint to them as if accustomed to long hours of reading in poor light.

The other was a slender willow of a boy with chestnut hair whom Athaya doubted was a day over thirteen. His build was lanky and somewhat uneven, arms and legs growing into maturity at rapidly different rates. Athaya thought it fortunate that the older man did not notice the way the boy was openly staring at her, seemingly bedazzled by the splendor of her gown and jewels. Although she did not object to this innocent, if blatant, admiration, Athaya suspected that his more genteel companion would find such behavior intolerably rude.

Just as the silence grew noticeable, Tonia sprang up from the cushioned stool she had only recently lowered herself onto and clapped her hands to her hips. "While Hedric's off puttering around in the next room, I suppose I can take care of the formal introductions," she announced crisply.

"I don't *have* to bring you any wine, you know," Hedric's good-natured reply came, slightly muffled from the clinking sound of pewter cups being arranged on a tray.

Tonia merely chuckled and ignored him.

"This is Dom Mason DePere," she said, gesturing to the slender man robed in gray. "The tutor at Wizard's College that Hedric told you about. And from what the regents tell me, he's one of the best, too." Tonia flashed him a sidelong glance laced with mischief. "I've know Mason for years, but I never dreamed he'd be crazy enough to go on a venture like this."

The tutor looked up, his face subtly aglow. "Then you never dreamed enough, Master Tonia," he said simply. He turned to Athaya and inclined his head courteously. "I've been teaching magic theory for five years, your Highness. My specialty is illusion spells—a very popular elective, if I may say so."

He waved his hand, and the carpet beneath them shimmered and turned to water, the chairs seeming to float atop the pool like driftwood. Another gesture, and the image was gone.

"Sure it's popular," Tonia said dryly. "That's because those urchins like to play practical jokes with all the trickery you teach them." The wisp of a smile that lingered on her lips made Athaya wonder just how many pranks of her own the young Tonia had played as a student.

"And why do you want to leave the College and come with me?" Athaya asked.

Dom DePere folded his hands gently in his lap. "My work is pleasant enough, Princess, and I do enjoy it. But in light of my specialty, I only encounter those students who have already passed the dangers of the *mekahn*, those who don't need to worry about survival and want to learn . . . well, the more 'decorative' parts of magic. But by joining you, I could reach those who need me most. There are enough tutors in Reyka to educate the Lorngeld here, and it's safe, steady work. But I want to do more—to help the ones who can't help themselves because your king and your Church won't let them."

"I'd love to say it isn't my king or my Church, Dom DePere, but as a Trelane I don't suppose I have that luxury."

"I know my reasons sound idealistic," he said, looking away. "But I never claimed to be a very practical man. I've always felt the desire to teach, but I've also dreamed of doing more than simply aspiring to a seat on the regent's council. I want to make a difference in the world." He shrugged self-effacingly. "I suppose all men dream of such things at one time or another."

"Don't be ashamed of being a dreamer, my friend. Very little would be accomplished in this world without people determined to do just that. My father dreamed of a united Caithe, and today such a land exists." She regarded the tutor with deep appreciation. "I'm glad to have you with me."

Her words were barely done when there was a loud commotion in the outside corridor, and Athaya sorted the various sounds into the shuffle of boots, the clatter of metal against stone, and a series of brusque voices punctuated by a few colorful curses.

"Damn your hide, I tell you I'm expected!" came a booming voice often found in drill sergeants and overly zealous priests. "Now move your carcass afore I move it for you."

"Ah," Tonia said with a satisfied nod. "That'll be Ranulf."

She made no move to get up, as if curious to see how long it would take him to gain admittance to the wizard's chamber. Within moments, the door to the study crashed open as if kicked in by a mule, but no one stepped through it. Athaya heard a sniffle, a cough, and a scratching sound as if someone were relieving himself of an itch. Then the air wavered in the doorway and the cloaking spell dissolved, revealing a broad-shouldered tree trunk of a man with an unruly crop of flame-red hair that sprouted from his head and chin like spring weeds. His massive body was clad in well-worn leathers and a sheepskin coat, thighs and forearms swollen with well-toned muscles. He snorted derisively as he shimmered into view, running one sleeve underneath his nose in lieu of a handkerchief.

"Damned if that runt wasn't going to let me in!" he bellowed, whisking off his wet coat and dropping it into a soggy wad on the floor. "I had to make like I was going back, then slip past him under a cloaking spell."

Alerted by the sound of the door being thrown open, a harried sentry clambered up the steps and lunged into the study, his sword at the ready. "My pardon," he said politely to the ladies, then glared at the burly man. "But I was told Master Hedric would be having only three visitors."

"It's all right," Tonia said. "Like it or not, this fellow's one of us. We had an extra," she explained, nodding at the boy.

Throwing the sentry a smug look, Ranulf kicked off his boots and propped his feet on the side table, much to the dom's visible consternation. Disgruntled, the sentry bowed and departed, though Athaya knew that with his slender build, he would have had the Devil's own time removing the newcomer by force if he had refused to go.

Tonia pointed to the massive, redheaded man, now seriously engaged with warming his toes by the fire. "And this scruffy-looking fellow who looks as if he's moved in already is Ranulf Osgood," she said, with a casualness that spoke of a close acquaintance. Upon hearing his name, Ranulf stopped studying his stockinged feet and gazed at Athaya directly, piercing green eyes filled with such candor and self-assuredness that it bordered closely on arrogance. Athaya was so struck by his boldness that she lost the first part of what Master Tonia was saying.

". . . born on the Isle of Sare and trained as an army man, although he hasn't done much fighting in a while. Not since the Caithans hired him, back when Kelwyn was still trying to put an end to the civil wars."

"And that was near twenty years ago," the Sarian replied. He offered Athaya a broad smile revealing the absence of two teeth. "I'd wager you weren't even out of diapers then."

Athaya blinked at the man's presumption of familiarity, but while Mason sat back looking scandalized, she found herself more amused than offended. She had flown in the face of propriety more than a few times herself, and was drawn to people unafraid to do the same.

"You were in my father's army, then?"

In an unexpected act of evasiveness for one so direct, Ranulf shifted his eyes away. "Well, not exactly." All of a sudden he seemed very interested in the patterns of the flames in the fireplace.

Athaya felt an unpleasant tremor of foreboding. "But I thought Tonia said you fought in the civil wars."

"And she's right," he said. Then he turned his gaze back to her, and the candor returned, as if daring her to listen further. "But I fought *against* the king, not for him." Ranulf paused for a moment to let his words sink in, and then added, "I was a mercenary under the earl of Tusel's banner."

Athaya drew her breath in slowly, completely at a loss for words. A mercenary? King Kelwyn's enemy? What had Tonia and Hedric been thinking? She had heard of the earl of Tusel— who had not? He had spearheaded a revolt that nearly lost Kelwyn his crown and was executed for treason when she was but a child.

Shaken by Ranulf's admission and unsure how best to react, Athaya was exceedingly grateful when Hedric and Kale returned at that moment, one carrying a tray bearing seven cups of hot spiced wine and the other a platter laden with a selection of cheeses.

"Oh my, what's happened now," Hedric remarked, seeing the silent tableau before him. "I wasn't listening." Lifting one brow in a wordless request for the Sarian to move his feet, Hedric set the tray of wine cups down on the table. Athaya wasn't particularly thirsty, but grasped for one of the cups as if her life depended on it, and swallowed half of it in one gulp.

"Ranulf here just happened to mention which side he was on during the Caithan wars," Tonia said, clearly wishing the Sarian had kept his mouth shut.

"Oh." Hedric bit into a wedge of yellow cheese with a bit more force than was necessary. "We were hoping that might not come up right away. I probably should have told you before, Athaya, but I didn't see any reason to alarm you. If Tonia had not vouched for his character and convinced me of his suitability for this enterprise, I never would have approved. But his past has no real bearing on the present, and—"

"No *bearing*?" she exclaimed. "He—"

"Was paid to render a service. There was no treachery involved. Even you will recall that at the time, Kelwyn had not yet reunited his kingdom and Sare was being independently ruled. Ranulf broke no oath of fealty to accept Tusel's offer, so don't fault him just because he happened to sign up with the losing side."

That piece of history did little to make Athaya feel much better, nor did it seem to appease the staunchly loyal Kale, who had an unusually marked expression of outrage on his normally placid face.

"And if you're concerned about the Sarian cultists that Basil mentioned during the Circle meeting," Hedric added, almost as an afterthought, "Tonia and I can both assure you that Ranulf was never involved with any of their ilk."

Athaya blinked silently. She wouldn't have remembered to worry about that if Hedric had not brought it up. Now she had two things nagging at the back of her mind instead of just one.

"And can I trust your loyalty?" she challenged, returning the mercenary's unswerving gaze.

Ranulf offered her a crooked smile. "Before you think the worse of me for fighting against the king of Caithe, you might want to remember what *you're* going back there to do."

Although the unadorned truth disturbed her, Athaya had to admit that the man had a point. She was, at least technically, planning to engage in an open act of treason by flouting the laws banning the teaching of magic. Anyone with a healthy respect for those laws and fervently loyal to the king who enforced them would be useless to her. And she could hardly find fault with Ranulf simply because he had taken up arms against a king long before she had.

"But putting it simple, your Highness," he added, using her title for the first time, "if it wasn't for somebody like you who found me in Caithe and smuggled me out, I'd have been dead twenty years ago. Absolved, they call it. You wouldn't think a man like me would care much, but sometimes I get to thinking of all the ones that got left behind."

Athaya mused on that quietly for a while, gazing at the mercenary with newfound insight. She still had misgivings about his past, but she knew he couldn't have falsified the sincerity with which he spoke those last words. And she also knew that it would be the height of hypocrisy for her to judge him based on nothing but vague suspicions. What if every citizen of Caithe judged her as nothing more than the mad wizard who murdered King Kelwyn, refusing to open their ears to the facts? That was exactly the sort of narrow-mindedness she was going home to eradicate.

"And what about you?" she said, turning her attention to the young boy at Mason's side. "Surely you have a less colorful tale to tell. What's your name?"

"Cameron," the lad piped up. He scrambled to his feet and dropped her a quick, if slightly clumsy, bow. "Cam for short. I'm from Leaforth—near the Forest of Else, by Kaiburn." Athaya nodded, vaguely recalling the location of the Caithan village and wondering what had brought the boy so far from home. "But I went to Delfarham once," he added exuberantly. "I saw you there—at a tournament. Except . . ." Cam paused to frown deeply. "Except you didn't look quite the same then."

"That's because I was probably dressed like our friend Ranulf here," she told him, motioning to the soldier's well-worn leathers. "I'm afraid I was something of an embarrassment to my family in those days. So, Cam, what brings you here? Hedric didn't tell me you were coming."

"He didn't tell you because he didn't know," Mason pointed out. He glanced at Cameron with a mixture of indignation and grudging respect. "The boy's only here because we couldn't shake him off our trail. He followed us all the way from Tenosce."

"And I'll follow you all the way to Caithe, too," the boy insisted, tilting his chin up defiantly.

"At least he's determined," Athaya remarked to the dom.

"He's a little thief, that's what he is," Mason countered, punctuating his words with a humorless laugh. "The three of us were in the market square at Tenosce buying a few things for the journey when this villain stole my purse and darted away like a rat running from torchlight. If Ranulf hadn't seen the direction he took and called up a few shielding spells, we might never have caught him."

Tonia gazed at the boy sympathetically. "Now, Mason, don't be so hard. He's a runaway. He had to put bread in his stomach somehow."

"He didn't have to do it with *my* money," the dom muttered, but without malice.

Athaya turned to the boy with newfound curiosity. "Well, Cameron, surely you didn't come all this way just to try to rob the king and his court instead of the folk in Tenosce. Why do you want to go to Caithe with us?"

Cam's eyes darkened with a maturity Athaya hadn't expected in one so young. "My brother," he said somberly. "The priest in our village took him away four years ago. I knew Mark wasn't possessed by the Devil the way the Father said, but I was afraid it'd happen to me and I'd have to die, too. I didn't want to die," he pointed out, as if feeling the need to explain such a desire. "But my parents thought they'd done the right thing. It didn't seem right . . . oh, I don't know. I just couldn't stay there anymore. I wanted to find out what wizards were really like, so I ran away to Reyka."

He ventured a glance at the dom. "Maybe it's true that I steal things sometimes, but only when I'm too hungry not to. I'm not really a thief. And when Ranulf caught me and took the dom's money back, I found out they were all going to Caithe to rescue wizards. So I decided to go, too." Cam lowered his eyes, suddenly absorbed with the patch of carpet he was turning under his boot. "I want to help prove that what the Father said about Mark was wrong. No one here thinks wizards are bad. They can't be—not if Mark was one."

Athaya closed her eyes, her breath catching in her throat. Tyler had said almost the exact same words to her. *If you have it, it can't possibly be evil.* She could only speculate on how many others in her homeland had whispered the same phrase to those they loved, suddenly doubting the truth of what they had believed for so many years when they realized that this time it was *their* wife, *their* child, *their* brother who was being taken away to die. It was easy to condemn a nameless man for any number of crimes, but when it was someone you cared for . . . oh, how easily minds could change.

"I understand, Cam." She gave him a smile, sad though it was. "And you're more than welcome to come with us. You may not be a wizard yourself—not yet, anyway," she added, knowing that it would be another six or seven years before any potential he might carry would surface, "but I can't question your reasons."

Then Athaya rose to her feet, hands on her hips, and studied her troops with an approving half smile. "A scholar, a mercenary, and a thief. An *alleged* thief," she amended, seeing the boy about to protest. "Add to that a disgraced princess, and we have three wizards, plus Kale and Cam. Not much of an army, but it's a start."

"Four wizards, my dear," Tonia corrected with a strange glimmer in her eye. She let out a wheezy laugh at Athaya's bewildered expression. "I'm coming along, too."

Hedric, who up to now had been unusually quiet, promptly

spit up the wedge of cheese he'd been eating, forcing Athaya to put aside the shock of Tonia's announcement long enough to clap him sharply on the back.

"*What*?" he exclaimed, as soon as he was able. His eyes bulged and for a moment he forgot to breathe. "Tonia, you can't be serious!"

Tonia tipped her chin up haughtily. "And why not? You went on a mercy mission to Caithe once. Now it's my turn. Can't very well let you hoard all the glory for yourself, now can I?"

"N-no, but—"

"You going to dare tell me I'm too old? I'm a damned sight younger than you are, you know," she reminded him, wagging a finger in his face. Then, seeing that his expression of disbelief did not diminish, she slapped her palm on her thigh and let out a hearty cackle of laughter, delighted to have taken Hedric so completely by surprise.

Athaya could only stare at her mutely, unable to piece her thoughts together. Her first reaction had been one of gladness— it would help to have someone as practical and cheerful as Tonia along for company. But she couldn't shake off a feeling of doubt . . . a feeling that there was something she wasn't being told. Why had Tonia suddenly made this decision? And why had she not mentioned it to any of them before this? *Unless she hadn't known herself,* Athaya considered. *Unless the decision had been made for her . . .*

The missing piece quickly slipped into place, and Athaya's expression quickly changed from simple surprise to smoldering resentment. "Lord Basil asked you to come, didn't he?" she asked, angry at the Overlord's apparent distrust. "He wants you to spy on me for him and make sure I don't break any of the Circle's rules, doesn't he?"

Tonia looked up, slightly guilty. "Well, I won't say he didn't suggest it," she admitted. "But I wanted to come. Can't very well send you off with just this motley assortment for company, now can I? Somebody has to do the cooking—I'll wager none of you know a frypan from a teakettle—and besides, you'll want another woman about. Who'll stitch up your underthings when they get worn, eh? One of them?" She jerked a thumb in the men's general direction and clicked her tongue disparagingly.

"I'd do it," Ranulf offered, leaning back and folding his hands across his belly. "Probably enjoy it, too."

"B-but you're one of the Great Masters," Athaya stammered, oblivious to Ranulf's ribaldry. "You're a member of the Circle! You can't go along just to be some sort of servant to us."

"We are all servants, my dear," she pointed out smoothly. "It's an admirable profession. Besides, in spite of everything Hedric's taught you, you're still young yet, and inexperienced. Basil and I agreed that it would be best if somebody came along who knew the ropes a bit better. Somebody who's trained many a wizard in her life, not just in the technical aspects of magic, but in the subtle ethics of it all. What should and shouldn't be done, and why. Such things take years to explore fully, and I dare say only a handful ever achieve a creditable level of true understanding in their lifetimes."

"And that handful . . . they become masters?"

Tonia shrugged modestly. "So we're told."

"Then I don't know how *you* got voted in," Hedric murmured grumpily. "This is the most half-cocked thing you've ever done, and I can't believe Basil talked you into it."

"Basil never talked me into anything in his life," she insisted. "I wanted to go. And I can't believe either one of you hasn't figured out the other reason why."

Athaya and Hedric exchanged glances, each hoping the other would provide the answer.

"Oh, use your heads, won't you?" Tonia huffed. "There's got to be somebody handy in case Athaya ever has to use the . . ." She glanced at the other wizards present and lowered her voice to a whisper. "The spell we talked about."

Athaya almost slapped herself for such stupidity. How could she have forgotten? What good would it do to protect herself with a sealing spell, only to have no way of getting it undone short of riding all the way back to Reyka?

"Are you done berating me," Tonia went on, "or do we keep arguing about this all afternoon?"

"Oh, Tonia, don't mind me." Hedric sighed and massaged his eyes as if he felt a headache coming on, realizing there was little he could do other than concede the argument. "God knows this is a worthy cause. I all but forced Athaya into taking charge of it in the first place, and logically there's nothing wrong with you going along. But it's going to be hard enough to see Athaya put herself in that kind of danger, much less you, too. I'll worry about you, that's all."

Tonia's eyes opened a little wider. "Why, Hedric Elson MacAlliard, I do believe you're getting sentimental in your old age." She offered him a consoling pat on the arm, then opened a new subject by asking everyone to begin listing the provisions they would need for the journey to Caithe.

After supper that night, Osfonin entertained Master Tonia and the other new arrivals with the best musicians to be found in Ath Luaine, inviting everyone to dance to the pipes and fiddles until the wee hours of the morning. Athaya saw Jaren vanish soon after supper was over, and though she tried to convince herself that he was tired or had pressing duties to attend to, she knew deep down that he was simply trying to avoid her. Briefly, she thought of following him—to try to explain that it was only because she *did* care that she had turned him away. But saying such things would only rekindle his hopes of returning to Caithe with her, and that he simply could not do.

After dancing a reel in turn with Mason, Ranulf, and Nicolas, Athaya worked her way around the edges of the Great Hall toward the vast table of cheeses, pastries, and ale. After choosing a rich, currant-filled pastry and finding an empty seat in which to eat it, she watched as Felgin took Master Tonia for a turn about the Hall and then offered his hand to several other ladies of the court. Courtesy dictated that as a guest in the palace, he ask Athaya to dance as well, but he had expertly avoided her gaze whenever he could, and so far, no one else in attendance appeared to have noticed the slight.

When the musicians broke from their lively tunes and began playing a series of lyrical ballads, Felgin returned to his place on the dais for some much-needed rest and refreshment. Before he could see her in time to move away, Athaya took the empty seat beside him.

"You've been avoiding me," she observed, not surprised when Felgin didn't bother to contradict her. "And Nicolas tells me you haven't said much to him all week, either."

Felgin gave her only the briefest of glances. "What is there to say?" He wasn't angry, just vaguely sad, and the slate-gray color of his tunic only added to his air of despondency. "Jaren's like a brother to me, Athaya. When he's hurt, I feel for him." Felgin helped himself to the wine flagon on the table and filled his cup to the brim. As an afterthought, he poured a cup for Athaya as well.

He didn't feel inclined to say anything else and quietly sipped at his wine as the silvery voices of the musicians sang a mournful ballad of two lovers who drowned at sea while sailing to their wedding. It was a haunting song, and Athaya's spirits were much subdued from what they had been only moments before.

"That song makes me think of something," she said, running a finger around the rim of her goblet. "But for my magic coming when it did, I'd be sitting here as your wife right now."

Felgin gave her a thoughtful stare, as if the notion had never entered his head before that moment. "I suppose you would at that," he said pensively. Then he looked away and shrugged. "I'd like to think it wouldn't have been the worst thing to ever happen to you."

Oh, I might have thought so once, Athaya mused, but she had to laugh at such foolishness now. Less than a year ago, she would have done anything to keep her father from pursuing her betrothal to the Reykan prince. And if anyone had predicted that she would actually come to like the man, Athaya would have sworn that such a thing would only happen if she went quite mad.

But of course, she told herself, *that's exactly what happened.*

Athaya pretended to consider his remark quite seriously. "Maybe not the *worst* thing," she replied, offering him a smile that she hoped would crack his stiff restraint.

Just then, Felgin sensed that perhaps he was being more surly than necessary, and without making a move he seemed to relax in front of her, the tension slowly receding from his face. When he looked at her again, his eyes were warm and unaccusing. "I can understand why you didn't want to marry me, Athaya. Nobody wants to be pushed into marrying someone he doesn't love just because his parents think it's a good idea." He paused and shook his head. "But Jaren . . . he's about the best there is. For the life of me I just can't see why you'd refuse him."

"Nicolas didn't tell you?"

"Oh, he told me all about your reasons," Felgin replied, subtly disdainful, "and I think the only person in this palace who would see any sense in them at all is Lord Ian. But don't worry. Nobody has told Jaren about them. Yet," he added, swirling his wine around until it came dangerously close to spilling out onto the tablecloth. "But I'm damned tempted to, Athaya. It's about time somebody stepped in to save you from yourself."

"Please don't tell him," she said quickly. "I'm hoping that if Jaren stays behind for a while, he'll eventually lose interest in joining me. Then he can go ahead and do . . . whatever he would have done before he knew I existed. I'm doing what's best for him, Felgin. As his friend, surely you can understand that. I'm not going to let him put his life in danger again."

"Then you don't know?"

Athaya set her cup down slowly. "Know what?"

The prince leaned forward and rested his forearms on the table. "Athaya, he's still planning to go with you. He told me so just this morning."

The wine she'd drunk seemed to sour in her stomach with those words, and the music in the Hall was muted, as if she were listening to it from a great distance.

"You've done your best to break his heart," Felgin went on, "but he still believes in your mission. He's already asked Hedric for an indefinite leave of absence from his post and has made up a list of several other wizards who'd jump at the chance to be assistant to a Master, even on a temporary basis. He's probably up in his rooms drafting letters to them tonight."

"But *why*?" she cried. She knew perfectly well why, but she was strangely unable to accept the fact that Jaren wasn't going to do exactly as she wished.

"As I told you, he wants to help. But of equal weight, I expect, is his hope that you'll come to your senses and change your mind about marrying him." Felgin gazed at her with a peculiar mix of admonition and admiration. "I've never seen Jaren in love with anyone before. It certainly is bringing out the streak of defiance in him." Felgin gazed out across the Hall, his next comment barely audible. "Strange how Lord Ian found that out long before you did."

Athaya slumped forward and buried her face in her hands. It had been hard enough to turn him away the first time. How would she ever be able to do it again? And if he had paid her no mind before, why should he do so now?

"Surely there has to be someone he'll listen to," she groaned.

Athaya jerked her head up sharply. *But of course there is,* she realized with a surge of hope. *Felgin just said so.*

"Excuse me," she said, abruptly rising to her feet. "I have to talk to someone."

Felgin put a hand on her arm. "He won't change his mind."

"It's not Jaren I'm looking for," she said over her shoulder as she stepped off the dais. But before she went any further, she turned back and smiled. "You're a good friend, Felgin. And not just to Jaren. I just wanted you to know that." And as the prince's face registered pleasant surprise, Athaya swept purposefully from the Hall.

Entering Lord Ian's private chamber called up memories of the uneasy self-consciousness Athaya used to feel when summoned into her father's presence for one of a countless number of scoldings, and it was a sensation she did not find pleasant to relive.

When the uniformed man at the door ushered her inside, Lord Ian rose to his feet and dropped his quill back into the inkwell on his writing desk. Loose papers surrounded him, each littered with ledger entries, cryptic markings, and an occasional blob of black ink. Although he was informally clad in an unadorned blue overrobe, and his balding head was left bare, Lord Ian's gaze was as stony as ever, and Athaya found herself anxiously winding her fingers around one another as if they were silver candlesticks in need of polishing.

"That'll be all, Brice," he said to the uniformed man, and once they were alone, Lord Ian looked at his guest inquiringly. "You wished to see me?" he said, his gruff voice carrying the tone of a field commander exasperated by an incompetent recruit.

"Yes, my Lord. I trust I'm not interrupting you."

He scanned the untidy assortment of papers on his desk with weary indifference. "I suppose not. I take little pleasure in reviewing my accounts. The drudgery of numbers is best left to my steward, I fear." He offered her a chair with a stilted jerk of his arm, but Athaya chose to remain standing.

"I came to talk to you about Jaren."

Although the duke did not move, a cloud of concern passed over his eyes. Muscles tensed, he jutted his chin out slightly as if silently daring to her to go on.

"My Lord, I'm not sure if you're aware of this, but your son proposed marriage to me last week."

For an instant, Athaya wasn't sure he had heard her, but the bulging veins on either side of his temples quickly told her otherwise. Then his cheeks flushed with outrage, and he slammed his fist down so hard on the desk that it upset the ink pot and sent a slender river of black ink flowing across his ledgers.

"That insolent boy! I forbade him to do any such thing, and this is how he heeds me!" Nostrils flaring, Ian glared at her as if convinced she had set out to deliberately ruin his family's good name. "The most gifted of all my sons and without a doubt the most obstinate!" he railed on. "I only want what's best for him and he—"

"I refused him, Lord Ian."

A more abrupt change could not have been possible. The duke blinked, suddenly struck silent. A moment later, he settled back down in his chair and began scratching at his chin, puzzled, but overwhelmingly relieved.

"That must explain why he's been so sullen these last few days," he mused. Then he rolled his eyes and snorted derisively. "And I thought it was because he had decided to obey me and was having a hard time swallowing his pride." The duke glanced up at Athaya, remotely aware that the woman he was ranting against with such fervor was standing right before him and would no doubt find his manners quite lacking. "Forgive my outburst, Princess. I may have my misgivings about you, but I should have had enough courtesy to keep them to myself."

"You're hardly the first to hold a bad opinion of me," she replied candidly. "I'm rather used to it." She took the chair she had refused earlier and leaned forward with an air of entreaty. "Lord Ian, your son is a kind and selfless man, and I care for him a great deal. His friendship is precious to me. But I also share your concerns that he remain here where it's safe and not get involved with my . . . 'crusade,' I suppose I should call it. I had no choice but to refuse his proposal."

The duke's eyes lit up with hope. "So you've convinced him to stay?"

"Well, not exactly," she admitted. "Felgin just told me that Jaren is still planning to follow me to Caithe. That's why I'm here. I thought you could help . . . maybe by asking him to go home to Ulard for a while. To see his family." She held out her hands, palms up. "Surely he'll listen to you."

"Bah!" Ian sputtered. "Not two weeks ago I specifically told him not to ask for your hand and look at how much good *that* did.'' The moment the words were out, the duke winced and offered her a gruff look of apology, but Athaya waved it aside.

"I understand, my Lord," she said. "And I can't blame you. I got Jaren into his fair share of trouble the last time he went to Caithe and I want to do everything I can to see that it never happens again.''

The duke sat back with furrowed brows, quietly tapping the tips of his fingers together like a king pondering the advice of his council. "You know, now that I think of it, he just might listen. I can ask him to come home just for a while, tell him he has to see his mother and brothers again before venturing off on such a dangerous 'crusade,' as you put it. If I couch it in terms of family duty and point out that he may get himself killed and never see any of us again, I'm sure I can lure him there . . . perhaps until summer.''

"That might be long enough," Athaya said, suddenly sad.

Suddenly the duke's eyes sparked with an idea. "Oh, but there may be a way to see that he stays for good," he said, a shrewd smile cracking across his face. "Claire O'Fadden.''

Athaya shifted uncomfortably in her chair. This was a twist she certainly hadn't expected. "Who?''

"The eldest daughter of my neighbors to the north. She and her brothers and sisters have been friends of my family for years. Claire is a few years younger than Jaren, but already widowed . . . a terrible accident it was, and her husband only twenty at the time. Jaren was always fond of her.'' The duke's smile broadened as he considered the idea. "Now that she's living at home again, I'm sure she'd welcome his company.'' And his tone made it clear that he would have no objections to a more permanent arrangement.

"A fine idea," Athaya offered, though the words stuck in her throat like honey, and she had to force them out.

After a few more minutes of contemplation, Lord Ian shifted his gaze to Athaya, studying her intently. "Perhaps I was somewhat hasty in my judgment of you, your Highness. It seems we both want the same thing in the end, doesn't it?''

"We do, my Lord. And I'm sure Jaren will come to thank us for it . . . eventually.'' *And if he doesn't,* she added inwardly, *then at least he'll be alive to hate us for it.*

Athaya left the duke's chamber confident of success. Surely

Lord Ian could convince Jaren to return home on a temporary basis, and once there, would insure that he stayed—even if what kept him there was the friendship of another young lady.

Oh, stop it, she told herself irritably. *You got what you wanted, didn't you?* All at once, she didn't feel as if she had succeeded at all, but failed miserably.

As she turned down the torchlit corridor leading to her own suite, she recalled something Felgin had told her during her first visit to Ath Luaine—something he said to comfort her when she admitted that her only dream was to marry Tyler, and that she never honestly expected it to come true. *In time you'll have new dreams,* he assured her. *Dreams that can be reached.*

Bitterly, Athaya banged one fist against the soot-streaked wall. *But you never told me what to do when the dream is well within your grasp, yet you don't dare reach out to take it.* Just this afternoon, she had told Dom DePere not to be ashamed of dreaming—that little would be accomplished if people did not— but now, as she rubbed the cold ash from her hands, she wondered whether it might be safer never to dream at all than to have all her desires snatched from her one by one until she had nothing left.

CHAPTER 8

※※※

U NDER A SKY THICK WITH GENTLY FALLING SNOWFLAKES, a small party of soldiers reined in at the crest of a rise on the wild and barren borderlands. The twenty-odd men were unnaturally silent, though whether it was from weariness or the unyielding stare of the black crags around them, none of them could say. The night was not as bitter as the last six had been, but it was extremely wet, and it had taken seven days instead of the usual four for the party to cross the distance between Ath Luaine and the Caithan border, unavoidably slowed by the patches of ice and ankle-deep mud that plagued the roads.

While Lord Gessinger and the rest of the Caithan guardsmen halted their mounts for a much-needed rest, Captain Parr surveyed the mean little village in the valley below, its dilapidated collection of cottages made only slightly less ugly by the blanket of fresh snow.

"Doesn't look fit for pigs, but it'll have to do," he muttered, trying to deduce which one of the shabby structures was large enough to accommodate his men. A cold breeze rippled the folds of his traveling cloak, and he pulled it tighter around him, grumbling profusely. "Damn this place, and all of Reyka with it. It shouldn't be this cold in late March."

"We're a good distance north of Delfarham, Captain," Gessinger replied exhaustedly. He shivered under his fur-lined mantle, looking more like a lost and wretched wanderer than a traveling duke. "But the road turns south from here. We'll be across the border by noon tomorrow." For a moment, he looked slightly less forlorn. "And that means we'll finally be free of Osfonin's 'honor guard,' " he added, glancing over his shoulder at the handful of blue-clad soldiers who had trailed them from Ath Luaine to insure that they crossed the border without incident.

As Parr turned back to study the Reykan guardsmen, his expression shifted, growing cold as the air around them. He exchanged a subtle, knowing glance with one of the men in his troop, then slowly sidled his horse closer to Gessinger.

"*You'll* be over the border, my Lord," he said pointedly, gripping the reins as if he feared his horse were about to bolt. "Not me. Or at least, not for long."

The duke eyed him with sudden distrust. "What do you mean, Captain? Explain yourself."

"I only rode this far to satisfy those men behind us. And to convince anyone spying on us with those hellish things—vision spheres, they call them—that we're really gone." His eyes narrowed underneath the cloak's snow-covered hood. "But the minute Osfonin's men turn back for Ath Luaine, so do I."

The announcement hung suspended in the air for several minutes, the silence broken only by the occasional jangle of a harness or a soldier's muffled cough. Gessinger fidgeted in his saddle, keenly aware that his authority was being usurped and that he was wholly incapable of regaining it.

"You can't disobey orders whenever the mood strikes you, Captain. I insist that you return with us." He held his chin up and tried to muster what dignity he could, but his lower lip twitched nervously.

Confident that the advantage was his, Parr saw no need to let the duke annoy him. Gessinger was an ineffectual man even at his best and wasn't worth the effort of a heated argument. Parr smiled thinly, conscious that Gessinger knew that as well—or better—than he did.

"I take my orders from the king," he countered, "and the king has charged me with finding Princess Athaya. I won't return without news of her." He locked his gaze onto the duke, staring steadily until Gessinger finally turned away. "Go back to Delfarham if you like. My business in Reyka isn't finished yet."

Gessinger huddled deeper into his mantle, chilled by the mere thought of the risks Parr was taking. "But what if you're seen?" he cautioned weakly. "Those men following us are sure to post sentries on the road. If you're caught, Osfonin has many wizards in his employ who could make you sorry indeed."

"And I can make those wizards just as sorry," the captain replied darkly. Pulling off a glove, Parr held up his left hand to reveal a heavy gold ring with a single corbal crystal embedded in its center. "The king gave this to me in case I needed some . . . 'incentive' to bring Athaya back." With a grim smile, the captain thrust his hand back inside the glove. "And we won't be seen. We'll leave off our uniforms for something less conspicuous and we'll take the seacoast road up to Torvik and cut south instead of using the main road we're on now. It'll take twice as long to get back, but we shouldn't run into any of Osfonin's sentries."

"Wait . . . you said 'we'?" The duke's eyes darted around him, hesitantly scanning the faces of the guardsmen and wondering how many of them were planning to desert him. But the grizzled faces were stiff and unreadable, as if they had been frozen into vacant stares by the crisp winter winds.

"Don't worry, my Lord, you'll have ample escort back to Delfarham," Parr said, the crafted courtesy in his tone rendering the words more condescending than comforting. "I've discussed this with my men, and while most of them volunteered to join me, I had to limit my choice to three. A larger number might cause questions."

The duke nodded absently. "I suppose."

"His Majesty will be grateful for our efforts, Lord Gessinger," Parr concluded, each word making a cloud of white mist in the wintry air. "What could be more important than bringing Kelwyn's murderer to justice?"

Before Gessinger could frame even the most impotent of replies, Parr snapped the reins of his horse and signaled for the men to proceed into the valley. They followed dutifully, guiding their horses around the duke as if he were a fallen log in their path. Then, when it occurred to him that no one would likely secure lodging for him unless he was there to claim it himself, Gessinger sighed deeply and spurred his horse ahead, wondering how King Durek was going to react when advised of the dogged persistence of his newly appointed captain, and the equally impassioned determination of his brother Nicolas, both quite unwilling to leave Reyka and abandon the quest for Athaya Trelane.

One week after the vernal equinox, on the night before her departure from Ath Luaine, Athaya was in Hedric's study weaving the crackling green coils of her fire-spell into various patterns, changing their intensity and direction as Hedric instructed. He had warned her that they would work on this spell again, much as she hoped he would forget, but today there were no bursts of panic; no unexpected translocations; and at long last, Athaya felt as if she were coming to be the master of the deadly green coils, instead of the other way around.

"Good, Athaya. Very good," Hedric said, nodding his satisfaction. "I think you've got control of it now."

Athaya let the crackling coils of fire dissipate from her fingertips and breathed an audible sigh of relief. "I hate that spell, Master Hedric. I may be able to cast it, but I'll always hate it."

"I know," he said with compassion. "But I wasn't about to let my prize pupil leave me without making sure she had mastered everything I had to teach her. Even if some of it *was* done under protest."

After offering him a crooked grin, Athaya sighed faintly and slumped back into the study's tree-chair. "Leaving," she said quietly, shaking her head in disbelief as she stared at the flames crackling briskly in the hearth. "I still don't feel quite ready . . . even with everything you've taught me."

Hedric chuckled with delight. "No one's ever ready, Athaya. In fact, the longer I live, the more I realize how very little I know about anything."

"I would have thought by now that you'd at least know everything there is about wizardry. With the possible exception of translocation spells," she added, playfully smug. "After all, magic is your specialty."

"Oh, I have my own theories about my craft. I plan to have several essays of my own on the general curriculum at Wizard's College someday, you know." His eyes twinkled with mischief. "So future students can revile my name as they pore over my eloquent words the night before their examinations." Hedric laughed merrily when he caught sight of the expression of pity that crossed Athaya's face.

Then he reached deep into the pocket of his robe. "That reminds me . . . I have something for you." He drew out a circular, coin-sized object and folded it into her palm. Then he rested his hand on her shoulder and gave it a paternal pat. "You've earned it."

Athaya opened her hand to find a brooch worked in solid gold. A cross, flared at each point and embedded with an array of colorful gems, set upon a circle—a design she had seen many times before. The workmanship of this piece was exquisite—crafted decades ago by the look of it—and Athaya could only guess at its value.

"It's beautiful," she whispered.

"It is the symbol of our people. The four points of the cross signify the four elements of fire, air, earth, and water. And the three gems on each point represent our own elements—the body, the mind, and the spirit. And the circle surrounding it all . . . oh, the endless task, perhaps, of trying to make all those elements work together in harmony."

"Is that how the Circle of Masters got its name?"

"Mmm, I really don't know," he mused, raising bushy brows. "Be careful, Athaya. I think that all of your studying is beginning to sharpen your mind."

Athaya couldn't help but smile broadly. *And that's as fine a compliment as I'll ever get out of you.*

Ignoring Hedric's good-natured barb, Athaya turned the brooch over in her hands, admiring the way the firelight played across the gemstones. "Does this mean school is out?" she asked playfully.

The master pointed a crooked finger at her in mock severity. "Hardly. School, as far as a wizard is concerned, is *never* out." Then his features relaxed, and he gazed at her with all the wisdom of the ages reflected in his eyes. "Remember, Athaya. In the end, it wasn't my duty merely to show you how to cast your spells, but to show you how to take joy in learning, to inspire you to go on and to seek knowledge on your own. And I fully expect you to challenge your own students as much as I've challenged you. The more you expect of them, the more they'll try to live up to your expectations. If you ask for mere competence, that's all you get. But if you demand perfection—if you insist that they try their best at all times—then you'll tap the greatness inside of them no matter what the extent of their gift.''

Slowly, Athaya pinned the brooch to the collar of her gown. She waited a long time before asking her next question.

''And have I lived up to your expectations, Master Hedric?''

For a moment, he looked as if he were going to offer her another backward compliment—another word of praise veiled in a friendly insult. But he changed his mind at the last minute, as if realizing he might not get another opportunity to speak with her privately before she departed, and surprised her with a light, dry kiss on the forehead.

''Yes, my dear, you have.'' He slipped his slender arms around her in a surprisingly strong embrace. ''I'll miss you, Athaya. More than you know.''

And with the gaze of the master upon her Athaya realized, perhaps for the first time, the scope of the task before her in leaving behind her role as apprentice and taking up the teacher's mantle.

The next morning—if it could be called that with dawn still hours away—was still and clear in the barren courtyard, the stars twinkling brilliantly in an ice-cold sky. A light layer of moonlit frost coated the ground, and it crunched loudly beneath Athaya's boots even though she tried to tread softly. Already shivering from lack of sleep, Athaya drew a heavy woolen cloak tightly around her and sought out the sanctuary of the stables. There she huddled in the doorway, blowing white clouds of hot breath into her gloves as she watched the subdued preparations taking place around her. She felt strangely detached from their activity, however—as if only a small part of her had brought her body outdoors this morning, while the rest of her was still curled up on a goose-down mattress, lost in dreams.

As well I should be, she thought, having no great love for being up and about at four o'clock in the morning. She took a deep breath of the crisp air to rouse herself. Although April was only days away, winter had yet to release its grip on Ath Luaine, and if anything about her departure could cheer her, it was the fact that it would be full spring in Caithe by the time she arrived.

In one corner of the yard, Kale and Mason were strapping leather packs to the horses and loading the rest of the provisions into a wagon. Cam was curled up in a mound of straw in the

rear of the wagon, and while they could have used the extra
help, the boy looked so peaceful that neither of them had
the heart to wake him. Tonia, who seemed to have more
energy than ever at this hour, was everywhere at once, making sure they had forgotten nothing, checking the map that
would take them south, and arguing with Ranulf over the
best road to take.

Leaning against the doorjamb, Athaya drifted into a dreamy
state of half-sleep, and didn't hear the approaching crunch of
footsteps until they were very close. When she looked up, raising heavy-lidded eyes, she saw Jaren beside her, all but obscured
under a warm, hooded cloak. He looked just like a monk on his
way to matins, hands tucked in opposite sleeves, head bowed—
but for him it was bowed in sadness, not piety.

He said nothing at first, content to lean against the stable wall
beside her and observe the activity in the courtyard. But he had
a faraway look in his eyes, as if he were not seeing the yard at
all, but images of the past, or dreams of a future that would
never come to be.

"I suppose you heard I'm going home for a while," he said
at last, absently grinding the snow beneath the toe of his boot.
"My father is leaving for Ulard in a few days, and I'll be following in a few weeks. I have to find a replacement, you know.
To help Hedric."

Athaya nodded, not trusting herself to speak. Lord Ian had
told her of his success in luring his son home, and so far Jaren
had not suspected the true source of that suggestion. But she felt
as if that guilty knowledge were written clearly on her face and
kept her eyes averted.

"I just wanted to come out and see you off." He leaned closer
to her for a moment, breath frosting the air between them, then
seemed to reconsider and drew back. "The last time you left
Ath Luaine, you told me to stay behind, but I wouldn't." He
paused to swallow, finding it hard to go on. "This time I'll
listen."

Athaya squeezed her eyes shut, remembering that day with
vivid clarity. How, in these very stables, she had furiously ordered him to stay behind, forbidden him to follow her to Caithe
and teach her magic, and even struck him for daring to accuse
her of cruelly ignoring the plight of a people Hedric had claimed
she was destined to save. Then, she thought his persistent con-

cern for her future was insufferable. Now she looked back on those days with affection, knowing that Jaren was the reason she was alive at all.

"But you understand why, don't you?"

Please, Jaren, she pleaded inwardly, *tell me you understand, even if you don't. Tell me what I want to hear, just this once, or I don't think I can live with myself for long.*

When he finally answered, his voice was weary and sad. "I understand, Athaya. But that doesn't mean I think you're right."

She waited for him to go on—to announce that he was still determined to join her later, after a brief visit in Ulard—but strangely, he did not. Athaya felt a sour emptiness in her stomach. Perhaps this neighbor Lord Ian had mentioned—Claire O'Fadden, was it?—was a more tempting reason to stay in Reyka than she had supposed.

"I can send word in a month or so . . . to let you know how I'm doing," she offered, but Jaren's nod of agreement was listless. He knew, as did she, that it was just one of many meaningless utterances people used when faced with the pain of knowing they might not meet again and choose instead to ignore the fact.

Then Jaren turned to her, gazing at her with quiet urgency. "I know you'll change the world, Athaya," he added, his voice edged with fervor, "or at least your small part of it. I have faith in you."

Quickly, as if afraid she might pull away if given warning, he leaned over and brushed her cheek with a chaste kiss. Before she could say a word, he spun around and walked away, boots crunching softly on the packed snow, unable to see the hands that Athaya instinctively reached out to him, silently trying to draw him back.

When he'd gone about ten yards, he stopped. He glanced up, as if asking the stars for counsel, then dropped his gaze again. Briefly, he drew a hand across his eyes and it came away moist and glistening.

"I still love you, Athaya," he said quietly, without turning around. "Always remember that." Then he paced quickly toward the castle keep, his head bowed low as if in shame.

Athaya felt the words leap unbidden into her throat. *Don't go! Stay with me . . . come with me! I'll marry you, Jaren, and*

*we'll spend the rest of our lives together . . . just don't leave
me now!*

But instead of calling out, she buried her face in the folds of
her cloak, biting her lip to hold back the tears. "Think of something else," she chided herself. "Don't do this. Think of
something else . . ."

And then, without consciously planning to, she closed her
eyes and began to recite, words tumbling out in an angry stream
as she forced her thoughts into other channels. "Credony, lord
of the first Circle, twenty-six years; Sidra, lord of the second
Circle, eleven years; Malcon, lord of the third . . ."

She continued with the recitation until her mind was numb
from the mechanical, memorized words, and the urge to run
after Jaren had abated.

Athaya's heart was heavy as lead in her chest, and just as she
was judging the day a complete loss before the sun ever rose,
she looked up and saw a small light winking from one of the
tower windows. Nicolas was perched in the bay window of his
chamber, his face made bright by the oil lamp he'd set on the
ledge before him. He blew her a kiss of farewell, and Athaya's
vision swam a little as she returned the gesture.

Then Ranulf barked out that they were ready to ride, and in
a matter of minutes he was leading them through the gatehouse,
with Mason and Tonia riding behind on the supply wagon that
held a still-dozing Cam. Athaya followed alone at the rear, behind the spare horses in Kale's care.

Fleetingly, Athaya wished she could have simply cast a spell
of translocation and taken herself to Caithe that very hour, sparing herself a long and tiring journey with nothing to do but brood
about Jaren and wonder if she would ever see Nicolas or Hedric—or anyone in this city—again. But even though Master Credony's ancient writings theorized that she could translocate
anything in her possession or anyone in physical contact with
her, the logistics of transporting five other people with all their
supplies and assorted baggage convinced her not to start experimenting with the spell now.

They took the south road out of Ath Luaine, heading for the
small port city of Alarvic, where they would hire a ship to take
them to the eastern shore of Caithe. Just before the spires of
Glendol Palace faded out of sight behind her, Athaya looked
back one last time, calmed by the sight of the silvery structure—

now touched by a rose-colored dawn—watching over the snow-bound valley. Soon the fortress would be buzzing with activity, but for now it still slept on, untroubled—but perhaps for one young man, wrapped in a cowled robe, who had loved her enough to let her go.

CHAPTER 9

※※

"**W**HAT IN THE NAME OF CREATION DO YOU MEAN Nicolas didn't come back with you?**" Durek raged, his voice rattling the foundations of the audience chamber in Delfar Castle. The ruby-studded band of gold circling his head glittered harshly in the candlelight as he pushed himself out of his receiving throne and glared at the shivering, gray-haired man cowering before him. "Are you trying to tell me you just rode off and *left* him in that godforsaken place?"

"Your Majesty, he—"

"Heaven only *knows* what those mind-plagued wizards will do to him! With our luck, they'll turn him into one of them, just like they did with Athaya." Durek threw his arms up in dismay, infuriated by his council lord's incompetence. "Whatever possessed you to simply leave him behind? Don't you realize the *danger* he's in?" The king jabbed a finger in the shivering man's face. "I've half a mind to retire old DeBracy and appoint *you* lord marshal of Sare in his place for this."

Lord Gessinger blanched, having no desire to be banished to that wild and storm-swept island. Even though some would claim the post to be an honor, Kelwyn had customarily used it as a subtle form of punishment for those of his court who did not serve their king to his satisfaction.

Swallowing loudly, Gessinger rounded his shoulders and hunched down as if trying to disappear inside the damp folds of his cloak. He had not changed from his riding attire since reaching Delfarham, and now a pool of water had formed at his feet, growing ever larger as the evening rain trickled off him. The king did not care to notice his apparent discomfort, however, and neither did Dagara or Archbishop Ventan, who lingered near the fire on the opposite side of the room.

"Prince Nicolas insisted upon staying, my Lord. I saw no evidence that he was being held there against his will. He—" Gessinger paused to clear his throat, visibly hesitant, but Durek's frigid glare convinced him to continue. "He appeared to be somewhat attracted to Osfonin's daughter."

Durek clapped a hand over his forehead. "Oh, God help us, I should have expected as much. I send him off on a critical mission, and he fritters away his time dallying with women."

"That boy will never change," Dagara muttered under her breath, viciously stabbing her needle into the embroidery she was working on. "Twenty-two years old and he acts less than fourteen of it."

"We saw nothing of Princess Athaya," Gessinger went on quickly, painfully aware that if his sister began expounding upon the various faults of Kelwyn's youngest son, he would be in danger of standing here all night.

"Of course you didn't *see* her," Durek retorted impatiently. "They would have been hiding her somewhere. Either that or she was standing right in front of you under a . . . what did Rhodri used to call those things? Cloaking spells? You know— those tricks they use to make themselves invisible."

"The same trick she used to sneak into Saint Adriel's for Kelwyn's funeral," the archbishop pointed out, nodding self-importantly.

Gessinger tightened his jaw at that, on the verge of asking just how he should have been expected to find someone who could fade into invisibility at will, but the king's stony gaze robbed him of that fleeting spark of rebellion, and he swallowed his objections and concluded his report.

"King Osfonin wasn't very cooperative. He told us that he didn't know where Athaya was, and that . . ." Another hesitant pause to clear his throat. ". . . that it was 'hardly his duty to worry about whether his esteemed friend, the King of Caithe, has misplaced his sister.' "

The queen dowager thrust out her chin in righteous indignation. "Why, of all the brazen audacity—"

"It means nothing, Dagara," Durek replied stiffly, his eyes growing dark. "I rather expected him to say something like that. After all, he's held his crown for over thirty years and I've barely worn mine six months. He's just seeing how far he can push me, that's all."

Durek paced in a wide circle around the room, his fingers working the dark, stubbly beginnings of the beard he was trying to grow.

"And Parr went back to find Athaya, did he?" the king murmured thoughtfully, nodding his pleasure. "Good. Very good. I did well in advancing him to the captaincy." Then he suddenly stopped midstride and turned abruptly to his councillor. "What about that cur who helped her escape? Jaren something-or-other. He's some sort of assistant to Osfonin's pet wizard. Was there any sign of him?"

"Oh, yes," Gessinger admitted, recalling Jaren's brief appearance on the night of the Caithans' arrival. "He claimed to know nothing, although Captain Parr didn't believe him. Later in the week, I spoke briefly with Osfonin's wizard . . . Hedric, I think the name was. But he refused to say anything other than he'd met Athaya in September and found her 'unusually gifted.' He advised us not to anger her."

Durek let out a snort. "Good advice, when you think of it. Just look what she did to Kelwyn."

The blunt truth of that statement precluded any further comment, and for the next few minutes the only sounds in the room were the crackling of the fire and the occasional drip of water from Lord Gessinger's cloak.

Then Dagara turned to her brother with a glare that could have curdled fresh milk. "Oh, Mosel, how stupid can you possibly *be*? Didn't you once stop to think that the only reason Nicolas stayed in Ath Luaine was precisely because Athaya *was* there? He's been devoted to Athaya all his life—why, she's probably had him under her spells ever since they were children. She wanted him to stay in Reyka with her, and so he disregarded everything else to please her. It's as simple as that."

"Possible, your Grace. But not irrefutably true."

Archbishop Ventan rose from his place near the fire and helped himself to a goblet of the king's wine. "Prince Nicolas has been quite despondent ever since Athaya fled the country. We have all noticed the way he keeps to himself much more than was his habit before. True, this could mean he misses her, but it could also mean that he feels betrayed—that he is finally beginning to see what she really is. If he loves her as much as you say, Dagara, then he'll have a care for her soul. Maybe he *is* waiting to see if she'll turn up in Ath Luaine. Or if she's been there all along and they've spoken, it's quite possible that Nicolas is trying to persuade her to come home and submit to absolution without feeling pressured by Lord Gessinger and his guards. As you said, if anyone can make her see reason, he can. Perhaps he merely wanted to do it on his own terms."

"Perhaps," Durek said reluctantly, "but I'm not sure I credit Nicolas with that much scope of reason. And even if that is what he's planning, who's to say some wizard—Jaren, Hedric, or even Prince Felgin—won't try to muddle his head with spells to insure that he fails?" Durek shook his head worriedly, then fixed his eye on the jeweled ring glittering on the archbishop's left hand—an excessively large diamond surrounded by a dozen tiny corbal crystals. "If I'd known Nicolas would be staying behind alone, I would have told the captain to leave him the corbal ring I sent along for their protection."

Ventan nodded gravely. "And he'll not find one in Reyka. With so many wizards about, the gem is even more rare there than it is here. But since no Reykan wants them anyway, corbals are practically worthless." The archbishop held his hand up to the light and admired the ring as if seeing it for the first time. "But they're far from worthless here," he added casually. "If I remember my history correctly, King Faltil nearly bankrupted the treasury acquiring them."

Durek scowled. He sensed he should know what the archbishop was referring to, but his mind was too full of other things to cooperate. "Bankrupted? What are you talking about?"

"He had to buy them all from Cruachi, of course. The crystals are abundant there and aren't worth half the price they could fetch anywhere else. And knowing how desperately Faltil wanted them, the old emir made him pay dearly for them. I'm told that the royal palace at Kapesch was gilded floor to ceiling with gold using the profits made on the exchange." The archbishop clicked his tongue. "Heathens," he grumbled to himself.

Dagara set aside her embroidery and bunched up her lips with impatience. "But why spend every last piece of silver he's got for a hoard of purple stones?"

"Weapons, my lady," Ventan replied, a glint of zeal in his tiny gray eyes. "How else do you suppose he was able to wash Caithe clean of the Lorngeld? When a corbal crystal is exposed to light, it tangles a wizard's thinking and renders his powers useless. You will recall that we used just such a crystal to secure the wizard Jaren in our dungeons."

"Yes," Dagara agreed acidly. "And it worked so well that he escaped the next day."

Lacking an adequate response to such an inconvenient observation, Ventan hastily continued. "King Faltil had some exquisite jewelry made out of some of the gems he acquired so that he and his courtiers would be protected from wizardry. And the Church was also given a generous allotment of corbals to insure that the Devil's Children stayed out of the houses of God. Many of the older altar pieces in the archives at Saint Adriel's are studded with corbals, but because of their value, we don't display them except on high holy days.

"And then, of course, there is Faltil's crown."

Durek looked up, suddenly curious. "His what?"

"His crown. Faltil had it made shortly after his coronation with the traditional crown of state. As proof that his magic had been bestowed by God, and was not the Devil's handiwork, he wore a crown made almost entirely of corbals to show that they did him no harm. There are dozens of crystals in the crown, and even the smallest of them are nearly the size of an acorn. I'd say Faltil's crown is probably priceless by now—easily the most valuable thing in the entire Caithan treasury."

The king knitted his brow, unable to recall the slightest mention of such a prize. It seemed strange that a piece of such obvious importance would not be among his own accoutrements of state.

"Why haven't I ever seen it?"

"Not many people have. It's been locked up in the strong room for over twenty years. A long time ago . . . oh, I'd say a year before Athaya was born, your father ordered the crown to be hidden away at Rhodri's insistence." Ventan paused to indulge in a gleeful chuckle. "Rhodri never actually saw the thing, but the very thought of all those huge crystals nearly made him incontinent."

The archbishop stifled further laughter, but smiled so broadly that his fleshy cheeks threatened to completely cover his eyes. "But the majority of the corbals that Faltil acquired were embedded into the hilts of swords and daggers. With one hand over the hilt to keep the gem in darkness, you could sneak up on an unsuspecting wizard, then uncover the crystal to unleash its power. The wizard would be rendered helpless, allowing the blade to do its work with ease."

Durek's eyes started to gleam. "I wonder what happened to all those crystals," he mused, increasingly absorbed with the idea brewing in his head.

"After Faltil's work was done, many of the gems were given to the Church as gifts—gestures of gratitude for the people's salvation. The rest, I would assume, are gathering dust somewhere, still embedded in their original weapons. But who can say where those swords are now?" Ventan added with a shrug. "The men who once fought with them no doubt passed them on to their sons, and so on. I'd venture to guess that a good number of your guardsmen possess one, although Kelwyn would have forbidden anyone to carry such a thing at court in deference to Rhodri. Such weapons are probably packed away somewhere, their owners having never thought to retrieve them once Rhodri was dead."

For the first time that day, Durek found himself smiling. Lapsing into silence for a moment, he took a turn about the room, stroking his chin. Then, in a burst of enthusiasm, he turned on Lord Gessinger so quickly that the rumpled councillor jumped back in surprise, having grown content with the assumption that the king had forgotten his existence.

"I'm going to find those crystals, Mosel," Durek declared, pointing a jeweled finger in the duke's face. "My guardsmen are going to be ready for any wizard who dares set foot on Caithan soil."

With newfound fire in his eyes, he snatched up a fresh sheet of vellum and began scribbling notes on it. "Daniel, I want you and every member of the Curia to find and display any of these old relics that are stored in their cathedral vaults. This order is to be carried out immediately in every province, and any surplus stones are to be distributed among the smaller parishes. I'll draft the order tomorrow and have you affix your ecclesiastical seal to it."

The archbishop nodded amenably.

"Now that Caithe is finally free of heretics, I want to make sure it stays that way," the king went on. "If either Nicolas or Captain Parr succeed in bringing Athaya home, the crystals will insure that she can't work any mischief with those spells she's learned. No matter how 'gifted' Osfonin's wizard says she is."

Durek glanced up from the notes he was making. "You can go now, Mosel. I'll send for you if I have any further questions. And get out of those wet things," he added disdainfully, as if he'd just noticed Gessinger's miserable condition. "You look like a drowned cat."

After the duke had bowed and departed, Durek dismissed Dagara and the archbishop as well, electing to spend the remainder of the evening in solitude. He drafted a few more lines of text, but soon set his parchment aside, too wrapped up in his plans to concentrate on the proper wording of a royal edict.

Dropping his quill back into the ink pot, he crossed the room and leaned against the window ledge to look out across the Sea of Wedane. The night was clear, the rain having moved off, and a crescent moon shed silver on the endless expanse of still-icy water. Even though the days were growing milder now that March had turned to April, the nights were still cold and crisp, and he could feel the chill drafts seeping around the fitted glass.

It was too late to go rummaging through the castle's strong room now, but tomorrow he was going to locate that crown of corbals and restore it to its proper place of honor. Perhaps he would even begin wearing it on formal occasions, to show his people that he refused to tolerate the practice of wizardry in his land. To earn by his actions the title that followed his name by custom—Defender of the Faith. To make them see that he was a worthy successor to his father.

As he gazed out upon that quiet sea, Durek resolved to do everything in his power to keep his realm safe from the Devil's brood. His people deserved such protection. And his God would expect nothing less.

That same night on another moonlit shore, Athaya bent down and scooped up a handful of cool, white sand, then held up her palm and let the salty breeze scatter the grains back to the ground. It felt good to touch Caithan soil again.

On the edge of the horizon, trailed by a silvery wake, was the silhouette of the Reykan galleon that had brought her here—a vessel owned by a wizard-friend of Ranulf's, which Tonia declared had a colorful history of piracy attached to it despite Ranulf's halfhearted assertions to the contrary. Behind her, stretching for miles along the coastline in either direction, was the vast expanse of the Forest of Else near Kaiburn. Athaya had chosen Kaiburn as the starting point of her venture not only because, as one of the largest cities in Caithe, it would provide a larger pool of potential students, but because Cameron was familiar with the area, and, being a relatively safe distance from Delfarham, Kaiburn was close enough to the sea routes to Reyka to afford a hasty retreat if need be.

Brushing the remaining sand from her hands, Athaya looked over one shoulder toward her mismatched collection of friends and their ragged assortment of baggage piled on the beach, all of it barely visible in the indigo night. Kale was sitting on one of the canvas bundles, quietly carving something out of a slender piece of wood while Tonia hovered over him, plying the poor guardsman with questions about what he was making and expressing acute dissatisfaction when he shrugged and briefly remarked that he had not yet decided. Next to them, Mason was perched on one end of a fallen log with his head tipped back, pointing out the patterns of spring constellations to Cam and trying his best to ignore Ranulf's unremitting stream of interruptions. And Cam, still wearing the red kerchief and gold earring that he'd acquired from the galleon's captain, sat cross-legged in the sand, paying scant attention to Mason's lecture as he turned a seashell over in his hand and watched how the moonlight brought out its hidden colors. All of them had risked a great deal to follow her here, and Athaya fervently hoped she was doing more than simply leading them to their deaths. She wasn't used to that kind of responsibility, and it threatened to overwhelm her if she thought too long on it.

Master Tonia, having finally accepted the fact that her conversation with Kale was futilely one-sided, noticed Athaya standing apart from the others and came to join her near the water's edge.

"Everything all right?" she asked gently. "You've been awful quiet tonight."

Athaya picked up a flat black stone and folded it absently between her fingers. "Oh, I'm fine. I've just been thinking." Then she tossed the stone into the sea, where it quickly sank into the darkness. "I'm starting to understand a few things I never did before."

"That's called life, Athaya. There's some things that only time and experience can teach you, no matter how bright you are." Tonia gave her a pat on the shoulder. "You're having second thoughts, aren't you?"

"No, it's not that. I'm just worried about us. All of us," she added, motioning to the four others lingering a short distance away. "I certainly don't expect that we're going to be able to march right out, work a few spells, and change the world by tomorrow. Durek will fight tooth and nail against us, and we'll be more than a little outnumbered. I just can't help thinking that I'm getting us in over our heads."

Her shoulders sloped inward, pressed down by the weight of her thoughts. "Now I know why my father acted the way he did when he knew a battle was imminent," she went on, watching the moonlight play across the waves. "He'd get horribly short-tempered and would bite the head off of anyone who dared to contradict him. But now I realize he was just scared. He had people's lives in his hands. He knew that at his word, men would die for him, and innocent people would likely be killed in the fighting. I never understood what a burden that must have been on him until now."

"Amazing, isn't it, the number of people who fancy they'd like being king," Tonia observed, shaking her head. "All most folks see is the trappings, and they don't have any idea of the responsibilities. Makes me glad I was born on a farm with only a few mangy geese and pigs to worry about."

Athaya felt rather envious of that, and when she tried to smile it ended up looking more like a grimace.

"But I think you're overlooking something," Tonia added. "Those men that fought for your father did it because they wanted to, not because he forced them. You didn't twist any of our arms to get us to come here. We were boneheaded enough to do it on our own." Tonia grinned at Athaya's grudging laughter. "And besides, I know you can do it. So do the rest of us . . . and Osfonin, and Felgin, and Hedric, and especially Jaren—'' Tonia broke off then, sensing she had touched on something sensitive. "Even Lord Basil has confidence in you, if you'll believe that."

"Now I *know* you're exaggerating," Athaya remarked wryly.

"Oh, he was damned nasty to you during the Circle meeting, but he did that on purpose. He was trying to rattle you—to see if he could make you crumble. And he couldn't," Tonia added proudly. "Sure, he complained for hours afterward about your being unruly and willful, but frankly, my dear, the only folk Basil doesn't complain about are the ones he doesn't give two figs for in the first place." Tonia gave her a gentle hug and then drew her back toward the others. "Come on. Let's have a bite of dinner and get some sleep."

Despite the hard ground near the forest's edge, Athaya slept so soundly that dawn seemed to arrive in an instant. By the time she had managed to dress herself and swallow a quick breakfast, the men had already broken down their tents and repacked the satchels. The first order of business that day would be to begin searching for a more permanent home.

"I know a place we can go," Cam said, swallowing the last mouthful of bread he was eating. He seemed eager to help by offering the information, but he fidgeted anxiously as he spoke, as if he didn't really want to bring up the subject. "It used to be an old church or something. It's not much more than a pile of rocks anymore, but there's a roof over most of it."

"Then lead on, Commander," Ranulf said lightly as he rolled up Athaya's tent and bound it with a cord. "Let's have a look at this rockpile of yours."

"Don't you think such a place might be too exposed?" Mason said doubtfully. "They don't build many churches in the middle of the forest, you know. It's probably too close to the city or the roads to be safe for us."

Cam shook his head forcefully. "But it *is* in the woods," he insisted. "And it'll be safe. Nobody ever goes there."

"Nobody but you, apparently," Mason observed, raising one brow. "And who knows how many other curious boys in this part of the country."

"Everybody else is scared to go there," Cam countered, looking somewhat proud of himself. "Even my parents and the village priest. But not me."

"Maybe it was a monastic retreat of some kind," Athaya suggested. "That might explain its being so isolated."

Tonia shook the breadcrumbs from her lap and got to her feet. "We can at least take a look at it. If it doesn't suit us, we'll simply look elsewhere." She gave Cam an approving nod, and he began studying the shoreline to determine which direction they needed to go.

"We have to head south, up that path," he said at last, scrambling over scraps of driftwood and broken shells toward a break in the trees.

"Are you sure you know where you're going?" Mason called after him. He peered skeptically into the dark tangle of trees before him, the crease in his brow revealing his doubts that Cam would remember the area so well after a four-year absence.

"Oh, don't worry. I know these woods better than the foresters do," Cam said, brushing off the dom's concerns without looking back. "My village is only a day's walk from here."

"We may as well follow him," Athaya said, turning to the others. "Unless anyone has a better idea?" Then, getting no response, she hitched up her skirt and caught up with Cam while Tonia, Kale, Mason, and Ranulf trailed after her.

They had traveled a good distance south since leaving Ath Luaine, and here all traces of winter were gone. The poplars and maples wore fresh green leaves, and the forest floor was carpeted with purple violets. Athaya had not ventured to this part of her homeland before, but while she had never actually seen the great forest where her father often went hunting during his younger years, she had heard many tales about the huge game-rich woodland that sprawled across much of eastern Caithe—tales which also told of bandits that made their home inside its dark confines and lingered near the forest roads to rob unwary travelers.

Athaya smiled to herself, feeling no fear. She suspected that any bandits hiding in these woods would be far more afraid of wizards than those wizards would be of bandits.

As morning wore on, it didn't take long for Athaya to realize that Cam's recollections of the forest trails weren't quite as vivid as he'd led them to believe. It took the better part of the day before they located the ruin he'd described, and Athaya tended to think the find was due to sheer luck rather than to Cam's somewhat deficient sense of direction. But if their circular wanderings served any purpose, it was to assure them that this dense woodland was not only rich in game, nuts, and berries but filled with potential hiding places should the need arise.

The tumbled-down collection of buildings was set in an overgrown clearing not far from a shallow creek. Cameron had exaggerated when he'd called the place a pile of rocks. The walls of the main building still stood, though they were overgrown with ivy and weeds, and despite being in desperate need of repair, much of the roof was still intact. Battered slate tiles, ripped from the roof by ancient winds, were scattered across the forest floor, looking as if they had been carelessly tossed away like an unwanted deck of playing cards. Traces of a cobbled walk circled the compound, leading around to what might have been an old brewhouse or kitchen, and in the midst of the clearing was a decaying bell tower. To Athaya's surprise, the bronze bell was still there, but the cord used to ring it was little more than a rotten ribbon of hemp. When she gave it a gentle tug, the rope disintegrated in her hands and crumbled to the ground.

Mason picked up a small pebble and flung it at the bell, and a rusty, low chime groaned ominously around them, like a spirit reluctantly awakened from a sound slumber. "The place is an old monastery, all right. But it doesn't look as if anyone's lived here in a hundred years."

"That must have been their chapel over there," Athaya said, pointing to the largest building, and the one in by far the worst condition. "Let's take a look."

As they approached, Athaya noticed that Cam was keeping close to the others instead of wandering off and exploring the place as she might have expected. He didn't look happy to be here and seemed jittery, as if he expected ghosts to be haunting this old, dead place. The mood was infectious, and Athaya found herself looking over her shoulder from time to time, paying undue attention to the otherwise innocent sounds of birds calling and wind rustling through the trees.

The double doors at the end of the sanctuary were open, their iron hinges long since frozen by rust. Athaya crossed the threshold and gazed at an aisle strewn with sticks, leaves, and decades of other debris that had either blown through the open doorway or fallen through the gaping holes in the roof. Pools of still water collected in the uneven stone floor, and Athaya saw the occasional glint of light reflected from a dirty shard of colored glass.

Athaya shuddered, though at first she was not sure why. She did not feel cold. But then she suddenly realized that here, in this place of worship, the walls were not broken with age, but had been smashed in by force. By men. The destruction was far too complete—far too methodical to have been done by nature alone.

But why attack a church of all places? she wondered. Such a thing had not been heard of in centuries. Not since . . .

With an acute sense of foreboding, Athaya stepped over a puddle of stagnant water in the center of the aisle and approached the broken stone slab that was once an altar. The marble was pitted with age, but several telltale stains could still be seen against the once-white stone. Flinching, Athaya was chilled with the certain knowledge that it was blood. The flagstone flooring was likewise soiled, though the color had long since faded from red to black.

"What else do you know about this place, Cam?" she asked quietly, without turning around.

"N-not much. My mother told me never to come here. She says the place is haunted by demons. She says they're the spirits of—" Cam swallowed noticeably. "—of evil wizards who lived here once."

"Demons?" Mason spat out. "What nonsense!"

Athaya laid her hands flat upon the cold altar stone. "It's logical when you think of it, Mason. The people here are taught that the Lorngeld are the Devil's children and that magic is his gift to them. If this wasn't just an ordinary monastery, but a brotherhood of wizards who lived here and studied their magic, then no wonder everyone thinks it's haunted."

Cam shuffled to Athaya's side, his eyes downcast. "That's why I came the first time. After my brother died. I didn't care about the stories. I thought . . ." His voice dropped to barely a whisper. "I thought if he was a wizard, then he might be here. Or his ghost. I didn't know. Maybe it was stupid. I was only nine years old. But my mother was furious when she found out where I'd gone. She said there was old magic here . . . that it was dangerous and might get me."

"Well, I don't know how dangerous it is, but in a way, your mother was right." Athaya stepped back from the altar and

cocked her head to one side as if listening for a distant cry.
"There is something here. A trace of . . . something, I'm not
sure what. Old magic, perhaps. It's faint, but it's there. Like the
way you can smell smoke from a fire hours after it's been put
out." She scanned the sanctuary with a distracted frown, as if
afraid that wizardly spirits were still lurking here, patiently waiting for someone living to haunt.

"I found some silver coins here once," Cameron went on.
"Enough to get me to Reyka. I wasn't going to take it. I'm not
a thief," he said with a pointed glance toward Mason, "or a
graverobber. But I thought that if it belonged to wizards like my
brother, then it was all right."

"It wasn't stealing," Athaya assured him. "Not if no one had
come to claim it in two centuries. Just think of it as an inheri-
tance . . . from your brother."

While Cam and Kale left the chapel to investigate the grounds,
the others continued to search through the old church for more
evidence of its history, shoving aside fallen beams and sweeping
away damp leaves as they went in an effort to make the place
somewhat more habitable. Most of their findings were unre-
markable—bits of pottery and glass; the random scrap of cloth.
But they also found bindings of books whose pages had been
torn away—one of them a copy of the *Book of Sages*—and altar
ornaments which were barely recognizable, so badly had they
been abused. The objects hardly merited such treatment. Plain
and unadorned, they were simply crafted expressions of devotion, their makers having no need for pomp and glittering gems.

A glint of metal amid a pool of muddy water caught Athaya's
eye, and she bent down to work the tarnished silver object from
its bed of mud. She wiped it clean, then slowly drew in her
breath as her suspicions about the monastery's past were unde-
niably confirmed. In her palm was a wizard's brooch—its cross-
shaped design almost identical to the one Hedric had given her.
But more disturbing than the brooch itself were the shards of
bone she found nearby, and a thick, curved object that could
only be a fragment of skull. Athaya could only assume that the
bones belonged to the brooch's owner—the bodily remnants of
one of the last trained wizards in Caithe.

In somber silence, Athaya piled her findings on the altar, all
of them traces of a long-ago violence that even the passage of
centuries could not wipe out. She conjured a small witchlight

and set it above the altar stone in lieu of candles. The light cast a ruddy glow over the collection of shattered altar vessels and broken bones, and as her mind relaxed, she could almost sense the tattered remnants of emotions as well. Pain. Outrage. Despair. The agony of losing all that one held dear. But underneath them all ran a current of faith—a faith so deep and unswerving that it took away the fear of death itself. Whoever these ancients were, they had loved and trusted their God above all else.

"I'll wager that's the first spell been cast here in quite a while," Tonia remarked behind her, gesturing at the softly burning witchlight.

Athaya ran her fingers over the tarnished wizard's brooch, then touched the golden one pinned on her own cloak. "But it won't be the last." Then, feeling an urgent need to leave this dismal sanctuary for the present, Athaya turned her back on the altar and walked quickly out into the clearing to take in a refreshing breath of clean spring air.

A few minutes later, she saw Kale and Cam returning to the chapel from the woods.

"We checked out the way to Kaiburn," Kale said. "I'd say it's an hour's walk, if that. The trail can be tricky, but it starts to follow the river about a half mile south."

Athaya rubbed her chin. "Would you say this is a good place to camp indefinitely?"

"I think so. We're deep enough inside the forest to be safe from casual wanderers, but not so far that the walk to Kaiburn would be unreasonable. Ideal, I'd say."

Ideal, Athaya repeated inwardly. *Except for the fact that it's the site of a massacre where magicians were slaughtered simply for being what they were. And what I plan to make them yet.*

Athaya discussed Kale's recommendations with the others, and they soon decided that despite its history, no better place could be found.

"In fact, it may even work to our advantage," she pointed out, as they began unpacking their belongings. "If everyone's terrified of coming near here, then we won't have to worry as much about being discovered."

"And with a strong set of wards and a few illusions, we can spell the place so tight that even Lord Basil couldn't get in," Tonia concluded, a renegade glimmer in her eye.

"Good thinking," Athaya said. "It's not going to take long

before news of what we're doing gets around. Someone's bound to come see if a few wizards haven't taken up residence here again. But if we can hide ourselves well enough, maybe they'll think this old monastery never existed in the first place.''

"Or that God wiped it off the face of the earth as a sign of His displeasure,'' Mason added dubiously.

Athaya gave him a sidelong glance. "We don't need you to play Devil's advocate with us, Mason.'' Then she laughed aloud. "The Devil's advocate. That's exactly what everyone thinks *I* am already.''

Tonia assigned Ranulf and Mason the task of warding their new home while the others moved their belongings into the dilapidated monk's dormitory. The dormitory was in relatively decent condition, and there was enough roofing left to provide each of them with a separate room. Athaya was given the most spacious room, most likely the former abbot's quarters, and immediately set about making it habitable. She swept the leaves and grime from the floor, hung a tattered blanket over the window as a makeshift curtain, and chased out a rabbit that had taken up residence in the fireplace. She laughed and hummed to herself as she went about her menial chores, reflecting on how far she had come down in the world, and more surprisingly, just how little she really cared.

Later, as the sky went from blue to dusty orange, Athaya left off her work and leaned against the cool stone sill, gazing out the window at the clearing. Ranulf was kindling a campfire under the bell tower, while Tonia and Mason sliced onions and carrots and tossed them into a kettle for stew. Cameron sat a distance apart cleaning fish that he'd caught in the stream, and Kale was beside him, putting the last touches on the wooden object he had been carving that morning—he had decided it would be a flute—and blowing a few tentative notes to test it.

From time to time, Athaya could hear a snatch of talk or a burst of laughter, and she waited a few minutes before joining them, content to watch from a distance and reflect that this could well be her last truly peaceful evening in a very long time. Once the trouble started—and she planned to start it first thing tomorrow—she doubted she would get a moment's rest until her work was over . . . or until she was beyond need of any sort of rest other than the eternal kind.

Quickly, she chased away that morbid thought and let her eyes fall over the rest of the camp: to the brewhouse, the kitchens, and the old chapel, all dark and deserted, their ruins only slightly illuminated by the campfire. She thought of how warm and joyous a place this must have been for the wizards who once lived and worshiped here. It felt good to have living folk here again, if only to assure the ghosts of those dead wizards that they had not been forgotten after all, and that not everyone wished to curse them.

Then she looked westward, pretending that she could see the bustling city of Kaiburn through the thick tangle of trees around her. Stars glittered above the dense wood as the orange sky slowly gave way to a deep, restful purple.

Rest while you can, city of Kaiburn, Athaya thought, as the scent of bubbling stew drew her out of her room to join the others. *Tomorrow the ghosts of this place shall rise again, and you'll not rid yourselves of them so easily this time.*

CHAPTER 10

ATHAYA PAUSED BEFORE A HICKORY TREE AND TRACED her fingers over the shaggy bark, waiting a few seconds before the runes she had drawn slowly began to appear, spreading outward across the bark like hoarfrost on glass. Since she and the others had left the camp that morning, Mason had performed this simple spell on various trees to mark the way back. Athaya asked him to show her the spell, but even when she created the runes herself, she was still fascinated by them. She reached out to touch the glowing patterns of red light, but the runes were as insubstantial as a well-crafted illusion, and her fingers passed right through them as if they were no more than mist.

She looked back down the forest path and saw Mason's trail of similar red marks, shedding their soft incandescence like clusters of fireflies on a summer night. Athaya turned to him and frowned skeptically. "But they're so bright . . ."

"To us, perhaps," the dom replied nonchalantly. "But not to anyone who's likely to be wandering through these woods. The runes are simply things that wizards can see and other people can't."

Cam studied the hickory tree with frustrated persistence, but finally shook his head and thrust his lower lip out in a pout. Lacking the wizard's sight necessary to detect them, both he and Kale were blinded to the runes. Accordingly, Kale was cautious, leaving a subtle trail of rocks and broken twigs in his wake, in the event that he or Cam got separated from the group and had no wizard in their company to guide them back.

Mason further assured them that the guiding runes would last up to a month without reinforcement. ''And unless there are any wizards in Caithe we don't know about, the only people that will be able to follow them to our camp are those we've trained ourselves. If we find that some of them can't be trusted not to reveal our hiding place . . .'' The tutor's brow clouded over. ''Well, that's something we can deal with later.''

The city of Kaiburn was set in the lush green hills of eastern Caithe, surrounded by fertile farmland and extensive sheep runs. Since the civil war of Kelwyn's time had been fought largely in the north and west, Kaiburn itself was not heavily fortified, and row upon row of neat, timber-framed houses and shops fanned out around its limestone walls. Dividing the city in two was the sparkling Sobonne River, flowing smoothly eastward carrying its load of merchant's barges, ferries, and gilded pleasure crafts of the city's wealthier residents. Two elegantly arched bridges joined the city at either end and were peopled with a variety of folk—older citizens with little else to do but watch the boats glide by and young lovers who tossed rose petals upon the rippling waters and made fanciful wishes for their future happiness.

No one gave them a second glance as Athaya and her band entered the city, not even the sparse contingent of guards stationed on the wall walks. Despite their benign appearance, however, all of them had daggers concealed under lightweight peasant cloaks. Even though the wizards among them did not require such defenses, it was wiser not to be forced to rely on magic for protection in a place so bitterly opposed to its use.

Standing at the foot of the easternmost bridge, Athaya set her hands on her hips and looked purposefully out over the sprawling city as if she'd just stepped into a filthy room and couldn't decide what to clean first.

''Let's split up into two groups so we can cover each side of the river,'' she told the others. ''Try to locate any *mekahn*-aged Lorngeld that need our help. In a city this size, there's bound to be at least a dozen or so.''

''And if anyone gets suspicious?'' Mason asked.

''Don't volunteer anything prematurely, but remember that

we're not ashamed of our mission, either. If it's appropriate, drop a few hints about what we're doing. If we do our job well, they're going to know all about us sooner or later."

Athaya motioned over the bridge to the far side of the city. "Ranulf, you and Kale come with me—we'll take the south end. Tonia, take Mason and Cam and cover the north. If we do stumble across a corbal crystal somewhere, that leaves at least one person in each group who will still have his wits about him." Athaya saw Kale and Cam exchange a subtle look of pride. Even in the company of wizards they had a unique service to offer, and she wanted to make sure they knew it.

While Tonia led her group down the northern riverbank, Athaya, Kale, and Ranulf crossed the bridge into the older, more prosperous part of the city. Towering above them were the majestic twin spires of Kaiburn Cathedral, the sculpted towers reaching up into the heavens like priestly arms imploring divine guidance. As they passed the wide expanse of marble steps leading up to the sanctuary, Athaya glanced briefly skyward and whispered a plea for luck to whomever might be listening.

"Let's head for the market square," she suggested. "That's where the most people will be this time of day."

Ranulf thought on that, working a sliver of something out of his teeth. "The most people, maybe, but not the most wizards. When I was struggling with my *mekahn*, the last thing on my mind was doing a bit of shopping. I tended to frequent other sorts of places . . . if you know what I mean."

Kale frowned inquiringly, but Athaya nodded slowly, fearing that she did indeed know what Ranulf meant. All too well.

"But at this hour?" she asked.

Ranulf's eyes grew grim. "It never mattered to me." He peered inside the small purse at his belt, mentally counting, and then nodded once. "Follow me."

Athaya let him lead her through the twisting cobbled streets, watching as the streets turned from stone to dirt, and the buildings lining them grew older, sagging with disrepair. From time to time Ranulf stopped someone on the street to ask a question or two, and Athaya noticed that he seemed to go out of his way to address his inquiries to the poorest and most wretched-looking person he could find. Within the hour, they had found the slum district in the city's west end, where the potent reek of rancid fish, fresh manure, and day-old beer made Athaya's breakfast rest less easy in her stomach.

Ranulf approached a filthy bundle of rags hunched in the mouth of an alley, and when he produced a pair of copper coins from his purse, a skinny arm darted out from within the bundle and snatched them. Ranulf nodded as the man said something in a rasping voice, then he returned to Athaya and Kale with a satisfied look on his face.

"It's this way."

Athaya and Kale followed him through the alley, sending rats scuttling into a hundred dark corners, and turned into a foul-smelling, narrow street that dead-ended some fifty yards ahead.

Squalid didn't begin to describe the place. The few windows that didn't have refuse piled in them ready to toss into the street below were tightly boarded shut, and only the blackened structure at the end of the street showed any signs of habitation. Two shadowy figures slipped furtively inside the building as they watched, and a short time later, another came staggering out, promptly collapsing in the mud with a muffled groan.

An acrid smell hung in the air here—a smell Athaya knew at once. The memory made her stomach churn.

Ranulf motioned toward the dilapidated hovel. "There. That's it."

"It doesn't look fit for rats," Kale murmured, increasingly uneasy. "What *is* this place?"

"A looca-den," Athaya replied, staring straight ahead. The figure that had collapsed in the mud had struggled to its feet, emptied its stomach, and was dazedly making its way back inside. Athaya gave the man's mind a fleeting touch, but flinched in distaste when she was jarred with the stupefying effects of looca-smoke.

"That isn't all they sell, either," Ranulf said, his voice bitter. "Looca, snow powder, pastle seed . . . anything that can rot your brain. I used to come to places like this when I thought I was going crazy—back before I knew my magic was responsible. The smoke helped me relax and made those damned voices in my head shut up for a while. If anyone in this city is suffering from the *mekahn*, they'd likely get desperate enough to look for some relief here."

Then he bent down and scooped up a handful of drying mud from the roadside. He almost grinned as he turned to Athaya.

"What are you . . . hey!"

Before she could stop him, Ranulf had smeared a liberal amount of dirt on her cheeks and rubbed some in her hair. "Now take a quick stroll through that gutter there," he instructed, motioning to a running sewer near the alley's edge. "You smell too good to be going where we're going."

She did as she was told, grimacing as the rank mud folded into her shoes. Ranulf dirtied himself as well, then dropped a few copper coins into her hand.

"Here—use these. They probably don't see much silver around here. And act like you know what you're doing—just follow my lead. Kale, I think you'd better stay out of here. Folks don't usually go to a den in groups, and we don't want to look out-of-place."

After assuring a very unconvinced Kale that she would be all right, Athaya trailed Ranulf to the end of the street and up the rickety flight of steps that led into the den. The door hung open, and inside, a leather-skinned woman monitored the doorway, carelessly knitting a grubby shawl. She set down her needles at their approach and silently picked up a tray cluttered with pipes, tubes, bowls, and other exotic implements, displaying it perfunctorily to them.

Ranulf tossed three copper coins onto the tray and selected a greasy-looking pipe that looked as if it had been used by every citizen in Kaiburn. The woman measured out a packet of looca for him and shoved it into his hand.

"Upstairs ain't full," she drawled, then turned dourly to Athaya. Just as Ranulf had done, she set down her coins and selected a pipe, trying to act aloof despite the flutters in her stomach. Heaven only knew it wasn't the first time she had indulged in a pipe of the sweet blue tobacco, but the odor brought back frightening memories of the *mekahn* that she preferred to leave dead and buried.

Clutching her pipe and packet, she shadowed Ranulf up a short flight of stairs where they emerged into a crowded smoking room. Athaya had to fight not to draw back in horror. If she thought the building's outside was bad, the inside far surpassed it in squalor. Bunks coated with ancient straw lined the walls, stacked so closely upon one another that the people lying in them could not hope to sit up. The floor was littered with pails of feces and vomit, much of it splattered in pools around the buckets. The air was tinted blue from looca-smoke, and the lack of windows left the room dark and stifling. The people huddled in the smoking room seemed oblivious to her presence, their red eyes blank and staring, and even though some were dressed in tunics and gowns made of fine cloth, those garments were long since ruined by the grime and smoke. Desperate moans were pervasive, at times punctuated by a shrill scream or laugh, and Athaya felt for an instant as if she had walked into the bowels of hell itself. She had never in all her life seen such misery and despair, and the enormity of it would have moved her to tears had not Ranulf grabbed her wrist and pulled her forward into the next, less crowded room.

The bunks were not stacked quite as tightly here, and Athaya and Ranulf were able to squeeze into one of them, hastily brushing a family of roaches out of the straw.

"Let's cast out," he said softly. "But you'd best at least light your pipe and make like you're using it."

As the blue smoke swirled around her, burning her eyes to tears, Athaya tried her best to relax without taking too many deep breaths. Then she reached out tentatively, and her mind instantly recoiled. The air was alive with hideousness, crackling with the currents of twisted and tortured minds, irrational thoughts and delusions—a cacophony of gibberish that sent ice streaming through her veins.

Ranulf gave her elbow a comforting squeeze. "There's all kinds of madness in the world besides a wizard's *mekahn*," he said quietly. "We'll have to sort out the kind we're after."

Steeling herself, Athaya reached out again, wading through the swamp of madness as if through a sewer of filth. She had to break away from time to time to reorient herself, but as long as she was already in this fetid place, she was determined to do her best to seek out anyone who needed her. There were so many here that could never be helped—at least not by the means Athaya had at her disposal—and it was difficult for her to pass them by, leaving them to their own private miseries.

Then it came, like a scream out of the darkness.

Athaya jerked her head around so abruptly that she got a painful crick in her neck. She wrinkled her nose and grimaced, as if assaulted by yet another, more hideous stench, and her eyes lost their focus for an instant. She blinked and glanced swiftly at Ranulf. His expression, though not as intense, mirrored her own.

"Disruptions," he said. "I can't narrow down where they're coming from yet, but whoever it is must be close by."

They probed again, touching mind after mind in search of one with newly forming paths. Most of the minds were voids, either mad or dulled with drugs, and they had to take care not to linger there too long and be sucked into those stupefying realms.

But they needed no further probing. All of a sudden, a piercing wail split the air, astonishingly unnoticed by all but Athaya and Ranulf. It was a man's voice, and came from the darkest corner of the room. Without looking as if they were doing so intentionally, Athaya and Ranulf slowly made their way to the edge of the disturbed man's bunk, led by his muffled whimpers.

Athaya estimated that he was about nineteen, and probably would be quite handsome if he were clean. Unfortunately, the curly brown locks were matted and pungent with looca-smoke, and there were dark, troubled circles under his eyes. In sharp contrast, his tunic was well crafted of the finest black wool, and the buttons were solid silver. Athaya was surprised that no one had stolen them long before this—just one of the buttons would have purchased a plentiful supply of looca—but then she realized that no one in this wretched place was probably alert enough to steal anything from anyone.

Then the man's eyes snapped open, wild and unseeing. "Be quiet, all of you!" he shouted, rolling from side to side in his bug-infested pallet. He clutched a handful of dirty brown hair in his fist and pulled at it despairingly. "No more, no more . . . *tacete, tacete! Procul estote . . . mentem mihi reddite!*"

It was all gibberish after that, then moaning, and more wild thrashing. The man didn't even notice when Ranulf knelt down next to the bunk and shook him vigorously, trying to break him from his delusions.

Athaya cast out to the young man's mind. "His paths are almost formed," she whispered, "but I think we've caught him in time. It's close, though."

She was just about to ask Ranulf for his assessment when she heard the wheezing sound of labored breathing very close behind her. Before she could turn around, a skinny arm snaked itself around her waist, the hand groping eagerly for her breast.

Gasping, she wheeled around sharply, disengaging herself easily from the man's weak grip and slapping his hands away. He was easily past fifty, and his bloodshot eyes were unfocused from the exposure to looca-smoke. Cheap homespun clothing, stiff from dirt and sweat, clung stubbornly to his skin. Her startled reaction to his advances made him chuckle gleefully, exposing a jagged row of black and yellow teeth, but his laughter soon dissolved into a brief fit of coughing.

"Keep your hands off her," Ranulf warned, his voice a low but threatening rumble. He rose to his full height, towering two heads over the older man. But his intimidations might have done better on a more clearheaded victim. As it was, the man only gazed up at Ranulf groggily, as if wondering where he'd sprouted from.

"Aw, be fair," he rasped, immodestly scratching his armpit. Then he glared down at the young man on the pallet and his reddened eyes took on a mischievous cast. " 'Sides, I thought that pretty boy there was yours."

Athaya saw Ranulf's cheeks flare red as his hair, but he checked his desire to deck the old man and simply reached into his pocket to draw out his packet of looca. "Here. Leave her be and take this instead."

Athaya hastily offered him the rest of her tobacco as well. "You may as well take it," she said. "We can't stay."

The man's recent bout of lust was forgotten at the sight of two barely used packets of looca, free of charge. He snatched up the packets greedily and shuffled away, coughing through his delighted laughter. Athaya brushed the hand-shaped grime from her bodice where the man had fondled her.

"Walking through that sewer felt better than being touched by that—" She broke off, shivering from disgust.

Ranulf, however, had an errant grin on his face. "Oh, he was harmless enough. Just think—before long that poor old sot's going to see your face on a reward poster somewhere and spend the rest of his short life bragging about the time he once had his very own hands on the royal bosom."

The humor of that prospect evaded her for the moment, so Athaya turned her attentions back to the problem at hand and cocked her head toward the unconscious man on the bunk. "So how do we get him out of here without someone getting suspicious?"

"Are you kidding? Most people would never leave this hole if somebody didn't come in and drag them out of it. Once they pay for their pipe, nobody in here gives a damn what happens to them."

Ranulf slid one arm under the man's back and hoisted him up and over his shoulder like a sack of meal. The young man made a dry, gagging sound as if he were about to retch, then fell still.

"Lead the way," Ranulf told her, steadying himself under the weight of his burden. "And tell me if I'm about to step in something unpleasant."

They had just reached the outer, more crowded room when the man began to thrash again, and Ranulf promptly lost his balance and dropped him, overturning one of the putrid buckets of feces dotting the floor. "They're coming again," the man gibbered, "God, they're coming again . . . louder, even louder . . ."

Then he closed his eyes and lashed out with his hand, striking Ranulf on the jaw before crying out: *"Ignis confestim sit!"* And from the tips of his fingers, a single bolt of green fire struck the ground only inches from where Athaya stood, igniting the dry straw cluttering the floor and sending up a rancid cloud of black smoke.

Athaya was so rattled by the sight of that familiar spell that she was paralyzed for an instant, unable to move. Even the muddleheaded folk crowding the den had realized something was amiss, staring at the flames as if dimly aware of danger.

"Don't just stand there—douse it!" Ranulf barked, wiping the blood from his lip as he tried to calm the man. His voice jolted Athaya from her shock. She quickly scanned the room for water or a heavy blanket, but seeing neither, she bit her lip in disgust, snatched up one of the scattered buckets of human refuse, and threw it unceremoniously on the flames. Athaya turned away, her innards feeling sour. If the liquid had not killed the fire, the smell certainly should have.

"Come on," Ranulf said, "I think we've worn out our welcome here." The young man had lapsed into unconsciousness— but luck or by Ranulf's tinkering, Athaya didn't know—and Ranulf hauled the dead weight onto his shoulders again and struggled out into the street, propping the man up against a greasy wall. Kale rushed to Athaya's side, his nose crinkling from the smell of looca—among other things—on her clothes, but visibly relieved to see that she had emerged unscathed.

"So what happens when someone starts talking about what caused that fire in there?" Athaya asked worriedly.

Ranulf didn't look the least bit concerned. "Athaya, with all the hallucinating that goes on in a place like that, do you honestly think anybody would take them seriously if they try to describe what they saw?"

He leaned over and slapped the young man's cheeks sharply. "Hey, can you hear me? Wake up, you."

The man's eyes fluttered once, but after letting out a feeble groan, his head lolled forward against his chest and he slipped back into oblivion.

"All right, then, if you won't tell us who you are, we'll have to try and find out for ourselves." Without hesitation, Ranulf began rifling through the man's tunic and breeches, searching for anything that might identify him. "He ain't poor, that's for sure," the mercenary remarked, displaying a generous handful of silver coins retrieved from inside the man's tunic. Replacing the money, Ranulf next pulled out a folded piece of parchment, its wax seal already broken. He scanned it briefly, then frowned and handed it to Athaya.

"It's from Selvallen," she said, squinting at the strange words. She had learned Selvallanese as a child—the proper education of a princess required that she be schooled in several languages—but she had lost most of that knowledge years ago. "The word *bevrio* means 'wool,' I think. And this list of numbers seems like an invoice of some kind. But look—there's an address on the other side. 'Jarvis & Jarvis Clothiers. Petersgate, Kaiburn. Caithe.' "

"Petersgate. Rich part of town, I'd wager," Ranulf said, fingering one of the elegant silver buttons on the unknown man's tunic. "Well, we may as well take him home. In his condition, that's the only way we'll find out anything more about him." Ranulf rubbed at his lip, still sore from where the young man had accidentally struck him. "Now all's we have to do is hire a cart to take us there. Damned if I'm carrying this lug the whole way."

Despite their disheveled appearance—and their scent—it wasn't difficult to find a cart for hire, especially after Ranulf flashed a pair of silver coins on a nearby street corner. The cart's driver asked no questions, and while he was clearly curious as to what sort of business a group of ragged-looking commoners would have in Petersgate, Ranulf offered no information other than that the driver would earn himself an extra three coppers if he could make his mangy horse go any faster. Athaya had quietly requested the extra speed herself. She sensed continuing disruptions even in the man's unconscious state and feared he might not be entirely lucid when he awoke. If he was going to burst into a streak of wild spells, she heartily preferred he not do it in public.

The driver set them down in the central thoroughfare of Kaiburn's wealthiest district, and by the time Ranulf and Kale hauled their charge out of the cart, the man was beginning to regain some of his senses. He coughed a few times and mumbled something unintelligible, but when his eyes opened, they were still glazed and sightless, as if he were slowly rousing himself from a deep sleep.

Athaya gazed at the man with growing concern. The sense of disruption in his mind was not receding.

"Now all we have to do is knock on doors and ask which of these houses he belongs in," she said, sighing at the unpleasant prospect. Suddenly, Athaya felt a powerful surge of empathy for her own father, understanding at last how mortified he must have been each time his guardsmen were charged to haul her back from some tavern or other, dirty, bruised, and smelling like cheap wine.

A flash of yellow caught her eyes, and she turned her head to see a young woman strolling up the street toward them, someone who lived in the area, judging from the elegant silk gown and tasteful collar of emeralds around her neck. She was chatting animatedly with her handmaid, who whistled cheerfully as she walked, swinging a basket stuffed to the brim with her mistress' purchases.

The women's footsteps slowed as they came closer, and the maid's jaw dropped, openly staring at the scene before her, convinced she was witnessing three thieves in the process of robbing the woozy man in their midst. But her mistress had eyes for only one of them, her gaze fastened on the man propped up on wobbly legs between Kale and Ranulf. In a horrified flash of recognition, her expression changed from bewildered surprise to outright dread.

"Cordry!" she cried. She rushed to his side in a flurry of yellow silk, sparing only the most cursory of glances for the three strangers around him. Wide-eyed, the maid promptly bolted down the street. Her basket flew from her hands as she ran, scattering rolls of twine, ribbon, and lace haphazardly over the cobbles. She careened into a nearby iron gate and started banging on it savagely, screaming for help.

Within seconds, a pair of black-clad servants gushed forth from one of the well-kept homes, urgently following the maid to her mistress' side.

"Excuse me," Athaya said, trying to gain their attention. "Is this—"

"Out of the way," one of the men said curtly, shoving her aside. The servants lifted Cordry up and hurried him inside, their eyes darting around furtively for signs of curious onlookers while the lady in yellow rushed ahead to hold open the gate. Athaya, Ranulf, and Kale followed behind them, all but forgotten in the excitement.

"Quick—run and find Sir Jarvis!" the woman cried to her maid, all but pushing her up the low flight of steps and into the house. "Tell him Cordry is sick again!"

The servants burst through the entryway and hustled their burden down the hallway and out of sight, the young woman trailing along in their wake. From somewhere in the rear of the house came a piercing wail, then the clatter of breaking glass, and finally the servants emerged again, pale and shaken, and disappeared into another room muttering something about the Devil's work under their breaths.

Athaya, Ranulf, and Kale had already crossed the threshold of the house and were about to find where Cordry had been taken when their way was barred by a bulky, narrow-eyed woman sporting a cook's cap.

"Who are you?" she snarled, waving a ladle at them as if it were a broadsword. "Get out."

Athaya stepped forward, holding her hands out in a gesture of entreaty. "Madam, we're the ones who brought him here. We found him near the river, and—"

Before Athaya could say another word, Ranulf lurched forward and grabbed hold of both her and the cook and pushed them roughly back against the wall. "Look out!"

A split second later, the wrought-iron chandelier over the entry hall snapped free of its chain and came crashing down, sending bits of broken candle wax skittering across the polished wood floor.

Ranulf let his breath out slowly. "I felt that one coming."

Athaya shuddered as she glanced at the broken chain, mentally gauging the weight of the chandelier. "Quick—we've got to get him calmed down before he tears the whole house apart."

The cook, still stunned by the close call, made no objections.

Athaya, Ranulf, and Kale followed the entry hall to a spacious sitting room. Heavy brocade drapes had been hastily yanked down over the windows, giving the chamber the wan appearance of a sickroom, and the floor was already covered with shards of glass from a pair of broken goblets. In the center of the room was a gray-haired man—an older image of the boy in his arms—using all of his strength to pin Cordry down on a pillow-covered settle. Behind them, the woman in yellow was wiping tears from her face with a lace handkerchief, and in the far corner of the room, a gaunt, aging man in an equally well-aged tunic gazed at the others with an expression of ill-temper and impatience. His fingers absently curled and uncurled as he watched the chaos before him, each hand looking like a large spider cautiously extending its legs before crawling forward.

"Be reasonable, my friend," he was saying, moving slowly out of the corner. "Let me send to the cathedral for help."

"Stay where you are, damn you," the other growled. "I swear you'd fetch a priest to give the boy last rites if he so much as blew his nose."

"Sir Jarvis, you can't keep denying it! Everyone in the city knows, and if you keep on like this, the bishop will accuse you of sheltering him!"

Jarvis wheeled on him like an angry dog, barely able to contain his fury. "You may have lost your wife, Gilbert, but don't be so quick to rob me of my only son!"

The man's sunken cheeks flushed purple with old rage, but before he could expel anything more than a series of strangled, half-formed sounds, Athaya strode into the room and elbowed her way past them to the young wizard's side.

The two men glared at her simultaneously, their argument temporarily forgotten. They seemed to be more startled by her mud-stained appearance than by the fact that she was an uninvited, and quite unknown, guest.

"Who the hell are—"

"Stand back and don't interfere," Athaya snapped back. Her voice carried the curt, inscrutably royal tone that her father had used all too often when speaking to her, and she had long ago committed every inflection to memory. She was pleasantly surprised at its effect. Bewildered, the men stepped back, yielding to the confidence in which Athaya took control of the situation. Only the lady in yellow remained where she was, her pale blue eyes reflecting equal amounts of suspicion and senseless hope.

Athaya sat down on the edge of the settle, where Jarvis' son lay writhing, his face slick with sweat. At her silent gesture, Ranulf came forward and gripped the man's shoulders while Kale took hold of his ankles. His struggles only seemed to worsen, however, and she quickly gripped his chin between her palms, forcing him to look into her eyes.

"Listen to me . . . Cordry, is that your name?" No response, but the woman behind the settle nodded vigorously.

"Cordry. Cordry Jarvis, hear me. Hear me and understand." Athaya locked her eyes on him, trying to wrench his thoughts out of their abyss of madness. She gripped his tortured mind with hers and held it psychically, not so hard that she would crush him, but hard enough so that he could not slip away. He tried desperately to squirm away—to escape her alien onslaught—but the stark terror in his eyes showed that he was under her control and wildly afraid of his helplessness. But despite his fear, brief expressions of hope flickered across his face, as if some deeply hidden part of him, trapped inside the walls of madness, knew that she could save him and wanted to cry out with joy.

Once Cordry stopped struggling, Ranulf tentatively released him. "I'll put wards up," he said quietly. "They'll contain any random spells he starts tossing around. But we'll have to be careful," he added. "Even though we can pass through the wards at will, an unleashed spell will ricochet around like a wasp in a glass jar. If he starts letting one fly, jump clear as quick as you can."

Ranulf's words weren't very reassuring, but she let him go about his task and make the necessary preparations. He walked in an oblong pattern around the settle, touching the occasional object—the mantel, a table, a chair—to connect the boundary points of the warded area. The barrier would be invisible to all but her and Ranulf—and Cordry, depending on how far his *me-kahn* had advanced—and soon she could see a faint whitish glow begin to surround them, as if a thin fog had permeated the room. Jarvis and the girl watched his movements intensely, vaguely aware that sorcery was being worked around them, yet too desperate to protest. Gilbert, however, dogged Ranulf's footsteps with blatant suspicion until the wizard turned and gave him a quick mental slap. Busy as she was with Cordry, Athaya sensed the overspill of Ranulf's command for Gilbert to stop interfering to get out of his way. Athaya held in a grin as the little man crept back into the corner then stood there futilely trying to remember why he had done so.

As Ranulf finished the last of the warding spells, a piercing screech split the air, rending the tentative rapport Athaya had forged with Cordry. Athaya glanced quickly toward the doorway and recognized the same bulky woman that had confronted her in the entry hall. The cook's face was white as flourpaste.

"Wizards!" she shrieked. "Heaven help us, *wizards!"* Her fingers clutched at her apron as if it were the only means of her salvation. "God have mercy, send for a priest!"

"Get her out of here and keep her quiet!" Athaya shouted to anyone who would listen. The cook's hysterical screams had destroyed Cordry's fragile hold on sanity, and Athaya had to shake her head violently to fight off the disruptions from his renewed mental ravings. Her thinking grew cloudy and muddled, and it took physical effort to keep her own paths clear and untangled.

"Megan, take Tess into the kitchens," Jarvis said to the woman in the yellow gown. At the edge of her vision, Athaya saw Megan put her arms around the cook's shoulders and gently guide her out of the room, murmuring words of comfort. Jarvis' companion, Gilbert, apparently incensed that his earlier advice—and the cook's—had been so soundly rejected, expelled a snort of frustration and scuttled from the room. The elder Jarvis relaxed his shoulders, visibly glad to see him go.

"I don't know who or what you are, young lady," he said, glaring down at Athaya, "and I'm not sure I *want* to know. But if you can help my son, then do it . . . I implore you."

It took several minutes for Athaya to calm Cordry enough so she could work, but with consistent prodding, his self-control gradually started to return. But he was still just out of reach, caught in a web of magic that he didn't understand. His eyes pleaded with her, somehow knowing she was helping him, but unable to comprehend how or why.

"Now, Cordry, listen to me," she urged, her voice low and fluid. "We're going to work a few spells together. Easy ones. Nothing that will hurt you or anyone else. Getting some of your power out will help ease the pain you're feeling. Then we'll be able to talk."

She brushed aside the dark curls framing his face and pressed her fingers against his temples, rubbing gently. *Can you hear me?* she asked, casting her words to him. *I'm here with you. I'm going to show you where the voices are . . .*

Tentatively, so not to startle him out of his precarious hold on reason, she led him through the twisting corridors of his mind, briefly explaining what paths were and how one used them. But he was afraid to the point of panic, and Athaya felt as if she were trying to coax a child, terrified of the dark, into an underground dungeon where any number of hidden terrors might be lurking.

She quickly set aside the idea of showing him a witchlight. Though it was one of the easiest spells to master, she thought he might be startled by a globe of fire suddenly burning in his palm. Instead, she took his hand and turned his thoughts to the place where the spell for guiding runes was kept. Although she had just learned the spell herself, it was a simple one and relatively easy to find. It took several minutes of coercion, but she managed to tap into enough of his logic to convince him to try.

He held up one hand and spoke in a shaking, raspy voice. *"Locus signetur."*

Within moments, the back of the settle was marked by a bright red rune, as if someone had painted it there with blood.

Athaya felt the intense pressure in his mind subside with the slight release of magic, and after letting him relax for a while, she bade him work the spell several more times, each one bringing him closer to his former self. After a half hour of such work, his personality had gradually resurfaced, and the wildness had ebbed from his eyes.

"Did I do that?" he asked aloud. He squinted at the runes intensely—they were bound to be fainter to him than to a fully trained wizard—but his eyes were touched with wonder, not quite sure the runes wouldn't harm him, but entranced by their existence.

Athaya encouraged his curiosity, continuing the gentle and undemanding rapport. He was easier to work with now that she had earned his trust, and she lured him toward acceptance of his powers like a deer who gradually lets go its timidity to venture into the open fields.

Now let's try a witchlight, Cordry. I think you're ready . . .

Then, like a blinding flash of light, dizzying pain assaulted her from all sides. She barely heard Ranulf's cry as he stumbled backward, cursing violently. She desperately wanted to move, to flee from the blinding hurt, but even thinking was a labor and her limbs refused to budge. Her carefully controlled hold on Cordry's mind shattered in an instant as she wrenched herself free of him, fighting for her own survival.

Cordry sensed the abrupt abandonment and panicked. Athaya could sense the wild, defensive power build up inside him, but she was frozen by pain, helpless to react, and unable to reason why his power was poising to strike while hers was all but useless. Ranulf was just alert enough to pull her clear of the wards before Cordry lashed out with a bolt of raw power; another bolt of green lightning, full of deadly force.

He was lucky not to be struck down by his own spell. Entrapped by the wards, the magic bolt ricocheted off the ward boundaries, missing Cordry by mere inches as it finally hurled itself into the straw mat near the hearth. The edge of the mat ignited, sending up tendrils of pungent smoke.

"Kale, the crystal!" Ranulf shouted. "Cover it up—get it out of the light—either that or smash the ungodly thing, *now*!"

Athaya was infinitely glad that Ranulf could still speak. When she tried it herself, her tongue felt thick and woolen and wouldn't form a single sound. She did not know who held the crystal or where it had come from. All she knew were the hot needles of pain coursing through her flesh, the pounding agony as her paths began to cross like bones being wrenched out of place, and the awful knowledge that even her skill with the sealing spell was useless now, the corbal hurling it infinitely out of her reach.

CHAPTER 11

✖

THE NEXT FEW SECONDS PASSED WITH AGONIZING SLOW-
ness, as if Athaya were entrapped by the mind-numbing
fog of looca-smoke. The fire that Cordry's spell had ignited seemed to burn for hours before Sir Jarvis beat it down
with his greatcoat, and Kale seemed to slog through mud as he
drove toward the blur of black cloth that filled the doorway—a
blur that held aloft a gleaming gold candlestick with a single
corbal embedded in its base. Then she recognized the traditional
black cassock worn by all ranks of the Caithan clergy and, gasping, tried to spring to her feet. The quick motion, however,
drove a thousand hot needles through her skull and forced her
back to her knees.

Through the fog of pain, she saw Gilbert Ames crouched in
the hallway behind the priest, watching the corbal do its work
with perverse pleasure. Sir Jarvis' cheeks puffed with outrage
upon seeing that his friend had taken it upon himself to send for
help, but Gilbert was oblivious to him. When he met Athaya's
eyes directly, he smiled at her torment.

He did not enjoy the victory for long. Whipping off his cloak,
Kale lunged forward and threw the garment over the gem-
studded candlestick, wresting it from the priest with ease. The
black-robed man tried to snatch it back, but he was a good deal
older and thinner than Kale, and his meager strength was no

match for a former member of the King's Guard. Thus robbed of his only weapon, he backed against the wall in terror, lips rapidly mouthing silent prayers.

Bellowing his outrage, Gilbert pushed his way into the room and tried to regain the crystal, but his wildly flailing fists could not compete with the cool instincts of a trained fighter. Kale kept him at bay with a well-aimed kick to the stomach, holding him off just long enough to get a solid grip on the candlestick.

A single blow was all it took. Gilbert slumped to the floor as if his bones had turned to powder.

Confident that his attacker was not liable to make further trouble for a while, Kale wrapped the candlestick tight inside the folds of his cloak to shut out every possible bit of light. The frantic pounding in Athaya's head gradually subsided like a thunderstorm blowing off to the east, and she managed to get up, gratified to find that her legs didn't buckle under her. With a dismissing glance at Gilbert, she turned to face her other assailant. Tiny beads of perspiration dotted the priest's balding scalp, and eyes as frightened as a cornered rabbit's flitted from Athaya to Ranulf and back again, rapidly calculating which of them was likely to strike first. As Athaya approached, the priest instinctively brushed his fingers from his heart to his forehead in a protective gesture.

She motioned to the bundled cloak tucked under Kale's arm. "Take that thing out of here." Although it was tightly wrapped, Athaya could still sense a trickle of disruption coming from the corbal, like an itch she couldn't quite reach.

"B-but you can't!" sputtered the priest, gaping fearfully at her as if she were a stone gargoyle that had suddenly come to life. "That's Church property! You have no right—"

"We're not thieves, Father," she said, smiling at the echo of Cameron in her voice. "I have every intention of giving it back. Kale, work the corbal out of its setting with your dagger and smash it. Then bring the candlestick in for Father . . ." She looked at the priest inquiringly.

"Greste," he supplied dutifully, as if trained from infancy to be polite no matter how bizarre the circumstances. "But the gem is—"

"Valuable, I know. And I'm sorry." At her signal, Kale sidestepped the priest and departed.

Although he looked more than a little rattled himself, Ranulf had already moved back to Cordry's side, calming his mind so that he could be made to sleep. Sir Jarvis hovered beside them worriedly, asking a string of questions without seeming to notice that Ranulf wasn't answering any of them. He wrung his hands on the greatcoat he had used to snuff out Cordry's fire, the once-fine wool now riddled with burn holes and stinking of soot.

Once Cordry was sleeping soundly, Ranulf dissolved the wards around him, and the whitish boundary melted away like morning fog. "*He'll* be fine," Ranulf told Jarvis, irritably rubbing his temples so that no one would overlook his own misery. "He was more startled than hurt." Ranulf glanced back at Athaya. "I expect that's why he lashed out like that, though I was damned surprised he could. But he's not through the *mekahn* yet, so he must have a few scraps of immunity left from those crystals."

Baffled by Ranulf's remarks, Father Greste shifted to a kneeling position at Cordry's side, giving Athaya and Ranulf a wide berth. He touched a blue-veined hand to the young man's wrist to assure himself that Cordry's sleep was not of the permanent variety.

"I thought corbal crystals were supposed to be rare," Athaya muttered, pressing down on her eyes to make the last few aches go away. "Where did you get one, Father?"

"F-from the altar at the cathedral," he replied haltingly. "There are others . . ."

"How *many* others?" she demanded, her voice suddenly edged with wrathful authority. She had an unpleasant vision of dozens of pieces like the candlestick—chalices, plates, thuribles—all potentially deadly weapons.

"It was the king's order," Greste went on, quick to shift the blame from his own shoulders. "The edict arrived not two weeks ago. Oh, he was right," the priest mumbled, rocking back and forth on his knees. "I knew there were wizards among us the moment those windows started breaking at the cathedral. The king was right . . ."

Athaya looked at him sharply. "The king? What edict?" Surely Durek couldn't know that she was in Caithe already. But that possibility, abhorrent as it was, could explain why Father Greste wasn't more shocked than he was to see a wizard in his midst after nearly two centuries. If the priests had been told to expect them . . .

"His Majesty commanded all corbal relics from Faltil's time to be brought out of storage and displayed. He vows to protect the souls of his people from sorcery." Father Greste swallowed nervously, no doubt yearning for some protection for his own soul at the moment.

"It's sorcery that needs to be protected, Father, not you," Athaya said softly. "The king doesn't understand that."

The priest blinked in surprise, timidity replaced by loyal indignation. "You dare to question the king's judgment?" he said, raising to his feet.

Athaya regarded the priest evenly. *Oh, yes, I dare because I know him, Father. Because he's always refused to tolerate any idea he didn't already agree with. The very notion that magic isn't the evil he thinks it is would turn his well-ordered world upside down and force him to admit that maybe he's not so blasted right about everything as he likes to think.*

"I doubt the king's motives are as pure as you say," she said, trying to cushion her scorn with a modicum of respect. "I'll grant you that perhaps he does want to protect his people—if he has even the smallest bit of Kelwyn in him, that must be so. Trouble is, he only concerns himself with a limited number of his subjects. The Lorngeld are Caithans, too, and just as deserving of their king's care."

Frowning deeply, Father Greste turned to Jarvis, extending his hands in supplication. "Sir, what is this woman doing here? The things she's saying—they are *profane*! Let me alert the bishop, I implore you. He has long been concerned with the . . . 'talk' . . . surrounding your son and sincerely wishes to be of service."

Jarvis, who up to now had remained a silent observer, did not welcome being drawn into the discussion. He looked profoundly torn, his tortured gaze shifting from Athaya to the priest and to his sleeping son, silently battling both sides of a war he never expected to fight. With a weary sigh, he moved to the polished oak cabinet and reached for a flagon.

"Come sit down and have some wine, Father. By the looks of you, you could use it. And by God, so could I."

The priest's eyes almost popped from their sockets. "In the name of all that's holy, how can you calmly sit back with a glass of wine when there are *wizards* under your roof?"

Jarvis laughed, but there was no mirth in it—only the high-

strung laughter of a man desperately trying to hide the extent
of his own pain. "Even you must admit that this is something
of a special occasion, Father," he said carelessly, like a man
who knows he's going to die no matter what he says in his defense. "I'll wager it's been many years since anyone in Kaiburn
has had a pair of wizards over for a drink."

Greste was left speechless by such levity and made a series
of sputtering noises in the back of his throat. Still, he did not
pull away when Jarvis led him to a cushioned chair and pressed
a goblet of wine into his hand. The priest didn't seem to notice
it was there at first, but when he did, he quickly gulped it down.

Kale returned a few minutes later and set the candlestick on
the floor beside Greste's sandaled feet. "I polished it up for you,
Father," Kale said by way of apology for the missing stone.
Then he unhooked a small pouch from his belt and sprinkled
the purplish dust of the crushed corbal over the cold ashes in the
fireplace.

"Now I've one other task for you," Athaya told him. She
pointed to Gilbert, still motionless on the floor. He was breathing steadily and looked quite peaceful—as if he'd merely decided to settle down on Jarvis' floor for a nap. "Since you put
him out, you can figure out how to wake him up."

While Kale saw to the lump on Gilbert's skull, Father Greste
glanced down at the corbal-less candlestick with acute regret.
"The bishop will be furious—it was part of a pair that was given
to the cathedral by his ancestors almost two hundred years ago.
Right after the Demons' Retreat was destroyed."

Athaya frowned at him. "The what?"

"An old ruin in the forest. Or at least it used to be. There's
probably nothing left of it now—so much the better," Greste
added, turning his lips down in distaste. "I've heard what they
did there. Sick, horrid things. Sacrifices to the Devil, lewdness,
dances—" He broke off abruptly, as if praying he hadn't given
them any ideas. "Ungodly folk. But they were already a distant
memory when my great-grandfather was a boy. King Faltil's
men got rid of them all."

"Faltil didn't get rid of anything," Athaya countered darkly,
simmering at the thought of her ancestor's flagrant act of stupidity and greed. "Did his scourge work? Are the Lorngeld gone?
No. They're born every day, all over Caithe. All Faltil managed
to do was murder everyone who knew how to use their power

so people like Cordry Jarvis would have no one to turn to for help. The Time of Madness never really ended, Father. It was merely 'put under control'—first by Bishop Adriel and then by all the others he duped into believing in absolution.''

Father Greste opened his mouth to object, but Athaya cut him off brusquely. ''Before you arrived, Cordry was out of control. We're just lucky that all he did was break a few goblets and singe the edge of a floor mat. He almost dropped a chandelier on my head and he could very well have sent the whole house crashing down after it. We're here to help him and we're not out to hurt anyone. Well, except for poor Gilbert over there,'' she added, ''but you have to admit, he attacked us first.''

Athaya watched the befuddled priest studying her, weighing her words. She could almost hear his thoughts as he tried to sort through them all, though she knew he was only listening to her because he was afraid of what she might do if he wasn't suitably cooperative.

''You don't know what to think of me, do you?'' she continued. ''I understand your confusion. You've been told all your life that the Lorngeld are crazy and destructive—''

''*And* the Devil's agents,'' he broke in with sudden vehemence. As if rudely awakened from a dream, his eyes lost every trace of their former apprehension, shining instead with new-found insight. He set his goblet aside and rose to his feet, gazing at her accusingly. ''And what better way to tempt me than to do exactly what you *are* doing, putting on a guise of compassion and goodwill! Your arguments are clever. *Too* clever.''

He wheeled around to face Sir Jarvis. ''They want you to think they are helping your son so that they can more easily steal his soul,'' he pleaded. ''They want to turn both of you away from God by offering you false hope that Cordry's life can be saved. Can't you *see* that? Can't you see the *danger*?''

Jarvis lifted up his eyes from the goblet into which he'd been deeply brooding and turned them to Cordry, still sleeping peacefully. When he spoke, his voice sounded like that of a much older man.

''All I see, Father, is that my son is far better now than he was an hour ago.''

Greste threw his hands up in despair, the black sleeves flapping like raven's wings. ''But it is deception! He is not recovered. He is only one step closer to damnation! These sorcerers have laid their mark upon him. His soul—''

"I'm worried about his *life* at the moment!" Jarvis shot back, jerking himself upright and sending fat drops of wine sloshing into his lap. "I'll worry about his soul when I'm damned well ready!"

Just as Father Greste was preparing to launch into another round of persuasion, a low, pitiful groan drew his attention to the opposite side of the room. Kale had succeeded in bringing Gilbert around, although the spindly man didn't look entirely grateful for the favor. He clutched his head tightly, as if afraid it would fall to pieces the moment he let go of it. His legs were wobbly, but because of his slight build, Kale was able to hold him up effortlessly.

"God's breath, what happened?" he mumbled, squinting in Jarvis' general direction and trying to make his eyes focus. "My head feels as if it's been under the mallets at the fulling mill."

"Father, I think perhaps you should escort Mr. Ames back home," Jarvis said, reluctantly rising from his chair. "He's in greater need of your ministrations at the moment."

The hardness in Jarvis' eyes convinced the priest that any further protests would be futile, at least for the time being. He retrieved the candlestick from the floor and motioned to Cordry with it. "Very well. But I cannot let this matter drop. Bishop Lukin must be told about what has happened here today. All candidates for absolution require his—"

"Lukin?" Athaya blurted out. She knew the name, and was not at all pleased to hear it again. "Of course—why didn't I make the connection before?"

"What's wrong?" Ranulf asked.

Athaya made a face as if she'd bitten into a lemon. "Jon Lukin, our honorable bishop of Kaiburn. He was one of Kelwyn's most adamant opponents when it came to any leniency toward the Lorngeld. Archbishop Ventan was always careful to tiptoe around Kelwyn to curry his favor, but Lukin was never so particular. At the Curia last summer, Kelwyn almost ordered Ventan to defrock him for his insolence. Durek took Lukin's side, of course, and he and Kelwyn didn't speak for days afterward."

The situation at court was so familiar to her that she couldn't help but speak casually of it. And she might have continued had Ranulf not thrown her a look of warning the moment she used her brother's given name and not his title.

Jarvis cupped his chin, rubbing it thoughtfully. "You are quite well informed about the Curia's affairs," he remarked, frowning at the bedraggled state of her dress and hair and trying to make sense of the incongruity.

"Sir Jarvis, you're straying from the point!"

Athaya let out her breath, grateful for Greste's timely interruption.

Jarvis' brow darkened; he was noticeably hesitant to return to the original subject, but he knew that the priest had to be appeased, if only temporarily. "Father, I don't think there's a need to tell the bishop about this. Not yet, in any event. And I'm sure I can make a generous donation to the cathedral if you'll allow me some time to ponder this matter."

"But that's—"

"Not exactly a bribe, my friend," he said, placing a hand on the priest's sloping shoulder. "Leave me to care for my son, and I shall give you funds enough to care for dozens of other needy folk. A fair and charitable exchange in which everyone benefits, don't you agree?"

"It's not just your son's life we're speaking of," Greste said solemnly, "it's his soul."

Jarvis massaged his eyes as if he felt a headache coming on. "I know. And I'm not sure what to believe anymore. But if I think he's in danger, I'll send for you immediately. I promise. Until then, I beg your silence. At least for a few days."

After a few seconds of private debate, Greste nodded. Athaya had not expected him to press the issue much further. Yes, the law was on Greste's side, but Jarvis was by far the wealthier and more influential—not the sort of man a simple priest wishes to acquire as an enemy. Athaya knew from experience that for better or worse, rank was quite useful in persuading those of lesser stature to mind their own business even if they suspect wrongdoing.

"And I'd appreciate your confidence as well, Gilbert," Jarvis said as Kale handed his charge over to Father Greste. "Your family's been in my employ for many years, and I've always done well by you. Don't repay me by speaking of this. You'll find me more than grateful . . . in fact, I'll go over those ledgers you brought by today and see if I can't add a little something to your week's pay."

Gilbert looked deeply muddled, still too woozy to recall exactly what he wasn't supposed to talk about. His eyes passed over Athaya and Ranulf as if he'd met them somewhere but couldn't recall where or when. He gave Jarvis a vague nod, but was far more concerned with staying on his feet and making his way out of the house without stumbling.

As Father Greste took Gilbert out to the hall, they passed a young woman coming in. It was Megan, the yellow-clad woman who had stayed by Cordry's side until she'd taken charge of Jarvis' hysterical cook.

"Tess is fine," she said in a gentle, refined voice. "She gulped down three glasses of brandy, so she'll not wake for hours yet." Athaya noted that while her words were for Sir Jarvis, her gaze rested solely on young Cordry. "Is it safe now?"

Jarvis drew her inside, patting her softly on the arm. "It's safe. And rest your mind about Cordry—he's just asleep. Although it was our guests and not a triple dose of brandy that did the trick."

"I doubt he'll remember any of this when he wakes up," Athaya told her, observing that the woman's blue eyes and blond hair certainly didn't fit in this dark-haired family. "Are you his wife?"

"Almost," Jarvis announced proudly. "This is my son's future bride, Miss Megan Loring." The warmth of his face showed that he loved her as his own daughter already. "She and Cordry have been betrothed ever since they were children."

Megan closed her eyes and turned her face away, as if the sight of her intended had suddenly become too painful to bear. "We are to be married next month. Or at least we were . . ."

Megan valiantly fought back her tears, and Athaya's heart reached out in sympathy. There couldn't be a single thought going through Megan's mind that she hadn't had herself. Athaya knew how it felt to love and be loved by the man you want to marry, and then to know what it was to fear for his life, to look at the specter of a future without him with the absolute surety that it would be worse than death; and then to be confronted with that reality . . .

And to face confronting it *again*.

"You'll be able to marry him," she said, pushing away the thoughts that hammered inside her. "I promise."

Jarvis' eyes lit up with hope. "Then you can cure him?"

"Yes. But only by making a wizard of him—as I'm sure you've already realized. And there's not much time."

In the heavy silence that followed, Sir Jarvis went to kneel at his son's side. He took Cordry's hand and held it loosely, gently caressing the youthful skin between his fingers.

"I've been training him to inherit the family business, you know," he said, not speaking to anyone in particular. "I'm a clothier—damned good one, too—but it's time a younger man took over. And Cordry is so quick . . . bursting with new ideas and energy! Why, last summer we invested in a new type of cloth—ray, it was—and made a fortune, all because of him." Jarvis's expression grew even more grim. "I've no other children. Cordry's my only hope . . . my joy. I don't know what I'd do without him."

The older man's eyes grew moist. "It's been so hard these last few weeks. Sometimes he looks at me as if I'm a stranger to him. And yet he's afraid—as if there's some part of him that knows what's happening and realizes what I'll be forced to do. Or what I thought I'd do . . ." Jarvis paused, struggling to keep his voice from breaking. "He looks at me with those eyes. Those wild, awful eyes . . ." Then, as if suddenly conscious that his painful monologue was being overheard, Jarvis cleared his throat and turned away, hiding his face and trying to pretend that it was the still-smoky air that was making his eyes water.

Athaya stepped forward, but not so close that Jarvis would consider it a presumption. "Part of his mind knows what's happening. It frightens him—and that's what causes his madness. Your son's magical ability is trying to express itself, but he doesn't know how to channel it. If I don't teach him, he'll destroy himself and very likely everything and everyone around him. And I know what that's like, Sir Jarvis," she said, her voice dropping. "I was the cause of more than one death before I managed to get my own powers under control. I don't want Cordry to go through the same kind of hell I did."

"So it is as we feared," Megan whispered. "He is one of them." The moment the words escaped her lips, she turned to Athaya with a sincere expression of contrition. "Forgive me, I didn't mean that as it sounded. I . . . I've known it in my heart for a long time, although Cordry wouldn't let me speak of it, even when we were alone. But I've already decided that it makes no difference. I love him and I don't care about anything else. I want whatever help you can offer, Miss—" Her cheeks reddened slightly. "I'm sorry, I never got your name."

Oh, Father Greste, where are you when I need you? Athaya thought inwardly. But while she fumbled for an answer, Jarvis rose to his feet, drawing back from her with peculiar caution. His expression of grief was gone now, replaced by hardness and mounting suspicion. His body made a sharp, jerking motion as if he were torn between whether to bow or attack.

"Your Highness." It was a statement, not a guess.

During those next few seconds, Athaya was sure that all of Kaiburn could hear the hammering of her heart. While Megan stared at her blankly, too stunned to even consider a curtsy— which would have been a laughable gesture considering Megan looked infinitely more respectable than Athaya did at the moment—Sir Jarvis' jaw went rigid, and every trace of compassion he had shown up to now vanished behind a mask of suppressed wrath.

"You spoke so easily of the king," he said, working through the evidence aloud. His face darkened with every word. "And now you speak of causing death . . ."

Athaya did not intend to weave falsehoods or make excuses for herself. She had much to answer for, and it was the people of Caithe to whom she owed the most explanation. They deserved that much from her, for taking their well-loved Kelwyn away. "I regret what I've done, but I won't deny who I am. That would be an insult to my father."

"Then the stories are true . . . what you did to him." Jarvis' eyes flashed like summer lightning, a hint of deep pain behind them. He was clearly one who had loved and been loyal to his late king. Under any other circumstances, Athaya could have severely upbraided him for such an open look of hostility, but since it was born out of respect for Kelwyn, and since her own royal status was an extremely moot point right now, she let it pass. But his glare caused Kale to gradually inch closer to Athaya's side, ready to protect her if need be.

Then the brewing storm erupted, and Jarvis could no longer hold in his anger. "Get out!" he cried, all the day's trials and strained emotions spewing out. "Get out of here! Leave my son and me alone!'' In a burst of rage, he snatched up the single glass goblet that Cordry had spared during his madness and threw it to the ground, sending up a shower of clear shards.

"Cedmond, please," Megan urged him gently, grasping his arm. "They only mean to help."

He jerked his arm from her roughly. "Help? Yes, she probably told our poor lord Kelwyn she was only trying to help—right before she *murdered* him. I won't stand by and let my son be her next victim!"

Cordry moaned softly, roused by his father's shouts, and Jarvis knelt at his side and whispered comforting phrases to him until he drifted back to sleep.

"I-I'm horribly sorry," Megan said, glancing apologetically at Athaya and the others. "He's distraught. Cordry's been getting worse for weeks. This isn't the first time someone's brought him home smelling like . . ." Then she realized that her guests smelled little better themselves and broke off quickly, cheeks pink.

"Megan, stay out of this," Jarvis ordered in a low voice. "I don't need you to go around apologizing for me." But looking at his son's anguished face sinking slowly back into peacefulness changed him somewhat, and when Jarvis got to his feet again, some of his anger had fled.

"I want him to live, Princess," he said slowly, every word a labor, "but I'm not sure I want to owe that favor to one such as you."

"If you ask me to go, I will," she said, calm but resolute. "There are others in this city who can use my help if you don't want it. But I suspect that if you were truly ready to give your son up for absolution, you wouldn't have purchased Father Greste's silence so readily." She paused to let Jarvis mull that point over for a moment, watching as his facade began to crack. She didn't like being harsh with him, but that was the only way to make him see what was at stake. "Or if you prefer, I can simply take your son back to the looca-den where I found him and leave him there until the priests come for him."

"No, don't!" Megan cried, looking imploringly at Jarvis, who said nothing.

Athaya took a breath to calm herself, her expression softening. "I caused my father's death because I couldn't control my spells. But I'm going to make amends for what I've done. That's why I'm here. True, I have taken one life. But I aim to save thousands. Including your son's, if you'll permit me." She noted the glimmer of light in Megan's eyes at hearing that. "My father always intended to do what he could for the Lorngeld. Less than a year ago, he assembled the Curia for that very purpose—to try to abolish absolution and legalize the practice of magic. I'm only carrying on what he started. If you don't trust my judgment, Sir Jarvis, then perhaps you can trust his."

Jarvis withdrew deep inside himself, pondering her words. Athaya could see the conflict playing across his face, one minute exhilarated at knowing his son might live, the next doubting her trustworthiness, terrified of the Church's wrath and conscious of the peril of Cordry's soul—and his own—if he made the wrong choice. His knuckles made sounds like snapping twigs as he wrung his hands together. He looked to Megan for support and found that her otherwise delicate face was the picture of resolve. She had made her decision long ago, and it lent him strength.

"Can you really hope to succeed?" he asked quietly. He needed to voice his doubts, afraid of letting his hopes rise too high. "I heard that King Durek has—"

"Sent his men out to bring me back," Athaya finished for him. She held her chin up defiantly. "He shouldn't have bothered. It was always my intention to return. By on my terms, not my brother's."

Jarvis didn't look at her and when he spoke, it was the voice of a man who knows he has lost the battle, but feels obligated to fight until all options have been exhausted. "But his soul—"

"Is not in danger," she assured him. "How could it be? All I want to do is let him use the gift his Creator gave to him."

Megan stepped forward, her face aglow. "You think magic comes . . . from *God*?" This idea so fascinated her that she looked like a child enraptured at hearing a fairy tale for the first time. The fact that it was heresy of the most blatant kind didn't seem to occur to her.

"Cordry isn't damned," Athaya assured them. "On the contrary, he's been blessed."

Jarvis' attention perked up at this, his eyes betraying proud surprise at such an unexpected honor. But he remained silent, either from confusion or from newfound awe at the source of his son's untrained power.

"Sir Jarvis, please," Megan said, folding his large hands

inside her tiny ones. "You must believe them. What she's saying
. . . it *has* to be true. No one as decent and loving as Cordry
could possibly be the Devil's child."

Jarvis sighed deeply, faced with a truth he could not contest.
"I know, Megan, dear. That I *do* believe." He stood a little
straighter after that, freshly redeemed, and almost smiled as he
turned to Athaya. "I must trust your judgment, your Highness.
Yours and your father's. Take my son and help him if you can.
I'll not betray you. On Kelwyn's name, I swear it."

His choice of oath touched Athaya deeply. "Thank you. And
we'll do what we can to protect you. All of you."

"There's just one problem," Ranulf pointed out, reluctant to
bring the subject up at a moment of relative victory. "No of-
fense, Sir Jarvis, but while you and the young lady have given
us your confidence, Cordry hasn't. And we can't risk taking him
back with us until we're sure he wants what we're offering, and
that we can trust him not to reveal our . . . 'headquarters,' so
to speak."

"And you can't teach him here," Jarvis said, "not when so
many people suspect what he is already." He settled back into
his chair, lost in diligent thought.

"There's an old sheepfold at the edge of my property," he
said after a time. "Cordry used to play there as a boy. The place
is run-down—just a heap of old rocks, really. When I bought
the adjoining land, I built a larger pen and never got around to
having the old one torn down. It's not much, but it's yours if
you want it."

Athaya smiled to herself. *No need to apologize, my friend.
We're getting quite accustomed to ruins.*

"I'll come back tomorrow. Cordry can take me to this sheepfold of yours, and then—if he's willing—we'll see what kind of
a wizard I can make of him."

Jarvis nodded, but his face was drawn with fear. "But if anyone asks what you're doing there, I'll deny knowing anything
about it," he warned her. "If I lose my place in this city, or my
mills, Cordry will have nothing. Nothing!"

"He'll have his life," Athaya reminded him. "But you have
to do what you feel is best. No one can ask more of you than
that."

As Athaya turned to go, she grinned up at Ranulf. "An old
sheepfold, eh? Take care to wager on how long it takes people

to start calling us shepherds leading their flocks down the road to damnation?''

Ranulf replied with a snort. "I never wager on a sure thing.''

In another city street, this one lined with well-kept shops and canvas booths, four plainly clad men lingered with carefully crafted nonchalance over a meal of molasses bread and honey butter, occasionally glancing up at the limestone walls of Glendol Palace a short distance away.

Captain Parr and his men had arrived in Ath Luaine the previous evening, their journey back to the Reykan capital having passed without incident—with the possible exception of a brief brawl in a seaport tavern in Torvik that left one of the men sporting an ugly purple bruise on his jaw. And if his men did have an annoying tendency to walk in step with one another, Parr tried to ignore it, knowing they were not otherwise recognizable as army bred.

As he had expected, it had taken twice as long to return from the border as it had to reach it, and already the equinox was a fortnight past and April nearly a week old. Even in the worst weather, Lord Gessinger would have reached Delfarham by now, but the captain remained confident that the king would understand his reasons for staying behind. And now it was time to get to work.

Finishing the last of his lunch, Parr wiped the crumbs from his mouth and turned to his lieutenant. "Berns, you come with me. Hugh, you and James cover that end of the street. We'll meet back here at the end of the day to see what we've found out.''

Hugh's hand jerked up briefly as if to salute, but he quickly transformed the motion and made as if to brush hair from his eyes. "And if someone wants to know why we're looking for her?''

"Then tell them something you think they'll believe,'' Parr replied impatiently. "But put a little truth in it—lies always work better that way.''

The men parted company, and Parr and Berns wound their way through the narrow street, absently looking at the goods for sale around them and trying to look inconspicuous.

"God defend us, they're everywhere,'' Berns murmured under his breath. He flicked his eyes toward another of the often-seen symbols, this one carved onto a wooden sign and hanging from a leatherer's window.

Parr nodded contemptuously. While he'd always found that one city looked fairly much like another, nothing in Caithe had prepared him for the sight of magicians freely advertising their services. Ath Luaine was peppered with such signs, the cross-shaped symbols posted outside any number of shops to attract potential customers. Parr had learned of the symbol—as well as other, more potentially useful facts—through King Durek's diligent studies, but seeing it displayed in such shameless abundance unsettled him.

Then, to his own surprise, Parr began to smile. "But who better to help us find a wizard than one who knows all of their tricks?"

Beside him, Berns swallowed noticeably. "Sir, you can't mean to ask a *wizard* for help?" he cautioned, careful to keep his voice low. "Our Lord might well strike us down for dealing in the Devil's work—"

"I don't think God will mind, given the circumstances," Parr replied dryly. "Besides, remember your history. Even King Faltil used wizards to rid himself of wizards, and it's well known what a holy man *he* was."

Berns made no reply, but followed with visible reluctance as Parr headed inside the leatherer's shop.

They were greeted with rapt enthusiasm by a stringy man of indeterminate years, his skin tough and brown as the scraps of leather and string scattered across his worktable. He quickly set aside the belt he'd been stitching and made a sweeping gesture around his shop, as if presenting his wares to royalty.

"Good morning, gentlemen," he said, his voice sweet as a courtier's despite his rumpled appearance. "I see you have an eye for fine work." He eagerly picked up another belt, this one finely tooled and inlaid with costly silver studs. "Now here's some of my best work. Notice the tight stitches, the artistry of the design, the suppleness of the—"

"It's fine work," Parr said, deftly cutting him off, "but we seek the services of a wizard. I saw your sign outside—" He raised his brows, prompting for a name.

"William," he offered cheerfully. "William Bain. Leatherer and wizard, though I'll confide to you, I'm a bit better at the one than the other." The man set his elegant belt aside and laughed modestly. "But I'll try to oblige you. What can I get you? A guidance stone? You do have a slight accent about you, and I'd think any visitor to Ath Luaine would welcome one. Or perhaps," he said, rubbing his chin as he grinned, "a charm to endear you to one of our fair ladies? The city is full of them, and some are quite partial to foreigners."

"No, nothing like that," Parr replied, fast growing impatient with the man's chatter. Still, chattering types were the best when looking for information—one never knew what they might say, thinking it trivial. "We're looking for someone, and it's quite urgent that we find her. We have a very important message."

William nodded as if their request was all too common. "Oh, certainly. My sphere runs true, even if some of my other spells don't. Have you a likeness, then?"

"A likeness?"

"A portrait . . . a miniature of the lady."

Parr shook his head. "No."

"Oh," the man said, shaking his head with regret. "I can't be seeking her without a likeness."

"I could describe her to you—"

"No good, I'm afraid. I'd need an exact image to pluck the right lady out of all the thousands in Ath Luaine. Unless of course, there's a chance I know her . . ."

Parr hesitated to tell the man who he was looking for, but if there was even a chance of success, he thought it worth the risk. This tradesman had an open disposition and an active tongue, and men such as he often prided themselves in knowing a great deal of what was happening around them.

"Maybe you have seen her," Parr began, molding his features into an expression of acute concern. "She's the Caithan princess who's been staying at the palace. We're loyal to her and have come all the way from Delfarham to warn her that she's in terrible danger. We'd ask the king himself, but what with things being what they are between Caithe and Reyka, we're afraid our intentions might be misunderstood. So we're trying to find her on our own."

William's face seemed to contract, hardening in thought like some of his boiled leather armor. "Princess Athaya," he said softly, nodding. "She rarely left the palace, they say. Only when the Master took her out for spellwork."

"Then you never saw her?"

"No. But she was here, sure enough. Things like that never get around us wizards, you know," he added with a touch of pride. "But the word is that she left a few weeks ago. Headed south for the ports, and a handful of folks with her, too. Talk's been rife in court all week about some sort of crusade in Caithe, so I'd wager that's where they've gone. If someone in this city is after her, my friends," he concluded, offering them a hopeful smile, "then rest assured they've missed their mark."

Parr tried to look pleased at that news, but it was more difficult than he'd imagined. He *knew* she'd been hiding at the palace, but it was scant comfort now. If only he'd risked riding straight back from the border instead of taking the route through Torvik! Then they might have caught her just as she was trying to escape.

Luckily, his lieutenant wasted no time with such brooding and turned to the leatherer with a pleading look. "We're grateful to know that, William, but we fear the man—we're sure he's an assassin—is still following her. We must find a way to warn her. Surely someone in this city would know exactly where she's gone."

Parr perked up at that. "Yes—perhaps you know if a certain friend of hers went with her?" he asked, careful to keep his eyes from narrowing. "His name is Jaren. Jaren McLaud. A wizard like yourself, I believe."

The man's eyes brightened, flattered by being put in such company. "Oh, yes, the McLaud lad! A fine young gentleman, he is, and such an honor to be assistant to Master Hedric, too. His family's got to be proud of that one, no doubt of it."

Parr bit his lip to keep from grimacing at that liberal dose of praise. "Then perhaps you could locate him for us?"

"Oh, surely. I know well enough what the young McLaud looks like, so it'll take no time at all."

As the man turned his back and settled in to conjure his vision sphere, Parr tried not to look revolted and kept a strong hand on Berns' arm to keep him from backing away. The orb hung between the man's palms like a soap bubble, and for an instant, Parr was tempted to puncture it with his dagger, knowing from Durek's studies how delicate such spheres could be.

A few minutes later, William banished the sphere with a smile of satisfaction. "You'll find him at Glendol Palace—at least for today. But he won't be there long, from what I hear. A fortnight back I saw his father the duke ride out the north gates—headed back to Ulard, he was—and word is that his son's to follow him any day now. A friend of mine is in the guard at Glendol, you see, and I get all my news firsthand.''

"Ulard," Parr said distractedly, "how far is that?"

"A good piece. Seven or eight days' ride, I'd say, given the rain holds off. But there's no sense waiting to talk to him there . . . not when he's but a stone's throw from you now. If you went to the palace and asked for him, I'm sure he'd see you. Especially if the princess is in danger.''

Parr merely nodded, laughing inwardly at the very thought of strolling up to the palace gates and asking for that duke's whelp of a wizard who'd already been brazen enough to lie about Athaya's whereabouts right to his face and taunt him in front of the court on top of it. It would be a tempting thing to bring that one down. A tempting thing indeed . . .

"You've been much help to us, William," he said, finally breaking the silence that had fallen over the three men. "What do we owe you?''

The man frowned briefly, but the clouds quickly cleared. "Ah, that's right—you're strangers here. There's no 'price' to speak of—how can one put a price on the Lord's gift?" he asked, holding his hands up. "For that, I can only take what people freely offer, for what they think my services were worth.'' Then he chuckled ruefully to himself. "Perhaps that explains why so many wizards are in other lines of work.''

Parr reached into his purse and handed the man a pair of gold coins, after which he was thanked profusely.

"God go with you," the leatherer said as they left, "and I hope you find the lady before she comes to harm.''

"She won't come to harm," Parr replied stiffly, not turning around. "Not until I get to her," he added under his breath.

Berns held the door open while Parr stalked out of the small shop riddled with indecision. It was a feeling he wasn't used to, having been trained for a command position, and it made him angry and ill-tempered. The princess was weeks to the south, and McLaud hopelessly out of reach behind the palace walls. The one was closer, but it was Athaya the king wanted most.

"I have to wonder," Berns said, as they leaned back against the wall outside the shop, "what Prince Nicolas has to do with all this. Was he lying to us all along, or was Athaya hiding even from him? Either he's still at the palace, or he's lost any bit of sense he's ever had and gone back to Caithe with Athaya. On this 'crusade'—whatever *that's* supposed to mean."

Parr glowered, saying nothing. He hadn't even bothered to worry about Nicolas yet—not that the prince was worth worrying about. He was more concerned with whether the leatherer's information could be trusted. What if the story of Athaya's departure was all a ruse, plotted by every wizard in this foul city? Perhaps it was a preplanned deception in the event that someone started asking just these kinds of questions. And even if it was true, what if McLaud wasn't in Ath Luaine at all, but back in Caithe with the princess, already stirring up rebellion?

"Sir?" Berns asked, noting his captain's silence.

Parr glared at the cross-shaped wizard's sign above the leatherer's shop. "Curse the whole damn lot of you," he grumbled, marching ahead of Berns at a rapid pace, and his lieutenant, familiar with his darker moods, trailed a safe distance behind.

CHAPTER 12

✳✳

"KEEP YOUR HANDS FARTHER APART—LIKE THIS,"
Athaya said, moving her pupil's hands into the
proper position. "The sphere forms better when
it's a bit larger."

Cordry let out a subtle sigh of displeasure and obeyed, but
when he spoke the words of invocation and called the mist from
his fingers, it shaped itself into a lopsided ball more akin to an
oddly shaped pumpkin than a globe. Master Tonia, who had
been studying his progress from across the earthen floor of the
sheepfold, merely raised one brow and tried not to grin.

"You're not trying," Megan scolded severely, before either
Athaya or Tonia had a chance to express an opinion. Megan
came to the sheepfold every day to watch Cordry's spellwork
and offer words of encouragement when he needed them, which
was pretty much all of the time.

"You need to concentrate, Cordry," Athaya said. "Calling a
vision sphere isn't a difficult spell, so it's easy to take it for granted
and make mistakes."

Megan nodded approvingly. "Listen to her, love. This is important."

"I guess so," Cordry said grudgingly, dispersing the badly
shaped sphere, "but so is making sure that next shipment of ray

is going to be ready by the end of the month. I don't trust Gilbert to get the figures right, and Father says—''

''Would you stop worrying about the mill for just one day?'' Megan folded her arms defiantly across her chest, blue eyes glittering like gems. ''We're talking about your *life*, for heaven's sake, and all you can think of is whether some silly old cloth gets loaded onto a boat!''

Cordry gaped at her, no more appalled than he would be if she'd just broken off their engagement. ''*Silly?* I'll have you know, Megan, that if we miss this shipment there won't be enough money to pay for our honeymoon, not to mention—''

As Cordry continued to inform his betrothed of the unmitigated disaster that would befall them should the mill not meet its commitments, Athaya rolled her eyes and silently relinquished him to Tonia, feeling an urgent need to step out of the sheepfold for a breath of fresh air. Megan and Cordry had the same quarrel every time she came to the sheepfold, and every time it ended with Megan convincing him to keep working at his spells, showering him with kisses and leaving his spirits much improved.

But Athaya was in no mood to listen to Cordry's grievances today, nor to witness Megan's affectionate persuasions. Their closeness vexed her, a constant reminder that she had no one to turn to when *her* spirits needed lifting, and worse, that she had no one to blame for that but herself. But the real pain came when Megan told Cordry she loved him and encouraged him to live up to his potential, for then Athaya heard Tyler whispering in her ear again, telling her to be what she was born to be, and Jaren, saying he knew she could change the world. She didn't begrudge Megan and Cordry their happiness, but sometimes she wished they would keep it out of sight, away where it could not harm her.

Athaya was blinded for a moment as she stepped out of the darkened sheepfold into the dazzling afternoon sunlight. Drinking in the smell of warm grass and wild lilac, she walked down the slope toward the dew pond a short distance away.

For the most part, Cordry was proving a cooperative enough student despite his obsession with his father's business. He remembered nothing of his ordeal at the looca-den a week ago, or of anything that had happened afterward, and might have thought it all a rather unfunny joke had Athaya not come to the house the following day to confirm his father's tale. He'd been confused, of course, to be so abruptly confronted with the idea that everything he'd been taught of magic was suddenly reversed, and that his father, for his own sake, was now a reluctant ally of the outlawed princess of Caithe. But when he truly understood that his choice was either to become a wizard, marry Megan, and go on with his life, or to succumb to his madness and be taken away for absolution, he didn't need long to think on it.

But while he hadn't refused their help, he hadn't exactly embraced it with open arms. In truth, he regarded it as little more than a nagging inconvenience. It had surprised Athaya to learn that none of his indifference had anything to do with the rightness or wrongness of magic itself—a topic that had rarely crossed his mind until recently—but that he simply found the manufacture of cloth far more fascinating a profession than that of wizardry. He saw few practical uses for witchlights and vision spheres, but knew perfectly well that people as far away as Selvallen would pay well and pay often for finely made cloth.

Kicking off her shoes, Athaya dipped her feet into the dew pond and watched the water ripple out toward the farthest edges. Her own magic had given her a direction for her life, a purpose she'd never had before. It had never occurred to her before now that someone else might have a strong enough direction already, thank you, and would regard his newly emerging powers as an unwanted encumbrance.

But it's only for a little while, Althaya thought, resigning herself to the situation. *Once he's trained, he never has to work another spell as long as he lives if he doesn't want to. It may be a waste of his gift, but at least he'll be alive to waste it.*

Shrugging off that gloomy thought, Athaya reclined on the warm grass and gazed at the little sheepfold-turned-magic-school, smiling her amazement at how quickly Ranulf and Kale had rethatched the roof and plugged the gaping holes in the walls with mud and straw. So far, however, Cordry was the only student the school had, but while she and Tonia shouldered the task of their lone pupil's training, Ranulf, Mason, and Kale filled their days by circulating through the city and planting carefully worded rumors about a band of wizards teaching magic in the countryside, in the hope that there might be a handful—or even one—soul desperate enough to seek them out. Athaya suspected

that most of these rumors were planted in Kaiburn's numerous
alehouses—an excuse for the men to take care of business and
enjoy a few mugs at the same time—but she knew that such a
place was the most fertile ground for a rumor if one wanted it
to spread quickly. As for Cameron, he had left them to pay a
brief visit to his family in Leaforth, with instructions to find out
if there were any Lorngeld in the village who could be brought
back to the sheepfold for training.

Not a bad bit of progress for such a short time, Athaya thought,
all the while aware that not all of her plans for Caithe were going
quite so smoothly. Her meeting with Jarvis the week before had
shown one thing to her quite clearly. It was too early even to
consider approaching her father's former allies to ask for their
support in her cause. Judging from the harsh reception Jarvis
had given her, she doubted that anyone without the pressing
need of saving his only child would accept her presence in Caithe
so easily. And those who had been Kelwyn's closest friends
would likely be more resentful than Jarvis had been, perhaps
going so far as to turn her in to the king. Later, once she could
prove to them that her crusade had a prayer for success, they
might have more reason to listen. She chafed at the delay, but
knew that acting prematurely might damage her cause more than
serve it; she had watched Kelwyn plan enough battles in her
youth to know that waiting was sometimes the proper course to
take.

A subtle movement caught the corner of her eye, and she
shaded her eyes and scanned the horizon, her gaze focusing on
a small patch of darkness in the distance. At first it looked like
the mere shadow of a cloud, dark and moving steadily toward
her, but the sun was nowhere near the clouds just now, and the
shape was still there.

Then she saw the glint of metal.

"I don't like the looks of this," she said aloud, scrambling
to her feet and hastily shaking the grass from her skirt.

Within minutes, the dark shape revealed itself as a dozen
rough-looking men trudging up the slope. Several of them carried torches and some brandished weapons—pikes, longbows,
and evil-looking hunting knives. The silhouette of one man,
slightly hunched over as he scuttled through the long grass, was
unpleasantly familiar to her.

She rushed to the door of the sheepfold, her abrupt arrival

startling Cordry out of the witchlight he was forming. "We've got visitors," she announced breathlessly, "and they're not friendly. Tonia, I might need you."

Curious, Megan peered through a small gap in the wall. "It's Gilbert Ames! He must have followed me here from the city."

"Why is he causing us so much trouble?" Athaya muttered angrily. "I thought he was a friend of Sir Jarvis."

"He's a bitter old man, that's what he is," Megan spat out, as angry with Gilbert for following her as she was at herself for having allowed it. "Sir Jarvis told me that Gilbert's wife was absolved almost thirty years ago, and ever since then he's gotten a sick kind of pleasure watching others go through the same agony he did—as if it somehow makes him feel less alone. He goes to all the absolution ceremonies at the cathedral—ghoulish, isn't it?—no matter whether he knew the poor soul or not. It must be killing him to know that Sir Jarvis and I are finding a way to save Cordry when nobody saved his wife."

Athaya turned to Cordry. "Stay inside and keep Megan with you. I don't want Gilbert to see either one of you here."

Leaving them behind, Tonia followed Athaya down the slope, setting her hands defiantly on her hips as she squinted at the unruly pack of men bearing down on them. Most of them were ill-shaven and shabbily dressed, and several announced their presence with an assortment of colorful curses and insults.

"Friends of yours?" Tonia asked dryly.

"That's the man I told you about," Athaya replied, pointing to the leader. "I just hope he hasn't got any corbal crystals this time. With Cam gone and Kale in the city, Megan's the only one here who's safe. She may be strong-willed, but she certainly can't fight off a dozen men."

"Let's not worry too much about corbals. Do you seriously think the Church would give their precious gems to a bunch of ruffians like that? They look more the type who'd sell the jewels for beer money, not chase off wizards with them."

Athaya wanted to believe her, but it didn't serve to lessen her fears as the men crept forward. They stopped as soon as they came within longbow range, keeping their arrows nocked and their knives firmly in hand. One or two of them glanced nervously up at the sky from time to time, as if afraid the wizards would drop something hideous on their heads the moment they let down their guard.

Gilbert stepped forward arrogantly and waved his torch from side to side as if he were trying to frighten rats away. "Mind-plagued wizards!" he shouted, full of bluster. "Go back to hell where you came from!"

His words were punctuated by a chorus of grumbling from his cohorts. One of the bulkier men looked as if he might lurch ahead and attack the two women with his knife, but another held him back, whispering caution in his ear.

"What do you want here?" Athaya called out. She held her hands out in a gesture of supplication. "We mean you no harm. And you have us at a great disadvantage. We are but two women, defenseless—"

"Defenseless, my arse," Tonia muttered.

"Your lies won't work on us!" cried a balding man of middle years. "The Devil is the master of lies—we'll believe nothing his kind say!"

The men grumbled louder and took a few tentative steps up the slope. Athaya did not want to use an unnecessary show of magic to scare them off, but the gritted teeth and hate-filled eyes of her attackers convinced her that verbal threats would not be enough. Moving as one, the men inched forward, closing in for the kill. And worse, two of the men had sharp, steel-tipped arrows leveled directly at her heart.

Faintly, she heard the taut snap of a bowstring.

Drawing in a sharp breath, Athaya threw her hands up and cast a shielding spell. The arrow, which would have pierced her cleanly through the chest, disintegrated into a shower of blue sparks as it struck the enchanted air in front of her. Ashes and burned fletching spiraled to the ground, settling harmlessly in the grass at her feet.

"You can't defeat us," she said, hoping to break their confidence, "and we don't want to fight. Go away and leave us in peace."

"No peace for the Devil's brood!" one man cried. With a howl of assent, the bowmen unleashed a flurry of deadly arrows, all of them well aimed. But like the first, each shattered against the shields that Athaya and Tonia held rigidly in front of them.

All right, Athaya resolved, staring at the pile of charred arrows on the grass before her. *We tried reason. Now all that's left are threats . . .*

She pitched her voice lower, like Kelwyn in one of his quiet rages, and little of her anger was feigned. "I can make you leave if I have to. Don't force me to do something we'll all regret."

"We aren't afeared of your spells, witch!" Gilbert shot back. "We have God on *our* side!"

Tonia grunted with disgust. "That's what they all say," she muttered, "right before they go out and rip each other to pieces for His glory."

Just then, Athaya saw a brilliant flare of light soar over her head, far out of range of her shield. The arrow was wrapped in pitch-streaked rags and set ablaze, and it flew in a graceful arc directly toward the sheepfold. The moment it touched the dry thatch, the roof erupted in a flare of brilliant orange.

Athaya heard a high-pitched scream and an instant later, Cordry and Megan rushed out of the building waving away clouds of black smoke.

"There he is! I told you Jarvis' son was one of them!" Gilbert shrieked with glee. "And the Loring girl is with him!"

The sight of their quarry and of the fire devouring the sheepfold roof gave the men a rush of confidence. Raising their weapons, they let out a series of battle cries and charged up the slope for the final onslaught.

Athaya was quick to realize that this situation called for much more than a simple shielding spell. She needed a more substantial defense. She didn't want to hurt her attackers—such an act would only prove to them that wizards were as bad as everyone said—but she had to come up with something impressive enough to convince them to leave her alone.

No careless mistakes this time, Master Hedric, she whispered to the air, and then, throwing her head back, Athaya raised her hands and closed her eyes, fixing her mind on every detail she'd ever learned about casting weather-spells. *"Erumpat caelum!"* she cried, using all the strength at her command to break open the heavens and call down as much thunder, lightning, and rain as God would give her.

Hedric would have been proud. The results were awesome and quick, and even Tonia looked mildly surprised. Black clouds billowed out of nowhere at Athaya's command, and a sheet of rain, hard and blinding, seared the sky. The attackers' torches sputtered and died, and they couldn't brush the water from their eyes fast enough to see where they were running. The ground rapidly turned to mud, and many of the men slipped into the thick brown pools while deafening bursts of thunder harried their ears, warning them away. At least half turned and fled at the first streak of lightning that scorched the ground, needing no further demonstrations of a wizard's power, but for those who stubbornly remained, Athaya continued to send down slender needles of white lightning, commanding them to strike just close enough to serve as fair warning.

"Leave us alone!" she shouted over the simmering thunder. "Leave us alone or I'll send another bolt of lightning right where you'll remember it!"

Beside her, Athaya heard Tonia choke on her laughter. "That wasn't the most regal threat I ever heard, but at least they're giving up."

Athaya let one last bolt strike the ground to drive her threat home. The scarred patch of earth that resulted convinced the ragtag band of men that they were definitely in over their heads. With their torches gutted, their bowstrings wet, and their footing precarious, they had no recourse but to retreat. Without a second glance at their leader, the men turned on their heels and bolted for the relative safety of Kaiburn, slipping and stumbling along the way.

"*Cowards!*" Gilbert screeched at their retreating backs, stamping his foot in the mud like an angry child. "Cowards, every last scurvy one of you!"

He wheeled around to face Athaya as if he might try to finish her off himself, but it didn't take long for him to realize that he was not only outnumbered, but vastly outmatched. Spitting out a curse, he stumbled away over the soggy grassland, flinging insults and shaking his fist futilely against her.

Only when he was well out of sight did Athaya disperse the tempest. With unnatural haste, the clouds rolled away to reveal placid blue sky and sunshine. Athaya shivered under the warm rays, brooding that her attackers weren't the only ones to have been soaked to the bone by the torrents of rain.

"A bit overdone, perhaps," Tonia remarked, squeezing the excess water out of her hair, "but at least it got rid o' the buggers."

"For now," Athaya replied, conscious that she was beginning to steam inside her wool dress. "But it should be awhile before they try again." Then she turned to Tonia with a wry grin. "You could have helped."

The Master only shrugged. "I would have. If you'd needed it."

Athaya and Tonia walked back toward the sheepfold to meet Cordry and Megan, who had been waiting safely out of range of the attackers' bows. After assuring herself that they had suffered nothing more than a rude surprise and a thorough dousing, Athaya examined the condition of the sheepfold. The smell of burned straw hung heavy in the air, but the damage was not that great. The rain had put out the flames before they spread to the timber framework, and only an ugly, blackened hole in the roof revealed that there had ever been a fire at all.

But Gilbert and his cronies had proven that the sheepfold was no place to be off their guard. Furthermore, the attack forced Athaya into making an important decision—one she hoped she wouldn't regret later.

She glanced at Cordry, his brown curls flatted by the rain. "I think you'd better stay at our camp from now on. It'll be much too dangerous for you in the city after today."

Cordry lifted his chin up in a show of courage. "I won't hide from the likes of Gilbert Ames. If he thinks I can do what you just did, then it should be enough to scare him into leaving me alone."

"Maybe. But will he do the same for Megan or your father?" Athaya countered. "He might very well accuse them both of sheltering you from absolution, and then they'll be in just as much danger as you are."

Megan saw Cordry about to protest and put a restraining hand on his arm. "Do as she says, my love. The princess is right—you'll be safer with her." Then she smiled, already starting to bubble with ideas. "Your father can claim you've run off and pretend to know nothing. And I can put on a fine show at having lost my betrothed to the Devil—I can even say I came here today to talk you out of learning your spells. In time, people will forget about you and find something new to gossip about. And later, once your lessons are over . . . well, then we can decide what to do."

"And where to go," Cordry added glumly, staring down at the sodden ground. "We'll have to start over in a new city, Meg. The minute Gilbert and the others start talking, everyone's suspicions about me will be confirmed. Even if no one can prove a thing, the scandal won't die away completely. I won't be able to take over my father's business—not if I don't want to bring it to ruin. And if we want to get married next month as we planned, we certainly won't be able to do it in Kaiburn Cathedral.''

Megan rolled her eyes, silently scolding him. "Cordry Jarvis, do you think I care two straws about that? Why, I'd marry you right here in this old sheepfold if I had to,'' she declared, giving him a quick kiss on the cheek to dispel his gloom. Then she pointed skyward and grinned. "But only after we fix the roof.''

That same afternoon, on a distant Reykan hillside lined with leafless trees only just beginning to bud, two riders followed the northbound thoroughfare that would carry them in another week's time into the remote shires of Ulard.

Ath Luaine was just a smallish blur in the distance now, still shrouded by the thin mist of a spring shower that had blown off in the early-morning hours. Since passing through the north gate an hour before, Jaren had reined in his chestnut mare and looked back at the capital several times, growing more pensive the farther away it grew, and knowing it would soon slip out of sight altogether. Not that he wasn't glad to be going home—it had been over a year since he'd seen any of his family besides his father—but the conditions of his visit disheartened him. It pained him deeply to leave Ath Luaine, as if doing so would snip the last slender thread that tied him to Athaya and cast him adrift to face his future alone.

"Looks as if it's clearing up,'' Brice remarked, aware that his young master had said nothing since leaving the city. "We'll have good road today once these puddles dry up.''

Jaren nodded sullenly, then smiled with embarrassment at his rudeness. Brice had been with his family as long as he could remember and was like a second father to all four of Lord Ian's sons. The man certainly deserved more than glum silence for his cheerful efforts at conversation.

"I'm sorry, Brice. I guess I'm not feeling very talkative today.'' Jarens' gaze wandered to the purplish crags off to the north. "I've had . . . something on my mind.''

"Something?'' the older man asked, stroking his stubbly beard, "or some*one*?''

Jaren didn't reply, but glanced sidelong at Brice as if trying to determine how much the man knew.

"It wasn't much of a secret how you felt about her,'' Brice

pointed out amiably. "Everyone knew that you and the princess were close friends."

"Close friends." Jaren laughed mirthlessly as he looked away. "That wasn't exactly what I had in mind."

"No, I suppose not," Brice said, sensing his master was in danger of slipping off into yet another period of silent despondency. "Maybe it isn't my place to say so, m'Lord, but I do know how you feel. I may be of an age with your father, but we old folks know what love can be like . . . and what it's like to feel you've lost it."

Jaren reached out for that simple dose of sympathy like a drowning man snatching at a piece of driftwood. "I thought she felt the same way about me, Brice. I thought we could spend the rest of our lives together. I thought—" He squeezed his eyes shut, shaking his head in futility. "I must have been crazy."

"Most wizards are, one time or another," his companion replied lightly. Brice guided his mount around a muddy slick in the road, then eased back to his master's side. "But just because a woman says she won't marry you doesn't mean she isn't in love with you. Trust a more experienced man to know."

Jaren stared at him incredulously. "She *refused* me, Brice. Flat out." His head drooped down against his chest. "She never even asked for time to think about it."

"Women are odd creatures, my boy, and royal ones are worse than most. I'll wager her refusal didn't have anything to do with whether she loves you or not."

Jaren made an impatient huffing noise. "That's nonsense."

"That's *women*."

Jaren was on the verge of saying something caustic when he suddenly jerked his head up. "Wait—how did you know I'd asked Athaya to marry me? I never told you about that. I never told anybody except Felgin and Nicolas. And Master Hedric, of course—he couldn't help noticing when Athaya and I suddenly began to avoid each other. But they all promised not to tell a soul."

Just then, Brice seem unnaturally preoccupied with guiding his horse around another mud slick, this one very small and hardly worth such meticulous attention. Jaren pulled back on his reins and stopped at the roadside, silently refusing to go another step unless his question got an answer.

"Brice, answer me."

The older man shifted uncomfortably in his saddle. "I . . . must have heard it said, that's all."

"From whom?" Jaren demanded, more despairing than angry. "Brice, you've got to tell me. If this is all over the palace, then I'm never going to be able to show my face—"

"Don't worry, m'Lord," Brice assured him at last. "It's a well-kept secret."

"Then who *told* you?"

Brice let out the wisp of a sigh, unable to see his Lord's son suffer any longer. "I heard it from your father."

That piece of information did nothing to alleviate Jaren's confusion. "I told Father I was going to ask her, but I never told him that I *did*. Especially after the answer I got—he would have said 'I told you so' a dozen times." Jaren eyed his father's manservant steadily, sure that he held the last piece to his puzzle. "Brice, you're hiding something. You've got that same sheepish look on your face as when I was a boy and you'd tell me we were going riding when you were really fetching me in for a bath." He drummed his fingers impatiently on his thigh. "Who told my father about the proposal?"

With an air of resignation, Brice cleared his throat like a herald about to announce an unwelcome visitor. "Princess Athaya told him herself. She came to see your father shortly before she left. To talk about you. They only want what's best for you, m'Lord," he added hastily. "You have to believe that."

Slowly, like a vision sphere coming into focus, Jaren began to understand. "That's why he said all those things about seeing the family again before I go back to Caithe. But he never planned on my going back, did he?" Jaren asked, his suspicions mounting. "He was going to try and keep me there, wasn't he? All that talk about Claire being home . . ."

"Don't be upset with him, m'Lord. It's only because he loves you."

Then Jaren rolled his eyes and sighed deeply, more exasperated than angry with his father. "Oh, I know that. Funny way he has of showing it, though."

"It wasn't all his idea, m'Lord. Princess Athaya asked him to persuade you to come home. She knew you'd be safer here than in Caithe and thought since you wouldn't listen to her, you might listen to him."

"So that's why she wouldn't let me go with her . . . why she didn't say yes . . .'' Suddenly, instead of being glum, a fire kindled behind his eyes. He broke out into a giddy smile, and even though it was still cloudy, he could have sworn the land was brighter than it had been a moment before.

"It's not that she doesn't care about me, Brice," he said, talking to himself more than to his servant, "it's all because she has some fool notion that I'll fall right into a pit of trouble the moment I set foot across the border."

Jaren swung his mare around, gazing back toward the south. In a few hours he could be back in the capital. Collect his things . . . tell Felgin and Prince Nicolas where he was going. And a fortnight later he could be in Caithe. He already knew she was heading for Kaiburn—certainly a city that size couldn't be hard to find, even without a map . . .

Brice seemed to sense the train of his master's thoughts, and his expression turned grave. "You promised, m'Lord. Your family is expecting you."

"Oh, I'll go," he said, reluctantly dismantling his castle in the air. "I'll keep my word." He turned and fixed his gaze directly on Brice. "But once I've spent a decent amount of time there, I'm packing up and going to Caithe. No matter what my father says. Better yet," he added, reconsidering, "maybe I just won't tell him."

"He won't like that."

"I know. But one of these days he's got to learn that his youngest son is twenty-six years old, not six or sixteen. I can take care of myself. I've gone to Caithe on my own before and I can do it again."

"You weren't a wanted man, then," Brice pointed out.

"They'll have to catch me first."

"They've done that once already."

Jaren brushed off that observation with an irritable wave of his hand. "Brice, stop being logical, will you? Besides, there's more to it than just that." He griped the reins tight, as if something inside was ready to burst. "My father just doesn't understand what it's like to feel you've never really worked for anything important. He was in the army—he had a chance to prove himself. But I never have. I've been given everything, and it's all come too easily. I even got my position with Hedric because the king owed my father a favor. But this! What Athaya's doing . . .''

He shook his head, almost at a loss for words. "God, I want to *work* for that and see it succeed."

Brice nodded, reluctantly captivated by his master's surge of idealism.

"But won't she be angry?" he asked a moment later.

"Athaya? Oh, I expect so," Jaren replied, cringing—with private delight—at the thought of what sort of reception might await him in Caithe. "But after she's yelled at me for a while, she'll have to realize that I have no intention of letting her slip away. Maybe then she'll give up all her fool ideas about protecting me and agree to be my wife."

Brice smiled broadly. "I hope it works out like that, m'Lord. Truly I do."

Somewhat reluctantly, Jaren snapped the reins and urged his horse on toward the north. But before he'd gone twenty yards, he stole another glance behind him, gazing over the heads of the other travelers in their wake, over the spires of Glendol, and farther yet, over the edge of the horizon, pretending that he could reach across the sea and glimpse the eastern shore of Caithe.

CHAPTER 13

✳✳

T HE RUMORS THAT RANULF AND THE OTHERS HAD CIR-
culated through Kaiburn bore fruit the following week,
bringing a second student to the sheepfold—a brown-
eyed, brown-skinned woman named Gilda who reminded Athaya
of nothing so much as a frightened doe. She spoke only rarely,
constantly scanning her surroundings for signs of danger. Athaya
went out of her way to be kind, but Gilda always appeared distressed and distracted, as if she was still undecided on whether
learning to use her magic was preferable to death by absolution.

On a humid afternoon in mid-April, while Mason was tempting Cordry with the illusion spells he would be taught if only he
would master his rudimentary spells, Athaya went to join Gilda,
who was sitting apart from the others in a patch of sun-warmed
dandelions. She approached cautiously, recalling how horrified
Gilda had been when introduced to the central figure in the tales
of King Kelwyn's demise. It had taken all the good grace and
patience Athaya could muster to persuade the girl gradually that
she was not about to be the princess' next victim, but Gilda still
tended to be exceedingly wary in her presence.

"You've been practicing your witchlight for quite a while,"
Athaya remarked, offering a friendly smile. "Tired yet?"

Shoulders sagging, Gilda avoided meeting her gaze. "A little." Keeping her head bowed, she plucked a dandelion from

the ground and rubbed it between her fingers until the skin turned yellow.

"You're making good progress," Athaya said, knowing that Gilda wasn't going to say a word to her without being prodded. "Don't tell Cordry I said this, but you're picking up your spells much faster than he is. Your gift runs strong."

Athaya hoped to earn at least an embarrassed smile from that, but the compliment only served to make Gilda more uncomfortable, and it looked as if she was about to cry.

"How much longer do I have?" she asked, speaking so quietly that the gentle breeze threatened to carry her words away.

Frowning, Athaya sat down cross-legged at Gilda's side. "You sound as if you're asking how many days you have to live. I assure you, the *mekahn* isn't fatal when it's detected in time, and you came to us early enough. A few more weeks and you'll be completely out of danger."

Gilda nodded slowly, but didn't look nearly as pleased with the news as she should have been. She squirmed as if she were sitting on a sharp pebble and plucked another dandelion, tearing the yellow bloom to shreds.

"What's troubling you? I can't help but notice how quiet and anxious you are when you're here. Are you afraid—"

"I'm not afraid of anything," Gilda retorted, with more force than Athaya had thought her capable of. Her oval face was set rigidly, convincing Athaya that her words were no mere show of strength.

In a vivid flash of insight, Athaya saw Gilda's behavior in an entirely different light. Just then, the girl didn't look frightened at all, but revolted. A mute, hidden revulsion that drained all the vibrancy from her face. Athaya had seen the look before at court—on the faces of men forced to exchange courtesies with those they despised—and suddenly wondered if it was the same for Gilda, tolerating something she found wholly repulsive because the fear of dying was just too great.

"Why did you come here, Gilda?"

For the first time, Gilda turned and held Athaya's gaze directly. "Because I had to. Not because I wanted to."

It wasn't the answer Athaya wanted to hear, but at least it was honest. "I can understand that . . . the idea of absolution—"

"It's not me I care about," Gilda cut in, affronted. A spark of anger flared in those brown doe's eyes. "I'd have accepted absolution if it wasn't . . . for this." She put her hand across her belly, stroking herself gently. "This child . . . it's my first. I want to give my husband a son."

Athaya stared blankly for a few seconds. That thought had never crossed her mind. Gilda couldn't be very far along—her belly was still flat and firm. But her concerns were very real. If she had ignored the symptoms of her magic, it would have been inevitable that the *mekahn*—or the Church—would have taken her before she could deliver the child.

"If I let them take me, that means they take my baby, too," Gilda went on, furiously tearing apart another dandelion. "If I have to learn magic to save my life, then I will. I can't bear to let my baby die because of my curse. But I'll never use the spells you're teaching me," she added defiantly. "I swear I never will. They're wrong and unnatural."

It was the lengthiest speech Gilda had ever made, and the contents of it affected Athaya to no small extent. No wonder Gilda was so wretched! She didn't believe in what she was doing, but was actively sacrificing her soul—or so she thought—to give her child life.

"Does your husband know you're here?"

"No," she answered quickly, "and I won't tell him. I won't give him cause to hate me. I kept all the signs secret . . . told him my forgetfulness was because of a physic the doctor gave me, and blamed my moods on the baby. Far as he knows, I'm just pregnant, not some crazy wizard."

Athaya sat still for several minutes as she pondered Gilda's words. She could hardly fault Gilda for not confiding in her husband when not a year ago she had avoided telling Tyler about her own powers for roughly the same reasons. The thought of losing him hadn't been worth the risk.

You're asking them to risk things you're not willing to, Athaya. Oh, be quiet, Nicolas. Who asked you, anyway?

"Magic can be used for many things, Gilda. I know you've been taught it's evil, but—" Athaya struggled to think of an example she could relate to. "But what about that witchlight I saw you working with? Essentially, it's little more than a lamp. Would it be so wrong to, say, leave one near your baby's cradle so he wouldn't be afraid of the dark?"

The bewildered suspicion that settled over Gilda's face gave Athaya a hint of encouragement. "You're the one who's ultimately going to determine whether your power is evil or not. You, and no one else. God gave us free will to apply to our magic as well as our other actions, but it's up to us to make the right choices.''

She left Gilda alone to work through her thoughts, but she departed with a queer feeling of uneasiness. Like Cordry, Gilda apparently had no intentions of pursuing the art of magic once its life-threatening stage was past. They would be safe enough that way, of course—no one need ever know what they were unless they came too near a corbal crystal. Athaya frowned as she considered how many others would likely come to them seeking out the knowledge of magic only to save themselves— or their unborn children—only to forsake their powers later and persist in despising their own kind.

As she was pondering the matter, she caught sight of Ranulf, Mason, and Kale returning from their day in the city. Almost instantly, Athaya knew that something had happened that troubled Mason deeply. The dom lagged far behind the others, and instead of his rigid posture and smooth gait, he plodded up the slope with head bowed and shoulders sagging, too immersed in thought to pay much attention to where he was going. Once, he absently stepped on the hem of his robe and tumbled headfirst into the grass, but quickly righted himself and pressed on, the incident instantly forgotten.

As Ranulf passed by on his way to the sheepfold, Athaya stayed him with a gesture and motioned back to Mason. "What's the matter with him?"

"He's daft, as usual," Ranulf remarked, rarely forsaking a chance to cast a barb at the dom. "But for once he's got a reason." He opened his mouth to say something more, then shook his head and continued up the slope. "I think he'd rather tell you about it himself, though."

While Kale trailed after Ranulf in search of the wineskins usually stored in the sheepfold, the dom slowly made his way to Athaya's side. Lifting his head at last, he regarded her with reticence, as if about to confess that he had misplaced one of her most priceless possessions.

"I have some news for you."

"That's an understatement if I ever heard one," Athaya said, having never seen him so distracted before. "It's bad news, I take it."

Mason straightened up a bit just then, surprised by her inference. "Oh, no, it's good. Quite good. Depending on how you look at it, I suppose." He bent down to pluck a stalk of grass and began meticulously shredding it lengthwise as he spoke. "When we were passing by the cathedral a week or so ago, Ranulf and I saw some glaziers replacing one of the transept windows. It reminded Ranulf of something he'd heard from that priest you encountered at the Jarvis house—something about windows breaking there all the time nowadays. Well, there's magic involved in it, all right."

Athaya's eyes glowed in anticipation, but the tutor merely frowned and discarded the shredded bits of grass. "I don't know how many hours I've spent just sitting in Kaiburn Cathedral waiting for something to happen. And from what you told us about those corbal relics, I had to be careful. It took some time, but while I was sitting there today, a pane of glass in one of the nave windows just shattered—and nobody so much as breathed on it."

There was a lull of silence, as if he was trying to see just how agitated he could get her before getting to his point. It worked remarkably well.

"And?" Athaya blurted out eagerly.

"And I've found another wizard," he said. "I touched his mind briefly, and it appears that he has a good deal of potential. Not an adept like you, but highly gifted." His eyes brightened briefly as he spoke, but the stubborn veil of apprehension quickly returned to shroud them.

But Athaya paid no mind to his unspoken concerns. With only two students in her care thus far, news of another—especially one with talent—was welcome indeed. "Mason, that's wonderful! Where is he? Did you tell him about the school?"

"N-no. I haven't approached him yet. I wanted to ask you—"

"What? Didn't you even find out who he was?"

Mason drew in a steadying breath. "Oh, yes," he replied with a disquieted air. "I found out."

Athaya cut off her next question, conscious of an acute pang of foreboding. The Dom was acting far too peculiar to ascribe it to mere absentmindedness. What was wrong with the man he had found?

"I know who he is," Mason explained, "but . . . there's a

slight catch." The dom pulled self-consciously at his sleeves as if he were reconsidering whether his news was altogether good or not. "His name is Aldus Moncarion. *Father* Aldus Moncarion. And he's Bishop Lukin's new secretary."

Athaya's eyes opened a little wider, but she didn't say a word. Her first instinct was to laugh, thinking that Mason had to be joking, but then she realized that while Ranulf might pull such a prank, the dom never would. He anxiously waited for a response to his news, but when it became clear that she was still too stunned to offer one, he went ahead and finished his tale.

"Aldus was assigned to the bishop's staff six months ago, right after his ordination. From what I've been able to gather, he's good. *Very* good. One of the other priests told me he was being groomed for high office—he's solidly grounded in theology, a fine speaker, and he's only twenty-five, which says enough for his learning since most men never leave the diaconate until they're over thirty. But twenty-five is fairly old to be approaching the *mekahn*. That could either mean he'll pick up his spells remarkably well, or that his power will be that much harder to channel."

Athaya closed her eyes and let out an exasperated sigh. "A *priest*?" she exclaimed, arms falling weakly to her sides. "That's more than a slight catch, Mason. How can we possibly convince a priest not to go through with absolution?"

"We have time yet," Mason told her. "He's barely begun his *mekahn*, so it could be weeks before the more serious symptoms show up. In the meantime, we can try to convince him that he's been called by God in more than one way."

"A priest," Athaya repeated, still disbelieving.

Mason smiled for the first time, trying to encourage her. "You wanted to spread the word that magic is divine, your Highness. Now's your chance to test your preaching skills on a professional."

"Thanks," she said dryly, raising an eyebrow. "That's *just* what I needed to hear."

"That's him," Mason said the next afternoon, tugging on her sleeve as he and Athaya stepped through the west doors of Kaiburn Cathedral. "The one talking to that old woman."

The sky was overcast, making the sanctuary markedly dim, lighted only by candelabras set near thick pillars running the length of the nave. As it was several hours until evensong, the cathedral was almost deserted, and only a few scattered people lingered in the sanctuary offering silent prayers or meditating. In the last pew, a young man in a black cassock sat with his hands folded over those of a weeping woman, her wrinkled face partially hidden by a tattered gray scarf. From time to time he would reach out and touch her cheek in a sincere gesture of reassurance. Once, Aldus turned his face toward Athaya, displaying fair, sculpted features framed by dark brown locks and large, warm eyes that shone as if they had once beheld the glory of God in all His splendor and never lost the wonder of it.

Athaya shrugged off her lightweight cloak, still damp from the light shower they'd had earlier, and handed it to Mason. "Why don't you wait outside. No sense making him feel as if we're ganging up on him."

"I'll be right outside if you need me."

Once he was gone, Athaya settled down on a pew across the aisle from Father Aldus and the old woman, trying to keep her wet shoes from squeaking on the tiles as she walked. Faintly, on the edges of her mind, she sensed the itch of the corbal crystal embedded in the candlestick on the high altar, but it was far enough from the rear of the nave to serve as little more than a minor irritant. Athaya bowed her head and folded her hands together, pretending to be at prayer while she listened to the priest and the woman speak.

"I can't go on without him, Father," the woman was saying, her voice broken with sobs. "We were married over forty years. I don't know how to live alone."

"You're never alone, dear lady. Not when you have God watching over you. And perhaps instead of grieving, you can rejoice in the knowledge that your husband is in heaven with our Lord. Just think of that!" he said, his voice swelling with rapture. "And you'll see him again one day, and live together in the presence of the Almighty forever."

The woman dabbed at her eyes with the corner of her shawl. "I want to believe you, Father. But how can you be so sure? How can you *know*?"

"I know it in my heart," Aldus said simply. "The same way I know that the rains don't last forever and that the sun always comes out again."

"But why should I wait?" the old woman groaned. "What's left for me here? I'd die today if I could be with him again."

"Death is a natural part of life and we should not fear it. But neither should we wish for it before our time." Aldus took her fragile hand and squeezed it gently. "Never give up on life, good woman. It's too precious of a gift."

The woman still looked sadly unconvinced, so Aldus continued, undiscouraged. "You feel pain now, I know. As if nothing in all the world can soothe you. But try not to be daunted by the burdens of living. Sorrow is a part of life, and without it we might never appreciate the joy. Dear lady," he added softly, "would you rather have never loved him at all?"

"Oh no!" the woman cried, stricken. "No, Father! It just hurts so much . . . so much . . ."

Athaya looked up from her pretended prayers, suddenly afraid. *And what do you want to have when you're old, Athaya? Memories of ones you have loved and shared joy with, or the cold reassurance that you have no one, and nothing to grieve for?*

She lowered her head again, wrenching her attentions back to the priest's words. "You have every right to grieve," Aldus was saying in conclusion, "but God will give you the strength to endure if you let Him. He must have some purpose for taking your husband before you. Trust Him, and perhaps He will reveal His plans to you in time."

Strengthened by new hopes, the woman embraced the young priest. She thanked him and shuffled away, her eyes no longer red with tears, and Aldus offered her a blessing as she went on her way.

To Athaya's surprise, however, the priest's quiet confidence faded away the moment the woman was gone. Slumping back down in the pew, he covered his face with his palms as if the discussion had thoroughly drained him. When he let his hands fall to his lap, he looked profoundly sad. Then he glanced back at the door through which the woman had gone, and his sadness changed to agitation, as if he desperately wanted to call her back and tell her that he was sorry, so very sorry—that he'd made a mistake and it had all been a lie to make her feel better, nothing more. But he didn't call out. He just remained where he was, staring at the assemblage of statues on the choir screen as if begging their assurance that he'd done the right thing.

"Father Aldus?"

Aldus snapped his head around quickly. He'd never noticed that Athaya was there.

"Yes?" He creased his brow slightly, questioning, but not unkind. "Do I know you?"

"I was watching you comfort that old woman," she went on, brushing his question aside. She crossed the aisle and sat down beside him on the pew. "With a few words, you gave her hope she never had before. You have a great gift, Father. More of one than you realize," she added, all too aware of the double meaning behind her words.

"I'm glad you think so, miss. Although . . ." His voice trailed off and he shook his head, unsure whether he should speak his mind.

"Please tell me," Athaya urged gently. "You seem the one in need of counsel now. I'm no priest, but I've an ear to listen."

"I think listening is all anyone can do for me at the moment," he said, suddenly glum. "I'm afraid this is a problem I have to deal with myself."

"Is it about that woman you were talking to?"

He turned his head, and the candlelight made a subtle halo on his hair. "No. Not directly. It's just that—" Aldus gazed up at the vaulted ceiling far above them, and his expression became melancholy again. "I want to inspire people. To make them feel God's presence as much as I do. But sometimes I wonder what right I have to ask people not to doubt things that I doubt myself."

Athaya held in a smile. *You're hardly the first with that problem, my friend.* She looked around her at the gilded statues, magnificent arches, and spectacular rose window above the altar and wondered, as she sometime did, if the beauty of this or any church was a product of heavenly inspiration, or merely a hollow shell—a divine monument to a human myth.

"Are you saying that you doubt God's existence?"

"Oh no!" he countered quickly. "Never that. I'm more sure of that than of anything in my life." His words sang with conviction, but the brief spark of energy was short-lived. "But I told that woman not to fear death. There's the contradiction. When I think of dying, it frightens me. And that makes me feel like a charlatan. I've never doubted my calling to the Church. Never. And it's still the only thing I've ever wanted to do. But I also want to be able to believe everything I ask others to believe. And lately I just can't seem to do that."

"I think you're far too young to worry about dying," Athaya remarked. Then she paused, choosing her next words carefully. "The only people our age who worry so much about death are those afraid they might be wizards. Those that might have to be absolved before they've gotten much of a chance to live."

Athaya saw her mark hit home. Aldus avoided her gaze, but she could see each muscle in his throat grow taut. His breath began to quicken, but he made no response to her comment.

"I've heard talk of wizards outside the city," she went on, idly running her fingers over the edge of the pew in front of her. "So many rumors . . ."

"They're more than just rumors," Aldus said worriedly, making a protective sign over his heart. "The wizards really exist. A band of men tried to chase them off a few days back, but were driven away by sorcery."

Athaya fixed her gaze on him. "What if you turned out to be one?" she said, quick and direct.

"Impossible." His reply was much more abrupt than was necessary. "I'm too old. And I've dedicated my life to God. The Devil has no hold on me."

"The Devil has nothing to do with it," she countered smoothly, "not according to them. They say that magic is from God. That it's a divine gift." Athaya didn't give him a chance to refute her, but pressed ahead before he had much time to think. "You've been confused lately, haven't you, Aldus? You feel moody—happy one day and miserable the next. You feel as if you're losing control of yourself. You break things a lot—like windows—without knowing how it happened. And I'll bet that candlestick on the high altar gives you headaches if you stand too close to it—"

"Stop!" he burst out, springing to his feet. He tried to make his fear look like anger, but his attempt failed miserably. "Stop saying things like that!"

"Why? Because they're true and they frighten you?"

"Who *are* you?" he demanded. "What do you want from me?"

Athaya stood up and rested her hand on his arm, but he recoiled as if her touch carried pestilence. Briefly, she touched his mind, confirming his potential. Although his paths had barely begun to form, she could sense the power building inside of them, just waiting to mature and blossom.

"Come with me, Aldus. Let me show you how gifted you really are. You've been called by God not once, but twice. And what He's given you is wonderful—"

Aldus was in such turmoil that it never occurred to him to flee. He stayed rooted to the spot, too terrified to move. His hands were shaking wildly as he gripped the back of the pew for support, and the color drained from his face so quickly that Athaya feared he might faint.

"Father Aldus, are you back there?"

The baritone voice that echoed down the nave sounded so much like the summons of God Himself that Aldus nearly jumped out of his sandals. He wiped the moisture from his forehead, babbling a prayer of thanks for the timely interruption.

"Y-yes," he squeaked out. "Right here, my Lord Bishop."

My Lord Bishop? Athaya instinctively drew back a step. *Oh, not here. Not now!*

The clatter of brisk footsteps grew closer. The bishop would be upon them in seconds, just after he passed by the next row of pillars. There was no time to run, but Athaya could not let him see her. As a member of the Curia, Bishop Lukin had spent several weeks at Delfarham last summer listening to—and soundly censuring—Kelwyn's speeches regarding the Lorngeld, and would surely recognize her on sight.

So, the moment Aldus turned aside to greet his bishop, Athaya shrouded herself under a cloaking spell, rendering herself all but invisible except for a hazy reflection on the polished marble tiles. If his gift was strong enough, Aldus might be able to detect her presence—the space before him might seem to shimmer, like the air above a candle—but if she were still and quiet, he would think it merely a trick of the light in the shadowy sanctuary.

She had barely faded from sight when Bishop Lukin strode regally into it.

At forty-five, Jon Lukin was one of Caithe's younger bishops, with jet-black hair just turning to silver on the edges. He was tall and muscular and could easily have wrestled a man ten years younger to the ground. He walked briskly, every step filled with purpose. The first time Athaya met him, she thought him a man who should by all rights have taken up the profession of arms rather than the cloth. When Archbishop Ventan had invited him to conduct services during his visit to Delfarham, Athaya had been unpleasantly struck by Lukin's loud, clipped voice, as if he sought to wrest the ear of God away from wherever it happened to be at the moment and bend it to his will. If one thing could be said about him, Athaya mused, it was that no one could possibly doze off during one of his fiery sermons.

"Ah, there you are, Aldus. I've been looking for—Lord, man, you're pale! Are you ill?"

The priest made a quick bow of submission to his superior. "No. I . . . it's this woman, she—"

The moment Aldus turned around, he began to sputter. "But she was right here—just a second ago. I *saw* her. She was standing right . . . there."

Bishop Lukin frowned deeply. "Who?"

Athaya held her breath as Aldus stared directly at her, and through her, squinting slightly before he rubbed his eyes as if his vision were blurring.

"A demon," Aldus mumbled distractedly, "it had to be! All that talk of magic—"

"Father Aldus, what the Devil are you babbling about?"

Aldus choked back a strangled cry. "The Devil! Oh, my Lord Bishop, we are in danger here!"

The rest of the story came out in a jumbled rush, but Aldus managed to convey the essence of it to the bishop. As Aldus spoke, Athaya watched the changes that came over Lukin's face of doubt, disbelief, and than a real, growing interest as he began to connect all the rumors of wizards in his city to the priest's bizarre tale.

But to Athaya's dismay, one piece of information seemed to be of special interest to him.

"Wait—go back. What did this 'demon' look like again?"

Aldus gave him a cursory sketch, and the bishop nodded slowly, fingers caressing his chin. "I think I've met this demon of yours," he muttered under his breath, a cold glint in his eye.

"I beg your—"

"Nothing," Lukin said shortly. "But I think you are right, my friend. This is indeed proof that the Devil is at work in Kaiburn. His children lurk in the countryside, and now he sends demons to tempt the priests of God."

"She wanted me to follow her, but I wouldn't. I—"

"You did well, Aldus," the bishop replied, curtailing the priest's explanations. "And you've had quite a shock. I think you'd best go lie down for a while. I'll have Father Greste assist me at evensong tonight."

Aldus was more than grateful to be dismissed. "Thank you, my Lord Bishop." He hurried out of the place of his temptation as fast as his legs could carry him, and Athaya had to jump back to keep him from careening straight into her.

After a few minutes of intense thought, Bishop Lukin strode up the aisle toward an elderly man polishing the gilt trim around the base of the choir screen. Athaya trailed behind him, unseen. Once, her wet shoes made a loud squeak, and Lukin whipped around, vigilant as a castle guard, but when he saw nothing, he muttered something and turned away. Athaya slipped out of her shoes and followed him.

"Father, attend me," the bishop ordered. "I must write an urgent letter to the king, and my secretary is unwell."

The elderly man dropped his polishing cloth and scurried to the bishop's side, his sandals clapping loudly on the floor. "Is something wrong, my Lord Bishop?"

"Oh, no, my friend. Quite the contrary," Lukin said, chuckling darkly. He smiled with grim pleasure, revealing teeth so white and sharp that it seemed he ate the bones along with his meat to keep them so. "You will, of course, keep this to yourself, but I think that I have just located his Majesty's elusive sister."

He paused as a good preacher will to let his words have their intended effect. "And if she is returned to him, the king should prove most generous in his gratitude. Come, we must hurry. My letter must reach the king in all due haste."

The bishop stalked away in a cloud of black robes with the elderly priest trailing excitedly in his wake. Although she was still under the protection of her magic cloak, Athaya was wary as she fled the sanctuary, half expecting Durek's guards to materialize out of thin air and seize her. But while it was only a morbid fancy at the moment, Athaya realized it wouldn't be long before she was forced to confront whatever royal troops Lukin was summoning, or worse, the king himself.

A week after leaving Ath Luaine, Jaren and Brice turned off the well-traveled thoroughfare onto the remote, winding road that would lead them deep into the shire of Ulard, and by the next evening, to the McLaud's ancestral home. They had the road to themselves this morning, since the day was wet and poor for traveling, but Jaren seemed not to notice the weather at all, nor had he for the past seven days, being too preoccupied with planning his future now that he had resolved to return to Caithe with or without his father's blessing.

"The first time I met her was in a tavern," Jaren said, passing the time by providing Brice with an exhaustive account of his history with Athaya. If Brice was bored, he hid it well—not that it would have compelled Jaren to stop talking.

"She was dressed in her brother's old clothes, had just cheated a man at cards, and had drunk a whole flagon of wine before I got there." Jaren shook his head and laughed. "If nothing else, it certainly proved to me that she was different from any other woman I'd ever met."

"Or will ever meet again, I'll wager," Brice said genially. "The Lord doesn't make too many like her. Not and make them princesses, too."

The narrow road curved and entered a wood of evergreens, the raindrops sparkling like icicles on the green needles. A wind had come up, cold for mid-April, but Jaren merely burrowed deeper into his cloak and went on with his story, undaunted.

"And from the beginning I knew she was going to do great things. So did Master Hedric. She has more idealism than she likes to admit, you know. Not many people can see that in her. She feels things deeply, so much that she shuts them away a lot and tries to tell herself she doesn't care so it won't hurt so much if things don't work out."

As they rounded another bend in the road, his chestnut mare balked in its steady gait, flaring its nostrils as if catching the scent of an animal nearby, but after a pat on the neck and a soft word, the mare snorted once and was persuaded to continue.

"It may take time," Jaren went on, "but I'm sure she'll work wonders for the Lorngeld in Caithe. And I want to help her do that more than I've ever wanted to do anything."

He heard the whistling sound first, only a split second before the pain struck, a sharp, biting pain that turned his left leg to fire and nearly sent him toppling from the saddle. But when he saw the slender arrow protruding from his thigh, thinking with surprising clearheadedness that an arrow wound should not cause that much pain—especially not the pounding in his skull—it was then that he noticed the ring tied securely to the shaft.

A corbal ring.

As recognition of the danger he was in began to sink in, he heard the rustling of shrubs and the clatter of mail as four armed men darted at him from either side of the road.

"Brice, get out of here! Go!" he called out, but there was no response. Only cold, resonant silence. The arrow that had struck his friend and servant had not been calculated to miss. Through slowly clouding vision, Jaren saw the man—the man he knew almost as well as he knew his own father—sprawled on the ground beside his horse, a brilliant red stain blooming like a rose on the front of his shirt. He wanted to cry out his grief, but the corbal made his throat go dry and constrict, robbing him of everything but pain.

He tried to spur his horse on despite the injured leg, but the scent of blood made the animal skittish and slow to obey, and by then the men were upon him. He had nothing to fight them with but his bare hands—corbals were all but unknown in Reyka, and he had never before needed any weapons other than his spells, now as far out of his reach as Athaya was.

A man with a fading bruise on his jaw yanked the shaft from Jaren's flesh with one rough tug, showing his disappointment when his victim refused to cry out. Two other men dragged him down from his mount and hauled him off the road into a thick copse of evergreens. A knot of wood bit into his back as they shoved him brutally against a tree trunk, pinning his arms back to expose his abdomen. Jaren thought he was struggling fiercely, but the crystal must have been muddling his senses, and he heard laughter at the futility of his labors.

Then the men's leader approached, a savage glint in his owl-like brown eyes. Jaren felt his innards go stiff. That face was all too familiar.

"We meet again, wizard," Captain Parr said, spitting out the words like curses. Smiling, he took the bloodied arrow from his cohort and toyed with it. The ring dangled from the shaft like a carrot on a stick, and he swung it lazily before Jaren's face, amused to see the reflections of pain there.

"A fine time I've had finding a secluded spot where we could have this little tryst," he went on. "I've been following you all week. But the waiting paid off handsomely, didn't it?"

Jaren didn't trust himself to speak, knowing whatever he said would probably earn him nothing but a beating. He kept wary eyes fastened to the corbal as if trying to shatter it by force of will alone.

"You didn't think we'd just give up and go back to Caithe, did you? Look at me when I talk to you, wizard!" Parr ordered, jabbing his captive roughly in the stomach with the fletched end of the arrow. Jaren glared daggers at him, but held his tongue.

Parr nodded once. "That's better. As I was saying, we came back for Athaya—don't think we were so stupid as to believe your paltry lies. But it appears she's left without us. And without you. That's curious. I'd gathered that the two of you were rather close." He paused to indulge in a rare chuckle. "But it shouldn't matter. Once she knows we have you, she might just do something careless and fall right into our hands."

That drew the reaction Parr was hoping for. Jaren kicked out wildly, striking the captain in the knee before he was pummeled into submission by a flurry of fists and the sharp shards of pain from the crystal.

"What's this?" the captain said, seemingly unhurt by the blow, "such a bold display of courage in defense of your lady? That's very noble. Too bad she doesn't deserve it." In punishment for the outburst, Parr drew off his mail glove and whipped it across Jaren's cheek, drawing four thin streaks of blood.

"I may not be going back home with the princess, but his Majesty should consider you the next best thing. He's been learning a great deal about your kind these last few months, you know. These crystals, for instance," he said, holding up the ring. "The pain they inflict depends greatly on their size and cut. Rhodri had many notes on the subject and in quite a surprising amount of detail."

Jaren, however, didn't find that fact remotely surprising. That was just the sort of information a wizard like Rhodri might collect for amusement, having had the same fascination for twisted knowledge as an inquisitioner eager to learn the finer points of torture.

"This particular ring should suit us perfectly," Parr went on. "The stone is large enough to hinder your cursed spells, but small enough so that you'll stay reasonably coherent during our journey home. That's not to say you won't be in any pain," he added, knowing full well that Jaren was feeling the bite of the crystal quite sharply, "but you should live through it well enough."

"You'll be seen," Jaren said at last, his muddled thoughts trying to find some flaw in their plan, "you'll be caught."

"Oh, I don't think so. We'll be sticking to the back roads so that our crystal won't alert any other wizards snooping about." Then, with a thin smile, Parr motioned to a wineskin strapped to his horse's saddle. "And you are about to develop a sudden tendency to drink too much. If anyone asks, we're just a group of friends helping their inebriated companion find his way home for the night."

At that, the captain leaned closer, and the amusement vanished from his face. "I hope your father has other sons, Jaren McLaud," he said darkly. "He'll need them."

"Sir," one of the men broke in, "we'd best go. There was another rider about a mile south of here, and he'll be catching up before long."

Parr stiffened his jaw, disappointed that his pleasure should have to end so soon. "All right. Berns, get those horses and tie them with ours. And Hugh, drag that man's body off into the woods and cover it with something—no one will find him until we're safely over the border. And somebody get me that binding cord we brought."

Then he turned back to his prey, baring his teeth as he spoke. "We're going back to Caithe, you and I," he said, his voice low and coarse, "and this time you won't find it so easy to escape."

And as Jaren's horse was tied to the others, and he was securely blindfolded, bound with cord, and led away through the wood, he almost laughed through his pain at the irony of it—that he had spent the better part of the week planning his return to Caithe, and was, in fact, setting out far sooner than he'd expected. But in all his pleasant daydreams, he'd seen himself riding off as a bridegroom in search of his bride, and not as a captive being led to the lair of his enemies and to a king who very much wanted to see him dead.

CHAPTER 14

✳✳

T HREE DAYS AFTER HER ILL-FATED MEETING WITH FATHER
Aldus, Athaya was still brewing a foul temper. While the
others were gathered around the campfire enjoying a supper of rabbit stew that Tonia had concocted, Athaya opted for
the solitude of her shabby little room in the dormitory, content
to lean on the pitted stone window ledge and watch them from
a distance.

Deep down, she knew she wasn't being fair to herself, but
that didn't help her from being angry about what had happened
at the cathedral. She had confronted Aldus with what he was,
letting him know it was no longer his secret, and then, at the
worst possible moment, had been forced to leave him in that
dangerous state without being able to convince him that his
power wasn't the Devil's mark. Twice she had returned to the
cathedral to speak with him, and twice he was nowhere to be
found.

How long would it take, she wondered, for Aldus to confess
his alleged sins to the bishop and admit to being of the Lorngeld?
How long before he sought absolution? She was furious with
herself for having given Aldus a reason to think she was a demon
come to tempt him. A *demon*, of all things! Perhaps the cloaking
spell had been her only option—or at least the only one she could
think of at the time—but that gave her little comfort. It wouldn't

take long for news of Aldus' "temptation" to spread throughout the city. And of course Bishop Lukin never bothered to tell Aldus that what he saw wasn't a demon at all. No, it was far too convenient for him to let his poor secretary go on thinking that her appearance had been an attempt by the Devil to snare him.

More than any of his other talents, Athaya wished she had inherited her father's gift of eloquence—his gift for inspiring people to follow him with just a few well-chosen words. Kelwyn could have swayed Aldus in an instant; she was convinced of it. But it wasn't just her failure to persuade Aldus to join her that distressed her. Even she had to realize that such a feat would take more time than the few moments they'd had. It was just that she wanted it so badly!

Slowly, Athaya was beginning to understand just how naive her initial hopes had really been. As a child, she had seen her father lift his troops into a feverish pitch of excitement with a few carefully chosen words, urging them on to victory in battle. She had seen it and knew it could be done. It was why part of her actually believed that people would flock to her side the moment they heard of the salvation she offered, without having to grapple with the right or wrong of it. Was that why she clung to the dream that all she had to do was speak the words to one glorious spell, and her countrymen would willingly fall in line behind her, cheering her cause?

She stole a glance skyward. "You're not going to make this easy for me, are you?"

Then, so soon after her remark that she thought it was some sort of unearthly response, Athaya heard a pitiful wail from deep within the trees. The band around the campfire jerked their heads up in unison, Ranulf and Kale instinctively reaching for weapons. A moment later, Tonia's voice broke through the confused murmur of voices saying with relief, "Cam, welcome back," but whatever she said next was drowned out by a chorus of concerned utterances and shuffling about as everyone dropped his or her bowl and weapons and scurried off to the edge of the clearing, out of Athaya's view.

When they returned to the campfire, two others had joined the group. Athaya knew Cam's lanky gait and tousled hair immediately, but she didn't recognize the weeping woman at his side until he'd drawn her closer to the fire, and the flames cast a ruddy glow upon her face. Even from this distance, Athaya could see that she was bruised and bloodied, her hair a tangled mass and her dress stained with mud and grass.

Athaya's eyes went wide. This was no new wizard he had brought back from Leaforth with him. It was Gilda.

Gasping sharply, Athaya bolted from her room, nearly breaking her neck on the narrow stair as she hastened down from the upper level of the dormitory. By the time she arrived in the clearing, Mason had given Gilda his cloak, set her on a log near the fire, and pressed a bowl of stew into her hand. Gilda didn't look the least inclined to eat it, but held on to the wooden bowl tightly, anxious to have something—anything—firmly in her grasp.

"I found her by the side of the river," Cam told Athaya solemnly, seeming twice his age just then. "I didn't know she was one of us until she mentioned the sheepfold. She was trying to find it, but lost her way once the sun went down."

"Why don't you and Kale go prepare a room for her. And take an extra kirtle from my room—she'll need a change of clothes."

As Cam and Kale went off on their errand, Athaya quietly asked Mason and Ranulf to check the woods for any unwelcome visitors who might have followed Cam and Gilda from the riverbank. Tonia hustled Cordry away to scour the dishes in the creek, and once they had relative privacy, Athaya sat down on the log at Gilda's side.

"Don't you come near me!" Gilda snapped, suddenly full of wrath. "This is all your fault!" Roughly turning away, she hunched miserably over her bowl, one or two tears dropping softly into the stew.

Athaya cast a puzzled glance up at Tonia, who settled onto the log on Gilda's other side and gently began to work the tangles from her hair. "Tell us what happened, my dear."

Tonia's compassion calmed the girl somewhat, and her anger melted back into bleak despair. "I was thinking about what you said that day," she said, turning her head only slightly toward Athaya. "About whether magic could be good if I wanted it to be. So I made a witchlight. I put it above the cradle—just to see what it would look like. The way you said," she added, faintly accusing. Then she slumped over even more, and her shoulders jerked once, as if she were trying to hold in emotions too strong for her.

"I never even heard him come in the house. He stared at me as if . . . as if I were the Devil himself. And then he did this," she said, touching her swollen cheek with blood-slick fingers. "He told me I was cursed and that our baby was . . . was the Devil's child. He said I knew what I was when I married him, and that our whole life together had been a lie . . ."

Gilda choked on her breath, struggling to go on. "I couldn't use the spells you taught me to fight him off. I just couldn't. My God, he's my *husband*. But then he went to fetch a priest, and I knew I had to get away. So I took what I could carry and ran." Her eyes glazed over with fresh tears. "I can't go back. He'll kill me if I do; or the priests will . . . me and my baby . . ." She couldn't say any more after that and hid her face in her palms, crying quietly.

"It's all right, Gilda," Athaya said, setting a hand on her shoulder. "You're safe here."

Gilda shoved her hand away. "Safe? From what? You people are the ones *causing* all the trouble! God in heaven, I wish I'd never had anything to do with you!"

The moment the angry words were out, the campfire suddenly flared up, flames blasting skyward as high as the ruined bell tower. Athaya tumbled back to keep the fire from igniting her skirt, the heat searing her face like boiling lead. Gilda let out a shriek of fright, but whether it was from the sudden burst of heat or the awful suspicion that she had been the cause of it, no one could be sure.

"Now, now, none of that," Tonia murmured, gently smothering Gilda's spell with one of her own. "We can't have you setting the whole forest on fire, now can we?" She went on muttering comforting phrases until Gilda's fear subsided, only to be replaced by numb deadness, as if she had slipped far out of reach of human consolation.

Cameron returned a short time later. He stared at the seemingly normal campfire as if he'd seen what had happened but knew better than to comment on it. "Her room's ready," he said, dutiful as a squire.

"Come along, then," Tonia said, gathering Gilda in her arms. "I'll find you a cup of something—something strong, I dare say—and sit with you until you fall asleep."

Her energy spent, and knowing she had nowhere else to go,

Gilda silently allowed herself to be led off to the dormitory, leaving Athaya and Cam alone by the fire.

"She's shaken, but not badly hurt," Athaya assured him, then rubbed her eyes, aware that her foul temper had receded only to be replaced by bone-deep weariness and discouragement.

Ranulf and Mason emerged from the woods a short time later. "Nobody out there," Ranulf said tersely, sheathing his dagger. "It was hard to tell, though, what with Mason stomping on every damnable twig he came across and making enough noise for a dozen men."

The dom's scowl could have set the campfire to flaring again, but Ranulf's remarks must have carried some truth in light of how quickly the tutor turned his attentions to Cam. "And how was Leaforth? I imagine your parents were glad to see you."

Cam shuffled his feet uncomfortably. "Not really. It was . . . awkward. As if it wasn't home anymore. And they were glad to see me leave again once I told him why I'd come back. But I found this on the way back," he said, abruptly shifting away from what had to be a painful subject. He reached into his trousers and drew out a pouch of copper coins, handing it proudly to Athaya.

"Found it?" Mason remarked dryly in her ear. "I'll bet he did. Probably slipped into the parish church and 'found' it in the poor box."

"I did not!" Cameron replied hotly. "Some men were fighting in an inn. The table fell over and coins flew everywhere, but folks kept watching the fight. Nobody bothered to go back to pick up the money and . . . well, I thought we might need it more than they did."

Athaya smiled at his good intentions, even though they were cloaked in thievery. "We'll need it soon enough," she admitted, aware that the money Osfonin had given her would not last indefinitely. "But try not to 'find' too many more things for us in the future, won't you?"

"Now tell me again, Cordry—what does Master Sidra write about the proper way to set protective wards?"

"What?" Cordry pulled his eyes away from the empty entrance to the sheepfold and gave Athaya a look riddled with guilt.

"You never even read it, did you?" Athaya scolded, folding

her arms across her chest. "You may be past the most dangerous part of the *mekahn*, Cordry, but that doesn't give you an excuse to ignore the rest of your lessons."

"I read it," he protested weakly. "I just didn't remember any of it." Cordry ran his fingers over the leatherbound book in his lap and made an obligatory expression of repentance. "I'm sorry. But how can I think about these dusty old essays when it's been almost two weeks and she hasn't come *again*? What if she's sick? What if she's in trouble?"

Athaya sighed, trying to hide her impatience. Megan had not come to the sheepfold since Gilbert's aborted attack, and without news of her or his father's mill, Cordry grew increasingly agitated and could barely concentrate on his spellwork.

"Maybe I should slip into the city tonight," he said impulsively, "just to make sure Megan and Father are safe."

Athaya glared at him severely. "Oh no you don't. One glimpse of you and everyone will know you didn't run away the way your father swore you did."

"But—"

"Do you want to put Megan or your father in that kind of danger? Gilbert Ames has probably told the whole city about seeing you here, and I'll wager that both your house and Megan's are being watched. The bishop knows about me, too," she added, "and he'll be cracking down hard on any reports of wizards that reach his ears. Father Greste has probably told him everything he knows by now, too. Megan's only showing good sense by staying away—and so should you."

At that, Cordry acquiesced glumly, but was somewhat cheered when Athaya promised that if another week passed without word from Megan, she would dispatch Kale to the city to investigate.

Leaving Cordry to reread the essay from the *Book of Sages* that he had neglected earlier, Athaya stepped out of the sheepfold and looked up at the gray clouds, wondering when—not if—the rain would come.

Cordry was certainly not the only one with worries on his mind today. She was worried about Gilda. Tonia, Cam, and Kale had remained with her at the camp instead of venturing out to the sheepfold, but even though she knew her newest pupil was safe, Athaya kept glancing anxiously across the meadows as if expecting Gilda's husband to appear any moment and demand her return. Not that there was any question of deserting the sheepfold—Athaya knew that someone had to be at the makeshift school each day on the off chance that someone heeded Ranulf and Mason's carefully nurtured rumors and sought help there. But it was a less peaceful place than it used to be now that news of its existence was widely known.

The sight of a solitary man trudging toward the sheepfold made her heart lurch to her throat, thinking for a moment that she might have wished up her worst fears and drawn Gilda's husband to the sheepfold. But soon she recognized Ranulf's lumbering gait and let out her breath with relief.

"I've got something to show you," he said bluntly, without any attempt at a greeting. "I went into Kaiburn today," he went on, the set of his jaw revealing that it hadn't been one of his happier jaunts to the city. He pulled a crumpled piece of parchment out of his tunic and handed it to her. "Feast your eyes on this. They're posted on walls all over the city."

One glance at the leaflet was enough to make her swear an oath ripe enough that even Ranulf's jaded brows went up an inch. Although the print was slightly smudged, as if its creator had been so eager to distribute it that he neglected to wait until the ink was dry, its meaning was more than clear. It bore a crude woodcut of Athaya's likeness, but she was startled and repulsed by the liberties the artist had taken. The Caithan princess was depicted against a backdrop of flames, her mouth twisted into a diabolical grimace. Two small horns were shown sprouting from her head, surrounded by wild coils of windblown hair. Lightning bolts shot from her fingers in triumph as her foot rested on the chest of the dead man at her feet, a king's crown resting on the ground nearby. Underneath it all in huge, bold letters was scrawled the word REWARD.

Had she been a man, Athaya would have spat on the ground in disgust. She was still tempted to do so, but refrained out of some little-used sense of propriety. "Bishop Lukin's letter has obviously reached the king. And this is his answer."

"It gets the gist across, even for them as can't read," Ranulf said. Then his voice dropped lower, marked with concern. "I'd watch your back from now on, Athaya. Every tongue in Kaiburn is wagging with the news that you're here, and I hear tell that a troop of the king's crack guardsmen are expected any day now from Delfarham."

Athaya glanced down at the parchment with detached curiosity. "I wonder how much he's offering."

Briefly, she wondered if she had anything to fear from Cordry or Gilda. Betrayal from within her own ranks distressed her, and while she suspected there was little threat from Cordry, she couldn't guess what Gilda might do in her bitterness at losing her husband. She might just consider a handsome reward a suitable recompense for her miseries. But Athaya couldn't afford to turn anyone away at this point, especially based on nothing more substantial than apprehension. Still, she made a note to be watchful in the future. Trust was a luxury she could not afford in large quantities.

"One of the bishop's scribes must have had a good time making this," she remarked, folding up the leaflet to hide its offending artwork. "Heaven only knows what he could do as an illuminator." Then she let out a tired sigh, suddenly drained. "Lately I've been considering going into Kaiburn and speaking publicly—like the itinerant friars that from street corners on market day. Rumors and hearsay are fine, but it's time we became more than just a few wild stories in people's minds."

"I'd not do it now," Ranulf advised. "Not yet, anyway."

"But there's got to be some way of fighting this." Her hands clamped down angrily around the leaflet, crushing it in frustration. "We can't just stand aside and let the bishop stir up even more resentment against us."

A renegade gleam appeared in the mercenary's eye. Ranulf smiled broadly, displaying the dark gaps left by his two missing teeth.

"They've picked the weapons. It seems only fitting to use the same ones. On those rare occasions when I mixed myself up in a fair fight, that was usually the custom."

"A little propaganda of our own, I take it?" Athaya said, gradually cracking a smile. It might not be as direct as a rousing speech, but such a tactic could serve their purposes well. "Yes, I think it could work."

Athaya and Ranulf presented the idea to the others that night at the camp, and were met with overwhelming approval. It took only minutes for Mason to locate the pot of ink and leather tubes of rolled parchment they'd brought from Reyka, while Cordry and Kale cleared off one of the large kitchen tables for use as a makeshift workshop.

Since he had already shown his talent for carving, Kale was selected to make the actual woodcut. He spent a better part of the next day diligently searching the monastery grounds for a suitable piece of planking or scrap of wood soft enough to make a decent carving, and then worked steadily through the night, first smoothing down the wooden surface and then meticulously carving the design into it, until his creation was completed.

Athaya's judgment of art was uneducated at best, but even she could see that the resulting woodcut was masterful. Following her instructions, Kale had crafted the image of a jeweled absolution chalice tipped on one side at the edge of an altar, spilling its poisoned wine to the ground. Tendrils of smoke curled up from the spilled pool of poison, proclaiming the wine's deadly intent as it slowly ate through the fine altar rug it soiled. At the top of the drawing, in bold script, was the simple word LIFE.

"It's beautiful, Kale," she breathed, holding up the slab of red cedar. "I'm surprised you didn't take apprenticeship in one of the craft guilds instead of joining the King's Guard."

"Oh, it's nothing," he said modestly, scratching his head in embarrassment. "The bowl of the cup is a bit too shallow, you see, and the stem . . . it's not quite even."

"Only an artist like yourself would notice."

With the woodcut finished, it was a simple matter to make the prints. By the end of the day, most everyone was marked by dark smudges of ink on their fingers, noses, and cheeks, like children who'd spent the day playing in the mud.

"Tomorrow we can start tacking these up all over Kaiburn," Ranulf said later, as the first of the prints began to dry. "But we'd best work at night—no sense asking for trouble. Even under a cloaking spell it could be risky."

Athaya picked up one of the drying prints and held it up to the glow of firelight, admiring it. "You realize, Kale, that before long this little carving could be the most famous—or infamous—piece of art in Caithe."

"Aye, my Lady," he agreed quietly. But the just-visible curve of his mouth told her that the thought of such anonymous fame appealed to his artist's soul.

In a matter of days, Ranulf reported that all of Kaiburn was buzzing with the news of the scandalous leaflets found posted on walls throughout the city—even, the most righteous of the citizens spouted indignantly, on the doors of the great cathedral itself.

"It definitely made an impression," he said, warming his hands at the campfire, "even though Lukin had his priests confiscate every one of the prints they could get their hands on. And the king's men were given the same orders now that they've finally arrived in the city."

"Then we'll make more leaflets," Athaya said resolutely. "And we'll keep on making them. As long as a handful of people see them before they're torn down, we've done our job."

"And whenever we saw one of the bishop's prints, we ripped it down." Ranulf tossed another stick into the campfire to stir it up against the cool evening, then got up and flung a quiver of white-fletched arrows over his shoulder and tested the string of his bow.

"Think I'll go fetch us some supper," he said. "What says everyone to a bit of venison tonight? There's deer aplenty in these woods."

"There's a reason for that," Kale said cautiously. "The Forest of Else is royal hunting land and those are the king's deer. You'll hang if the forester catches you shooting at them."

"Oh, don't worry," Athaya said languidly, dangling one shoe from her toe as she tried to keep from giggling. "If you get caught, just tell him that the king's sister gave you permission."

Ranulf slapped his thigh and expelled a hearty guffaw. "I expect that would only speed up the hanging, your Highness."

Athaya tossed back her hair in feigned haughtiness. "What a thing to say."

"Shh!"

Rudely waving her silent, Ranulf suddenly went rigid, every muscle poised on the alert. His face was set hard as boiled leather, and his eyes were wary as he slowly drew an arrow from the quiver and nocked it.

"Anybody hear that?" He turned his ear to one side. "Somebody's out there . . . near the deer trail."

After a painful moment of silence, broken only by the distant hoot of an owl, Athaya detected a faint rustle, like an animal moving slowly through the brush.

"Outlaws?" Cordry asked, eyes dancing from the anticipated adventure of such an encounter.

"Possible," Ranulf murmured. Then in a lower, almost

amused tone, he added, "but don't they know their own kind when they see 'em?"

"Could they be Durek's men?" Athaya whispered anxiously, all the while wondering how soldiers—or anyone, for that matter—could have avoided the carefully placed illusions ringing the camp. Cameron had known what and where they were to guide Gilda past them, but no one else should have found the trail nearly so easy to navigate.

Kale responded quickly to his soldier's instincts and ducked quietly inside the bell tower to fetch a crossbow, its bolt already loaded and ready. "How many, do you think?"

"I can't tell. Not many. Maybe just one." Ranulf turned back, firing out orders so rapidly that it was hard to believe it had been many years since his last skirmish.

"The rest of you stay here. Act as if nothing's wrong so they don't know we're wise to 'em. Cam, you stick close to the others. If our visitors have corbals, you'll have to help everybody else out of this. Athaya, if there's trouble, you get out of here—*no* heroics. Tonia, I want you to make sure her Highness takes that advice. I don't want to do the king any favors by letting her get taken. Cordry, go join Gilda in the kitchens and stay there until I tell you otherwise. Kale, come with me. Mason, you too—*if* you can be quiet about it this time."

"Oh, thanks," the dom muttered, hastily stuffing his feet back into the leather slippers he'd discarded earlier.

The three men stole toward the far side of the camp, passing behind the brewery shed. She saw Kale double back around one end of the camp, and a moment later she detected Ranulf and Mason as they emerged from the other direction, silently stalking the intruders under cover of cloaking spells. Two faint, shimmering blurs moved against a backdrop of pines, looking like nothing more than smudges on a glass as they passed steadily through the brush, and only Athaya, with her adept-level vision, could make out any trace of them as they delved deeper into the woods.

Athaya lost track of them a few minutes later, all three men swallowed up by the brooding night woods. Her heartbeat sounded loud as war drums in the stillness of the night, and with every spark of the fire or murmur of the wind, she imagined another intruder, clad in the burgundy livery of the King's Guard, creeping ever closer with his sword poised and ready, waiting for the ideal moment to strike.

Then Ranulf's triumphant voice boomed out like thunder.

"Got you!" he cried, his words immediately followed by a frantic scuffle and a series of panicked yelps and grunts. "There, hold still, you little bugger. You ain't going nowhere."

Ranulf beamed with a hunter's pride as he, Mason, and Kale hauled their prize into the clearing. Their captive was bundled in a black hood and robe, a slender white cord wrapped around his waist. They pulled him near the fire and roughly deposited him on a fallen log, tying his arms behind his back with a strip of leather. Once Athaya and the others gathered around him, the intruder, realizing he was vastly outnumbered, finally stopped squirming.

While Mason and Kale kept a tight hold on their prisoner, Ranulf sauntered around to face him, holding up an arrow so that the firelight would flash menacingly off the steel tip.

"Now then," he began, grabbing a handful of the man's woolen cowl, "what are you doing skulking around in the woods all alone? Planning to rob us, were you? Or do a bit of spying?"

With one rough jerk, Ranulf yanked back the man's hood.

Athaya's hand went instantly to her mouth, stifling a gasp of surprise. The harsh glare from the fire drew shadows on the smooth, sculpted cheekbones and lent a wild, otherworldly gleam to the priest's expressive, terror-filled eyes.

"Father Aldus," she whispered.

CHAPTER 15

✖✖

"YOU KNOW THIS GUY?" RANULF ASKED, LOWERING his arrow. He glared down at Aldus with contempt, grumbling his disappointment that he had been so hastily robbed of his first chance to interrogate a prisoner.

"He's Bishop Lukin's secretary; you remember, the priest that Mason told everyone about. Kale, quickly—let him go," Athaya urged, and with the flick of a knife, Kale cut the bonds around the priest's wrists. That done, he backed away with a fleeting glance skyward, as if fearful that lightning might well strike him for handling a man of God so roughly.

While Mason offered a stream of profuse apologies to Aldus, Ranulf set his arrow aside, albeit reluctantly. Soldiering for pay had taught him suspicion if nothing else, and he wasn't as quick to accept their new guest as was the dom.

"You *did* come here alone, didn't you?" he growled, his cold stare silently warning the priest that the results would be unpleasant if the answer was anything but yes. "Didn't bring your boss with you . . . or maybe a few of the king's men?"

Aldus winced as he rubbed his wrists where the leather straps had chafed them. "Of course I came alone. Do you honestly think I want anyone to know I'm here?"

Ranulf scowled deeply as he folded his meaty arms across his chest. "Unless the bishop already knows. Unless he sent you out to find us, so you could turn us in to the king's men."

Mason shot Ranulf an indignant glare. "Would you please stop treating this like some sort of inquisition? This man came here for help, not to be dragged over the coals."

Ranulf slowly scratched his beard, considering that point, but a moment later he wheeled around sharply to face Athaya.

"Wait a minute," he said, eyes narrowing, "how in hell did he find this place? People know about the sheepfold, all right, but nobody knows about our camp except Cordry and Gilda. Or *do* they?" he demanded of Aldus, grabbing a handful of black wool from the priest's collar.

Aldus was doing his best to remain calm under Ranulf's scrutiny, but it was clearly beginning to strain what little composure he had. "I didn't want anyone seeing me near your . . . 'school,' if that's what you call it. I had to find you secretly. I guessed you might be living in the forest . . . like the other outlaws," he added, with just a hint of scorn.

"Oh, and you just happened to stumble across us on your first try, eh? We set a mess of illusions all around this camp just to keep people from wandering in. Brambles, false paths . . . how was it they didn't keep you out?"

Aldus stared at him in bewilderment. "Illusions? I don't know what you—"

"How did you get here?"

"You left a trail as plain as day!" Aldus shot back, his patience finally breaking under Ranulf's demands. "Didn't you expect somebody might have the sense to follow it?"

There was a minute of puzzled silence before Mason blinked and said, "Of course. The guiding runes . . ."

Athaya exchanged a startled glance with him. "But I thought only a *trained* wizard would be able to see them. Cordry can make them out, but he's been with us for weeks. And Gilda can't see them at all yet."

"Maybe Aldus is more talented than I thought at first," Mason admitted, vaguely chagrined that he had underestimated the priest's potential. "Either that, or he's farther along in his *mekahn* than most Lorngeld who exhibit his level of symptoms. If he's as good a theologian as they say he is, maybe all that mental discipline has allowed his mind to fend off the madness longer than normal."

"Look, if you're going to kill me, then do it," Aldus burst out, channeling his fear of them into anger. "From the tales I've heard of you people, I'd say killing is all in a day's work."

Athaya couldn't help but notice that Aldus stole a glance in her direction as he spoke, and she felt something tighten inside of her as she silently looked away.

"Ranulf, go into the brewery and fetch our guest some ale," Tonia said, tactfully dodging what could have turned into a pointless and unpleasant argument. "He looks in need of it."

Father Aldus relaxed only slightly when Ranulf had taken his imposing bulk elsewhere. He seemed all too aware that the others were waiting for him to speak, but sat on the fallen log and anxiously fingered the tassel of the white cord at his waist. Then, when the silence became oppressive, he reached inside his robe and drew out a tattered piece of parchment that looked as if it had been hastily crumpled and then later smoothed out again.

"I saw this," he said, holding up one of the bishop's leaflets with Athaya's likeness on it. "Then I knew it was no demon I saw that day. It was you, your Highness." Despite that knowledge, Aldus didn't look the least bit comfortable in Athaya's presence. He shrank from her in distrust, clearly unsure whether being a notorious wizard and murderess was any improvement over being a demon.

Ranulf returned with a tankard of ale, generously filled to the brim as if to make amends for his earlier hostility. Aldus gulped it down eagerly, though his hands were shaking and he spilled a good bit of it on the front of his robe.

Once he was reasonably calm, Athaya sat down beside him on the log. He started to move away from her, but then remained where he was, as if realizing there was nowhere to run.

"Why did you come to us, Aldus?"

Swallowing another mouthful of ale, the priest hunched over as if every ounce of strength was slowly ebbing from him. "I don't know. Something made me come. I don't know what—or who." He sighed deeply. "Maybe I just want to listen."

"We can't ask more than that," Athaya said quietly.

He nodded slightly, but did not turn to look at her. "What you said that day was true, your Highness. I don't feel at peace the way I used to. I feel as if I'm spending each day poised on the edge of a cliff, wondering whether this will be the day I fall off. And I break things all the time. But it's worse than that," he added, hanging his head. "Every day, people come to me, trust me with their problems, and sometimes . . . sometimes I *forget* them." Aldus' face was lined with pain, deeply ashamed that he could neglect such a sacred duty. "And yesterday, when the bishop came into the sacristy and asked me to write a letter for him . . . I couldn't remember his name. I tried . . . but I couldn't *remember*!" Aldus covered his face with his hands, his body trembling uncontrollably.

No one else spoke, sensing that Aldus would go on in his own good time. And after a moment's silence, he raised his head and took a steadying draught from his mug.

"I've wanted to be a priest all my life," he said dreamily, gazing out into the darkness of the night woods. "I've never doubted my calling. But why would He *do* this to me?" Aldus cried softly, looking skyward as if expecting to find an answer in the stars. "Why call me to His service and then allow the Other to call me away from it?"

Tonia stepped forward, absently prodding the campfire with a stick as she spoke. "Tell me, Father . . . when you grew from a boy into a man, did you hate what you became? Did you ever consider killing yourself because you had changed into something else?"

Aldus drew himself up, vaguely affronted. "Of course not."

"Then what's so different about this?" she asked simply. "Your magic is maturing now, just as your body did then. You won't be a worse creature for it. Just a different one."

Aldus paused to think on that, but the simple logic of her words only seemed to add to the confusion seething inside him.

"Remember what you told that old woman, Aldus?" Athaya said. "You told her that life was a gift. Well, your magic is a gift, too. And don't you tell your parishioners every day that they should be grateful for the gifts God saw fit to give them? Grateful, instead of rejecting them?"

"Well, yes, but—"

"Then why single out this particular gift as something to be afraid of?"

Aldus gazed deep into his tankard, now almost empty. "Then tell me what kind of gift it is that makes me feel as if my entire life is spinning out of control—that makes me destroy things, and forget things, and think I'm hearing voices? Tell me why I should be grateful for *that*?"

"That's not an easy thing to explain," Athaya told him, thinking back to how long it took her to understand the notion of magic commanding its price, and that the threat of madness was part of obtaining its rewards. Then she thought of Gilda, who had made much the same complaint when she first came to them, and got an idea that might help persuade them both. "Life may be a gift, Aldus, but if you tried telling that to a woman while she was going through childbirth, she might not be in any sort of mood to agree with you. For a few hours, it might not seem worth all the blood and pain. But later, when the baby comes . . . somehow the trial was worth it."

It was hard to tell, but Athaya thought she might have gotten through to him—at least a little. Aldus was quiet for a long time, content to stare at the red embers of the fire and struggle with his thoughts.

Athaya refused to be discouraged by his hesitance. At least he was here, and that meant that some part of him wanted to listen to what she and her fellow wizards had to say. "If you like," she offered, "I can take you into the chapel so you can be alone for a while."

Aldus jerked his head up in surprise. "A what? You mean—"

"Yes, we have one," she said, cracking a smile as she gestured to the shabby old sanctuary. "It might surprise you to know that in other places—like Reyka, for instance—magic and religion are basically the same thing. If it helps put your mind at ease, we've put our camp on the site of an old monastery."

We just won't mention what happened to those ancient brothers, will we?

Slowly, Aldus set his tankard down on the damp grass and got to his feet. "I'll have to go back to the city soon, but . . . yes," he said, a faraway look in his eyes, "I think I would like to pray for a while."

As Tonia and Mason accompanied Aldus to the sanctuary, Ranulf sidled up to Athaya, his eyes still full of distrust. "There's one to keep our eyes on," he said darkly, hooking his thumbs in his belt. "How do we know he won't turn tail and tell Bishop Lukin exactly where to find us?"

"We don't know that," Athaya admitted, slightly piqued that the mercenary persisted in being so suspicious. "But I doubt he would have come here alone if that was the case. Besides, how do we know Cordry or Gilda might not turn us in if they were pushed hard enough? We run the same risk with anyone we teach. All we can do is hope for the best.''

Ranulf made a disgruntled noise in the back of his throat as he threw a bucket of water over the embers to douse the fire for the night. He made no more cynical remarks, but Athaya found herself less hopeful than she had been a moment ago. Wizards had been slaughtered on these holy grounds before. Who could say that it might not happen again?

Father Aldus came to the forest camp each evening, leaving word at the cathedral that he was making nightly visits to a sick parishioner. Since he was well known for busying himself with such selfless tasks, none of his fellow priests questioned his long absences, and to Athaya's surprise, Aldus said that not even Bishop Lukin seemed to find anything amiss.

Despite his continued visits to the camp, Aldus remained precarious in his decision to explore his burgeoning powers. In light of this, Athaya asked Mason to take responsibility for his training, hoping that Aldus would find common ground with a fellow theologian and scholar and be less likely to change his mind and confess his powers to the bishop. Although he never said as much, Aldus seemed visibly pleased that he was not entrusted to Athaya's care. He knew she was no demon, but there was still the slight matter of what she had done to Kelwyn. He did his best to hide it, but it was obvious that he was still deeply in doubt of her sincerity.

In that, he and Gilda found much in common. While Cordry welcomed Aldus openly, finding it only fitting that a blessing such as magic would be found in a priest, Gilda had been deeply shaken by Aldus' appearance among them, as if it was unwanted proof that her powers were not as evil as she'd thought. But after the initial shock was past, she and Aldus began to kindle a friendship—out of a shared sense of spiritual crisis, if nothing else—and were often seen praying together in the battered old chapel, pleading for guidance.

On a chill evening in late April, Athaya decided to see for herself how Aldus was progressing, having kept her distance from him during his first week among them. On the far side of the clearing, Mason sat cross-legged on a patch of dry ground while Aldus positioned himself near the forest's edge, whispered a brief prayer, and began to craft an illusion. By the time Athaya sat down beside the Dom, Aldus had transformed the trunks of two towering oaks into a pair of marble pillars, adding detail to his creation with unusual speed and skill.

"He certainly casts a fine illusion," Athaya remarked quietly, not wishing to break Aldus' concentration. "But I thought you said it was better to master the basics before going on to something this advanced."

"I did," Mason admitted, "but, frankly, it's the only type of spell he isn't timid about practicing. Oh, he's got his basics down well enough—witchlights, wards, vision spheres—did I tell you he can even contact someone through a sphere already?—but he's skittish about casting all of them. All except for illusion spells," he added, gesturing to the priest's increasingly lavish creation. "He's got a real passion for them; I'm not sure why. Maybe because they let him 'see' all those unseeable things he reads about in the scriptures. His illusions do tend to have something . . . otherworldly about them."

As she looked upon Aldus' creation, awed by its beauty, Athaya thought that the Dom's explanation was entirely correct. Between the marble pillars was now an elegant gate nearly ten feet high, its bars made of gold and encrusted with pearls and colorful gems. White mist shrouded the grass, making the gate seem to be floating on a cloud, and near each pillar, Aldus was adding a few final touches by creating a pair of rosebushes, each in full bloom.

"Be careful of adding too much too quickly," Mason told him in a hushed voice. "An illusion is somewhat like a house of cards. You have to handle it very delicately until it's done or the whole thing will fall apart."

Aldus progressed well for another few minutes, adding a dozen blooms to each rosebush, but the moment he stepped back to survey his work, his control wavered. Behind him, the bronze bell in the tower suddenly began chiming incessantly, pealing out in warning, and soon his entire creation came crashing down around him. The rosebushes flared into two columns of very real flames, while the marble pillars turned black with decay and the jewels shriveled and dropped from the golden gates like rotten fruit.

Aldus, when Athaya next saw him, was white with shock.

"Try not to let it upset you, Aldus," Athaya said, while Mason was busily crafting a counterspell to douse the flames and silence the bell. "I can tell you from experience that not all of your spells are going to work reliably right away."

"I was almost finished when I started hearing the voices again," he said breathlessly. "I tried to ignore them, but I just couldn't. The only thing I could think of was that our prayers must sound just like that to God . . . the babble of a million voices, all whispering at once, neither one louder than any other . . ." He let his words trail off and rubbed his eyes wearily. "I got so distracted that I lost control over the illusion."

Aldus still looked profoundly shaken, but Athaya smiled encouragingly. "The more you practice, the less distracted you'll get. You're bound to have some false starts, though—it's all part of learning to master your magic. Until you get full control over your power, you'll inevitably cast spells that you weren't exactly planning to cast, and sometimes at very inconvenient times. If you think this was unnerving," she added, "I once cast a spell that took me three miles away in the blink of an eye and had no idea how I'd done it." She went on to tell him about her unexpected discovery of translocation, and of Jaren's astonishment when she had materialized in the palace library unannounced.

"You can *do* such a thing?" he said when she was done, his eyes wide and staring. "Cross such distances at will?"

Athaya nodded. "Once, anyway. I haven't tried it since. It gave me quite a start, let me tell you. Especially when I realized that the spell used up all of my strength—I couldn't cast so much as a witchlight until over an hour later. But you shouldn't worry about anything quite so drastic happening to you," she assured him. "You won't be venturing that deep in your paths for quite a while yet."

Instead of being comforted, Aldus only nodded listlessly and slumped down on the ground to think, looking at the empty place where his illusion had been with eyes full of chaos.

"Is something else the matter?" Athaya asked quietly.

"The spell . . ." He bowed his head and clasped his hands tightly. "When I pray, I feel a surge of strength and inner peace . . . as if I'm touching on something far larger than myself. And when I work magic—especially illusions—I find it's the same." His eyes grew even more troubled. "Too much the same."

"And that frightens you?"

Aldus turned his head slightly. "Yes . . . and no. I think it frightens me because it . . . it *thrills* me so. As if I can actually feel His power flowing through me. It's like offering a prayer and actually *hearing* Him respond, telling me He's listening."

"Perhaps you're simply more in tune to God's gifts," Mason said, dispersing what was left of Aldus' illusion and taking a seat beside him. "It's natural that prayer and spells should feel the same to you, since both of them touch upon the power of God."

Mason paused for a moment, steepling his fingers as he prepared his next point. "I believe that much of the joy we take in our gift is because it lets us create. It allows us to bring something into existence that wasn't there before—like your illusions. Creative power is the core of what we wizards are, and the thing that draws us closer to the bestower of our gift. Look—"

With a whisper, Mason conjured a small witchlight and cupped it in his palm. "An effortless bit of magic, this light in the darkness. Called from the void to do my bidding. And just as I called this little orb into my hand, so did God, with His infinite power, conjure the earth out of nothingness—perhaps as simple a trick for Him as this light is for me." He smiled at Aldus, his face awash with intensity. "Our Lord, you might say, is the greatest wizard of all."

Aldus could do little more than look at him blankly, his mind struggling to absorb that concept. But after several moments of pointed silence, he realized that he was staring and let out a nervous laugh. "Bishop Lukin would die of apoplexy if he heard you say that."

"I'm sure he would. But how else would he explain the miracle of creation? Miracles are by their very definition things of magic. And what else could the world be, but a thing of impossible wonder and magic, bidden into being by a wave of God's almighty hand."

Mason closed his palm and snuffed out the light with ease. "A somewhat disconcerting end to my analogy, I suppose," he offered dryly, "but I hope you see my point. The reason why you find prayer and magic so similar, Aldus, is simply because they *are*. They're reflections of each other . . . different sides of the same mystery."

He laid one hand on Aldus' shoulder. "Come—it's late, and you look badly in need of rest. Ranulf, Cordry, and Kale are going out to distribute another batch of our pernicious leaflets tonight, so they can walk with you as far as the river if you like.''

"No,'' Aldus said quietly. "If you don't mind, I'd rather go alone.''

He shuffled across the clearing with his head bent slightly, his black robe quickly blending into the dark night woods. Once he was out of sight, Mason let out a heavy sigh. "He's got talent—a lot of it—but he's still tenuous in his commitment. Every night I wonder if he'll come here or go to the bishop and confess everything." The Dom shook his head worriedly. "It's not easy to undo a lifetime of teaching in such a short time."

If it can be done at all, Athaya thought glumly, recalling all of Ranulf's suspicions. But Mason's thoughts on prayer and magic had inspired her, and she could only hope that they would do the same for Aldus, making him see that he did not have one divine calling, but two.

Just before dawn, while she was still comfortably wrapped inside two woolen blankets, Athaya felt a hand on her shoulder, shaking her urgently. Opening one sandy eye, she saw Tonia hovering over her bed, her face lined with worry.

"What is it?'' Athaya murmured, still half-asleep.

"Get up, Athaya. We've got trouble.''

The tone of Tonia's voice jerked her awake in an instant, and after throwing on a heavy woolen robe, she followed Tonia out to the clearing where Ranulf and Kale were talking quietly amongst themselves, their faces tired and clouded. It was then that she noticed the stains and jagged tears in their clothes, and saw that the strip of cloth around Kale's right arm was crusted with dried blood.

"Cordry's been taken by the king's men,'' Kale reported solemnly.

Athaya felt as if a cold knife had been thrust into her belly. "What? How?''

"By being a damned fool,'' Ranulf replied. "They've been watching the Loring house for days, just waiting to see if he'd come. And the minute he showed up, they pulled out a fancy sword studded with corbals and hauled him away.''

"Weren't you watching him?''

"What is he, an infant?'' Ranulf retorted, bristling out of concern rather than anger. "He slipped away from us when we weren't looking. We knew where he was headed the second we realized he was gone, but by then it was too late. We got to Megan's house just in time to see him being marched off by the king's men.''

Athaya sat down on the edge of a damp log, her feet unable to support her. ''Where have they taken him?''

''To the bishop's palace. But we can't get to him,'' Ranulf added quickly, knowing it would be her next question. ''He's heavily guarded, and some of the king's men have corbals. We tried to sneak around back and climb up the trellis, but two of the guards saw us and sounded an alarm. We might have been able to get inside if we'd killed them, but then everyone would know who did it and enough folks think we're a bunch of murderers already. As it was, we fought just hard enough to get away.''

Athaya rubbed her eyes wearily, cursing herself for not having sent Kale into the city to check on Megan's safety as she'd promised. In all the excitement of Aldus' arrival, it had completely slipped her mind.

''Lovestruck fool,'' Ranulf grumbled on, unable to contain his frustration. ''Risking everyone's neck for one stupid glimpse of a girl he's going to be looking at the rest of his life anyway. Didn't he realize that both of them would have been a hell of a lot safer if he'd just kept his distance?''

Athaya absently prodded the damp earth with her toe. ''It's hard to stay away from someone you care about,'' she said quietly, not addressing anyone in particular, ''even if you know it's the best thing for both of you.''

Kale stepped forward, his expression grave. ''Cordry is scheduled for absolution the day after tomorrow.''

Athaya shut her eyes tight, wishing that the day was over before it had ever begun. ''What about Megan and Sir Jarvis?'' she asked suddenly, snapping her head up. ''My God, they haven't been—''

''No, they haven't been arrested,'' Ranulf assured her. ''Nobody can prove they've done anything wrong. But until the absolution ceremony is over, you can bet neither one of them will be able to use the chamber pot without the king's men knowing of it.''

''And that isn't all,'' he went on, turning his mouth down in a grimace. ''Bishop Lukin has already decided to perform the absolution ceremony himself. He says it's out of his respect for the Jarvis family—one of his ancestors was a lord of some kind, I guess—but I think he just wants to be there in case the infamous Athaya Trelane tries to pull off some sort of rescue.''

"Which, of course, she'll have to do," Athaya murmured. Absently, she pulled up a handful of tender grass and began to shred it between her fingers, but a minute later she hastily brushed it away and jumped to her feet, a ray of hope in her eyes. "And I know just the man to help her do it."

"No! I couldn't possibly get away with something like that!" Aldus backed away from her and shook his head resolutely, but Athaya paid no heed to his refusals. She knew it was far too soon to be asking such a thing of him, but there was simply no other way.

Athaya pulled the hood of her cloak closer around her face. She had risked a great deal coming to the cathedral in broad daylight, but she couldn't wait until evening to speak with him— not when time was so short. Even in the relative privacy of the vigil chapel near the apse she felt exposed and on edge, in constant readiness to slip under a cloaking spell at the slightest provocation. And the chapel was close enough to the corbal candlestick on the high altar that she could feel errant disruptions from it that, while they caused nothing worse than a dull headache, made her nerves grow even more taut.

"Aldus, you're our only hope. You're the only one who can make sure the chalice isn't poisoned during the ceremony. We can't get Cordry out of the bishop's palace beforehand—he's too well guarded."

"But can't you—what was the word—'translocate' him?" Aldus asked, desperate to find a solution that did not require his participation. "You said you could cross distances at will. Why not use the spell to slip inside at night and rescue him?"

"Because I've never been to the bishop's palace and I have to know what a place looks like before I can go there. And besides, Ranulf says that the guardsmen have orders never to leave Cordry alone. Even if I could get in, I'd never get able to get out again before the guards captured me, too—I told you before that the spell takes all of my strength."

Wringing his hands anxiously, Aldus began pacing in circles around the tiny chapel, occasionally pausing to gaze at the vigil lamp burning peacefully on the cloth-covered altar. "You don't understand—"

"I know I'm asking you to take an awful risk, Father, but a man's life is at stake. You have a holy obligation to help him. And so do we."

Aldus stared at the vigil lamp for a very long time. It seemed to offer him a modicum of peace, for when he spoke again, his voice was much less shrill. "Are you commanding me to do this, your Highness?" he said at last.

Athaya wiped the slickness from her palms on the front of her cloak. *I'm damned tempted, Father, believe me.*

"No," she said. "You answer to a higher power than mine, I assure you. But I beg you as a friend—as someone who shares your gift—don't turn your back on Cordry. He's one of us. And if we don't protect each other, every Lorngeld in this country is going to keep on suffering."

"But I can't!" he protested, wheeling around in a billow of black wool. "It's not that I wouldn't, but . . . the bishop asked *me* to assist at the ceremony. Don't you see? I have to refuse. The crystals on the high altar—they're starting to hurt so badly that I can't get near them anymore. I'll have to make an excuse and tell him I'm ill. There's no way I could go through with it and not have him suspect me."

Slowly, Athaya rose to her feet and joined him in front of the chapel's small altar. *No, there is a way,* she thought to herself, *it's just totally out of the question.*

Athaya thought long and hard, but as she saw it, the only possible solution was to teach Aldus how to cast the sealing spell—the spell that Athaya had been warned never to discuss with anyone outside the Circle—so that he could protect himself from discovery. With his powers locked away, he could handle the corbals without pain and Bishop Lukin would be hard-pressed to suspect him as a wizard.

Surely the Circle would understand . . .

"Come to the camp tonight, Aldus. I may have an answer by then." And before he could argue further, she hurried from the chapel, her face enveloped by the hood of her cloak.

I'm not going to stand by and let Cordry die when I have a perfectly good way of saving him, she swore to herself, striding rapidly down the ambulatory. *There aren't enough of us yet to risk losing even one.*

Rules or no rules, Lord Basil.

CHAPTER 16

"But you *have* to allow it, Tonia," Athaya pleaded later that morning. "Without the sealing spell, the bishop is bound to find out about Aldus, and there's no other way to keep Cordry from being poisoned during the ceremony."

"Shh! Keep it down, would you?" Tonia glanced rapidly out the window of the monastery bakehouse, where she was kneading the dough for the day's bread. "Nobody's supposed to know you can work that spell."

"But Aldus wouldn't tell anyone, and . . . I know!" she added with a burst of enthusiasm, "I'll ask him to hear my confession and then tell him about the spell. He'd never dare breathe a word about it to anyone under those circumstances."

Tonia threw up her hands in despair, leaving a cloud of flour in the air between them. The idea sounded entirely too logical for her taste. "Saints protect us, Athaya, the Overlord sent me here to make sure you stayed *out* of trouble, not to help you find more of it!"

"If you have a better idea then I'll gladly hear it," Athaya replied, "but God knows I can't think of another way. And we don't have time to convene the entire Circle and ask their formal permission."

Tonia responded with a series of indecipherable mumbles,

continuing to knead her bread with unnecessary force, but Athaya thought she caught the phrase "Why me?" escape the Master's lips somewhere in the midst of those mutterings. After another minute of silence, Tonia expelled a sigh and dumped the sticky lump of dough unceremoniously into a pan.

"Oh, all right. I don't see how I can possibly say no without looking like an ogre. But Lord above me, don't *ever* tell Basil about this or he'll have my liver for breakfast. But I'm damned well going to be there when you start teaching him about the seal," she declared, wagging a flour-whitened finger in Athaya's face. "That spell is nothing to fool with, and it's my responsibility to make sure the two of you know what you're doing."

After her earlier talk with Aldus, Athaya was afraid that he might not come to the camp at all that night. She was relieved when he eventually appeared, although it was almost an hour after his customary time, and he was far more apprehensive than usual.

The idea of hearing Athaya's confession troubled him to no small extent, and only when Athaya assured him that she wasn't going to burden him with what had happened between her and Kelwyn did he agree to hear it. They went into the chapel alone and settled down beside one another on the cold stone pew nearest the altar. He had barely finished sanctifying their meeting under the necessary vows of secrecy when she poured out her plans for how to save Cordry and protect Aldus' magical identity all at the same time.

"A spell I can cast on myself?" he exclaimed when she was finished. "So I can't feel the corbals?" Being unable to work his spells or be disturbed by corbals was clearly appealing to him; the answer to all his worries—or his prayers.

"But it's dangerous, Aldus," she cautioned him. "The sealing spell may protect you from corbal crystals, but it won't make your powers go away. Quite the opposite, in fact." Athaya went on to explain to him the risks involved if the seal was left on too long, how the mind would gradually weaken and eventually rupture under the growing pressure of the imprisoned power. Aldus' eyes grew wider and more horrified the longer she went on, appalled that such a potentially grisly spell—like the demons he feared so terribly—was living inside of him.

"You can't tell anyone about this spell, Aldus. Not *anyone*. I could get in some very serious trouble just for telling you, but there was simply no other choice."

"And you told me about it during confession just to make sure I'd keep quiet," he replied, drawing away from her with wounded pride.

Pricked by guilt, Athaya looked away and let her eyes fall on the bits of bark and leaves still strewn across the chapel floor. "It's not that I don't trust you," she said, all the while wondering how much she *could* trust someone who had taken vows to uphold the very beliefs she was trying to destroy, "but keeping the sealing spell a secret is important. I had to make you see that. And using the seal is the only way to save Cordry." She lifted her eyes from the litter-strewn floor and gazed at him imploringly. "Will you do it?"

It was quiet for a long while, the silence broken only occasionally by the hoot of an owl outside the chapel. Aldus closed his eyes, searching inwardly, then unclasped his hands and let them drop weakly to his lap. He nodded stiffly, as if it took great effort. "All right," he said, his voice barely above a whisper. "Tell me what to do."

Within minutes, Athaya had fetched Master Tonia to the chapel, and together they spent the rest of the evening teaching Aldus everything they knew about the sealing spell. He picked it up rapidly—it was not a difficult spell to learn—but he did voice a complaint when he realized that the seal unsettled his balance and made him feel as if he had a head cold.

"Better than the bite of a corbal crystal," Tonia said, shuddering at the thought. She touched his forehead and gently released his seal. "Oh, and one more thing," she added, "be careful that you're not physically touching anyone when you cast the spell, or it'll set the seal on them instead. If they're a wizard, that is. If they're not . . ." Tonia paused to think. "I don't think anything will happen, but I can't be sure. Better not take chances."

"Just don't set the seal until you have to," Athaya reminded him. "And afterward, come find one of us to release you. The seal shouldn't do any real harm—I was taught that the worst effects don't manifest for several weeks—but since your power is still maturing, I don't think it's wise to restrain it any longer than necessary."

Aldus nodded at all this advice, desperately trying to remember every shred of information. Something else was troubling him, however, and his face was creased by worry lines. "But what about later, after the ceremony is over? There will still be corbals on the altar and they hurt more and more with each passing day. I can't spend the rest of my life running to one of you every time I've had to shield myself from them."

Athaya and Tonia exchanged a look of concern. That dilemma had already occurred to them, but neither one had come up with a solution yet. "Let's worry about that after Cordry is safe," Athaya said, pushing the problem to the back of her mind. "Right now we have to find some way of letting Megan and Sir Jarvis know what we're planning."

Athaya glanced hopefully at Father Aldus, and the pained look of inevitability that crossed his face told her that he already knew what she was going to ask him to do next.

The next evening was sultry and still, more like late summer than the first day of May. Athaya's clothes stuck stubbornly to her skin as she sat on a tattered blanket in the back of a rented cart, silently muttering curses at the prickly bits of straw and clods of damp earth clinging to her peasant gown. Dom DePere was just as irritated with the shabby accommodations, but Tonia and Ranulf merely chuckled merrily at their companions' discomfort, blaming it on an overprivileged upbringing.

Snapping the reins of two sorry-looking mares, Kale urged the cart forward to the mouth of a squalid little alley and pointed across the cathedral square. "It must be about time. They're starting to go inside."

Squinting against the harsh orange sunset, Athaya watched the city's foremost citizens, each clad in his finest spring attire, climb the spacious steps and file into the sanctuary with what Athaya thought to be ghoulish dispatch. Most of the congregation was already inside before the bells in the cathedral's tower sounded the call to the ceremony, announcing the commencement of Cordry Jarvis' journey to the next world.

As Athaya had expected, Bishop Lukin had taken precautions against any attempt at a rescue. She had seen no fewer than two squadrons of the king's burgundy-clad guardsmen file into the sanctuary—apparently with the bishop's sanction to enter the church fully armed—while another two squadrons remained outside to guard the doors and watch the surrounding streets for signs of trouble. Along with their daggers and swords, Athaya noticed that each man who entered the sanctuary had a small hand mirror hanging from his belt. Durek had clearly warned them of at least one wizards' trick in advance. No doubt Athaya's appearance at Kelwyn's funeral last September had reminded him how easily wizards could slip into places they were not wanted.

"Time to go," Tonia announced, signaling Mason to join her. "The rest of you stay out of sight until you hear the chimes, then come around to the east gates as soon as you can. We'll want to beat it quick the minute we've got Cordry."

Ranulf nodded grumpily, still piqued that he could not take part in the more interesting part of the evening. But Aldus had informed them that Father Greste was to be Lukin's other assistant that night and would recognize Athaya, Kale, or Ranulf from their meeting at the Jarvis house. Thus, it was their duty to remain with the cart while the others obtained Cordry's body. In the meantime, all they could do was monitor the ceremony through vision spheres and hope Father Aldus fulfilled by far the most critical part of the plan.

When Tonia and Mason had gone, Kale moved the cart even deeper into the narrow alley, and Ranulf settled down beside Athaya on the straw.

"I'll cast a cloak over us while you keep an eye on things with your sphere," he said, grasping her arm so that his cloaking spell would shield them both from sight. Then he snorted under his breath. "Finally get a pretty girl into the hay with me and I can't try a damned thing," he muttered, chuckling when Athaya's eyes opened just a little wider.

Athaya cast her sphere and conjured a clear image of the sanctuary. It was bedecked with sprigs of lilac, and brightly lit with white candles; an obscenely festive setting for such a morbid ritual.

"Do Megan and Sir Jarvis know what to do?" she asked quietly, catching sight of them in the pew nearest the altar. If they did, they were certainly playing their part well. Megan's eyes were red and puffed from crying, and Jarvis stared straight before him, seeing nothing and surely not hearing a note of the preparatory anthems being sung by the choir.

"I hope so. But they'd better turn out to be damned good actors or this could blow up right in our faces."

And Aldus will be suspected for certain, she thought. The priest had openly visited both the Loring and Jarvis houses that afternoon, ostensibly to offer prayers of condolence, but actually to inform them of Athaya's plans. And according to Aldus, enough people—the king's men among them—had witnessed both visits so that his involvement in the plot would be undeniable should anything to wrong.

"Megan is meeting Cam and Gilda at the sheepfold later," Ranulf went on, his voice a coarse whisper. "They'll bring her to the camp, and she and Cordry can leave from there. But Jarvis says he won't leave Kaiburn. Loves his mill too much."

"It's hard to start your life all over again." Briefly, Athaya's mind flashed back to the tumult of the past year, and the image in her sphere blurred for a moment. *God knows it was hard enough for me.*

"He should be safe enough. Even if someone finds out Cordry was never killed, there's no proof that his father was involved. And I suspect Bishop Lukin appreciates Sir Jarvis' generous donations to the cathedral far too much to make unnecessary trouble."

Athaya commanded her sphere to focus its image more clearly now that the ceremony was under way. The choir fell silent as the bishop stepped into the pulpit, his bright red stole streaming over snowy white robes like fresh blood. When he offered the opening prayers, his booming voice sounded like a field commander calling his troops to attention.

"Beloved children of God, we are gathered here in the sight of God to proclaim His rightful rule over this world and all her people and to proclaim our loyalty and submission to His word. One of our number has come forward to renounce the gift given to him by the Dark Angel upon his birth, who, in his eternal evil, seeks to lure his children back to him through the temptations of magic. But as this supplicant forsakes his life, so shall he find life, and as he meets death, so shall he conquer death, and dwell in the house of the Lord forever."

The vestry door to the side of the altar area opened, and Father Aldus and Greste emerged, both clad in somber black cassocks. Supported between them, clad in an unadorned white robe, was Cordry. His knees wobbled noticeably, and Athaya could tell by the vacant expression in his eyes that he had been heavily sedated with looca-smoke.

Once Cordry had been placed in a kneeling position at Lukin's feet, the bishop moved to the head of the altar steps. "Who brings forth this man for the sacrament of absolution?"

Reluctantly, Sir Jarvis rose to his feet, one white-knuckled hand clutched around the end of a walking stick. His face was deathly pale, certain that he was seeing his son for the last time. When he spoke, his voice was flat and lifeless, the words devoid of spirit and hope.

"I do."

"And do you freely deliver him into the care of God's holy church, such that his soul may be cleansed and his spirit transported unto God?"

There was a long pause, and for one terrifying instant, Athaya thought that he might refuse to offer the traditional response. His eyes flared. He was clearly tempted by the thought, but instead he whispered quietly, "I do."

As the choir began to sing a plainsong chant, Lukin gave a curt signal to Father Aldus. Athaya thought the priest looked unusually nervous as he turned his back to the congregation and began to mix the wine. His eyes flickered once to the corbal-studded candlestick on one side of the altar, but he showed no signs of pain—only a tendency to walk with a slight lack of rhythm, his balance distorted by the sealing spell.

As he lifted the chalice, Aldus lurched forward and spilled some of the wine on the altar cloth, leaving an ugly red blotch on the embroidered white linen. He quickly recovered himself—not before Lukin scowled at his clumsiness, however—and handed the chalice to the bishop with a suitably apologetic look on his face.

Holding the cup aloft, Lukin turned to face the congregation. "O Heavenly Father, bless this cup and bless he who shall partake of it, for in so doing he partakes of your divine nature."

The bishop motioned Cordry to stand, which he did only with Father Greste's assistance. "Now rise, my son, and take this cup, and do not wish it to pass from you, for what you do now is good in the sight of God."

As Cordry's hands grasped the cup, Athaya saw Jarvis slump back into his seat and look away, while Megan buried her face in the shoulder of the young woman beside her, presumably a sister. The rest of the congregation was unnaturally silent, and Athaya thought she could almost hear the sound of their collective heartbeats as they watched Cordry drink from the chalice. The soldiers in the cathedral relaxed their grip on their weapons as he drained the cup and handed it back, their faces showing a touch of disappointment that their services had not been required.

All along, Athaya had expected Cordry to simply drift off to sleep. To slide to the floor at the bishop's feet and then be carried swiftly away. She did not expect to see Cordry's muscles twitch violently—the first effects of *kahnil* poisoning—nor did she expect to see Megan jump to her feet with an expression of utter terror on her face, eyes darting only once to Father Aldus in silent, desperate query.

Cordry did not cry out in pain, but his mouth fell open in a silent, timeless gasp. Snatching one last moment of lucidity, he stumbled backward and tried to flee. "Megan, where are you?" he called wildly, but before he could escape the altar area, the assistant priests took his arms and restrained him. Only after a bout of violent trembling did he finally crumple to the ground, the white robe settling down around him like a gentle snowfall.

Athaya kept her eyes fixed on the image in her sphere, conscious of the growing fury inside her. *If you've killed him, Aldus, I swear I'll take you to hell myself.* But Aldus didn't seem surprised by what had happened, only anxious to proceed with his task by shrouding the body with an embroidered cloth and helping Father Greste and two other assistants carry it back to the vestry.

As the body was being taken away, the chimes in the bell tower pealed out in dissonant victory. Hearing the signal, Kale snapped the reins and coaxed the two mares to move the cart into position.

"Is it over?" came Ranulf's voice in her ear.

"Almost. There's still the closing hymn and benediction," she said, keeping the rest of what she had seen to herself. If Ranulf had the slightest suspicion that Aldus had betrayed them, he might very well burst into the sanctuary and break the priest's neck. Athaya remained silent as the cart circled around to the cathedral's east end, concentrating on keeping the image in her sphere from dissipating.

"Behold, O Lord," Lukin was proclaiming, lifting his palms toward the vaulted ceiling. "We have acted according to your laws and delivered this man's soul unto you. Bestow upon his soul the blessings of life ever after and fill him with your grace and heavenly peace."

As the choir began to sing the closing hymn, Athaya shifted the sphere's image to the vestry. She saw Aldus bending over Cordry's body, the face draped with a thin white cloth, while Greste motioned the other two black-robed men to rejoin Bishop Lukin in the sanctuary for the final hymn and benediction. The moment they were gone, Athaya saw another door open, and Mason and Tonia stepped inside. They were clad in the somber black costumes of house servants, and kept their eyes dutifully lowered.

"We've come for him, Father Aldus," Mason said, bowing courteously. "There is a carriage waiting outside."

Greste frowned deeply. "Come for whom? What carriage? Father Aldus, what is he talking about?"

"I'm sorry," Aldus said, trying his best to sound casual. "I neglected to tell you. These are servants of Sir Jarvis. When I spoke with him this afternoon, he expressed his wish that his son's body be laid out at home for a few days before the burial."

Greste grimaced, his tongue working inside of his mouth as if he'd bitten into a too-sour apple. "I didn't think anyone adhered to that gruesome old custom anymore," he remarked, so quiet that only Aldus could hear.

"I'll take care of this. You can join the others for the benediction. I'll be out shortly."

The moment Greste departed, Athaya banished her sphere. The cart was now directly behind the door nearest the vestry, just outside the wall of the cathedral close. Aldus hurried forward to hold open the iron gate, while Tonia and Mason carried Cordry between them. They quickly placed him on the cart and tossed a few woolen blankets over him to hide the sight of the glaring white robe.

"Is he all right?" Athaya demanded, catching Aldus' sleeve. But Aldus jerked away, mumbling something about getting back in time for the benediction, and retreated inside the cathedral. She couldn't tell if he looked guilty or simply nervous, but she couldn't very well follow him into the sanctuary to ask.

"Now stay under there and keep quiet," Ranulf ordered, tossing a rancid-smelling wool blanket over Athaya's head as well. "Last thing we need is for some sharp-eyed soldier to catch a glimpse of you."

The odor of old sweat and manure clung to the blanket, and Athaya had to busy herself with other thoughts so that her stomach would not grow queasy. The cart rumbled away, wheels clacking over uneven stones, and for an instant Athaya felt her muscles relax, confident that they had made it.

"Uh-oh," came Tonia's muffled voice. "Look there. A couple of the king's men are patrolling the wall up ahead."

Athaya didn't dare look herself, but listened frantically to the whispers being exchanged around her. She heard Ranulf expel air through his teeth in suppressed anger. "Didn't the fools hear the chimes? What should they care what we're doing here now that Cordry is supposedly dead?"

Tonia whispered a curse. "Kale, turn down this—oh, damn it all, they've seen us. We'll have to bluff our way past this."

"We won't stand a chance if they poke their noses under that blanket," Mason murmured. "Any of the king's men will know Athaya on sight, and Cordry will be a little hard to explain in that absolution robe. And look—the man on the right has a mirror."

"God almighty, now what?" Tonia said. "We can't turn back without making them suspicious, and we certainly can't up and kill them . . ."

Huddled under the foul-smelling blanket with a still-unconscious Cordry, Athaya listened to the hushed talk around her with a gnawing sensation of dread. A cloaking spell would be useless against mirrors, and even if she could duck out of the cart and slip into an alley somewhere, after a generous dose of Aldus' sleeping potion—if indeed that's all it was—Cordry certainly wasn't going to be able to escape on his own.

"Tonia?" she whispered."

"Shush up and don't move," came the harsh reply. "They're only about twenty yards ahead of us."

Athaya bit down hard on her lip. There was only one way to get out of this and it wouldn't help them all. But it was the only chance Cordry had left.

"Tonia, wish me luck," she whispered, and before the Master could admonish her again, Athaya closed her eyes and began to drift. She sank deep into her paths—deeper than she'd ever gone, save once, when she yearned to escape from yet another threat and find a safe place to hide.

"Halt there," came the brusque voice of a guardsman, perilously close. "State your business."

Athaya took hold of Cordry with both hands, and when she found the proper spell, she channeled every bit of energy she had into it.

First there was a jolt, then a blinding white light riddled with colorful images, each giving off its own noise in a dizzying chorus of nonsense. In the space of two heartbeats the clatter died away, and she felt the ground go solid beneath her again. Around her, she heard nothing but the gentle rustle of an evening breeze.

And when she opened her eyes, she saw Cordry sleeping peacefully on the damp grass beside her underneath the shadows of the ruined bell tower.

"I always believed you could do it, Athaya," Tonia said later, once the others had rejoined her at the camp, "but when I looked back and saw the two of you gone . . . it was incredible!"

Cam and Gilda had escorted Megan from the sheepfold, where she'd agreed to meet them after the ceremony, and while she sat with Cordry in a spare room in the dormitory everyone else gathered around the fire beneath the bell tower to hear the tale of his deliverance. "How did you know you could take somebody with you?" Tonia went on, eager for details on the little-known spell of translocation.

"Frankly, I didn't know. But I thought I remembered Master Credony's essay speculating that you could translocate with another person so long as you were in physical contact." Athaya shrugged resignedly. "I figured it was a good time to test the Master's theory."

"A damned good time," Ranulf stated. "Those soldiers searched the cart not two minutes after you and Cordry vanished. And they had one of those damned leaflets with them, with orders to look for somebody answering your description." Ranulf tossed another log on the fire and let out a sigh of relief. "Lucky for us they didn't have any corbals with them or I don't know what we would have done. Let Kale come to the rescue, I guess. Again."

Just then, Megan came out to join them, swinging her arms contentedly.

"How is he?" Athaya asked.

"Oh, he'll be fine. I don't know what Father Aldus gave him, but it wasn't enough to put him to sleep for too long. He's resting now, but he's awake. Awake enough to start mumbling something about building a new mill in Kilfarnan," Megan added, pursing her lips in mock disdain, "so I left."

"I just hope our wizard-priest hasn't been found out by the bishop," Tonia said with concern. "I'll be worried about him until he checks in with us tomorrow." She exchanged a glance with Athaya, both of them knowing that the sealing spell would not harm Father Aldus for quite some time, while being discovered by the bishop was a much more immediate and potentially disastrous threat.

Megan held her hands up to the fire, a vagrant grin playing about her face. "Actually," she said, "he'll be here later tonight. When he came to the house to tell me about your plans, I asked if he could marry Cordry and me before we left Kaiburn. No one else in the city could possibly have done it, so he agreed. Didn't want us going off together without being properly married, I suppose," she added with a touch of mischief in her eyes. "And when he told me that you had a chapel here, I knew it would be the perfect place."

True to his promise, Aldus arrived at the camp an hour later. Subtly, Tonia touched him briefly to release him from the sealing spell, and he squeezed her hand in silent thanks, making no mention of the spell in front of the others. Athaya offered him a somewhat sheepish greeting, finding it difficult to meet his gaze as she thanked him for his help. Since realizing that Cordry had obviously not been poisoned, Athaya felt deeply ashamed for doubting Aldus' word and suspecting he had betrayed them.

"I can't stay long," Aldus said, his voice still unsteady. His anxiety melted a bit as he smiled at Megan, who knelt in the grass near the fire. "But I promised to perform a wedding tonight."

It was a brief and simple ceremony, but that didn't bother Megan at all. She didn't mind being married in a run-down old chapel strewn with debris and lit by a ring of witchlights, nor did it bother her that the groom still wore the stark white robe of an absolution candidate. Cordry was woozy and only half-awake during the ceremony, and Mason stood at his side to make sure he didn't topple over. Shortly after midnight, Cordry and Megan were pronounced man and wife, and Cordry kissed his bride and promptly drifted back to sleep, still muddled by the effects of Aldus' drug.

"Ah well, I suppose I can wait one more day," Megan said with a smile, touching her husband lightly on the cheek as Ranulf, Mason, and Kale carried him out of the sanctuary. The reddish light of the witchlights flickered in her eyes as she turned back to Athaya. "At least now I know we belong to one another. No matter what happens."

Athaya felt a chill ripple down her spine as she banished the witchlights and escorted Megan from the sanctuary. *I just want to make sure we truly belong to one another,* Jaren had said. *That we have our share of happiness in case one of us doesn't make it.*

Suddenly, walking at Megan's side, Athaya felt quite cowardly.

Shortly after the absolution ceremony was over, and Bishop Lukin had offered a few personal, if obligatory, words of consolation to Sir Jarvis, he busied himself with setting everything back in its proper place, folding away his stole, and pouring out the rest of the tainted wine.

"Sir Jarvis seems to have accepted it at last," Father Greste told the bishop after the last of the congregation had departed. "But I fear it will take longer for Miss Loring. Her family says she has been slow to admit that Cordry was one of the Devil's own."

The bishop nodded absently, unable to offer much sympathy for the wizard's betrothed. Rumor held that she had tried to turn Cordry from his ways weeks ago, but now that the boy was dead, such tales hardly seemed to matter.

"Has the body been taken for burial?" Lukin asked, his tone cool and clipped as if he were merely checking one more task off his list.

"No, it's been taken to the Jarvis house," Greste reported obediently. "Sir Jarvis wished to have his son laid out for a short time, so folks could pay their respects."

Lukin furrowed his brow. "What? I was not told of this request."

"Nor was I, but two of his servants were waiting by the vestry door to pick up the body. Apparently they had made arrangements with Father Aldus. Sir Jarvis probably didn't wish to bother you with his request, my Lord Bishop. It's not been easy for him to talk about it, and—''

''I suppose not,'' the bishop said curtly. He frowned his displeasure, even though there was little reason to. None of the king's men had reported anything amiss in the sanctuary, and the men patrolling the surrounding streets found no one attempting to stop the ceremony. The bishop's perfectly orchestrated evening had gone off without a hitch—although he had held his own hopes that the king's renegade sister might dare to appear—and this one slight irregularity irritated him. But no matter. The wizard was dead—absolved of his curse. What did it matter if Jarvis wished to indulge in such a barbaric custom by displaying the corpse?

He waved his hand carelessly toward the altar. ''One more thing. I expect you'll have to change the altar cloth. Father Aldus spilled a good bit of wine on it during the ritual, and *kahnil* is very acidic. It's probably eaten a hole in the cloth as large as my palm by now.''

''I've already removed it, my Lord Bishop. But the cloth is fine. Stained from the wine, of course, but that'll come out in time.''

The bishop frowned again. Another slight irregularity. ''Let me see.''

Greste handed him the folded cloth, but after examining it thoroughly he found little evidence that *kahnil* had touched it at all.

Slowly, Lukin picked up the chalice from the altar and ran his finger around the bowl. He sniffed it carefully, then touched it to his tongue. His heavy brows folded in toward one another.

''A simple soporific,'' he murmured, and for a brief moment, one end of his mouth curled up, grudgingly impressed by his secretary's ingenuity. Admittedly, there was a trace of *kahnil* in the mixture—enough to cause a muscle spasm or two, but hardly enough to kill.

He set the chalice back down. ''Where is Father Aldus?'' he asked with calculated indifference.

''I don't know, my Lord Bishop. He left right after the ceremony.''

''To bed, I assume?''

''No. He went into the city. Perhaps he was called out for last rites,'' Greste suggested. ''One of his parishioners has reportedly been ill for quite some time.''

''Yes. So I've been told.'' Lukin turned around slowly, careful to keep his expression placid. ''If you see Father Aldus later tonight, send him to my study. He seemed a bit disoriented during the ceremony, and I want to make sure he's feeling all right. Especially since he's been tending the sick,'' Lukin added, properly pious.

The older priest nodded dutifully and scurried about his tasks, while Lukin remained at the altar, glaring at the empty chalice.

''Father Aldus,'' he said aloud, soft enough so Greste would not hear. ''You are being led into temptation of the worst kind, I fear.''

CHAPTER 17

✳

WHEN JAREN OPENED HIS EYES, IT WAS STILL DARK, BUT with the cruel promise of dawn perhaps an hour away. The smell of saltwater and rotting seaweed was strong in his nostrils as he tried to shift his weight to a less painful position on the hard, damp sand. The flap of the tent was pulled back, and a chill wind snaked underneath his cloak and sent shivers rippling through his limbs, each movement piercing the cramped muscles like a needle.

But at least he was alert enough to know where he was, and that alone was something new.

Since being seized by Captain Parr and his men nearly three weeks before, this was the first morning Jaren had awakened with anything remotely resembling a clear head. Before crossing the border into Caithe, the men had constantly kept him on the very brink of unconsciousness, forcing him full of sour-smelling wine whenever they could and letting the corbal do its work whenever he spilled up what his stomach could not hold.

Between exhaustion, hunger, sickness, and the constant stab of the crystal, Jaren's power never had time to fully rejuvenate. But over the last few days, during the scant moments of lucidity they allowed him, he began to notice that the men were growing more careless the closer they drew to Delfarham, confident that even if their captive were to escape, he would be trapped in hostile lands for weeks before reaching the safety of the Reykan border and could easily be apprehended. They had not been as diligent about keeping him senseless, nor had they been as careful to awaken before he did to guard against his slipping away during the morning hours when what meager powers he had were strengthened by sleep. Bit by bit, Jaren could feel the effects of their negligence and this morning he sensed a long-awaited trickle of magic moving through him like the welcome warmth of a campfire on a chill winter's evening.

Not that he was fully recovered by any means. As he shifted his weight from the stones beneath his blanket, he made the mistake of moving too quickly and his head started whirling in circles. A surge of bile rose halfway up his throat, lingered indecisively, and then receded, leaving a foul, pasty taste in his mouth.

Aware that there was not much time before the men would rouse themselves and begin another grueling day's ride, and even more aware that he needed to make good use of what consciousness he had before it was brutally taken from him again, Jaren rolled over with his back to the tent's opening and tried to splay his hands far enough apart to form a vision sphere. The ropes made it difficult, but at least the bindings around his wrists were looser than those around his ankles. If he pressed his forearms together, he could force his hands backward far enough to support the sphere.

Or at least he hoped so.

"Occulta me," he whispered, startled at the parched, tone-less sound of his own voice. His mouth went dry as he waited to see if the tendrils would come. A sphere did not take so much strength, and he only had to sustain it long enough to call . . .

It felt like the better part of an hour, but within a few nerve-racking minutes, a tenuous orb appeared, suspended gingerly between his fingertips. It wasn't perfectly round, nor did it look as if it would last very long, but he was already sweating from the effort and dared not try to make it sturdier for fear it would drain what little power he had.

Concentrating as hard as he could, he willed an image into the sphere—demanded it to come, as hard as he had ever commanded an image before. Blood pounded through his head and blackened his vision like a sudden tide, then gradually subsided. He almost cried out his joy when a faint image appeared.

Colors swirled lazily about—shades of green wrapped in the misty whiteness of the sphere like a forest in a snowstorm. When the image took shape, he saw a shabby little room somewhere with even shabbier furnishings: a rusty oil lamp, blankets drawn across the windows to serve as makeshift shutters, a broken ale barrel for a table. But it was the most welcome sight he'd seen in weeks, for on the pallet in the corner, nuzzled under a tattered quilt, was Athaya.

His hands shook with the thrill of finding her, and he had to breathe deeply for a moment to steady himself. The last thing he needed was to break the sphere; he doubted he could summon it back again, not to mention suffering through the throbbing headache that a shattered sphere promised.

Athaya, he sent to her, using as much strength as he dared. *Wake up—hurry, there's not much time.*

The image was blurred and unsteady, like trying to peer through rain-streaked glass, but he saw her shift under the blankets as if reluctantly floating up from the depths of a pleasant dream.

Athaya, can you hear me?

He was so desperate to reach her that he almost lost the image, and it took every ounce of concentration he had to rein in his emotions and keep the sphere under control.

Anxiously, he licked the salty drops of perspiration from his lips. *Athaya, please . . .*

Then she rolled onto her back, and her eyes snapped open. "Jaren?"

And just as he drew breath to go on, his head exploded into fireworks of pain, and instead of the delicate sphere between his hands he saw the wicked blade of the dagger that had pierced it, steel glistening from the orb's sticky residue. Instantly, the pounding in his skull began, and somewhere in the midst of that pain he felt the dagger bite down into the flesh of his throat.

Captain Parr looked down on him in loathing, eyes and teeth glowing white in the darkness. With a flick of his wrist, he pricked the tender skin under Jaren's jaw with his blade, coaxing out a few drops of blood.

"Mind-plagued wizard . . . you'll get no more chances like that between here and Delfarham."

Then Jaren felt the sickly crack of the dagger's hilt against his skull, and the brilliant burst of stars before his eyes quickly melted into darkness.

"Jaren?"

Her own voice sounded strange in her ears and jerked her awake sooner than she would have liked. Athaya glanced around warily, half expecting to see someone in the room with her—or at the very least, a ghostly remnant of her dream—but once she realized she was alone, she sat up and rubbed the sand from her eyes.

Something had pulled at her then let go abruptly, but it lingered still, somewhere in the back of her mind. Not since the *mekahn* had she been so rudely jolted awake by too-real dreams, and that fact gave her cause for alarm.

Those dreams had always boded ill.

Even though it was still dark, Athaya doubted she could go back to sleep. The sensation—it had been so real! And more, it was not fright that had waked her, but a sudden rush of joy at hearing his voice—joy, because she had reacted purely from instinct. Her conscious self, still asleep, had forgotten to remind her that she had rational reasons for wanting him to stay away and that she should not want to see him here.

I think that her unconscious mind knows more about magic than she does right now, Hedric had remarked once, when she was struggling with the onset of her power.

Knows more about magic? Athaya wondered suddenly. *Or more about everything?*

Wrapping herself in a thick woolen cloak, she slipped out of the dormitory and went into the chapel to think. She curled up in one of the stone pews, shivering as its coldness seeped through her cloak, and gazed at the altar where Megan and Cordry had been married less than six hours before.

"Why do I get the feeling someone's just about to tap me on the shoulder and say 'I told you so'?" she murmured, then dropped her eyes from the altar and fixed her gaze on the moonlit cluster of dead leaves in the corner of the chapel.

Even in the predawn silence Athaya had no peace, her mind echoing with voices clamoring for her attention. One insisted she had made the right choice, but another, more seductive voice—her all-knowing unconscious, perhaps?—asserted that she still had a chance to atone for her mistakes. But as with the *mekahn*, the more she tried to ignore the voices, the more they persisted, refusing to die away until she turned to face them.

She didn't know how she could have dozed off during such a quiet turmoil, but the next thing she knew, bright rays of green-filtered sunlight were streaming into the chapel, and Tonia was gently nudging her awake.

"Usually folks don't fall asleep in church unless the preacher's talking," she remarked, eyes wrinkling at the edges as she smiled.

Athaya was too groggy to appreciate Tonia's levity; if the Master had one fault it was being far too cheerful in the early-morning hours. Shivering, Athaya tucked her feet under her cloak, wishing she had thought to bring a pair of slippers.

"I've been looking for you," Tonia went on. "Cordry and Megan are just about to leave, and I thought you'd want to come out and see them off. He looks none the worse for wear after yesterday, although he isn't too happy about having slept straight through his wedding night." Grinning, she let out a merry chuckle. "Ah, well. I expect they'll make up for it."

Tonia took in a refreshing dose of crisp morning air and expelled it with vigor, then realized that Athaya hadn't said a word yet. "Something the matter?"

Athaya shrugged listlessly. "I don't know. I had a dream that Jaren was calling to me. At least I assume it was a dream," she added, frowning slightly. "It seemed so real . . . I'd swear I actually *heard* him."

Tonia settled down in the pew next to her, smothering a squeal at the cold stone. "I doubt he'd be calling you in the middle of the night. Besides, even an adept would have trouble reaching you from Ulard—spheres do have their limits, you know." Tonia smiled at her indulgently. "Could it be just a bit of wishful thinking on your part?"

Athaya cast her a sidelong glance, trying to guess how much Tonia already knew about the situation. "Maybe." Then she looked away, suddenly feeling very much alone. "I think I've made a terrible mistake, Tonia. I don't know if you heard, but Jaren asked me to marry him. Right before we left Ath Luaine."

Tonia tipped her head to one side. "I thought there was something afoot between you two. I tried to get Hedric to tell me what it was, but getting a secret out of him is like getting a smile out of Lord Basil. Old mule,'' she added, shaking her head in mock disdain. "Both of them."

"I said no," Athaya told her, feeling the pain of her refusal all over again. "He was so hurt, Tonia . . . I wouldn't be surprised if he never spoke to me again."

"Oh, don't be silly. I've known that boy since the day he came into this world, and he's not the type to carry grudges. Too much old-fashioned compassion in him. His father's the same way, although you'd never know it underneath all that bluster." Then Tonia folded her hands in her lap, the familiar playfulness in her eyes changing to sincere concern. "Do you love him?"

Athaya glancing skyward as if the answer could somehow be found in the shadowed ceiling of the chapel. "Master Tonia, I've been asking myself that question for months. Funny thing is, I think I've known the answer all along."

You wouldn't be so torn up about this if you weren't hopelessly in love with him already.

Athaya bowed her head. *Oh, Nicolas . . . you know me far too well.*

"I feel safe with him, Tonia. And confident, as if nothing in the world can beat me when he's near. He's the best friend I have in the world—he and my brother Nicolas. I don't know when I started to feel differently about him," she added, shaking her head. "One day I just . . . did. Like the way it can rain for hours during the night before the patter on the glass finally wakes you up enough to notice. You don't know exactly when the rain began to fall . . . but only that it's there now."

Athaya picked up a dead leaf from the floor and began to shred it between her fingers, its brittle powder falling on her cloak like ash. "I guess I didn't want to admit what I felt for him. That would have made it real. And I could see everything happening all over again—it just scared me too much."

"And that's why you refused him?"

"I didn't want him risking his life for me, Tonia. Not after what happened to Tyler." She glanced up uneasily, hoping she wouldn't have to explain. "Hedric told you about that, didn't he?"

"As much as he thought I should know. But tell me this, Athaya," she said, pressing her palms together, sagelike, "if it hurt that much to lose him, would you rather have not known him at all?"

In her mind's eye, Athaya saw an old woman in a dimly lit cathedral and a young priest trying to comfort her, and remembered pondering that very question. But the answer that had eluded her that day now asserted itself with surprising force. "Tyler? God, no. He's one of the few happy memories I have of the past three years."

Tonia smiled gently. "Then I think you've answered your own question." The Master paused for a moment, touching one finger to her lips as she arranged her thoughts. "It seems to me, Athaya, that you've placed yourself under a different kind of sealing spell. A seal that only you can release."

Athaya frowned at her inquiringly. "What do you mean?"

"Every one of us has an inner voice, Athaya. It tells us what we really feel, what we know will make us happy—things that should be quite obvious except that most of us spend the better part of our lives fighting it, insisting on doing what we *should* do instead of what we truly *want* to do. But you can no more deny that voice than you can deny your own magic. And if you lock it away and refuse to face what your soul is trying to tell you, it can be just as damaging as any sealing spell. It might not kill the body, but it can kill the spirit. And sometimes," she added, her eyes growing distant, "that's even more of a tragedy.

"Oh, listen to me—I'm droning on like an old philosopher," she said, breaking the solemn atmosphere with a chuckle. "All I'm really trying to say is that second thoughts usually surface for a reason."

"But how can I be his wife knowing that every day when I wake up beside him it might be for the last time?" Athaya cried, an edge of desperation in her voice. "It took a long time for that pit in my stomach to go away, Tonia. I know what it feels like and I don't want it to happen again! I'm just not that strong. Maybe I was once, but—"

"You're stronger than you think, my dear. You wouldn't be here otherwise. You'd be hiding in Reyka, still brooding over the past and not getting on with the future. Not doing what the Lorngeld in Caithe need you to do."

Tonia clasped Athaya's hands firmly between hers, as if steadying her for a blow. "This may come out sounding harsh, Athaya, and I don't mean it to . . . but what are you more afraid of? Jaren dying for your cause, or the pain *you'll* feel if he does?''

Athaya was struck silent, stripped of the power to speak. The bare, ugly truth of those words pierced her to the quick, and she felt trapped in an emotional ambush, defenseless, and knowing there was no one to rescue her. The dark secrets of a selfish soul had finally been held up to public scrutiny, and she felt her flesh grow hot with shame as she was forced to step forward and recognize that soul as hers.

''A man who sticks his hand in the fire remembers what it feels like, Tonia,'' Athaya snapped, suddenly finding it much more difficult to defend what she had done. ''He'd have to be crazy to go off and do it again.''

''Maybe. But you'd call the same man brave if he knowingly takes the risk of . . . say, running into a burning house to save someone trapped inside. Knowing what the pain of fire is like and yet risking it again—that's true bravery.''

Athaya pondered that point for a long time, thoughts tumbling over themselves in a frenzy. Once made, it would be an irreversible decision, but somehow it felt less daunting now, as if by talking things out, some long-sought source of strength had finally come to her. Megan had risked herself for Cordry; Aldus had risked himself for both of them. Why should she, as their supposed leader, lack their courage?

You're asking them to risk things you're not willing to, Athaya.

For the first time that morning, she smiled, certain what she must do. *No, Nicolas. Not anymore.*

''I have to go back,'' she said at last, speaking as much to herself as she was to Tonia. ''Before he really does forget me. I could use my translocation spell to get to Ath Luaine, and then ride to Ulard . . .'' Her voice trailed off while her thoughts spun on ahead, weaving a tapestry of the future that she hadn't dared to envision before. And it was a glorious thing . . .

''Then take the day to think on it, Athaya. Make sure it's what you really want. And if you feel the same way tomorrow, then go to him. Go with my blessing.''

Offering Athaya a kindly wink, Master Tonia got up and cocked her thumb in the direction of the camp's clearing. ''Now that you've settled your own future, don't you think it's time to wish Cordry and Megan off on theirs?''

When they joined the others in the clearing, Megan was nuzzled next to Cordry, arms linked, chattering on about their plans. Gilda and Cameron were stacking up the breakfast dishes beside the campfire while Mason was busy packing a satchel of cheese, fruit, and dried meats for the couple's journey.

"We'll be heading west," Megan said. "Cordry's got it into his head to build a new mill near Kilfarnan. And unfortunately," she added, rolling her eyes lovingly, "with the money that Aldus brought us from his father, he can do it."

The mere mention of the mill made Cordry's eyes gleam. "The river's fast there, I've heard, and the water's hard, so we can make a fine broadcloth with—"

"Oh, quiet now," Megan scolded. "You can talk my ear off about it later, but show our friends some mercy, won't you?"

It was only then that Athaya looked more closely at the satchel that Mason was packing, and realized it was his. When he caught her puzzled stare, he set the bundle aside. His eyes were expectant, earnestly hoping for approval.

"There wasn't time to tell you before, your Highness, but I've decided to go with them. Not that our newlyweds need a chaperon," he added dryly, "but Cordry's training is still limited to basic spells. By the time we reach Kilfarnan, I'll have him up to snuff."

"Will you be back?"

"Not for a while," Mason admitted. "With your leave, I'd like to take word of what we're doing to other parts of Caithe. If nothing else, it should make everyone think there are more of us than there are."

Ranulf grunted his laughter. "Just take to the woods, my friend—you make enough noise for a dozen men."

Knowing he would soon be leaving Ranulf's gibes behind, Mason responded with a tolerant smile. "Once I find a suitable place, I'll set up another school like our sheepfold. Who knows?" he went on, eyes reflecting a fountain of possibilities. "Maybe it will become a full-fledged Wizard's College someday."

"You're thinking on a mighty grand scale," Tonia remarked, not at all displeased.

"I told you I was a dreamer, Tonia." Then he turned back to Athaya. "As for Aldus, I think he'll adjust to someone else taking over his training. By now, he might even trust *you*," Mason added, grinning at her. "And after the way he came through for us at the cathedral last night, I think his jitters are cured. I'll try to return before too long, if for no other reason than to see what kind of master-wizard my former pupil has become. If he only channels half the energy into his spells as he did into worrying about the right and wrong of it all, he'll be marvelous.''

Athaya nodded silently, growing wistful as she watched Megan, Cordry, and Mason gather their things and prepare to set off on the long trek to the western shires of Caithe. She had to smile, however, when she saw Cameron offer the dom the pouch of copper coins that he had ''found'' on his way back from Leaforth, and her smile grew even broader when Mason, despite his stern gaze at the boy, promptly packed the money into his satchel and muttered a humble word of thanks.

While Mason examined a tattered old map in search of the best route to Kilfarnan, Cordry approached Athaya and offered her a respectful bow. ''Before I go, Princess, I just wanted to thank you for saving my life. Twice,'' he added, somewhat abashedly. He offered her a penitent gaze. ''I can't promise that I'll be much of a wizard. Magic just isn't as vital to me as it is to you, I'm afraid. But I know that I wouldn't be alive right now if it wasn't for you. And I wouldn't have Megan. I can't begin to repay you for that.''

''Yes, you can,'' she replied. ''By telling anyone who'll listen what my mission is. By telling any wizards you find to seek me out. Think of all the others who deserve to be as fortunate as you are, Cordry. And tell them.''

Cordry nodded solemnly. ''I will, your Highness. That much I can promise you.''

''And as long as we're exchanging thanks, I'm grateful to you and Megan as well,'' she went on, laughing softly at his puzzled expression. ''The two of you helped me understand a few things, even if you didn't know you were doing it at the time. I know you'll be happy together. Lord knows you've risked enough for each other to deserve it.''

Athaya felt an exhilarating surge of confidence as she watched him return to Megan's side and wrap his arm around her.

Now it's my turn.

Later that night, as a steady rain drummed steadily against the shutters, a noticeably smaller group collected in the monastery's kitchen to make another batch of leaflets while they waited for their supper to cook. The scent of onion soup and roast rabbit made her stomach growl as Athaya dipped the carved cedar block into a pan of ink, dabbed it on a rag, and then pressed it down firmly on a clean sheet of vellum.

Beside her, Gilda picked up the freshly made print, gazed at it intently for a moment, and then set it onto another table to dry. "I wish I could show this to my husband and make him understand that I'm still the same person, with or without my magic. Why can't he see past *what* I am to *who* I am?''

A few weeks before, Athaya would never have expected Gilda to say such a thing. But Aldus' presence among them, and especially his part in Cordry's rescue, had caused her to re-examine her old prejudices—if a priest had magic, how could it be so wicked?—and Athaya knew, with deep satisfaction, that Gilda had finally crossed that all-important threshold and accepted her gift.

"He might change his mind," Tonia said, tossing a handful of cabbage into the soup kettle. "Once he realizes how much he misses you. Once he sees his child."

Gilda touched her hand to her belly and nodded. "That's what Father Aldus thinks," she said, a glimmer of hope ch in her eyes. "I hope he's right."

Glancing up from her work, Athaya realized that Aldus had not come for his lesson tonight. She didn't let it worry her, however. He hadn't left them until very late last night, and the bleak, steady rain no doubt convinced him to stay home and catch up on some much-needed sleep.

"And even if your husband doesn't take you back, you've still got all of us," Ranulf observed, propping his feet up on the edge of the table. "Oh sure, we're heretics and outlaws and all, but at least we're sincere." He drew in a deep breath and smiled in keen anticipation. "And we can cook, too."

While the others chatted on about how Mason, Cordry, and Megan would fare in the west, Athaya drifted away from the conversation, thinking instead of her plans for the following day. Since talking with Tonia that morning, her resolve had grown even stronger. She would go back to Reyka tomorrow and tell Jaren she had been horribly wrong; that she loved him and wanted to marry him; that only her blind fear had made her push him away. Tonia was right. Everything had its price and this time the price was fair. If she wanted Jaren here with her, she had to accept the fact that every day might be their last. But that, she knew now, was no excuse for not being happy with one another while they had the chance.

Athaya smiled to herself as she dipped the cedar block into the ink, free of worries and giddy with optimism. Megan and Cordry were safe, Aldus and Gilda had grown more comfortable with their magic, and Mason had taken word of their mission to the west so that others could know there was hope. And the moment she spoke with Jaren, Athaya knew—*knew!*—he would come back to Caithe with her. And Father Aldus could perform yet another wedding . . .

Then suddenly, out of the dull buzz of conversation around her, a distant voice pierced her consciousness and shattered her peaceful reverie like a warning bell.

Athaya, answer me!

"Jaren?" she said aloud, dropping the cedar block onto the floor in a shower of black ink. But only an instant after her heart began to race, thinking it had *not* been a dream that morning, she realized that it was not Jaren's voice at all.

The others turned to stare, unable to hear the call, but Tonia soon realized what was happening and waved them silent. Dropping down onto a stool in the corner, Athaya closed her eyes and cleared her mind, opening herself to the message being sent.

Athaya, please answer, came the desperate cry. *It's Aldus. I need your help. Please—I'm in trouble. Terrible trouble . . .*

"What is it? Aldus, where are you?"

In the vigil chapel—where we met once before. The bishop knows everything, your Highness. He found out that I didn't poison the chalice. The king's men are everywhere. They've got crystals and mirrors . . . there's no chance I can get away. They're taking me to Delfarham tomorrow, he went on, his voice rising in pitch as it grew more despairing.

"Delfarham? Why—" She broke off abruptly as the answer came to her. Absolution of the clergy was a special case, and required the archbishop's writ. But such a writ could easily be sent by courier, Athaya realized, and that meant that Aldus was being taken to the capital for a different reason.

So that the king could speak to him.

To find out what he knew. And whom.

With a sharp wave of her hand, Athaya summoned her sphere and sought out the chapel. She'd only been there once, but her memory of it was accurate enough to give her a clear vision. When the orb's mist cleared, she saw a mirrorlike image of Aldus bent over his own sphere, calling to her, white candles surrounding him like sentries.

Extending her vision, she saw a quartet of soldiers in the corridor outside the chapel. Each man had a small mirror strapped to his belt, and one of the men had a leather hood tied over the hilt of his sword, no doubt to keep the corbal embedded there from harming Father Aldus . . . unless he caused trouble.

To her relief, Bishop Lukin was nowhere in sight.

The bishop promised to leave me alone so that I can pray throughout the night, Aldus explained, running short of breath. *And the men have orders not to come in no matter how I try to persuade them.*

"Lukin's afraid you might trick them into letting you go," she muttered. "You probably could, too. A fine preacher like you could make them believe almost anything."

Please help me, Princess. I don't want to be absolved. I want to live. I believe you. There was no time to tell you before, but seeing Cordry safe again . . . Oh, Athaya, I believe!

The image in the sphere began to waver, and the priest's voice faded to eerie silence. "Aldus? I'm losing you—" But the sphere now showed her nothing but grayish fog, and though she called to Aldus twice more, he never answered.

After banishing the sphere, Athaya quickly related to the others what Aldus had said. "We've got to find some way inside that chapel before morning," she concluded, scanning the faces around her in hopes of hearing an idea.

Ranulf's face was dark and solemn, as if recalling a failed campaign from long ago. "Athaya, it's impossible. Believe me, I've slipped into a lot of well-guarded places in my day and I know a hopeless situation when I see one." Seeing her about to object, he held up his hand and continued. "Look—I'm not just saying this because I've had my doubts about whether we could trust him. I'm saying it because he's surrounded by men with mirrors and corbals. And I'll bet there are more soldiers inside that cathedral than the four you saw. We'll never be able to slip inside unseen. Not without leaving a trail of bodies behind us, anyway."

"But we can't just leave him there!"

"It's not that I don't care, Athaya, but if being a hired fighter taught me anything it was that sometimes you have to leave one man behind on the battlefield rather than get ten men killed trying to save him. And it's not as if Aldus doesn't have a chance," he added hopefully. "If he's alert, he might be able to make a break for it on the way to Delfarham. Believe me, it would be less risky for him to try and slip away from the guards than it would be for us to go in and get him."

"Good time for him to see if he can work a translocation spell of his own," Tonia muttered, peering sullenly into the soup kettle.

Athaya stood up so fast that she felt the blood pound in her head. "Tonia, that's it! The translocation spell. I'll get him out of there the same way I got Cordry out of that cart."

"No, Athaya," Tonia said bluntly, waving a ladle at her as if brandishing a weapon. "It's much too dangerous."

"But I have to go. Nobody else can do it."

"Then you're taking me with you," Ranulf declared.

"And me," Kale said, quietly firm.

Athaya shook her head resolutely. "Out of the question. I know I can take one person with me, but I don't know if I can take two—much less three, since we'd have to bring Aldus back. Now is hardly the time for experiments. He's alone, and nobody's coming for him until morning. That'll give me plenty of time to recover my powers and get both of us out of there well before dawn. And Aldus can shield me with a cloaking spell if anyone comes in—"

"But what if you're captured?" Tonia demanded. "Who's going to pop in and get *you* out of there?"

Athaya started pacing around the kitchen, trying not to dwell on that possibility. "Is my life worth more than his? With his faith and his strength, he's worth a dozen of me. And he's talented, Tonia! He's *good* with his magic. God knows we can't afford to lose that kind of potential if we don't have to."

Brushing aside the next chorus of warnings, Athaya went to the dormitory for her cloak and shoes. When she returned, she was greeted by strained silence.

"Don't look so morbid," she chided them. "Save me some dinner. I'll be back in a few hours."

Tonia looked at her sternly, but with profound concern. "And if you *don't* come back?"

Athaya clasped the cloak around her neck, knowing that it was a possibility, however slight. For a moment, she listened to the sound of rain falling on the leaves, thinking that it wasn't so heavy as it had been a moment ago. "Then tell Jaren I love him, Tonia," she replied softly. "Tell him I should have said yes."

And before anyone said another word, Athaya retreated into the chapel, somehow hoping to draw extra power for her spell from that quiet place. The ruined sanctuary was dark and peaceful, and she felt a subtle nudge of courage as she placed her palms flat upon the altar and began to relax.

She knew where the spell was kept, but it was buried deep in her paths and took several minutes to reach. And then, when she thought she was ready—when the image of the vigil chapel had formed in her mind's eye—she pushed all of her power outward and hurled herself across a void of light and color, the discord of a thousand voices set to music. Her body drifted away, caught between the moon and stars with no earth on which to put her feet. Her head reeled with dizziness for a moment— or an eternity, she didn't know which—and then it stopped, harshly abrupt.

When her feet touched down on the stone floor, her knees promptly buckled, sending her crumpling to the ground. Aldus was beside her in an instant, cradling her, and patting her cheek to rouse her.

"Your Highness, are you all right?"

She cracked open her eyes and saw a hooded face against a backdrop of candles, his whole form framed by golden light like a visiting angel.

"I'm fine," she whispered. "Just a little dizzy. I'll have enough strength to get us out of here in an hour or two. Maybe you should cast a cloaking spell over me until then, in case anyone comes in unexpectedly."

"Yes . . . I suppose I should," he said, but made no move to do so. Athaya thought she heard a stiffness in his voice that wasn't there before; an edge of regret, as if he wasn't entirely happy to see her.

Then she saw the candles flicker in a sudden draft, and knew full well that neither she nor Aldus had moved.

"My thanks, Father Aldus," came the strong, baritone voice

from behind them. "You do Caithe a great service keeping this sorceress from seducing souls away from God."

Despite her lightheadedness, Athaya twisted out of Aldus' grasp and scrambled clumsily to her feet. There, lingering near the chapel's entrance, was Bishop Lukin, all in black but for the bloodred stole around his neck. He approached her without a trace of reservation, and Athaya's stomach turned over with the certain knowledge that the bishop did not fear her magic precisely because he knew how pitifully weak it was.

"Princess Athaya," he said, making her name alone sound like an accusation. "The last time I saw you was at your father's funeral. But then, you probably wouldn't remember my being there. You were, I recall, quite busy trying to burn the cathedral to the ground."

She didn't trust herself to respond, but merely stared over the bishop's shoulder toward the chapel's entrance, wondering how she could have failed to see his presence in her sphere. Lukin smiled at that. "I think Aldus called them 'wards,' " he said, glancing back casually. With her weakened strength, Athaya could barely detect the filmy white outline of the boundary that had kept her scrying powers from revealing the bishop's presence. Mason had taught Aldus well—too well, perhaps. His wards had deflected her sphere with appalling ease.

Then, as the gravity of her situation took hold, she wheeled around on Aldus, full of rage. "How could you do this? How could you *lie* to me like this?"

Aldus could neither look at her nor answer her and turned away in silent desolation. But the bishop was more than willing to answer for him. "What is one more lie to a child of the Father of Lies?" Lukin replied, his eyes narrowing. "There was a bit of truth to what he told you, however. We *are* going to Delfarham. All of us," he added, smiling thinly. "Your brother wishes to speak with you."

About what? Where I'd like to be buried? Athaya had not seen her brother since the day of Kelwyn's funeral and she felt her palms grow moist thinking of the wrath he must have stored up against her since then.

"I have friends in this city," she warned then, hoping to wipe that self-confident smile from Lukin's face. "If I don't return at once, this chapel will be brimming with wizards—"

The bishop inclined his head slightly. "An admirable bluff,

your Highness. But Father Aldus has already informed me that you are the only wizard capable of crossing distances by sorcery. If you are waiting for a rescue,'' he added with a sneer, ''you will be waiting a very long time.''

The bishop clapped twice, and a quartet of uniformed men streamed into the chapel. In deference to their new ally, they did not threaten her with a corbal crystal, but that only made Athaya even more conscious of how little they had to fear from her weakened magic.

Then Lukin gestured to her negligently. ''Father Aldus, if you would.''

Athaya backed away as the priest reached out to her, but the soldiers arrayed themselves behind her, closing off all routes of escape. Delicately, Aldus laid a hand to her forehead as if offering a blessing. There was a painful yearning in his eyes as he gazed at her, desperate that she understand.

I'm sorry, Athaya. But it's the best thing for you. His Grace has shown me . . . it's truly the best thing.

Then the subtle pressures in her mind grew more insistent, more compelling, and she quickly succumbed to them, unable to use her own powers in defense. She collapsed against him, slowly drifting out into the darkness, and heard one whispered plea for forgiveness as Aldus cast her gently into the unwanted realm of sleep.

CHAPTER 18

✳✳

THE FIRST SIGHT THAT GREETED HER WHEN ATHAYA cracked open her eyes was the austere figure of Bishop Lukin sitting across from her in the richly cushioned coach, his demeanor infinitely serene and self-assured. She needed no more encouragement to snap herself awake, although part of her remained clouded and lethargic, stubbornly refusing to rouse itself.

Ignoring the bishop's tranquil gaze, Athaya pulled back the heavy velvet drapes covering the coach's window. It was still dark, but she could see the shadowy forms of the soldiers that escorted the coach, pale moonlight lending their mail shirts an icy gleam. The moon also shed enough light on the landscape for her to realize it was wholly unfamiliar.

Wherever she was, it was nowhere near Kaiburn.

Awake, her troubles came streaming back to haunt her like a flood of ghosts. She did not know how long she had been asleep, or what had happened during that time. Were Tonia and the others safe? Were they even alive? Athaya couldn't bear to think about that for very long. If Aldus had confessed everything to the bishop, wouldn't that have included detailed instructions on how to find the forest camp? And the names of everyone he had seen there?

Then yet another unpleasant thought struck her, and she glared

at the bishop with deep suspicion. "Where's Aldus?" she demanded. If the bishop had accepted his confession, had he also
been gracious enough to administer the sacrament of absolution,
before the priest could change his mind?

Lukin shrugged mildly. "Behind us, traveling in another
coach. I didn't think it wise for him to get too close to you," he
added, slowly lacing his fingers together. "You might try your
trickery on him again."

"How do you know I won't try it on you?"

The bishop smiled indulgently, teeth glowing menacingly in
the darkness of the coach. "Father Aldus has assured me that
you will not. Or *can*not, to be more precise."

Athaya's show of confidence faltered. Lukin knew something
and was obviously going to enjoy watching her try to figure out
what it was. Sullenly, she let the drapes fall back into place.
Lukin surely couldn't watch her every minute—she would have
to be allowed some privacy to wash and use the chamber pot.
Perhaps if she was left alone long enough, she could call to
Tonia. Warn her to evacuate the camp and clear everyone out.
If it wasn't already too late . . .

Oh, Athaya, how stupid can you possibly be? she scolded
herself, suddenly infused with hope. *Just get out of this mess
exactly the same way you got into it.*

Feigning defeat, Athaya leaned back against the plump, red
cushions and closed her eyes. It was so simple! All she would
do was pretend to doze off and then throw all of her strength
into a translocation spell. Even if she had slept only a few hours,
her power would be fully restored. Athaya fought to stifle a grin.
She only wished she could see the bishop's face after she vanished before his eyes.

Lukin didn't make a sound as she settled into a comfortable
position and relaxed, drifting through her paths, deeper and
deeper still, following the endless, twisting corridors. Her
breathing quickened as she found the spell and she forced her
lungs back to a slower rhythm so that the bishop would not
suspect what she was about to do.

She focused her mind intently on her room in the dormitory,
picturing every detail in vivid clarity, and then, with a single
thrust of force, she opened her mind to the runes and cast the
spell.

And a moment later, she was still in the coach, listening to the low sound of the bishop's laughter hammering in her ears.

Then it all fell into place—the bishop's confidence, the vague feeling of imbalance she had sensed when she awoke. *The seal,* she realized in horror, her heartbeat wildly erratic. *Aldus set the seal while I was asleep . . .*

"Now you see," Lukin remarked, seeing from her expression that she had discovered the full extent of her imprisonment.

Athaya clenched her teeth, tempted to reach out and rake her nails across those hard, sculpted cheeks. She knew there was time—while cause for alarm, the seal was not as immediate a threat as her upcoming meeting with Durek—but the bishop's haughty gaze told her that Aldus would never be given opportunity to release her. But her next thought quickly robbed her of all anger—something she could not believe that Aldus had done willingly.

Her hands fell limply to her lap. "He *told* you," she said, deeply shaken. "He told you about the seal . . . after I confided it to him during confession."

"His vows of secrecy were not binding, Princess," Lukin said, in a voice thick with contempt. "I shouldn't be surprised that such an insignificant fact would slip your mind, but you are excommunicate. And have been for several months, I'm told." His lips twisted down with scorn. "God's seals—the seals of the confessional—hardly apply to you."

Then Lukin drew himself up proudly, determined to show her how completely she had been defeated. His eyes blazed as if he were about to launch into an exceptionally passionate sermon.

"Late last night I confronted Aldus with the subject of Cordry Jarvis. He denied everything, of course—he claimed to have placed the *kahnil* in the wine and denied ever having sought you out. And I almost believed him at first—after all, he handled the corbal candlestick that night and didn't show a hint of pain. But, by the grace of God, once he realized that my first concern was the state of his soul, the tenuous bond he had with you was severed. He went down on his knees and wept as he begged for guidance. He told me of a spell that protected him from the crystals and how he had deceived me. We spoke for many hours, but I finally managed to extricate him from your grasp. To bring him back to the fold and cast out the demons you had sent to plague him." The bishop unfolded his hands and pointed an accusing finger at her. "The power of the Almighty is greater than that of *your* master, my Lady."

"But God is my—"

"It was the purity of his calling to the Church that saved him," Lukin went on, abruptly cutting her off. "His faith was too strong to be corrupted by your seditious teachings. Magic is a gift?" he mimicked, twisting her own words so that they sounded base and corrupt. "With madness its cost?" Then his eyes grew dark and threatening, like angry clouds about to send down a bolt of lightning. "And you dare to call God Himself a *wizard*?" he spat with contempt, tendons growing taut in his throat. "What next? That you are His angel, sent to save the world?"

Athaya felt herself trembling with rage and clamped her fists together to keep at least one of them from finding a place somewhere on the bishop's jawbone. She wasn't going to bother arguing theology with him. She had tried it with Archbishop Ventan once and failed. And Lukin was twice the churchman he was—if being a good churchman meant one who believed without question and cut down anyone who refused to do the same.

"What are you going to do with Aldus?" she asked, eager to abandon the subject of her teachings. She smiled scornfully. "Grant him the comforts of absolution?"

Ignoring her insolent tone, Lukin's expression softened somewhat. "No, he'll not be absolved. Not if he continues to follow the path he's chosen," the bishop added, letting the enticing words linger there a moment before obliging her with an explanation.

"Despite his grievous legacy of magic, Aldus is one of the finest priests I have ever encountered. And he may be quite useful because of that. If he vows to use his . . . 'abilities' to keep those like you from contaminating this country with your heresy, then I think his Majesty and the archbishop can see fit to postpone his writ of absolution. Perhaps indefinitely, if need be. As long as he proves worthy."

"You hypocrite!" Athaya shot back, unable to contain her fury any longer. "You're just *using* him! If you believed all that rubbish you preach about saving his soul, then why keep him alive? Why endanger him that way?"

"For the greater good," Lukin responded coolly, like a field commander calculating how many men he could afford to lose and still carry the day. "His soul may be at risk, Princess, but if he does as he has promised, I think our Lord will understand."

Arrogance! she cried out bitterly. *How would you know what He would or would not understand? How can anyone?* But she said nothing, and fell sullenly back against the cushions, too drained to argue. The bishop, pleased at having won the battle, rummaged through the basket beside him and began nibbling contentedly on a small loaf of bread.

Unwillingly, Athaya found herself remembering how delighted she had been when Mason brought her the news of Aldus' potential—of the gifted magician he had found.

You were right, Mason, she thought grimly. *He definitely has potential.*

Potential to kill us all.

After three days confined inside the bishop's coach and three nights locked inside spartan cells in the abbeys where she and the bishop's party slept, Athaya realized that the landscape was growing disturbingly familiar. She recognized the open fields, the ridges of trees dotting the horizon, and the low hills on the outskirts of the capital. The smell of salt grew stronger as they drew closer to the sea, and finally, as the coach crested the next hill, Athaya saw the castle's limestone towers, almost white against a steel-gray sky.

She was expected; that much was clear by the staggering number of curious faces and pointing fingers that swarmed to their windows to watch the coach pass by as it rolled through Delfarham. More adventurous folk crept as close to the coach as they could without touching it, like children testing each other's bravery. "Kill the witch!" someone cried out, and after a tense pause, others saw that Athaya had not used her sorcery to strike the man down for his mockery and quickly joined in. "Death to the Devil's Child," they called out, shaking their fists. "Send her back to hell where she belongs!"

Athaya jerked the drapes shut when she could take no more, but the bishop merely drew them back again and waved genially to his flock.

Delfarham's noisy streets were soon left behind as the coach proceeded up the incline toward the castle gates. Only seconds after passing through the gatehouse, Athaya heard the metallic groan of iron chains, punctuated by a decisive thump as the portcullis was lowered. The king was clearly taking every precaution to insure she didn't slip away this time.

"Welcome home," the bishop said ominously, but Athaya only scowled at him.

The courtyard was nearly deserted when she disembarked, with only a select group of men waiting to take her inside. She didn't know if Durek had ordered everyone away or whether they were hiding voluntarily, and if she hadn't been in such deep trouble, Athaya might have been rather proud to know that she had been the cause of such turmoil. Briefly, she glanced behind her to see if Aldus had embarked from his coach as well, but he, too, was staying—or being kept—out of sight.

When she turned back, she saw a portly, black-robed figure padding across the courtyard, and sighed her displeasure as she recognized the archbishop.

"Your Excellency," Lukin intoned politely. He went down on one knee—a clipped gesture not unlike a salute—and brushed his lips against Archbishop Ventan's ring. Athaya knew that the ring was made up of tiny corbal crystals, but with her magic tightly sealed, she felt nothing.

"Welcome, Jon," Ventan replied warmly. "It's good to see you again." Athaya thought she detected a bit of unnecessary emphasis on the word "you." The archbishop cleared his throat and snatched a quick, wary glance at Athaya. He offered her no greeting.

"The king will see her immediately," he told Lukin softly, and then offered to show the bishop and his party to their chambers while the castle sentries escorted Athaya to her fate.

None of the men said a word to her as they directed her to the king's private audience chamber. She hardly needed their guidance. She had been summoned to that chamber for scoldings so many times she could find it blindfolded from any given point in the castle. But now it was Durek she was to face, not Kelwyn, and to her surprise, she feared this meeting even more. Kelwyn had been stern, but always just. Her brother, however, was such a stranger to her that Athaya did not know whether he would concern himself with such a lofty concept.

Durek was alone in the chamber. He stood motionless before the window, his somber gray doublet blending in perfectly with the clouds rolling in from the sea. He kept his back to her long after the guardsmen had departed, as if carefully bracing himself for the sight of her.

When he finally turned around, Athaya felt a tremor of shock. He had aged greatly these last few months. He was twenty-nine, but his hair was already growing thin and showing streaks of gray around the temples. His face was more gaunt, despite the stubbly beard that tried to lend it bulk, and his pale eyes were remote and cold. But more than anything else, what she saw was a young man clad in his father's clothes, pretending that they suited him even though he would not grow into them for years. The image made her vaguely sad, as if despite all his efforts, Durek would never be more than Kelwyn's shadow.

She did not fear him after that. She couldn't.

Durek approached her slowly, his face an unreadable mask as he stepped silently across the carpet. He appraised her with a faint grimace, scanning her shoes, her gown, her hair. Athaya shifted her weight self-consciously. She had been wearing the same woolen kirtle for almost five days—still peppered with ink from printing leaflets at the camp—and her hair was dirty and tangled. Worse, she strongly suspected she was in need of a bath.

His assessment made, Durek snorted and turned away. "I see you haven't changed the way you dress."

Athaya bit back an unbecoming reply. *Ah, yes. The same old Durek.*

He sat down at the writing desk—Kelwyn's desk—and bade her take the chair across from him. But as she stepped forward, she felt a peculiar sense of menace, as if the very air were hostile to her, enraged at her presence. Some part of her relived what had happened the last time she was in this room; seeing the hideous onslaught of power that drained her father's life; hearing his cries for mercy. She tried to shut out the memory, but somewhere in the caverns of her mind, she still heard the echoes of those cries.

"What's the matter, Athaya?" Durek asked mildly. "Afraid of ghosts?"

Athaya glared wordlessly at him as she took her seat, and Durek merely shrugged. "Well, I must say that this is the longest you've managed to keep quiet in recent memory." Then he sat forward and brusquely put all triviality aside. "I won't say welcome home, Athaya, because we both know what a ridiculously insincere remark *that* would be. This is no longer your home, and you are quite unwelcome here.''

Athaya swallowed a disdainful laugh. *So what else is new?*

''You brought me here,'' she pointed out. ''If you don't like it, then send me away.''

Durek opened his mouth to say something, then hastily reconsidered. He leaned back and steepled his fingers, tapping them gently against his chin.

''Well? Do you have anything to say?''

Athaya paused just long enough to annoy him, absently surveying the chamber, the furnishings, the man. ''The beard doesn't suit you,'' she remarked.

''You know what I meant,'' he snapped back. He gripped the edge of his desk as if trying to keep it from sliding away. ''It was bad enough when you were nothing but a pathetic embarrassment to this family, Athaya, but this time—'' He broke off, gritting his teeth. ''—this time you've gone too far.''

Athaya gazed at him cynically. ''That's what you said the last time.''

''That's because I thought that killing Father might have been enough for you!'' he roared. ''I never dreamed you'd come back and start stirring up some sort of revolt. Now you're not just a plague on this family, you're a plague on Caithe itself. Its pride, its honor . . . its very existence. I won't have it, Athaya. Do you hear me?'' He pounded his fist on the desk, sending an empty ink pot toppling to its side. *''I will not have it!''*

His rage put her on guard. This was not Kelwyn, who had never allowed anger to rule his head, but Durek, who tended to be far more irrational about such things. As he took a deep breath to calm himself, Athaya studied him intently, looking past his accusations to what lay hidden behind them.

''What are you so afraid of, Durek?''

''Afraid? Don't be absurd! I'm simply trying to keep you from tearing my country apart. I think I have a right to do that, don't you?''

''I'm not trying to tear it apart,'' she countered, keeping her voice steady. ''I'm trying to put it back together again. If you'd set aside your prejudices long enough, you could *see* that. And besides, this isn't *your* country. It's everyone's. Including the ones you and the Church keep exterminating. As their king, don't you feel a duty to them? They're your people, too.''

Durek rolled his eyes skyward. "Oh, Lord, now you're starting to sound just like Father.''

Athaya felt some of her pent-up hostility melt away just then. "I'll take that as a compliment, although I doubt you intended it as one. Father understood the Lorngeld, Durek. He just never lived long enough to make you understand, too.''

"And whose fault is that?'' Durek asked bitterly. "The fact that you have the gall to sit there and tell me how wonderful your cursed magic is not six months after you used it to murder Kelwyn only proves how much it's corrupted you.''

"If you understood what magic really *is*, you wouldn't be so intent on destroying it.''

Durek shook his head in disgust, continuing as if he hadn't heard. "And worst of all is the shameful way you use Kelwyn as a banner for your cause. You're pitiful, Athaya,'' he said acidly. "You didn't give a damn for the man while he was alive, but now that he's dead, he's suddenly the hero of your life!''

Athaya felt every muscle in her body grow stiff, but she forced herself to stay in control and not be baited by her brother's allegations. Durek's words were true, but only in part. Yes, Kelwyn was her idol. He always had been. But sadly, through the years she had learned that the only way to gain his attention was not to worship more fervently, but to make herself the object of his wrath.

"I always cared, Durek,'' she said softly. "You're wrong if you think I didn't. But now I understand him. I know what he wanted . . . I can picture the visions he saw of what Caithe could become. Don't blame me because you can't see them, too.''

Athaya saw Durek's face go red at that, but she went on in spite of the warning. "Father ended one civil war, and he was just beginning to end the second. To heal the rift between those with magic and those without. To unite this country. Learn that lesson, Durek. Not from me, but from him. Because until you start caring for all of your people, your Majesty,'' she said, putting extra emphasis on his title, "you'll never be the king— or the man—that Kelwyn was.''

Durek lurched to his feet so quickly that she didn't have time to react before his palm lashed across her cheek. He breathed in angry, ragged gasps, and quickly jammed his hands behind his back to hide their shaking.

Then she recalled something Nicolas once told her, and realized the magnitude of what she'd done. *Deep down I think he's terrified that if people start comparing him to Kelwyn, he won't come off looking so good.* She had dealt a deeper cut than she'd intended, and for a moment, Athaya almost regretted the hurtful words.

She looked away from him, turning her eyes to the window and watching the clouds darken and turn green, thick with portents. No magic storm, this, but only one of the frequent tempests that blew in from the sea in the spring.

"What do you want from me, Durek?" she asked softly, without rancor.

Durek pushed himself away from the writing desk, working out his store of rage by pacing rapidly across the carpet. "What I want, Athaya, is for you to stop this ridiculous crusade of yours! This country has been plagued by civil war for centuries, and now that we finally have some peace, you come along and start stirring everything back up again. I want to stop this madness before it gets worse."

"But that's exactly what *I'm* trying to do. Stop the madness. Put it under control."

He wheeled around on her, incensed. "Don't play word games with me, Athaya. I'm trying to make you see reason—"

"No, Durek. You're trying to make me see things the way *you* see them. It's not the same thing."

Then he threw up his hands in exasperation. "I won't waste my time arguing with you, Athaya. It's futile. And it isn't why I summoned you here." He strode back to his desk and jabbed a finger at one of the papers. "Tomorrow morning you are to be put to trial both for Kelwyn's murder and for spreading heresy in Kaiburn."

Athaya had expected as much, and Durek was vaguely dismayed that she didn't act surprised. "Why bother with a trial? We both know what the verdict and the sentence will be. I'll wager you've already gotten rid of anyone who might have the least favorable thing to say about me in my defense."

"Really?" he said, glaring at her shrewdly. "What about Nicolas? Odd that you haven't asked to see him yet."

Athaya felt herself stiffen, caught so easily by that trap, but

Durek merely laughed. "Oh, don't panic. I'm perfectly aware that Nicolas is still in Reyka and I have no doubt that you were party to that decision. But Nicolas is a fairly minor problem at the moment. And by the time he returns, your situation should be completely resolved."

Resolved, she repeated inwardly. *A tactful way of saying I'll be dead by then, isn't it, Durek?*

"And once you're taken care of," he went on, "I'm going to find out who else has been consorting with you and where they're hiding."

This time, Athaya was indeed surprised, but she tried not to show it. Durek obviously had no idea who her allies were or where the camp was, or he would have already ordered his men to attack. Did she dare hope that Aldus had not entirely betrayed them? Perhaps his confession was not so complete after all.

"And how exactly do you expect to do that?" she challenged. "It's not easy to find a wizard who doesn't want to be found."

Durek smiled confidently. Too confidently. "I'll do it the same way Faltil did. And using some of the same weapons," he added. "I'm sure you noticed that many of my men are armed with corbal swords. Kelwyn wouldn't let the Guard carry them, but I think it's a fine idea." Then he motioned to a darkened alcove in the corner, and Athaya detected a hint of cunning in his eyes. "Come—there's something else I want to show you."

He led her to an alcove in the rear of the chamber, where a circular object of some kind was set on a pedestal and hidden underneath an ornate, embroidered cloth. Again, Athaya felt that same sense of menace, and the hair on the nape of her neck pricked up. Durek smiled proudly as he drew the cloth aside.

Instinctively, Athaya stumbled back in sheer terror, flinching from pain that did not come. A crown . . . a crown made entirely of corbals! She forgot to breathe, transfixed by the beauty and the hideousness of such a thing. All those gems. All those horrible, deadly gems . . .

"If a single crystal causes a wizard such pain, then what would a hundred do?" Durek mused, running his fingers over the glittering purple stones. "I could find out, if I asked the good Father Aldus to unlock your magic, couldn't I? Or showed the crown to him as well?"

Athaya was dazed by the very thought. She remembered the hot, stabbing pain of the large crystal that Father Greste had brought to the Jarvis house and couldn't begin to comprehend the pain magnified a hundredfold. This crown would be a death-blow to any wizard who ventured too close to it. Madness and death, in a matter of moments. Even with her magic sealed, she could detect a faint buzzing from the crown, like the hum of a thousand angry wasps.

"Beautiful, isn't it?" he said softly. "I've been reading a lot about corbal crystals lately. How they work . . . where they can be found. Rhodri left many notes on the subject." Durek's voice softened to a rhythmic lilt, his seemingly idle words creating a palpable aura of foreboding. "Even Saint Adriel writes about them; you might have remembered that if you'd attended to your scriptures as a child. He calls the crystals—let's see, how did he phrase it?—'the holiest of gems, put on earth by God to thwart the Devil's wicked designs and cause his children grief.' "

Athaya backed away from the crown and tried to shake off her fear with an attitude of disdain. "Oh, don't be absurd. If he'd discovered that sheep dung did the same thing he'd have fallen on his knees and called *it* holy, too."

Durek only smiled at her, like a cat contemplating what to do with the half-dead bird still struggling in its claws. He drew the protective cloth back into place.

"Is that to be my sentence then?" Athaya asked, turning her back on the pedestal. She clasped her hands tightly to keep them from shaking. "Not the dignity of a headsman's ax, but death from that loathsome crown?"

Durek strode casually back to his desk. "The council will decide on your sentence, Athaya. If they find you guilty, of course," he added, with unnecessary diplomacy.

Athaya fervently hoped she looked less worried than she was. Not only because of her own plight, but because of the ominous array of weapons that Durek had assembled to combat the threat of wizardry. Not only was there the random corbal crystal to worry about, but an entire crown of them, its beauty promising an unspeakable kind of death.

But even more than the crown, she feared Father Aldus. If he could be persuaded to use his spells in the interests of protecting Caithe from heresy—and why would he dare disobey his bishop or his king by refusing?—he could become a weapon too potent for her fledgling crusade to defeat. A weapon that she herself had helped to create.

Her stomach churned as the implications grew. Aldus could become as dangerous as Faltil himself, claiming that his powers came from God—claiming that he was commanded to rid Caithe of all wizards. *It's the best thing for you,* he had said, just before overcoming her with magic. Worse yet, in his precarious state of mind, he might even come to believe such a thing, seizing a way to fulfill both his magic birthright and his holy vows. Seizing a way to keep himself sane when the world seemed to be crumbling beneath his feet.

As Durek summoned his guardsmen to take her away, Athaya realized that the ground was quickly crumbling from beneath her own feet as well.

CHAPTER 19

IT WAS DIFFICULT FOR ATHAYA TO PULL HERSELF OUT OF bed the next morning, relishing the sensation of the feather mattress beneath her, not a straw pallet or lumpy, hard earth, but *feathers*. It almost made her feel like a king's daughter again.

When her eyes first opened, the past year had vanished from her memory. She was in her own bed in her own room, everything exactly as she remembered it: the same blue satin coverlets, the same scratch on the wardrobe where she'd thrown a cup at it during a childhood tantrum, and the same, familiar sounds of horse tack and muted conversation in the courtyard below her window. Fleetingly, she anticipated a typical day: breakfast with her family, dull lessons with her tutor, a few hours of riding. But reality swiftly forced itself upon her, the tumult of the past year whipping by in a dizzying kaleidoscope of faces—Kelwyn, Rhodri, Tyler, Jaren, Hedric; then newer, less familiar ones—Tonia, Mason, Ranulf. Aldus.

The seal. The trial . . .

Once, this room had been her sanctuary. Now it was her prison.

But in a sense, it always was, she mused, and grudgingly threw back the soft coverlets and got up to dress.

Durek's guardsmen came for her shortly before noon. She recognized two of them as having served under Tyler's command, but all six men eyed her in wordless condemnation, no doubt hoping that she would earn the same punishment as had their former superior.

It was quick—a single stroke, Nicolas had told her, shortly after it was done. *He couldn't have felt any pain.*

Athaya bit her lower lip as she descended the tower stairs, thinking it likely she would get to test the truth of that for herself.

Even before she reached the council hall, she could hear the low murmurs of the king's councillors exchanging predictions of what the day's events would bring. They broke off immediately when Athaya appeared, the spacious hall suddenly hushed as a winter dawn. With a conspicuous amount of throat-clearing and rustling of cloth, the lords of Caithe found their places on the tier of benches to either side of the empty throne and waited for the arrival of the king.

Athaya was motioned to the backless prisoner's chair in the center of the hall. She scanned the musty-smelling chamber, studying faces. To her dismay, she saw only hard eyes, hateful frowns, and jaws firmly set in attitudes of contempt. From their ordered bank of seats, the council looked like a choir ready to sing out her guilt with zeal. She expected little sympathy for the Lorngeld here; the majority of Caithe's councillors had vehemently opposed Kelwyn's plans for abolishing absolution, and Athaya doubted that they had changed their minds since his death. Lord Gessinger was among the more sympathetic, but the general opinion of the court was that having Dagara's brother as an ally was worse than having no allies at all. Universally dismissed as meek and ineffectual, only the warmhearted Cecile was ever openly kind to him. Even today he sat alone at the end of the council bench, speaking to no one, his chin pressed dejectedly against his chest.

No allies here, she thought dismally. *Not even Cecile or Nicolas.*

After several tense moments of waiting, the door to the antechamber opened slowly. Archbishop Ventan and Bishop Lukin strode out, both sumptuously clad in formal white cassocks and bloodred stoles, the traditional liturgical colors for the sacrament of absolution. The significance of their raiment was not lost on Athaya, nor was it intended to be. And if that was not bad enough, each wore a silver Saint Adriel's medal around his neck.

Durek emerged after them, and if Athaya had been nettled by the clergy's choice of attire, the king's nearly set her blood to boiling. Not the plain gray doublet or the light woolen mantle, but the glittering crown of Faltil perched menacingly atop his head. In the bright sunlight slanting through the oriel windows, the corbals swelled with power, and although the sealing spell protected her from harm, Athaya still sensed a distant, high-pitched ringing in her ears—painless but distracting.

As he settled into his throne, Durek gazed at her with vague disappointment, as if hoping she would have appeared in her travel-worn peasant clothes so he could show the court to what depths his sister had sunk. But she had chosen a gown of somber black silk, adorned only by a strand of pearls and a simple white veil—an ensemble solemn enough so that even Durek would have to approve of it.

He flicked a glance to the silver-haired man at the end of the council bench. ''Lord Chancellor, you may read the list of charges.''

The aging man rose, bowed respectfully to the king, and unfurled a surprisingly lengthy scroll of parchment. He did not look at her as he spoke, and Athaya felt a prickling of anger snake up her spine. The trial had not yet begun, and already she was furious; furious at the taunting white and red of the clergy; furious at the crown her brother wore so vindictively, as if proud that the trial's verdict was a foregone conclusion; furious that Durek would proceed with such a travesty in the first place, pretending he was dispensing true justice, pretending he was a king.

''The first charge, that her Highness, Athaya Chandice Theia Trelane, daughter of our late Lord Kelwyn, did willingly seek the knowledge of magic—''

Willingly? Athaya thought inwardly, recalling how vigorously she had once denied her power. *You don't know the half of it, my Lord . . .*

''Second, that she did refuse absolution—''

Absolution is for sins, my Lord. I have committed many, but not the ones you claim . . .

''Third, that she used such powers to murder our Lord King Kelwyn, her father—''

Athaya's blood grew warmer. *Murder, no—a defense against madness!*

"Fourth, that she used such powers to murder Kelwyn's companion and tutor, Rhodri—"

As if that should be a crime! her mind cried out. *He's the one who caused the madness! And he tried to steal my power—his greed killed him, not me!*

"Fifth, that she did refuse to repent of her crimes and has proceeded to spread foul heresy in the city of Kaiburn, offending both Church and Crown and endangering the peace—"

It's often offensive when you tell people something they don't want to hear, my Lords. Especially when they know it's true.

"Sixth, that she did coerce a priest of God's most holy Church to interfere with the absolution of another, thereby risking both their souls—"

Their souls were already at risk. By denying who they were. That's true for all of us, my friends. Not just wizards . . .

When he was done, the chancellor handed the parchment to the king. Durek scanned it carefully as if to assure himself that nothing had been omitted.

Well, that's an impressive list, Durek. The only thing you left off was the time I beat you at archery nine years ago. Why not punish me for that while you're at it?

Then Durek put the paper aside and gestured to Bishop Lukin, who stood and produced yet another scroll. His well-trained voice boomed through the hall, projecting each word with relish.

"As evidence to the sixth charge, my Lords, I have here a document signed by Father Aldus Moncarion detailing his coercion by the accused, and how she dared promise him life in this world knowing that his magic demanded his absolution." The bishop held the paper up for display as if it were a holy icon worthy of reverence. "This document also contains a full account of his transgressions and a formal request for atonement, and states his willingness to obey his temporal and spiritual superiors in all things from this day forward, for the glory of God and the honor of Caithe."

Athaya glowered at him, eyes burning like coals. *And I'll just bet you helped him write that little treatise, didn't you?* she thought maliciously. *In fact, I'd be surprised if he even knew what was in it, save for his signature.*

"Have you anything else, my Lord Bishop?" Durek asked formally.

Lukin nodded once. "Just this." He held up a crumpled leaflet, holding it by one corner as if it were on fire. Athaya recognized Kale's woodcut immediately.

"The bishop was quick to distribute his opinions of me," Athaya explained steadily. "I merely thought to respond in like fashion."

"You have not been given leave to speak," Durek warned, turning his head so the corbal crown glittered menacingly. He gestured for the bishop to go on.

Lukin scowled at her, waving the leaflet contemptuously. "You promise life for the damned! Are you God Himself, to grant such favors?"

"They are not damned, my—"

"Athaya—" Durek warned again.

"Ah. So you know more than Mother Church," the bishop countered acidly. "And how came you by such wisdom?"

"I was taught by men more godly than you, my Lord Bishop. People who don't use religion as a weapon to prove to the world that they're better than everyone else."

"And isn't that exactly what *you* are doing?"

"That's enough," Durek broke in irritably. "It isn't our place to debate theology here, but only to establish the guilt or innocence of the accused." He expelled an impatient sigh. "Well, Athaya, since you seem so anxious to speak, how do you answer to the charges made against you?"

Athaya rose to her feet, clasping her hands in front of her. "I will admit to having done the things that our Lord Chancellor has so graciously recited," she began, "but I thoroughly deny that they are crimes. If what I've done is against the law, your Majesty, then the law is wrong."

Before Durek could reply, Lukin rolled his eyes and lifted one hand imploringly toward the heavens. "So Athaya Trelane descends from her tower to impart justice to us all. Just as she plays the savior to her people, promising them things she cannot grant."

"I'm not promising anything. I'm simply telling them not to be ashamed of what they are." She gazed at Lukin directly, and his haughty demeanor lent her confidence. "Magic may make you uncomfortable, my Lord Bishop, and you may not like it. Well, you make me uncomfortable, my Lord Bishop, and I don't like *you*, but I'm not calling a council to debate the matter of *your* execution because of it. The only reason my father died is because I was not permitted to learn how to use the power I was born with. It was a senseless accident—one that never has to happen again unless you want it to. If you leave the Lorngeld alone, my Lord Bishop," she pressed on, unyielding, "if you let them respond to their own calling, *then they will not endanger you.*"

Before Bishop Lukin could sputter a reply, Athaya turned her back on him and addressed the other members of the council. "Has anyone here bothered to recall what Caithe was like before the Time of Madness? Before the idea of absolution ever existed? There were wizards here—a great many of them. Trained ones, and relatively harmless because of it. And I certainly wasn't raised on endless tales of horror about what a godless, Devil-plagued land this was before Saint Adriel came along. No . . . those tales came later. *After* Faltil's scourge."

"Saint Adriel spoke to God and heard His wish," observed Archbishop Ventan. Compared to Lukin, Athaya was startled at the meekness of his voice. "Absolution was revealed to him as the answer—"

"To a problem that never should have existed in the first place!" she countered. "All I'm trying to do is return Caithe to what it used to be. To let the Lorngeld know that they don't have to die because of a hideous mistake one misguided bishop made two centuries ago. Kelwyn wanted this, my Lords, and each of you knows it. I'm not out for revenge or power or anything *like* that; I'm only trying to finish what my father set in motion. I've explained all this to his Majesty," she added, glancing at Durek, "but he cannot understand it. If any of you can, my Lords, I implore you to assist him."

She let her gaze rest on every man assembled in the hall, each face more dour than the rest, searching for a sign of sympathy. But except for the forlorn Lord Gessinger, whose attention seemed to be wandering, she saw only distrust and suspicion. A surety that she was mad—nothing but a mind-plagued wizard—and deserving of whatever judgment the king saw fit to recommend.

"And as for that confession supposedly written by Father Aldus," she went on, gesturing to the scroll in Lukin's hand, "why didn't you let him come here and speak for himself? Are you afraid he'd break down and tell the truth? You're trying to confuse him by—"

Then her mind went blank. No thoughts, no emotions—only

a black, soundless void. She had no idea what she had been saying or why she had been speaking at all, and she steadied herself against the prisoner's chair, chasing off a jolt of dizziness.

"Yes?" Durek prompted her.

"I . . . what was I . . ."

Bewildered, she gazed at the sober faces surrounding her. Where was this place? And what was she doing here? It had to be quite important, to have captured the interest of the king and his council. But just then, she could not *remember* . . .

The king's voice was more impatient this time. "Have you anything else to say?"

Athaya looked at him, and at the corbal crown resting ominously atop his head, and her memory snapped back, as if the lapse had never occurred. But she felt her hands shaking from shock. Such a thing had not happened since—

Since her *mekahn*.

She drew in a sharp breath. *The seal—it's starting to affect me already* . . .

"Yes, I have more to say," she responded coolly, cloaking her fears in defiance. "More than you'd ever care to hear. But we both know it won't do me any good, will it?"

Silence was the only answer she received.

At Durek's signal, she heard the chink of metal as the guardsmen approached to escort her from the hall. She was taken to a small, windowless cell where she would wait until the council sent for her.

Somehow, the thought that a group of men were at this moment deciding whether she would live or die did not distress her overmuch. In fact, the entire trial had felt vaguely familiar, as if she were performing once again the steps to a dance she already knew by heart. Then she laughed in resignation, resting her weight against the cold stone wall. *And why shouldn't it seem familiar? I've been on trial for one thing or another my whole life. I should be used to it by now.*

She thought back, letting each piece click into place. Kelwyn had judged her since the day she was born, comparing her to her mother and forever finding her lacking. Her own magic had tested her, trying to break her before she learned to master it. The Circle had summoned her, rebuking her for breaking their laws. And now Durek called her to answer for what he termed crimes, branding her a seditious heretic.

Athaya sighed inwardly. *God's own judgment is going to seem mild by comparison when it finally comes to pass.*

The guardsmen returned for her within the hour—far too short a time for Athaya to imagine that the council had debated her case with any diligence whatsoever. In the back of her mind she could almost hear the sharpening of the headsman's ax and morbidly wondered if it would be the same one used on Tyler.

The moment she stepped back into the hall, she knew her situation was not good. Few of the men dared to look at her directly, and both Durek and Bishop Lukin seemed uncommonly sure of themselves. Archbishop Ventan nervously fingered his Saint Adriel's medal, and Lord Gessinger had his face buried in one shoulder as if he had just dropped off to sleep a few moments before.

This time she was not invited to sit. The king's chancellor took one step forward, his face noticeably pale as he pronounced the results of the assembly.

"Athaya Trelane, Princess of Caithe, you have been found guilty of all charges against you."

Athaya shifted her weight to her other foot, trying not to smirk. *God's breath, what an astonishing surprise.*

"Therefore it is the judgment of this council, in accordance with the laws of Caithe—be they right or wrong," he added pointedly, "that you be taken to the place of execution three days hence where you will be set afire and burned until you are dead. And may God have mercy upon your soul."

Silence shrouded the hall, and the sound of the chancellor's footsteps as he returned to his seat were loud as war drums, reverberating in her mind like distant thunder.

No, Athaya thought, strangely calm. *No, that's not what you were supposed to say. You were supposed to say that I will be taken to the block where an ax will take my head. That I will die a noble's death. Quick. A single stroke.*

He couldn't have felt any pain, Athaya.

She choked on her next lungful of air, realizing she had forgotten to breathe. Slowly, the truth of what she'd heard began to register in her mind. They meant it. *Durek* meant it. The crown of corbals told her so.

"The council is aware that this punishment is rarely administered to those of high birth, your Highness," the chancellor explained, "but it is the decision of this body that, while it would be respectful to your father's memory to spare you such an end, the severity of your crimes merits it.''

Athaya dropped down weakly onto the prisoner's chair, unable to stand any longer. With sudden clarity, she remembered the dreams that had tormented her during the *mekahn*: people screaming in torment, writhing in flames; images of eyes melting, of skin crisping to black, of blood boiling. And the heat. The *heat*. A kind of pain that even a crown of corbals could not begin to inflict.

She wanted to shriek in horror, but her mouth was dry and her tongue would not obey her. All she could do was stare disbelievingly at the king—at her brother—and think back to the days when they were children, when arguments between them were settled by a tussle in the dirt and a few sharp words, and wondered how they had ever come to this.

Then Durek leaned forward. "However," he said, and obtained her immediate attention.

"I am prepared to suspend this sentence on one condition." He paused, letting her grow even more frantic. "That you publicly recant. That you renounce everything you have said on the subject of magic. And that you do so in Kaiburn, where your heresies flourish.''

It took several minutes, but Athaya found her tongue. When she spoke, however, her words sounded pitifully fragile. "And if I refuse?''

"In that case, Athaya, your next day of judgment will come sooner than you might like.''

Already Athaya could feel the heat and feel her gown clinging to sweating skin. She could smell the pungent smoke swirling around her, choking her. And could not think of a way to save her life and still have it worth keeping. Rhodri had offered her the same sort of senseless choice—give up your magic and live, or refuse and die. And that time, she had nearly lost everything by agreeing.

"You'll kill me no matter what I do," she replied softly. "Why should I recant?''

Durek smiled faintly, but it was a scornful smile. "Because if you do, Athaya, then you will be allowed to keep what life is left to you. I will arrange that you spend the rest of your days in the convent of Saint Gillian's to reflect upon your sins and beg

God's forgiveness. With your powers held in check, you will no longer be able to cause mischief. I can afford that much mercy.''

She had heard of Saint Gillian's—a bleak, remote place on the northwest coast of Caithe, miles from anything or anyone. And because of its isolation, it had a long history of housing royal prisoners—recalcitrant wives of ancient kings, mostly—who had been lucky enough to escape a death sentence. No one would ever find her there.

And even if they did, there might not be anything left worth finding.

Mercy?

Oh, Durek, if you only knew.

She had seen what ruptured magic could do; she had seen how it had blown Rhodri's body into random scraps of flesh and bone. And Hedric had been quite clear in warning her of the dangers of a sealing spell left on too long. In time, she would drift once again into madness—an ordeal she thought forever behind her—and when the strain grew too great, her magic would break free of its prison.

And nothing would happen after that, Hedric had said. *It would be the last thing to ever happen to you. You'd be dead shortly after it occurred.*

And the only question left unanswered in her mind was whether the carnage would be inside her paths, invisible to those without the means to see, or whether it would blow her head apart like a pumpkin dashed against a rock, innards scattered with grisly abandon.

"Do you accept this condition?" Durek asked. His voice was infuriatingly gracious. He knew what she would be forced to answer. And if Aldus had told him the true nature of the sealing spell which bound her, he also knew that what he nobly called mercy was only a short reprieve. The only hope she had now was time. To buy a few days and hope she could think of something. She had friends in Kaiburn—perhaps when news of her arrival came, Tonia and the others would find a way to rescue her. All it would take was the Master's touch to restore her power, and then she could save herself.

"You don't offer me much choice, do you?" Athaya answered at last, hanging her head. It was intended to be only a false show of submissiveness to her king, but deep inside, she knew her chances for escape were remote at best.

Durek nodded crisply. "Very well. We shall leave for Kaiburn at dawn tomorrow. My Lords," he added genially, taking off his crown, "this council is dismissed."

There was little to be grateful for, but once Athaya was locked securely inside her chambers, she whispered a prayer of thanks that she was in Delfarham alone, that she had not taken anyone with her when she answered Aldus' call for help, and that she was not responsible for anyone's fate but her own.

She slumped down on her bed and thought back to the last time she was a captive in this castle, back before she realized that men could die for her sake and could suffer for believing in her too much.

Oh, Jaren, she thought, burying her face in the blue satin coverlets, *I'm glad you're not here to see this.*

As the horizon flared into a brilliant orange sunset, Father Aldus closed the thick, gilt-edged book in front of him and returned it to its place on the dusty shelves. Sighing, he slid the reading lamp aside and rubbed his eyes, trying to work out the motes of dust that had lodged there. He had been in this chamber for most of the day, obeying his Majesty's command to sift through the writings that the wizard Rhodri had left behind in hopes of finding a useful weapon against the Lorngeld—perhaps something as valuable as the sealing spell.

"One more, and then I'm retiring," he promised himself, eyeing the last book on the top shelf. Despite the many hours at his task, he had uncovered little of use. A few hastily drawn path-maps, a timeworn copy of the *Book of Sages*, and an assemblage of notes on the various properties of vision spheres and what factors affected their scrying range. Nothing that he felt could be used as a weapon, although as the king had pointed out, mere knowledge was often weapon enough.

Aldus squeezed his eyes shut briefly, still conscious of the dull, swollen feeling inside his skull. Just before midday, he had been buffeted by an unusually severe headache, and only now was it beginning to fade. Between that and his lack of success, he was surprised he had stayed at his task quite so long. But he found the dead wizard's possessions—dare he admit it?—seductive. The writings on magic and its aspects spoke to him like nothing else ever had save for the scriptures. It forced him to recall that prayer and spellcasting gave him the same sensation of rapture, the same thrill of touching upon something larger than himself, and he wondered, when he dared, whether faith and magic were more closely linked than men cared to admit.

As he pulled the last book from its shelf, a folded sheet of vellum slipped out and fell to the floor. Curious, he unfolded the paper, and when he caught Athaya's name sprinkled liberally throughout the text, he began to read.

And wished he had not.

"Oh, dear God . . ."

He read on, mesmerized, the paper shaking his hands like dry leaves in an autumn breeze. Without shifting his gaze from the parchment, he groped for his chair, lowering himself into it as if afraid he might faint.

He never heard Bishop Lukin enter the room. He only noticed the looming shadow on the wall when it finally moved and gasped in startled shock, nearly knocking the oil lamp to the floor as he lurched to his feet.

"By our Lord, Aldus," Lukin said, chuckling his amusement. "One might think I was the ghost of this Rhodri fellow from the look on your face."

Aldus rested a hand over his heart, as if to confirm that it was still beating. "I . . . didn't hear you." He glanced worriedly at the paper in his hand. "Is the trial over?"

"Oh, yes," the bishop said indifferently. "I hadn't expected it to take long."

Aldus swallowed hard. "If I may ask, my Lord Bishop, what was the council's decision?"

Lukin creased his brows, then decided that the question was harmless enough. He shrugged casually. "She is to be burned, as befits a heretic."

"What?" Aldus shrieked, stumbling back into his chair. "But you promised they wouldn't burn her! You said she would be sent to a convent, to fast and pray, and seek redemption for her soul—"

"You didn't let me finish," Lukin admonished, not unkindly. He leaned forward, pressing his knuckles against the hard surface of the table. "She won't burn. Not if she agrees to recant. And she has agreed. In fact, we are returning to Kaiburn tomorrow." The bishop picked up a book from the table and flipped through it absently. "And when she has renounced herself and put an end to this foolish crusade, the king will take her to Saint Gillian's, where she will cease to be a problem for all of us.''

Aldus nodded silently, somewhat mollified. He had only agreed to help lure the princess into the bishop's trap after being assured that she would not be put to death. Granted, Athaya would spend her life in confinement, and constrained by the sealing spell, but at least she would have a life to spend. And despite what he had been taught about the seal's danger, he had great faith that the good nuns would protect the princess with their prayers, and that God would see fit to grant her deliverance from the spell's threat.

Lukin gazed at him warily. ''I hope you are not reconsidering your commitment to us, Aldus.''

''N-no, my Lord Bishop,'' he replied dutifully, as if offering the ritual response in a liturgy.

''Good. Because his Majesty has another task for you.'' Lukin's eyes gleamed with anticipation. ''The captain of his guard has just returned from Reyka. It appears he has brought us another wizard. Some foreign name . . . ah yes, McLaud—that was it. The king wishes you to seal this wizard's powers just as you did for Athaya. You shouldn't have any difficulty subduing him. The young man isn't in very good condition.''

Aldus nodded again, but only slightly.

''Then shall we go?'' Lukin proposed, setting the book down and motioning to the door.

Only as Aldus bent down to snuff out the lamp did he recall the paper clutched in his grasp. Gasping, he jerked himself upright. ''My Lord Bishop, I found something that may interest the council. They may wish to reconvene and consider this evidence.''

He handed the paper to the bishop. ''It says here that Kelwyn's death was undoubtedly an accident. Look,'' he said, pointing to the proper passage. ''Right here it says that Rhodri sensed Kelwyn's spell lash out first. He knew all along that Athaya was only trying to defend herself, but he didn't tell anyone to avoid getting into trouble himself. And he also explains that Athaya only went to her father's funeral to beg forgiveness for what she'd done, not to do further harm. His tone is rather proud and scornful, but the facts remain the same.''

Lukin's face clouded ever darker the more he read, like a god who suspects his people are ceasing to revere him. Aldus backed away, half expecting the paper to catch fire from that angry gaze. "And do you actually think this changes anything, Father Aldus?"

"It proves that her father's death wasn't the cold-blooded murder most people think it was."

The bishop shook his head, profoundly disappointed. "I fear you still possess a disturbing amount of loyalty to the princess, Father Aldus. Whether King Kelwyn's death was an accident or not, Athaya Trelane is still quite guilty of heresy, is she not? Besides," he went on, crushing the paper contemptuously, "this testimony was written by a wizard, and a reputedly vile one at that. You can hardly put any faith in it."

He strode to the fireplace and thrust the sheet boldly into the flames. When he turned back, his face was hard, lines of concern cracking the skin of his cheeks like fissures in rock. "I don't think I need to remind you that your own situation is precarious at best. If the archbishop finds your resolve lacking, he will sign the order for your absolution. For the good of our Church, our country, and your own personal welfare," he added darkly, "I suggest very strongly that you remain silent about what you've learned. Now come," he said sharply, heading toward the door, "you must set the seal on our new wizard in all due haste."

Aldus hung his head in shame, his face hot from the bishop's rebuke. He looked back toward the fireplace only once, watching the blackened edges of Rhodri's paper slowly curl inward upon themselves. For an instant, he imagined that it was not paper that burned, but human flesh, giving off a greasy stench of death as the fire ate its way to the bone beneath. Hastily putting a hand across his mouth, he hurried from the chamber.

As he crossed the threshold, he drew his cowl over his eyes to hide his misgivings, suddenly feeling the conflicting calls of his powers and of his vows more strongly than ever before. Ever since he had betrayed Athaya—for the good of her own eternal soul, of course!—he had been praying for guidance. And not merely praying—begging. He was begging for confidence that he had done the right thing, begging for reassurance.

And when he thought again of the paper he had found, now nothing more than blackened wisps of ash, he trembled with a growing terror that his Lord might have granted him an answer.

CHAPTER 20

ATHAYA WAS MORE HEAVILY GUARDED ON HER RETURN TO Kaiburn than she had been on her departure over a week before and she felt grimly flattered by the amount of caution that Durek thought necessary to insure her captivity. He was taking no chances that any of her "fanatical converts," as he termed them, would attempt to rescue her before her public disavowals were complete.

Yes, her disavowals. The outskirts of Kaiburn were already visible on the horizon, and Athaya still had no idea what she would say when called upon to make her recantations. Up to now, her energies had been completely devoted to devising some means of escape, and to her dismay, all efforts had been fruitless. If she could have spoken to Aldus, perhaps she could have persuaded him to release her from the seal, but he had been forbidden to see her since the day she was taken into custody nine days ago.

Nine days? Or was it more? Or less? Frowning, Athaya counted on her fingers to track the time. Despite her best efforts, her memories of the past few days were strangely fuzzy, and she found it difficult to remember the sequence of events since leaving Delfarham. Although her symptoms were still quite mild, she feared that the pressure of the sealing spell was growing steadily worse, and it was with uneasy haste that she tried to convince herself that four days confined inside an airless coach would make anyone lose track of the hours.

Just keep telling yourself that, Athaya, she said inwardly. *You have plenty of other things to worry about right now.*

Word of the king's arrival had reached Kaiburn well ahead of them, so there was no shortage of folk lining the streets to cheer when the string of four coaches, all of them richly trimmed with velvet hangings and solid-gold fixtures, rumbled into the western end of the city. Had she been an impartial observer, Athaya might have found this majestic entrance quite impressive; as it was, it only served to remind her that she possessed a spectacular talent for making enemies of very powerful people. The king's coach led the procession, followed by the bishop's coach bearing Lukin and Father Aldus. Athaya was in the third coach, and the fourth, presumably carrying the king's personal belongings, trailed a few yards behind her, with a half-dozen burgundy-clad soldiers, Captain Parr among them, bringing up the rear. Briefly, she wondered why Durek's new captain had not been present at her trial . . . four days ago, was it? Surely the man who had helped bring her to justice once before would not have missed such an opportunity unless the circumstances were dire indeed.

The procession halted briefly, and by the swell of cheers that erupted around her, she knew that Durek had emerged from his coach to ride the rest of the way, showing himself to his people. The citizens of Kaiburn had not yet seen their newest king, crowned but seven months before, and judging by their clamor, they were determined to give him a fitting welcome.

"Long live King Durek!" the voices cried. "And death to all wizards. Death to the Devil's Children!"

Athaya rubbed her eyes wearily, sinking back into thick cushions that offered no real comfort. *At least nobody will have to explain to them why we've come,* she thought. Curtly, Athaya snapped the heavy drapes back over the coach's window. Even the skies over Kaiburn boded ill—the day was overcast and chilly, a perfect complement to her mood of growing despair.

Athaya felt her stomach lurch with dread when the coach finally rolled to a stop. She peeked out from behind the drapes, orienting herself. As she'd anticipated, they had brought her to the great square before Kaiburn Cathedral. Today, however, the area was so crowded that she saw little beyond the stately spires of the church rising out of that restless sea of faces.

As the king dismounted from his mottled gray stallion to greet his people, Bishop Lukin and Father Aldus emerged from their coach. The bishop toted a bulky, locked box in one hand, which he promptly handed to a waiting pair of guardsmen. In deference to Aldus, those soldiers who possessed corbal-studded swords had the hilts wrapped tightly with woolen hoods and leather thongs to shut out the light.

Then her time came at last, and the iron bolt securing Athaya's coach was thrown back. A chorus of hisses and jeers jarred her ears as she stepped down from the coach, a brisk wind snapping at her cloak. For an instant, the ground wavered before her eyes and she missed a step, and had to grip the frame of the door to keep from falling. The disorientation was gone as soon as it had come, but she knew its cause was due only in part to the nerve-racking taunts of the crowd pressing in around her.

"Murderess!" came one harsh voice, perilously close. "She's the one who killed our Kelwyn!"

Athaya didn't turn to see who had spoken, but kept her teeth firmly clenched as the guardsmen led her to Durek's side. She had no doubt that, but for them, the people gathered in the square would have happily torn her apart, each hoping to seize a scrap of flesh to display proudly to his neighbor.

As she neared the cathedral, she noticed that the crowd was thicker in one spot, just at the foot of the steps. And as the people crept back to let the guardsmen pass, Athaya saw what had drawn such a terrible crowd and worked it into such a frenzy. *What can draw so many, except the promise of an execution?*

There, at the foot of the limestone steps sweeping toward the cathedral, was a rough-hewn stake, a pair of heavy iron shackles pounded into the wood at its center. Its base was surrounded by a sinister mound of faggots, a thin trail snaking through to ease her approach. And if the sight of the stake alone was not enough, she realized to her horror that it was a slow fire. No damp leaves were packed into the pyre, so that she would be overcome by smoke before the flames licked flesh. No, the wood was dry and exposed, the cruelest death of all.

A wave of dizziness brushed over her again, but this time it was born of sheer horror, and not the seal. Her knees barely able to support her, she turned to Durek. "You really don't trust me, do you?'' she asked, using every bit of self-control she possessed to keep the fear out of her voice.

"Have you given me reason to?'' he responded coolly. "I wanted to make sure you did what you promised to do.'' His mouth turned down in a expression of disdain as he absently flicked a speck of dirt from the front of his somber gray surcoat. "Strong measures are the only ones you seem to understand.''

Looking away from him in disgust, Athaya surveyed the horde of folk around her. Some faces showed compassion, one or two even revealed genuine sadness and regret, but most looked hungry for her death. "You've promised them an execution today. How will you explain that there won't be one, after I've recanted?''

Durek shrugged negligently. "I am the king. I need not explain myself.''

Kings must explain themselves more than anyone, she thought, but knew that Durek was not likely to take such counsel to heart, especially coming from her.

When Bishop Lukin and Father Aldus had taken their places nearby, Durek climbed the timeworn cathedral steps and held up his hands to silence the throng. It took several minutes for them to quiet, but since much of the din consisted of cheers for his long life, the king merely smiled and let them indulge themselves.

"People of Kaiburn, I greet you,'' he shouted, trying to make himself heard throughout the square. "And I am proud that today, in this fair city, the threat of wizardry plaguing our land will be obliterated forever!''

Durek's voice droned into oblivion as Athaya shifted her gaze back to the stake not twenty yards from where she stood. The sight of such an instrument resting at the foot of the most beautiful cathedral in Caithe was so obscene that Athaya wondered if there was any hope at all of eradicating the long-held hatred of the Lorngeld, which plagued her land more brutally than any wizard had ever done.

Any hope of getting out of this alive.

She hadn't realized Durek's speech was over until a pair of gloved hands urged her forward, and the sharp tip of a halberd in her back invited her to take the king's place on the steps.

Durek gave her a subtle look of warning as they passed.

"Choose your words well, Athaya," he whispered. "They are the only thing between you and your Maker now."

From the top of the steps, Athaya had a view of the entire square, and what she saw obliterated any hope of being helped by any of her fellow wizards. Every conceivable entrance to the square was solidly blocked by soldiers, at least one of whom held the hilt of his sword aloft, no doubt to allow the corbal crystal embedded there to absorb as much light as possible. Tonia, Ranulf, and Gilda would be thoroughly barred from the square, and even if Kale or Cam could get close to her, what could they do against the dozens of armed men that Durek had brought with him? Even Sir Jarvis, with all his wealth, could use none of it to help her now.

And worse, she knew that did not change what was required of her. What her duty called her to do.

She was broken out of her reverie by a handful of rotten melon rinds that splattered against her feet, staining the hem of her gown. She looked up in time to see a small boy smirk at her before he darted away, giggling with delight.

Annoyed at her continued stretch of silence, Durek glared at her pointedly to begin. She closed her eyes briefly, summoning strength. *Father help me,* she whispered inwardly. *Give me the right words.* She had directed her plea to Kelwyn, and not to God, but her choice of words made her realize that, considering her plight, she would be grateful for the aid of either—and preferably both.

"People of Kaiburn," she began, cringing at the initial frailty of her voice. "I am Athaya Trelane."

The level of jeering increased dramatically, drumming at her ears like driving rain. An overripe tomato exploded on the step beside her.

"And I am not ashamed of it," she added quickly, loud and with confidence. That was enough to diminish the taunts; many of those gathered were visibly surprised that she would admit to such a thing.

"Over the past few weeks, you have certainly been aware of my presence and my purpose in this city. You have heard what I and those with me have said about the Lorngeld. You have seen the tracts we have printed assuring them of life."

She swallowed once, steadying herself. Despite the chill of

the day, she grew warm under her cloak. Warmth. Heat. The
purification of fire . . .

Duty, Athaya! Vows mean nothing unless you keep them!

"His Majesty—my brother—wishes me to speak to you regarding these acts. Wishes me to tell you that I was wrong."
She lowered her head, assuming a posture of meekness and
humility. "He wishes me to say that these were all lies. That
the Lorngeld are a cursed race, and I along with them. That
absolution is the only route to salvation for those like me.

"These are my brother's wishes."

She steeled herself, curling fingers into fists. Then she raised
her head, chin high, in one final show of defiance.

"And I will not heed them."

Dozens of startled jaws dropped in unison, and quickly, before the shock wore off, Athaya surged ahead, shouting so that
her voice might reach heaven itself.

"Magic is a gift from our Maker, and if you cast it off with
scorn, you may as well cast *Him* off as well, for what is of you
is of Him! Those of you that have lost husbands, wives, sons,
or daughters to this insanity have lost them to a lie! But it isn't
too late. You can give their lives new meaning! Help me. Join
with me, and together we can erase this lunacy from the land,
and found a new era of peace. Don't let men like these lie to
you," she cried, pointing directly at Bishop Lukin, stiff with
rage at the king's side. "They fear you. Fear you for what you
could become! Incarnations of the miracle, and better messen-
gers of God than they themselves!"

Unbidden, the words flowed out of her at a furious pace until
a squadron of armed men surrounded her, one of them clamping
a hand securely over her mouth. Without any attempt at dignity,
they hauled her from the cathedral steps and back to Durek's
side.

And waited.

Athaya closed her eyes and caught her breath. Yes, she had done
it. She had gotten the courage from somewhere—or someone—
and done it. But she could have done nothing else, preferring death to a life tormented by the knowledge she had failed—
failed herself; failed Tyler; failed Kelwyn. And failed everyone
who had ever died or lost someone beloved to absolution.

She noticed then that the crowd was oddly hushed, their fervor
dampened by the strength of her unexpected words and the fate

she had sealed by saying them. Father Aldus, little more than a
shadow at the bishop's side, was ashen and trembling—as if her
words had physically wounded him, forcing him to see his soul
and loathe the sight of it. But her victory lasted mere seconds.
When she braved at glance at Durek, his face was purple with
rage, and it was only a supreme effort of self-control that kept
him from reaching out to snap her neck in one fierce explosion
of fury.

"That was your last chance, Athaya," he said, his voice so
low it was little more than a whisper. "Now you will see what
your defiance has wrought." Curtly turning away from her, he
signaled to the half-dozen guards stationed near the fourth coach.

*I know what I've wrought. But some things are worth dying
for, Durek. Tyler knew that. And now I see it, too.*

Wiping moist palms on her skirt, Athaya watched another
group of soldiers herding people away from the area closest to
the stake. Somewhere nearby, she caught the acrid smell of
smoke from a torch being readied.

Her only thread of hope lay in Aldus' inborn compassion, and
she prayed that he would be merciful enough to reach out with
his magic and put her to sleep before the flames licked up against
her flesh. She gazed imploringly at him, hoping he would pick
up her thoughts, but his face was firmly buried in his palms as
if trying to hide from God Himself.

Athaya turned back to her brothers with an eerie sense of
calm. "In a sense, I owe you thanks, Durek," she said steadily.
"You've let me speak to more people in one day than I would
have been able to reach in months. Perhaps that *is* worth dying
for."

The smile that crossed Durek's features sent icy shivers rippling down her back. "Come now, Athaya," he replied, darkly
amused, "did I say that the stake was for you?" Then his expression abruptly turned to contempt. "I'm not about to make
a martyr of you, Athaya. I never intended to; God knows the
last thing I need is to give the few people you've managed to
recruit a reason to keep making trouble. But there was nothing
lost by seeing whether the threat alone would have persuaded
you to recant. Pity," he added scornfully. "If it had, I would
have done you the courtesy of not making you watch this."

At the snap of his fingers, the uniformed men surrounding
the fourth coach began moving forward. Amid the sea of bur-

gundy surcoats, she caught a glimpse of bare flesh and the crest of a tousled blond head.

And when the men stepped aside, revealing their captive to her sight, her blood turned to acid and began to burn her flesh from the inside.

"Jaren!" she cried, lurching forward, but strong arms seized her by the shoulders and dragged her back. Her head began to split apart as magic boiled furiously inside its prison, outraged at its helplessness. And for the space of a heartbeat, she was swept into that in-between place of swirling images and their earsplitting din, a place she had only been during the wink of a translocation, giving her the sensation that her feet had no earth on which to stand, and that she had become nothing but a flesh-less spirit—a spirit now made only of pain.

He had not seen her at first. He allowed the men to lead him wherever they would, the desolate gait and anguished lines around his eyes revealing that he knew too well what awaited him. He had expected to find no friends here. Athaya doubted he even knew what city he was in.

But when Jaren heard her voice and beheld her standing but a few short yards away, his eyes went wide with horror and shock. They had not told him she was here. "Athaya!" Wildly, he tried to jerk free from his captors, only to be sharply wrenched back by Captain Parr, who gripped the other end of the fetters binding his wrists. "Athaya, whatever they want, don't do it—"

But the captain cuffed him soundly, warning him to be silent.

They brought him nearer to her; painfully near. He was clad only in a pair of rough woolen breeches and sandals, allowing full view of the scattered red lash marks striping the flesh of his back. But his eyes were clear and unclouded by looca-smoke; Durek wanted him to feel every moment of his dying and find no sanctuary in numbness.

Before, Jaren might have met his fate more willingly. Now there was the brutal sting of regret in his eyes.

"Captain Parr has certainly outdone himself," Durek remarked, nodding gratefully to his officer. "Since he didn't find you in Ath Luaine, he was good enough to bring me this wizard instead. And thanks to Father Aldus, this one's powers are locked away just as yours are." Durek glanced at Jaren with a grim satisfaction. "He'll not escape me this time."

Without doubt, Athaya knew that the sealing spell was the only thing between Durek and his grave that day. Had her power reigned free, it would have lashed out with killing strength, oblivious to the blow it would do to her cause. And for a tempting moment, her cause did not seem to matter, but only that her brother pay dearly for this outrage . . .

"My God, Durek, how can you be so vicious?" she lashed out, wondering how the same man could have possibly fathered them both. "What has he done to deserve this? You haven't even given him a trial!"

"I sent word to Reyka warning he would die if I ever found him in Caithe again," Durek replied indifferently. "He appears to have disobeyed my wishes."

"As if that bastard gave him a choice!" she shrieked back, flailing an arm toward Captain Parr. "Jaren was going to Ulard, not to Caithe—your men *kidnapped* him!" As her voice rose in pitch, she realized that she was slipping dangerously out of control. Time was running out, and even now she could hear the ominous clatter of irons as Jaren was released from one set of fetters and transferred to another—those that would bind him to the stake.

Then she whipped around and cast a withering glare at Aldus, who looked only slightly less shaken than she. He chattered wildly in Lukin's ear, hands clutching desperately at the bishop's smooth woolen sleeves. But the bishop was in no mood to listen, and abruptly detached himself from Aldus' grasp and stepped away to get a better view of the execution to come.

"I hope you're satisfied, Father," Athaya said, her voice trembling, full of fury. "You must feel glad, *saving* him like this."

Aldus looked beseechingly at her, his face ash gray. "I . . . I thought they were going to send him to a monastery," he blurted out. "Like you. The bishop gave me his word!" Aldus wiped a trickle of sweat from his brow. "He can't do any harm now—not with his power sealed. I thought he would be sent to an abbey to pray for guidance . . ."

"Until he sees the error of his ways?" she shot back, disgusted. "There's nothing for him to repent, Aldus. You're the one who should be begging for mercy right now. *You*. Because you're no better than they are now." She motioned sharply to Lukin and the captain, speaking in low tones together, partners in this gruesome conspiracy. "You may as well step up and light the pyre yourself. Go on! Let the fire *purify* him—that's what you think it will do, don't you? *Don't* you?"

As she drew breath to continue, Bishop Lukin hastened back to Aldus' side, his eyes clouded with concern that her cutting words might tempt the priest to repent what he had done and return once more to her side. Shooting a smoldering glare at her, the bishop wrapped one hand around Aldus' arm and force-fully guided him a safe distance away.

By then, Durek had returned to the cathedral steps, again preparing to address his people. He gestured dramatically toward the stake a few yards away, and to the man now bound there by heavy irons. "Good citizens of Kaiburn," he called out, pointing an accusing finger at Jaren. "This creature before you is a wizard. He is guilty of teaching my sister all manner of atrocity, and giving her the knowledge that led to King Kelwyn's death. For these crimes, he dies today. Witness this, and remember it well, for it is my proof to you that I shall protect all of Caithe from the demons that ravage us."

He glanced at Athaya once, just long enough to remind her that this was her doing, that even if she were to fall on her knees and beg forgiveness and recant everything she'd ever said about the grandeur of magic, it was now too late. And though it pierced like a blade through the heart, Athaya knew that even if he were to offer her that chance, she would have no choice but to refuse it. It had been a hard and painful lesson, but she could not betray all of Caithe for the sake of a single life. Not even if that life was the most precious one in the world to her . . .

And why couldn't I admit that before? Why only now, when I'm just about to lose him?

As if sensing her anguish, Jaren turned his eyes to her and offered a silent nod of acceptance. He had always been willing to risk himself for her and had not forsaken that commitment. From the beginning, he taught her that the liberation of Caithe was worth the sacrifice; that the persecutions would never end unless she continued in spite of whatever blows might be dealt her. She learned that lesson in her hour of deepest grief, but never had she expected to be faced with another such hour so soon.

Duty, Athaya. Vows mean nothing unless you keep them.

She knew he couldn't hear her—not with his powers sealed—but she cast him what thoughts she could, thinking perhaps that, somehow, he would know what was in her heart.

And at last, as she watched the captain's approach with a burning torch, she knew that Jaren did not regret having to die, but only having to leave her behind.

Jaren, I want to marry you, she cried inwardly. *I wanted it all along but I was afraid! Afraid this would happen!*

And like a divine reproach, she realized that he would have been safer with her than without her—safer in the Forest of Else than in the heart of Reyka, where she bade him stay because she would not take the risk of losing him.

Athaya glared up at the clouded gray heavens, accusing them. *Is this how I'm to learn my lesson then?* came the silent scream from inside her. *Can you teach me nothing without using death to do it?*

His role in the drama over, Durek drew away from the stake and bade the captain to approach. Parr smiled grimly as he approached his victim, relishing his time in the center of attention. The torch in his right hand burned hungrily, flames snapping skyward and leaving a black trail of smoke as he walked. The crowd fell silent as he passed, making the crackling flames sound even louder.

Athaya's vision wavered and went dim, an abrupt journey into twilight. She felt as if she were seeing everything before her through the fog of a vision sphere, as if she were trapped outside, able only to watch as events unfurled in some other place and time. And seeing Jaren there, scant footsteps from her side but an eternity away, was like seeing the gates of heaven appear in all their glory before her, and be rent with the sure knowledge that they would never open, and that their promised bliss would forever remain just out of reach.

She tried to look away, but could not. If Jaren was going to die for her, the least she could do was suffer what she could in watching.

And her last thought as Parr began to lower the torch to the kindling was that if the price of her magic was to be this high, then she deserved to be every bit the God-chosen savior that Hedric proclaimed, and Lukin denounced.

And who are you? he had asked scornfully. *His angel sent to save the world?*

Briefly, Athaya closed her eyes. *I should be, my Lord Bishop. By God, after this I should be.*

CHAPTER 21

✸

"WAIT, PLEASE," ALDUS SAID SUDDENLY. HE turned to his king with palms extended in entreaty. "Could I not offer him a final blessing? He may be a wizard, my Lord King, but surely we can see fit to send him into the next world with a prayer instead of a curse?"

"He hardly deserves such a kindness," Lukin grumbled impatiently, eager for Captain Parr to set the pyre ablaze.

Athaya glared at Lukin with unbridled contempt. "Your compassion has no bounds, your Grace," she said acidly. "And you dare to call yourself a man of God."

"Hold a moment, Captain," Durek called out, much to the dismay of his officer. The king scanned the crowd, aware that a gesture of compassion would help to endear him to his people, and cocked an inquiring brow at Bishop Lukin. "Is there any harm?"

Had the request come from anyone but his king, Lukin might have rolled his eyes and said something unbefitting to one of his profession. Instead, he merely sighed irritably. "Oh, very well, but do hurry up about it, Aldus. The captain is quite anxious to begin."

Sandals clapping on stone, Aldus quickly crossed the few empty yards separating the king and his prisoner. Jaren gazed at him warily as the priest picked his way up the thin path through the waiting fagots, his black woolen robe snagging on the sharp, grasping tips.

Then Athaya drew in her breath sharply, struck with the suspicion that perhaps the priest meant to show mercy by killing Jaren now, before the fire could do its work. As much as she desperately wished he would show such mercy, another part of her desperately hoped he would not, holding out for something—some miracle—that would keep Jaren alive.

Aldus murmured a few words of prayer; then, after a moment's pause, in which an unseen blanket of peace seemed to settle over him, he touched his hand to his heart, then to his forehead, and finally extended it toward Jaren in benediction. His fingertips rested gently on the flesh at Jaren's temple and lingered there—not long, but longer than was customary. The priest tipped his head to one side, eyes holding Jaren's as if engaged in silent rapport. Then Athaya saw a subtle tremor go through Jaren's body, as if cold water was slowly dribbling down his back. And when the moment passed, his face showed mute surprise.

"And may God have mercy upon your soul," Aldus concluded, his voice steady and clear.

As the priest turned back to rejoin the others, his gaze went immediately to Athaya. And in those eyes was a strength and conviction radiating from deep within, as if he had been touched by the very hand of God, and she realized what Aldus had done, what his "blessing" really was. It was release. He had undone the seal. And he was walking back to her side with even steps, intent on doing the same for her.

One touch, Father, she thought, heart soaring. *One touch, and I can deliver us from this!* Fleetingly, she wondered whether she could take both him and Jaren to safety with the spell of translocation, and more, how she would get them both within her grasp long enough to try. And only then did she wonder very soberly whether her power, after nine days' imprisonment, would be strong enough to do anything at all.

The brief blessing done, Durek once again gave his captain the signal to set the pyre alight. Parr moved quickly this time, unwilling to let another delay spoil his enjoyment. He murmured something to his victim—something vile by the flash of fury that crossed Jaren's face—then set the torch to the kindling and backed away, watching the flames feed until he had to draw back from the growing heat.

Hot beads of sweat broke out on Athaya's forehead as Aldus came ever closer, seeming not to hurry toward her for any particular reason. Jaren eyed Aldus' progress with keen attention as well, timing his escape to the last possible moment. If he broke free of his shackles before Aldus reached her, the ploy would be exposed. But if he waited much longer, the flames, already leaping dangerously high, would eat their way around the circle and trap him inside a lethal prison.

Hurry, Aldus . . .

He was within ten yards of her when Durek addressed him, forcing him to linger, and Athaya very nearly shrieked out for her brother to be silent and leave the priest alone. Aldus listened to his king with as much patience as possible, trying to appear humble as Durek mouthed his gratitude for the priest's loyalty, but was unable to avoid casting one or two nervous glances in Athaya's direction. His movements temporarily arrested, Athaya tried to inch toward him instead, but one of the guardsmen gripped her firmly by the shoulder and gruffly instructed her to remain where she was.

Frantically, Athaya watched black tendrils of smoke spiral around Jaren's head, stinging his eyes and making them run with tears. The growing heat had prompted the guardsmen to move the crowd back several more yards, and Athaya shuddered with disgust when she saw a cluster of cityfolk jostling one another to gain the best view.

Then a lick of fire spat violently skyward, searing Jaren across one arm. He gasped with the shock of pain, and knew he could wait no longer. Spying a narrow path behind him that the flames had not yet reached, he snapped open the locks of his shackles with one desperate burst of magic and bolted from the stake, holding up his arms to shield himself from the flames closing in around him.

"Mother of God, he's escaping!" Bishop Lukin cried, his cool composure abruptly shattered. "Captain, after him!"

Parr, however, was already in motion, furiously ordering a trio of men to join in the chase. His eyes burned as angrily as the pyre, its flames now whipping up against the stake itself and setting the iron shackles to glowing like hot coals. But the outrage on his face grew even more intense when he saw a former comrade force his way out of the crowd and run to Jaren's side, rapidly pointing the way to safety.

"It's Kale Eavon!" Parr barked out. "He's one of them—I want him arrested!"

But then, from the same direction that Kale had come, Athaya saw another welcome face emerge from the crowd. As the soldiers rushed in, Sir Jarvis, in a well-crafted display of clumsiness, stumbled forward and dropped his bulging purse of silver coins, spraying riches over the cathedral steps. Eager folk swooped on the coins like pigeons on breadcrumbs, paying no heed to the captain's vicious howls that they clear the way.

Free of the seal, Jaren hastily conjured a cloaking spell, gripping Kale's arm to hide them both from sight. But his powers were weak from disuse and he could not sustain the cloak for more than a few seconds at a time. Athaya could see both he and Kale flicker sporadically in and out of view, scrambling up the cathedral steps toward the great west doors.

But one spell, even badly cast, was enough for Bishop Lukin to realize the full extent of what had happened. The moment he saw Jaren shimmer out of sight, he whirled on Aldus in a fury, his face twisted with untold rage. "*You!* Damn you, Aldus, you freed him! You've betrayed us!"

"*No!*" Aldus cried, facing his king and his bishop with newfound defiance. "I've only betrayed myself by denying what I really am! I feel the Lord inside me, your Grace, and it is a glorious thing!" His eyes shone with inner rapture—the final realization that his magic and his faith were not incompatible, but merely different reflections of the same mystery. And although others might have seen his face and thought him mad, Athaya knew that it was not madness, but unearthly bliss, immersed in the ecstasy of a second ordination.

Aldus assessed the situation rapidly, first noting the distance between him and Athaya, and then realizing that Parr and his men were successfully shoving the cityfolk aside and gaining on Jaren and Kale, now only a few steps away from the sanctuary doors. The bishop, however, sensed what Aldus was planning and shouted a warning to the soldiers guarding Athaya.

"Get her back! Don't let the priest get near her!"

The men rapidly formed a solid ring of flesh around her, halberds at the ready to fend off any who would dare try to free her. But even though Athaya was a head shorter than any of the men, nothing could have blocked the sight that came next.

"Holy mother of God . . ." came Durek's hushed voice, but his words trailed off as he lifted his eyes to the sky.

"Figuram visionibus praesta!" Aldus was calling to the heavens, his arms spread out at his sides like wings. His voice was so laden with joy that each word he spoke seemed to be a song of praise to his Maker. *"Turmam angelorum mihi praebe!"*

At his command, swirling gray clouds descended from the sky, shrouding the city square in a blanket of fog. Mist churned and swirled, like a vision sphere slowly molding an image. And then, taking shape from the fog itself, hosts of graceful, winged creatures appeared, gracefully circling above the square. Athaya shielded her eyes, blinded by brightness. The creatures were bathed in soft, white light, and glistened like sunlight on the ocean. Athaya felt the rush of cool wind on her face, and the air was thick with the scent of roses as the creatures flexed their wings—delicate, insubstantial things of fine lace.

"What are they?" she heard frightened voices cry, many of them belonging to the normally imperturbable soldiers around her. To her surprise, the man at her right dropped to his knees and began muttering fervent prayers of forgiveness, his duty all but forgotten.

The light dimmed slightly, just enough for Athaya to perceive that each creature had a human face. But those faces, neither male nor female, were not of the flesh, but smooth as polished marble, as if all the statues of the saints in the cathedral had been infused with life and given wings. Golden locks of hair swirled around their faces as they looked down upon the crowd, their unnaturally large eyes bestowing kind glances upon some and glares of fury upon others.

Then, in unison, they began to beat their wings with unearthly strength, silently fulfilling the task they had been summoned to perform. Without hesitation, they swooped down upon their targets, driving the soldiers away from Athaya and forming an ethereal barrier between Jaren and the captain's men. Their wings fanned the flames of the pyre ever higher, but the flames did not alter their progress; the creatures flew through the fire unsinged, as if it were nothing more than the mist from which they had come.

A cluster of them broke off to harry the bishop and the king with special fervor, forcing them back against the coaches where they clutched one another in dreadful disarray. Athaya stumbled back, prepared to flee herself, but one of the winged things paused in its task long enough to smile upon her, briefly bowing its head in respect.

"Stay," it bade her. "He shall not forget you." It fluttered away in a blaze of light before Athaya realized that she had never seen its mouth move, but only heard the echo of its words in her mind.

Then she looked to Aldus, awed at the change in him. Gone forever was the tormented, desperate man of only an hour before. In freeing Jaren, he had made his soul's commitment. Now he was the essence of confidence, hands raised aloft, head thrown back, and eyes wide open, drinking in the visions before him.

An illusion, Athaya realized at last, gazing at the spectacle before her. *But on a scale unlike anything I've ever seen.*

Abruptly, she remembered what Mason had told her—that Aldus' talent for illusion was phenomenal, and his depiction of holy images uncanny in its detail. She remembered the jeweled gates he had crafted at the camp, and then looked with speechless wonder at the hosts of angels above her. For what else could they be? Aldus was giving form to all the visions of divinity in his mind's eye, for a short time setting his own fantasies of heaven within his reach upon the earth and using his power so that others could see the glory he saw when he mused upon his Lord.

But as she watched his conjured angels sweep the crowds back, she had to wonder, if only for one, daring moment, whether it *was* all an illusion, or whether Aldus' powers of prayer, now combined with his powers of magic, had somehow created a thing the world had never known before.

It was only then that she was able to shake off her shock long enough to realize the effect that Aldus' work was having on those around her. Dozens of folk had fallen to their knees, faces stiff with the fear of imminent judgment, while others were pushing their fellows aside, fleeing from the square.

"The priest is a wizard himself!" came one hysterical voice from the crowd. "Lorngeld in the priesthood—we are undone!"

"No," cried another, "he wields the power of God! Can't you see? Even the angels come to do his bidding!"

"Heretic!"

Harsh words exploded into a brawl, and in a matter of minutes, fear caused the fighting to spread like pestilence, escalating into a full-scale riot. One man snatched a burning stick from the pyre, waving it wildly to clear a path for his escape. Fists flew as people argued over the source of the creatures—were they demons or angels?—but many others used the wild disorder as an opportunity to loot the surrounding shops and brazenly rip purses from each other's belts.

Durek's men tried their best to keep the cityfolk under control, but they were vastly outnumbered and just as shaken by the winged creatures circling above them. Thus it was that most of the soldiers and cityfolk were too busy in their rioting to notice that Aldus was beginning to tire and that his angels were gradually fading away, drifting one by one back into the clouds from whence they had come.

Briefly, Athaya glanced toward the cathedral doors where she had last seen Jaren and Kale, but they had vanished, as if they, too, had dispersed like the angels into the clouds.

Then, before too many people had a chance to gather their wits and realize the creatures were gone, Aldus turned and bolted to Athaya, his arm extended.

"Give me your hand!" he called out, his voice stronger and more powerful than she had ever heard it.

But in the same instant, she heard her brother's voice as well. "Stop him!" Durek shouted at his men, none of whom looked particularly eager to attack the one who had caused such an awesome spectacle. "Keep him away from the princess!"

Warily, one of the men drew his sword and stepped in Aldus' path, formally ordering the priest to halt. But Aldus looked straight through him, as if he were merely another illusion made of swirling clouds and light. He calmly cast a shielding spell and pushed the blade aside without breaking stride, the spell sending up a shower of blue sparks in the soldier's astonished face.

Then two pairs of hands clamped down around Athaya's arms, dragging her back from the priest's dogged approach. Shoving aside the fleeing citizens in their way, the guardsmen retreated as far as they could go, until they were backed up against the coaches with nowhere else to turn.

Athaya stretched out her hand, reaching through the wall of men between her and Aldus. Unruffled, the priest cast another shielding spell and thrust it at the guardsmen, causing them to yelp and stumble aside, rubbing their arms from the sting.

Then Aldus reached out, and his hand locked down on Athaya's with a savagely strong grip. "A moment," he whispered, and began to gather enough strength to release the seal. She only hoped that his masterful illusions had not robbed him of too much power.

Bless me, Father. Just the way you blessed Jaren.

It was only then that Athaya realized that Durek and the bishop were frantically fumbling with the locks on the mysterious strongbox that Lukin had lifted out of the coach when he had disembarked. The king tore the leather straps aside and threw back the lid, and Athaya's eyes went wide with dread as he lifted up the crown of Faltil in all its glittering horror, the light from the blazing pyre fueling the crystals' lethal power.

"Feel the wrath of God upon you, Aldus!" the bishop cried out. "His holy jewels shall judge you now!"

Aldus' hand went limp in her grasp, life draining out of him in the space of a heartbeat. His eyes glazed over with unthinkable pain, and then grew grimly distant as his mind snapped from the blow. For a moment, he did not cry out at all, too numb with shock, but then, when he did scream, it was like the howl of a soul abandoned in the deepest pit of hell. His wails echoed through the square with such piercing violence that all who heard them were struck motionless. Even the folk busy brawling and robbing one another paused, many glancing skyward in fear that some other arcane creature was about to swoop down upon them.

"Aldus," Athaya whispered, but knew it was too late. His face was vacant but for the pain. The staggering collection of corbals had stripped him of his very self, leaving only the husk behind.

And leaving her magic imprisoned.

Then, spinning about like a trapped animal, Aldus fled, running from the corbal crown. His eyes were wild, devoid of reason, seeking only release from his torment. And when he turned toward the pyre, he paused for only an instant before rushing across the square and hurling himself into the crackling column of fire.

Athaya covered her mouth, choking back the bile in her throat as she watched the priest's robe erupt into flames with a sickly whooshing sound, his body catching like dry kindling. She wanted to look away, but something forced her to keep watching. To keep watching, as the screams drifted to her ears, then faded away into grisly, gurgling sounds. To keep watching, as the ground ran red with blood, and two blackened arms still cursed with life—those arms which had only moments before called angels from the sky—thrashed wildly in the air, begging their mercy.

A greasy column of smoke trailed up from the pyre, carrying the acrid stench of burned wool and flesh. And for an instant, the smoke seemed to take the shape of a graceful, winged thing, hovering only briefly before dispersing into the air like the mist of a vision sphere.

Within minutes, there was nothing left. Aldus' body was consumed like paper, leaving nothing behind but bones, as if he had not been made of flesh and blood, but something far less common.

Irritable, and more than a little nauseated, Durek handed the crown to one of his men. "Put this thing away," he snapped, and the guardsmen obediently packed it back inside the strongbox and secured the leather bindings. His face pasty white, the king glared at Bishop Lukin, failed to find anything useful to say, and then folded his arms angrily across his chest, brooding. Around him, soldiers still attempted to clear the square and stop the looting and brawling, but Aldus' death had caused the riot to worsen. The day had degenerated into a complete disaster, and the king was not pleased.

Then, just as Athaya saw her brother turn slowly toward her, his face dark with fury, a slender, lanky arm slipped between two of Durek's soldiers, snatched the strongbox by a leather strap, and darted away through the crowd with the most spectacular prize any looter could hope to acquire that day.

"The crown!" one of the guardsmen shouted. "After that boy! *Thief!*"

Durek's temper exploded at this last indignity, his face as purple as the corbals themselves. Shaking with rage, he thrust an accusing finger in the bishop's face. "Lukin, this is your foul, godforsaken city, and if I don't get that crown back from whichever one of your loathsome citizens stole it, I swear I'll—"

He broke off sputtering, too angry to go on. The bishop did not brave a reply, as if only now realizing the precariousness of his position, both temporal and spiritual. He was visibly relieved when the king spun around and stalked away.

But to Athaya's dismay, he came directly to her.

They studied one another, neither daring to speak, and Athaya wondered just then if Durek would strangle her now or have the decency to wait until they were out of the public eye.

"Get in," he threatened through his teeth, all but shoving her inside the coach. He climbed in after her and slammed the door shut with bone-jarring force. At his signal, Athaya heard the sound of the deadbolt being slipped into place. The driver whipped the horses into motion, and in seconds, the coach was thundering out of Kaiburn, leaving utter chaos in its wake.

Avoiding Durek's demonic stare, Athaya pulled back the curtain and peered out of the tiny rear window. As the coach fought its way out of the crowded square, the driver's whip soundly convincing folk to move out of the way, she saw an ugly kaleidoscope of bloody faces, freshly set fires, and unbridled looting—a city completely out of control.

And receding in the distance was the pyre, its fire now starting to die, leaving a shapeless form in its center shrouded by wreaths of smoke.

The people had come to see the death of a wizard.

And so they had.

CHAPTER 22

✳✳

"OW—TONIA, THAT HURTS!" Jaren jerked his arm away, but moving the limb hurt more than the salve, and Tonia quickly reclaimed it and proceeded to grease the puffed, ugly-looking burn with a grayish, sludgelike mixture.

They sat in the corner of the monastery's kitchen, a late-afternoon breeze carrying in the scent of fresh rain and apple blossoms. The room grew chilly as the sun slanted away from the southern windows, painting the room in pale yellow hues.

"Are you sure you're all right?" she asked, her face reflecting fierce concern. Although the advantage of youth would help him recover from his physical hurts easily enough, Tonia studied Jaren closely for any lingering effects of the sealing spell, tentatively touching his mind to insure that the paths were unharmed and the magic flowed freely within them.

Jaren shrugged weakly. "I don't know how I feel. Empty, I guess. I . . . can't feel much of anything yet." He squeezed his eyes shut and opened them again, his face slack with despondency. "It doesn't even seem real," he added, straining to sort out the harrowing events of the day. "It probably won't hit me until tomorrow, and then I'll realize what almost happened and start gibbering."

"Here's more of that salve you wanted, Master Tonia," said

Gilda, wiping one hand on a ragged apron as she stepped into the kitchen. She set a fresh pot of grayish stuff on the pock-marked table. "I'll go cut up some clean cloth for bandages."

"Thank you, my dear," Tonia replied, smiling warmly. When Gilda was gone, the Master let out a sigh of relief. "Good thing that girl stayed at the camp today. I suppose morning sickness can be a lucky thing sometimes," she added, chuckling faintly to lessen the air of melancholy bearing down on them.

Ranulf and Kale trudged into the kitchen a few minutes later, both liberally covered with dirt. A shovel was propped against Ranulf's right shoulder. Cam shuffled in behind them, his eyes fixed on the flagstones under his feet.

"We buried the strongbox underneath some loose stones in the chapel," Ranulf announced. He set the shovel aside and proceeded to brush clouds of dirt from his leggings. "Once we fill it with mud and replace the stones, no one will ever find that damned crown again."

Tonia nodded her approval, then gazed admiringly at Cameron. "You ought to be proud, my boy. You risked your neck stealing that thing."

"I'll bet even the painfully proper Dom DePere would praise your thievery to the skies *this* time," Ranulf added, tousling the boy's hair.

Cam nodded sullenly, unable to appreciate his accomplishments at the moment. "But it still didn't help Athaya," he whispered, scraping the toe of his boot across the floor. "And now she can't even use her magic to get away."

The room fell silent at that, Cameron having voiced the one subject they had all been evading for hours. At first, Tonia was reluctant to inform the others about the sealing spell that Aldus had cast on Athaya and Jaren. But later, when she heard Cam's gruesome description of how the crown of corbals had driven the priest to madness, she could not bear for the others to assume that such a fate had been Athaya's as well. Tonia had sworn them all to secrecy, murmuring yet another prayer that Overlord Basil would never hear of this. Already, she could hear his lengthy lecture about flagrant violations of ancient edicts, and the inevitable calamities that ensue when those outside the Circle are entrusted with Circle spells. And worst of all, this time he would be right.

"I knew we never should have trusted that priest," Ranulf

mumbled, angrily grinding his teeth together. "This is all his fault."

"He wasn't trying to hurt anyone intentionally," Jaren said. "He didn't have much time, but right after he released me, he said that his prayers for guidance had been answered and that God had shown him he was wrong to deny his power." Jaren slumped back exhaustedly in his chair, rubbing his eyes. "All along, he was only doing what he sincerely thought God wanted him to do. You can't ask much more of a man than that . . . even if he turns out to be wrong."

Such a show of forgiveness, coming from the one who had nearly died in Aldus' place, promptly shamed Ranulf into abandoning that topic.

Then, in a burst of suppressed frustration, Ranulf slammed a meaty fist on the table so hard that the pot of salve leaped a handspan into the air. "It's just so damned frustrating, Tonia. If only we could have gotten close enough to *do* something!"

"Lord above, Ranulf, it's not as if we didn't try."

"Then you were both in the city?" Jaren asked.

"For all the damn good it did," Ranulf grumbled. "Tonia and I got just close enough to the square to realize that we couldn't get through the blockades, and before we could think up another plan, that miserable little oaf Gilbert Ames saw us in the crowd and set a squad of soldiers on us."

"That's the man from the fulling mill I told you about," Tonia clarified, proceeding to rub more salve on Jaren's arm.

"One of the men had a corbal dagger and another had a mirror, so it was no mean trick giving them the slip. And by the time we lost them, the trouble in the square had already started. But I managed to pay back our friend Gilbert," Ranulf added proudly. "Once the riot started and folk started running out of the square, we just happened to meet up again. I clubbed him a good one, let me tell you. And he was so slow to get up that a good twenty people stomped all over him trying to escape." Ranulf paused and snickered grimly to himself. "He'll be remembering those bruises for a while."

"And I'll be remembering my headache for a while," Tonia added, her mouth twisting up in distaste. "Ranulf and I were a good distance away from the square at the time, but that ghastly crown nearly made our skulls explode."

"I can't figure how *you* managed," Ranulf remarked to Jaren, shaking his head.

"Kale and I were almost out of the city by then," he explained. "While the air was full of . . . whatever those things were that Aldus created, we slipped into the cathedral and went out the east end."

Kale grinned slightly. "I happened to remember a certain vestry door from the night of Cordry's absolution."

"I *did* feel a jarring pain at one point," Jaren went on, "but it wasn't so bad that Kale couldn't help me along until it passed. Until he brought me here and we learned about the crown, I just figured headaches were a side effect of the seal." Then Jaren looked up at the guardsman with a wan smile. "It seems you're making a habit of rescuing me from the king, aren't you, Kale? First in Delfarham last October, and now here."

"I only wish I could have saved Athaya, too," he said, lowering his eyes solemnly.

Then Cameron broke out of his sullen silence and glanced up at Jaren, studying him intently. "You're the one Athaya wanted to marry, aren't you?"

"*I* wanted to marry *her*," Jaren replied quietly, his shoulders drooping slightly. "I'm not so sure about the other way around."

"I like her," Cam declared. His face was set with profound seriousness, as if his formal approval were somehow required.

Jaren smiled at him warmly, but with a heavy air of sadness. "Yes, Cameron . . . so do I."

Tonia made an impatient huffing noise as she went about putting the salve away and collecting various pots and pans in preparation for supper. "You'll be getting one hell of a brother-in-law if you do," she remarked acidly. "Durek has tried to kill you twice already. I can only imagine how he'll react to having you as a member of the family."

Without waiting for a response, Tonia waved a small stewpot in Ranulf's general direction. "Now why don't you and Kale take yourselves off and wash those clothes in the stream. You could even go snare us a couple of rabbits for supper if you feel useful enough. Cam, go help Gilda fill up some flagons of ale from the brewhouse. We can sit around moping for the rest of the night if we like, but we may as well do it on a full stomach."

They all took the suggestions willingly, eager to keep busy. Only Jaren stayed where he was, cradling his injured arm and permitting himself to look as miserable as he felt once the others were gone.

"I just can't believe she's not here, Tonia. And it's all my fault. If I hadn't bolted too soon, Aldus would have reached her in time."

"Now, Jaren—"

"Aldus *told* me to run; he told me he'd free her and we'd meet later at a camp in the forest. God, I never even looked *back*, Tonia! Kale came to me, then the next thing I knew, the air was full of . . . I don't know *what* they were." He shook his head, not quite convinced he hadn't been hallucinating. "We just ran, after that. One of the creatures flew past me and said Athaya would be safe, and so we ran. I never saw her again . . ."

Tonia abandoned the stewpot and sat down beside him. "Jaren, we've been through this a dozen times. What were you supposed to do? Rescue her all by yourself? There was at least a full regiment of soldiers in that square, and with that blasted crown floating around, you probably would've gotten yourself killed, too."

"But what have they done to her?" he cried, pouring out all the helplessness and anger trapped inside. "Where have they taken her? My God, Tonia, how do we even know she's still alive?"

"She's alive," Tonia assured him. "I've already cast out for her with my sphere. She's in a coach somewhere. With her brother," Tonia added sourly, "and a generous assortment of his soldiers."

"Then what are we doing just sitting here?" he exclaimed, jumping to his feet. "We have to go after her!"

Tonia took him by the shoulders and pressed him back into his chair. "Jaren, let me finish. We know she's in a coach, but we haven't a clue where that coach is or where it's headed. The fall of the shadows made it look like she's traveling north, but I don't know Caithe well enough to recognize the few scraps of landscape I managed to see in the sphere. She could be any-where—"

"But we have to do *some*thing! He'll kill her!"

"He would have done that today if it was his intention. No, I think the king is too afraid of Athaya to risk making a martyr of her." Tonia sighed heavily, brushing a lock of gray hair from her brow. "But what he *is* planning to do, I haven't the faintest idea."

Jaren bowed his head dejectedly. When he spoke next, it was barely above a whisper. "But even if the king doesn't kill her, Tonia, the seal will. Eventually."

"I know. But we still have time. Not much, I'll grant you, but some."

Tonia set about slicing up a few large onions and tossing them into the stewpot while Jaren quietly stared at the dying sunlight, barely moving a muscle except to breathe. But when the silence grew oppressing, Tonia set her knife aside and turned back to him, muttering something about the onions making her eyes moist.

"She realized she was wrong, Jaren," Tonia said softly. "And she was planning to go to you—to tell you so—the day before she was taken. Right before Athaya left us, she said that if she didn't come back, I should tell you that she loves you and that she should have said yes; that she'd marry you if you still wanted her to."

A brief spark of faith kindled in his eyes, but then he hung his head, unable to take much joy in the news under the circumstances. "I don't know whether that makes me feel better or worse," he groaned, covering his eyes with his hands. "To know how close we came . . ."

He lapsed into silence again, but after a time he said, "I was planning to come to Caithe, you know—right after I left Ulard. No matter what my father had to say about it. I wanted to tell her that I wasn't going to give up on her—that any risk was worth taking as long as we could take it together. And now . . ." His voice broke once, and his eyes flared angrily at the unfairness of it all. "Now I may never get the chance."

"What's all this talk of 'never' all of a sudden?" Tonia said, wagging a finger at him. "You're giving up too easily for a man who fancies himself in love." She reached out and patted him on the shoulder. "But I suppose you've had a more harrowing day than any man deserves. You'll feel better after a good night's rest."

Smiling, Tonia bent down to embrace him. "We'll find her, Jaren. For your sake—and for Caithe's—we'll find her."

Then, gravely quiet, she added, "We've *got* to."

* * *

The coach bearing the king and his sister slowed its feverish pace only after putting sufficient distance between itself and the chaotic city of Kaiburn.

It was not yet dark, but a brilliant moon shone overhead, a gentle silver beacon amid the reddish glow of sunset. Despite tedious hours trapped inside the coach, Athaya was too agitated to sleep, but across from her Durek dozed fitfully, curled up against the cushioned seat like an exhausted child. His linen sleeves were wrinkled, the white feather in his cap was drooping, and each time the coach hit a rut in the road, he whimpered in protest and shifted to a more comfortable position.

Athaya wished he had chosen to ride in another coach, vastly preferring being alone to being in her brother's company, but she doubted that Durek would let her out of arm's reach until she was safely locked away behind the walls of the convent which was to be her prison.

I suppose a convent is better than a dungeon . . . or a grave, she mused, idly wondering how the good nuns would react to their notorious prisoner.

Nuns. But of which convent? Athaya frowned deeply. Damn, she couldn't remember. And she was certain Durek had mentioned it. She vaguely recalled that the place was quite far and that it would take well over a fortnight to get there, but try as she would, the name would not come to her.

She pulled the drapes of the coach closed, blanketing herself and her brother in darkness. At the moment, being imprisoned in a remote convent was the least of her problems. The sealing spell was of far greater concern. With Aldus dead, Tonia was the only one in Caithe who could release her. And Tonia had no idea were she was being taken.

For that matter, neither do I, she reminded herself testily, cursing her lapse of memory.

But Athaya had endured the ravages of the *mekahn* once and did not plan to do so again. Even if she could trust Tonia and the others to find her, her first priority was to channel every bit of strength she had into fighting the sealing spell, to keep it from eating away at her mind and sending her spiraling back into madness. And most of all, to keep herself rational enough so that the nuns could not persuade her to succumb to absolution— something they were certain to attempt. But in spite of her resolve, Athaya knew that her brief lapses of memory were only a foretaste of things to come. Even now there were times when she felt her power straining against its chain, simmering with anger to be free, and knew that such anger would destroy her if not kept at bay.

Memorization is a form of discipline, Athaya, Hedric had instructed. *It strengthens the mind just as physical exertion strengthens the body. And a disciplined mind stands the best chance against the effects of the seal.*

Athaya leaned back against the cushions and closed her eyes, willing her muscles to relax. "Credony, lord of the first Circle, twenty-six years," she whispered under her breath. "Sidra, lord of the second Circle, eleven years; Malcon, lord of the third . . ."

She went through the entire exercise, reciting the lords of the Circles until she came to Basil himself, lord of the eighty-ninth Circle of Masters. *Basil.* Expelling a sigh, Athaya mused that if the Overlord learned what had befallen her by sharing knowledge of the seal with Aldus, he would doubtless proclaim that she got exactly what she deserved.

But although her own fate seemed bleak, she was profoundly grateful that she did not have to despair over Jaren. Something deep inside had told her he was safe, even before Captain Parr had rejoined the king's party and grudgingly admitted that his prisoner had eluded him. But her heart felt like cold iron in her chest when she thought of all the things she wanted to say to him. Things that might now go forever unsaid.

He would have been safer with me all along, she told herself for what had to be the hundredth time since leaving Kaiburn. *I was afraid he'd get hurt if he followed me, and he was almost killed because he stayed behind*—a not-so-subtle dose of irony compliments of the Almighty.

Or whoever persists in doing these things to me, she grumbled inwardly, flicking a scowl skyward.

Then she gazed at Durek, unthreatening in his repose. His sleep was growing more troubled, and Athaya felt a twinge of satisfaction each time he frowned and whimpered, as if trapped in dreams inhabited by spellcasting wizards.

"All right, Durek," she said aloud, leaning forward. "You've won . . . for now." The king let out a muffled snort at the sound, but did not awaken. "But you haven't beaten me. Not yet. You can lock me away behind a dozen stone walls, but I won't let this seal defeat me. Damn it all, I *won't*. I have too much to live for this time.''

Slouching back in defiance, Athaya shifted her thoughts away from her own private battles and stepped back to survey the larger tapestry she was trying to weave. She was pleased at what she saw. Not three months ago she had still been at her lessons in Reyka, but now her presence in Caithe, and the reason for it, was widely known.

''And it won't stop there, Durek,'' she warned the oblivious king. ''We've set something in motion that's too powerful to stop. What happened in Kaiburn today will spread throughout Caithe in a matter of days. It should draw out dozens of new students. And inspire more angry mobs to try and kill us,'' she conceded, inclining her head to her brother. ''You ought to feel glad about that. But what I'm doing is bigger than both of us, Durek, and it's going to change the world.''

I know you'll change the world, Athaya, Jaren had said. *I have faith in you.*

''Then hold on to that faith, Jaren,'' she whispered under her breath. ''I think I'll need every bit of it.''

But instead of feeling despondent, Athaya felt an unexpected surge of hope, a feeling that instead of being buffeted by winds she couldn't control, she was—perhaps for the first time in her life—the master of her own destiny. *An odd thing to think on my way to prison,* she mused, smiling wanly. Somehow, however, she knew that Tonia or Jaren—or someone—would find her. Eventually. And if she could resist the worst of the sealing spell until then, it was only a matter of time before she could return to Kaiburn and continue what she had begun.

''I won't let you down, Jaren. I won't let any of you down.'' She thought of everyone who had risked their lives to come to Caithe, leaving the safety of Reyka behind. And she thought of those who had already put their trust in her: Jarvis, Megan, Cordry, Gilda—and Aldus, at the end—and knew that, in time, their numbers would multiply from a handful in one city, to hundreds and thousands in cities and villages all over Caithe. And the grandeur of that prospect only fueled her resolve to battle the seal even harder, so that when her rescuers came, they would find her strong and whole and able to resume her duty.

''And they *will* come,'' she vowed to the still-sleeping king, his face now buried in a red velvet pillow. ''Do you hear me,

Durek? And when they do, I will be set free from both my prisons.''

Athaya opened the velvet drape and watched the clouds drift lazily across the moon, temporarily blocking its light. Then she began to recite her lesson a second time, this time with the hint of a smile on her face. *Credony, lord of the first Circle, twenty-six years; Sidra, lord of the second . . .*

And she continued her recitations until the sunset left behind a glittering expanse of stars, the coach rolling through empty lands beneath them toward the remote northern shores of Caithe.

ABOUT THE AUTHOR

Julie Dean Smith was born in 1960, and has been writing since the age of five. Her first published work was a single sentence included in *Bride of Dark and Stormy*—a compilation of entries from the Bulwer-Lytton Fiction Contest.

She studied economics and English at the University of Michigan, during which time she became an avid football fan. She played the trumpet in the marching band, and on New Year's Day of 1981, was fortunate enough to witness Bo's boys actually win a Rose Bowl.

In 1984, she earned her M.A. in English at Western Michigan University, and her interest in computers developed while she was painfully handwriting the rough draft of her research thesis on Charles Dickens. Ms. Smith currently works for a software company in Ann Arbor, Michigan, producing reference manuals and user guides (another form of fiction entirely).

Her other interests include Celtic music, medieval history, and computer games. Repeated viewings of *The Adventures of Robin Hood* and *Star Wars* have also given her a weakness for old-fashioned escapist entertainment, and she hopes one day to fulfill a lifelong dream of being swung by a rope over a gaping chasm, clasped in the arms of an attractive hero wearing a billowing white shirt.